Twilight Years

Twilight Years

vali gyenge

iUniverse, Inc.
New York   Bloomington

Twilight Years

Copyright © 2008 by Vali Gyenge

All rights reserved. No part of this book may be used or reproduced by any means, graphic, electronic, or mechanical, including photocopying, recording, taping or by any information storage retrieval system without the written permission of the publisher except in the case of brief quotations embodied in critical articles and reviews.

This is a work of fiction. All of the characters, names, incidents, organizations, and dialogue in this novel are either the products of the author's imagination or are used fictitiously.

iUniverse books may be ordered through booksellers or by contacting:

iUniverse
1663 Liberty Drive
Bloomington, IN 47403
www.iuniverse.com
1-800-Authors (1-800-288-4677)

Because of the dynamic nature of the Internet, any Web addresses or links contained in this book may have changed since publication and may no longer be valid. The views expressed in this work are solely those of the author and do not necessarily reflect the views of the publisher, and the publisher hereby disclaims any responsibility for them.

ISBN: 978-0-595-51382-6 (pbk)
ISBN: 978-0-595-50398-8 (cloth)
ISBN: 978-0-595-61874-3 (ebk)

Printed in the United States of America

iUniverse rev. date: 11/11/2008

Dedicated to all my friends who inspired me and to all my fellow seniors. It is never too late to find love, peace and happiness!

Chapter 1

The drive from Milan was short but demanding. The highway was jam-packed, and enormous, noisy trucks passed them constantly. Elsa turned off at the first exit to a secondary road, but Lili was not a good navigator. They got lost twice and drove in circles for hours before they found the route to Lake Como. A short while later, the road led them to the Piazza Cavour, the centre of the town at the south end of the lake.

The sight was disappointing. The piazza was nothing like what someone would expect in a small resort town, especially not at the famous and romantic Lake Como. No statues, no fountains, no century-old buildings … it was square and ugly. The piazza stretched out to the harbour, where a few sightseeing boats were moored. Beyond them, the lake was covered with a dense mist and seemed small and insignificant. Both ladies were tired from the long, busy drive, so they decided to stay for the night.

At the tourism bureau, a dark, pretty girl told them to follow the road on the left side of the lake to the street named Passeggiata Panoramica. If the ladies then turned toward the lake, they would find a good hotel on the lakeshore. The girl called ahead and reserved a lake view room for them.

The hotel was two stories tall, smart looking, and the room was bright and comfortable. The sight from their window was entirely different from that on Piazza Cavour. Beyond the narrow channel of the harbour, the lake was dark blue and immense, and it was surrounded by a high mountain range with sparkling snow on its peaks. It was a breathtakingly beautiful sight.

Elsa opened the windows wide to let the fresh breeze in from the lake. She stood there for a few minutes and inhaled deeply, her eyes drinking in the beauty of the place. She then turned towards Lili, who was hanging up her things in the closet.

"I am so happy we decided to come here instead of hanging around in Milan," Elsa said to her friend's back. "This is a breathtakingly beautiful place, don't you think? Aren't you glad we came? Let's stay for a few days, okay?"

Turning around, Lili said, "We'll see. I like it too, but I'm still sorry about the two fashion shows I'll miss in Milan because of your disdain for the city. Those promised to be very interesting, and the models could be bought off at a very reasonable price."

"I'm sure you will learn all about the shows in the papers next week. Besides, you have more than enough fashionable rags to wear," Elsa said with a bit of mockery.

For the most part, Elsa did not like what she had experienced in Milan. As the busy, industrial town of northern Italy, it was a truly modern city with one-and-a-half million inhabitants. The streets were always clogged with traffic, and the stench of gasoline fumes trapped in the canyons between skyscrapers was suffocating. There were nice districts too, of course, with wide, tree-lined avenues and countless historic treasures.

They had planned for a week's stay in Milan, thinking it would give them enough time to see the sights. Elsa sat through a poor, afternoon performance of the ballet, *Ondine*, at La Scala of Milan, just to see the newly rebuilt auditorium. After the performance she met Lili, who had spent the afternoon at a fashion show. They walked around the Duomo—the large, ornate structure with a domed roof near the historic centre of town—window shopped at the arcades around it and admired the statue of Leonardo da Vinci. The next day they were lucky enough to get into the Church of Santa Maria delle Grazie with the first group of visitors and were able to see one of the most famous wall paintings in the world—*The Last Supper* by Leonardo da Vinci. It had been newly restored by long years of hard work by a group of artists. As she admired the enormous painting, Elsa could not help but wonder about how many artists' paintbrushes had touched it up and how many lines remained from the original master. Still, the expressions of the many faces, the depth of the painting, and the vibrant colours filled her with admiration. By the afternoon of the fourth day they had enough of the traffic jams, the noise, and the crowded streets, so they had left for Lake Como.

∼

Elsa sat on a bench by the lake. The sun shone on the gently rolling waves, and the water reflected all the hues of the blue of the sky. The high Alps across the lake seemed to be floating in a light green mist, with their peaks hidden in heavy, grey clouds. On the lake, small and large boats passed each other and honked their horns in greeting. Elsa sat close to an ancient (a few hundred years old at least) harbour gate. The old stone pillars of the gate depicted what she assumed was a Roman crest.

She had been always fascinated by the relics of history, so before the trip she had researched the history of Como on the Internet. She learned that it became a city around 195 BC. Ruled by the Romans, it was an important trade route to northern Italy. Como suffered many wars and ruler-ships until, with help from Garibaldi in the 19th century, it won independence from Austria and joined the Kingdom of Italy for good. Elsa liked to fantasize and make up stories about the places she happened to be in. From her seat she imagined that this cove was a safe haven for small fishing boats and tall ships in stormy weather. She pictured burning fires on top of the crumbling, gray stone walls to help boats reach the safe refuge of the harbour. She imagined sailors warming themselves at the big bonfires, singing, and drinking—celebrating their good luck in arriving safely.

Her bench was near one of the low, crumbling stone walls. The centuries-old wall was thriving with life. White and pink flowers grew from the cracks, and small lizards ran around like lightning or lay motionless, sunning themselves atop the stones. Elsa turned slightly to look up the wide, rambling stone steps leading to the large park behind her, where a few aged stone statues were scattered around. The park was beautifully kept. The bushes and trees were trimmed so precisely that not one little branch or leaf was out of place. It seemed as if a giant had trimmed them with an enormous cutter. It reminded Elsa of the formal gardens of the Habsburg Castle, the Schloss Schönbrunn, just outside Vienna. But here, even if the trees and bushes had been just as formally cut, the park missed the German-influenced rigidity. The landscaping in Como demonstrated classic Italian charm. A gravel path cut the park into two halves and led to an old, yellow, one-story building called Villa Olmo. Built in 1783, it had seen much better days long ago and was now a museum.

As she sat on the bench looking at the mountains across the lake, a sad, melancholic mood came over her all of a sudden. It was unexpected and she could not find a credible enough reason for it. She was not disappointed by the scenery. The travel books were justified in saying, "Lake Como is one of the most beautiful places in Europe." The name "Lake Como" sounded so sentimental to her somehow. But she had to admit that her favourite lake would always be the Gossau Zee south of Salzburg. It was much smaller than Como and ringed by the highest mountain range in Europe. The mountains hugged the lake so tightly that when she walked on the narrow walkway around it, she felt as insignificant as an ant in the sand. Gossau Zee's magic atmosphere had put her in a spirited solace. She was moved by the beauty of Como too, but it did not stir any deep emotions in her soul. She wondered if her earlier visit to Villa Olmo had made her melancholic. She knew she had felt sad after viewing the past splendour of the bare, now-neglected rooms, with dust covering crystal chandeliers and the dark, stern-looking portraits of ancestors on the walls. The few colourful posters she had noticed announcing an international fencing competition in the coming month, to be held in the large hall on the ground floor of the villa, also made her feel sorry for the glorious past of the place.

She looked out at the lake, following the shoreline with her eyes. Not far from the old harbour she noticed another inlet. It was enclosed by a fancy, rusting, wrought-iron gate to prohibit anybody from docking there. Two tall, white-and-red-striped poles rose high above the waterline. An old cigar-shaped wooden boat was tied up between the poles and rocked on the gentle waves. A small, colourful flag fluttered on its bow. As she watched the flag, Elsa realized the reason for her mood. Venice ... Tom ... the unforgettable past of her life ... the unforgettable, glorious past...the painful ending by her own fatal determination.

Before she could sink into reminiscence, she was disturbed by a noisy commotion from around the side of the villa. As she craned her neck to discover the source, a wedding party came in sight. Leading the group, the bride wore a long, yellow dress and a small, silly-looking hat with a short veil, and the groom was dressed in black and had a yellow rose pinned on his lapel above his heart. A photographer followed them, desperately trying to shoo away a group of children so he could start his work of taking beautiful photos of the present happiness for reference in the years to come. After the newlyweds came a group of smartly dressed people with tall glasses in their hands. Elsa watched them, astonished that they did not spill any of the champagne in their busily gesticulating hands. They talked and laughed, happily and loudly as only Italians can. Elsa watched the bride and groom smile happily as they posed for the photographer. With a deep sigh, she whispered to herself, "I hope they are going to be happy for a long time," and wished them good luck in her heart. She stood up and started to walk towards the hotel.

Elsa was in her early fifties but moved with a younger person's energetic walk. She was not small, and if she remembered to straighten her back, she was a bit over an average height. She knew her figure was still attractive. She felt most comfortable in her current, casual garb—pants and a shirt, and soft moccasins on her feet. She had decided a long time ago that no matter what the fashion magazines said, she would not be influenced. At her age she could afford to ignore the fashions and traditions.

Before she got very far, the afternoon sun suddenly disappeared. An enormous, dark cloud had escaped from the mountaintops and opened up. Heavy rains started to pour, drenching everything. Elsa was soaking wet by the time she found shelter under a tree with dense foliage and settled in to wait for the downpour to stop. She looked at her watch. It was after five. She thought, *Lili must be up from her afternoon nap and wondering where I am in this weather.* Just then, the storm left as quickly as it had come. As she started again for her hotel, carefully avoiding the big puddles on the bumpy pavement, she looked back towards the villa. The wedding party was no longer anywhere to be seen.

By the time she got back to the hotel, the sun was out again. Its dark red rays were warm and friendly, and they seemed to ask forgiveness for the sudden downpour.

Ignoring the waiting elevator, Elsa walked up to the third floor and used her key to open the room softly, because Lili might still be napping. But Lili was sitting on her bed smoking.

"Where the hell were you in that downpour?" Lili demanded, clutching her cigarette between two fingers. "I was worried. Look at you, you're soaking wet!"

"You shouldn't worry. You know I can take care of myself and always get back on time no matter what. How much have you smoked? This room smells like a bar in Algiers!" Before changing out of her wet clothing, Elsa opened the windows wide.

"Leave me alone about my smoking. I've told you many times that I want to be a happy corpse! I will never quit. You'd better get out of those wet things fast before you catch a chill."

"So, what are we going to do?" Elsa asked after she had put on her robe and dried her hair. "Are you going to laze on that bed or get up so we can go for a walk and find a restaurant? The air smells so lovely after the rain!"

"For a walk? Didn't you just come back from one? And who knows when it will start to pour again! Those mountains are full of surprises! Why don't you *force* yourself to sit down. We have some wine left in that bottle—let's have a glass and relax. It's too early to go to dinner."

Lili got up from the bed, filled two glasses with wine and handed one to Elsa. As she sat down again, she lifted her glass to Elsa, who sat on her own bed.

"Here we are, in Como!" Lili said. "Aren't you happy we came? Cheers!"

The two friends sat on their beds and smiled fondly at each other. They were bosom buddies, childhood friends from elementary school. They were inseparable. Lili had spent most of her days after school at Elsa's place. She was a lonely, only child longing for love, and Elsa's family was close knit, easy going and demonstrative. Lili enjoyed the warm atmosphere and was always on her best behaviour when Elsa's parents were present. The whole family took Lili in as a third daughter. The two girls had developed a strong bond, and it did not matter how different their personalities were. When they were thirteen years old, they made an oath that they would never ever part, no matter what. They pricked their thumbs to seal the oath with blood. When in their teens and later, very few friends could understand their deep friendship. Elsa was quiet, withdrawn and conservative. Lili was a loudmouth and liked to be the centre of any kind of attention. Fate later threw them to different parts of the globe, and though they lived different lifestyles and with different values, they managed to keep their friendship alive and well.

Elsa smiled and said to Lili, "Well, I must say we did age gracefully." Elsa lifted her glass in salute.

"Speak for yourself," Lili cried in mock outrage. "I'm not aged yet! I have plenty of drive left. I bet I still can seduce any guy if I want to!"

"Oh, come now, Lili. And how would you know if he let himself be seduced because of your charms or because of your money? Or did you forget the last handsome disaster!"

"You are forever a sceptical lady! That's why you have never had any hot affairs! You do not know what have you missed!"

"What I did not have I could not miss! Let's get dressed, find a nice, little family trattoria and have a fantastic Italian dinner! Move your ass. Let's go!"

"Okay, but it must be one where I can smoke at the table."

"Okay, okay ... I'll die of second-hand smoke for all you care! But we are going to walk, or no dinner!"

When they came outside, the air smelled wonderful. It was Elsa's favourite time of the day. The twilight started to swallow up the lake as the dark, towering mountains stood sentinel. Birds flew low, close to the water to gather a last bit of food before settling down in their nests for the night. People strolled leisurely on the streets, browsing the brightly light shop windows.

After a short walk, Elsa and Lili found a small, friendly looking restaurant in one of the winding side streets. It was just like a picture on a postcard. Through the window, Elsa could see the tables were covered with red-and-white-checkered table cloths, and the old Chianti bottles in the middles of the tables were hardly recognizable from all the wax dripping off the thick candles. Small platters of olive oil and balsamic vinegar, as well as a basket of warm, Italian bread, were placed near the centres of the tables. A friendly, portly proprietor greeted them at the door, led them to a window table and lit the candle for them. They ordered the wine first, and after a few glasses they ordered their dinner. The wine and the good food made them happy and reminiscent. Elsa's mood from the afternoon disappeared, and she felt content.

At times like this, the two women always talked about their favourite subject—adventures around the world—and it never mattered how many times they had repeated a certain story. When talking about old times or memories from their childhoods, they used their mother language: Hungarian. The emotions and sentiments deep in their hearts could only be truly expressed in their mother tongue. They both spoke fluent English, but they both, of course, had thick Hungarian accents. Lili's accent was an Australian-English-Hungarian mix, and Elsa's was Canadian-English-Hungarian. This combination always amused their "first English" friends who mercilessly teased them. Lili's Hungarian was a bit rusty, as she had only a handful of Hungarian friends in Sydney and her husband was Australian. On the other hand, Elsa's ex-husband was Hungarian and she visited her family in Hungary quite often. She regularly scolded Lili when her friend mixed the two languages into one sentence.

"Isn't it heavenly to sit here without any worries, or, pardon me, to just forget the problems for a while and be happy?" Lili asked, lifting her glass to Elsa. "For your health, soul mate. Cheers."

"Aren't we two lucky witches," agreed Elsa. "Suddenly I can't count how many times we have clinked our glasses in how many places in this wide world. Hopefully we are going to do it for a long time yet!" Her smile widened, and she continued, "Remember when we played 'Shirley Valentine' in Greece? We carried the round table from the patio almost to the sea before we sat down beside it. And how the old, limping, white-bearded waiter looked at us sternly but served the food there anyway? I have never since tasted such good calamari."

Lili grinned and took over without missing a beat, saying, "Do I? That was when we went on a one-day trip to Santorini and stayed for a week at that mountainside bed and breakfast. We had breakfast every day on the small balcony facing the sea. I remember watching with malicious joy as the big liners discharged their hurried tourists for the one-day sightseeing trip and donkey ride up the hill. It was one of our best trips ever."

Elsa pointed an accusing finger at Lili and said, "Except, I never forgave you for not letting me rent a scooter to commute to the beaches with."

Lili bowed her head as if asking for forgiveness. She replied, "Yes, my friend, but if you had, we would have never taken the boat to the most remote beach on the island, and we would never have spent the day with the nude gay guys basking in the sun, lazing on the warm sand and watching the gorgeous, tanned, naked bodies pass by."

"And you kept moaning, 'what a pity, what a pity'!" laughed Elsa, continuing the reminiscence. "And that German family? The big, fat father with pink skin like a piggy, the robust wife with a blond bun on top of her head and the two white-haired kids—all of them stark naked? And how later on they looked like cooked lobsters?"

"Speaking of lobsters," Lili said, rolling her eyes, "I will never forget the lunch we had in the restaurant on that beach."

"Like you'd ever forget any lunch or dinner," Elsa replied, smiling at her friend. "Lately, you remember first of all where and what you ate and secondly where and with whom you had sex!"

"At least I had it, not like you, mate!"

"Oh, okay. I shut up, I capitulate! Let's order some more wine."

Sipping the light red wine, they observed the sights through the large window of the restaurant. The sky had cleared up and the twilight tried to hang on, but night soon took over the streets. People were walking in groups, talking and laughing. Couples strolled by absorbed in each other. Dogs sniffed around from the ends of their leashes as their owners walked them. Elsa noticed a young woman pushing a pram. A small boy hung on to the handle. Elsa turned back from the window and took another sip from her wine.

"I'm glad I am not young anymore. My son has grown up and has a life of his own, freeing me of parenting responsibilities."

Lili turned back from the window too and looked at Elsa. "You were an overachiever in that area for most of your life. You put everybody and everything before yourself, and where did it get you?" Lili asked solemnly.

"To a nice trattoria in Como! Nothing to be sorry about!"

"Damn, don't make me scream—you know very well what I'm talking about! You have been living alone for how many years now? Fifteen?"

"Not that many. But it was and is my own choice."

"No, it was not! What about the love of your life after your divorce?"

"It was great as long as it lasted. No regrets."

"But it could have lasted for much longer or maybe forever, if your son had not interfered! He was jealous of your happiness and, might I add, he was afraid that he'll inherit less if you spend your money on travelling with your lover!"

"You are a cold-hearted, cynical bitch! David has never worried about money. He wanted to protect me from getting hurt. As you well know, Tom was younger than I ... and he did have money on his own. I was not a 'sugar mama' like you were for a couple of good-looking guys."

"Who's bitchy now? Okay, okay, I withdraw. Peace ... let's enjoy the evening," Lili said, filling up both their glasses. "Here is one for eternal friendship."

After dinner, they walked along the lakeshore back to the hotel, feeling relaxed and happy.

Lili said, "It's too early to go to bed yet. Let's have a nightcap on that terrace above the water."

"Didn't we have enough to drink?" asked Elsa.

"You'll sleep better and we don't have to drive. Don't be such a square!"

They sat on the dimly lit terrace sipping grappa, the Italian dessert liquor usually made by distilling the grape residue from the winemaking process.

The early fall air felt like velvet on their faces whenever a light breeze blew in from the lake. The sky was black, but the rising new moon was slowly breaking up the complete darkness of it. The anchored boats' glittering yellow lights looked like fireflies over the water. Elsa's afternoon mood was back. The scenery bought back her memories in full force. She did not fight against it this time and let the memories flood her heart.

Chapter 2

As Elsa watched the dark water and the blinking yellow lights of the moored boats, sipping her grappa. Her mind was wondering in the past,.

~

She was married for twenty-three years. The marriage worked well at first and she loved Sàndor very much. They had mutual roots, as he emigrated from Hungary in 1956 just like her. They met in 1957 at a party in Toronto, and a year later they were married. It was not passionate love but rather a realistic union, a meeting of two lonely people who needed to share the hardships of building a new life in an unfamiliar country so far from their old habitat. Both were lonely and homesick, and they comforted, respected and cared for each other. Both of them adored their only son David, who was born in the third year of their marriage. Sàndor was an insurance salesman when they got married and worked himself up the corporate ladder to become an executive of a large insurance firm. He was pleasant looking, captivating and could charm everybody. Even with those characteristics, he was honest in his dealings to the last details. He lived for his business.

Elsa accepted this and never complained. She kept herself busy bringing up David and educating herself through correspondence courses and writing workshops. She wanted to be a writer. Years passed pleasantly without serious financial or personal problems. Then came the year when David started his university studies to become a lawyer. He flew out of the nest to lead his own life. Their big house in the prestigious part of Rosedale, in the heart of Toronto, became empty and depressing no matter how hard she tried to revive it as a warm and cozy family home. Sàndor travelled more frequently and stayed away longer every time. Elsa trusted him and did not want to pursue the reason. Soon, however, rumours reached her that Sàndor was travelling with a woman when on business. Elsa was hurt and felt betrayed.

She had gone through the same painful sensation when in her twenties, but she was older and wiser now. She didn't want to know the truth. She dealt with it in her own way, pretended that nothing had happened and waited.

Her own affair started before the divorce, in the last year of her marriage.

That year she travelled with Lili to Rome and Florence. They dutifully visited most of the museums, cathedrals and graveyards in Rome. They read the guidebooks, looked in awe at the giant paintings by Raphael, spent hours in the Vatican and observed the breathtaking ceiling by Michelangelo in the Sistine Chapel. In Florence, they could not tear themselves away from Michelangelo's *David* at the Galleria dell'Accademia. At the end of three weeks of intensive sightseeing, they decided to spend a relaxing week in Venice. Money was plentiful at that time for both of them, so they stayed in the five-star Hotel Danieli a few steps from St. Mark's Square.

Both of them had visited Venice more than once before, and this time they just wanted to spend a relaxing week doing nothing. They sat on the terraces around St. Mark's Square, drinking outrageously expensive bitter espresso from tiny cups and listening to the music played by a tuxedoed band. They watched the people stroll by and the tourist groups lining up at the foot of the bell tower and the entrance to the cathedral. Thousands of pigeons took off every time the bells tolled, forming a large, dense cloud. Laughing, they stayed as far from the cloud as they could.

They shopped for souvenirs around the alleys at Rialto Bridge, and Lili looked for shoes and dresses in the posh boutiques along the very narrow streets around St. Mark's Square. The weather was sunny, and the late spring brought warm, soft breezes from the direction of the Grand Canal.

On the afternoons when Lili was having her "beauty sleep," Elsa would board a vaporetto (canal boat for public transportation) without looking at the timetables or where it was heading and get off wherever she felt like it. On one sunny afternoon, she found herself on the island of Burano. The village covering the small island was like a postcard. Houses were painted in every shade of many colours—blue, purple, green—with differently coloured window mouldings and shutters. She especially admired a dark blue house with green shutters and a red bicycle beside its white front door. A narrow canal ran through the middle of the village's main street. Several arched bridges connected the two sides, and small boats and gondolas were neatly tied to their posts. Fruit shops, sidewalk restaurants, fish markets and souvenir shops lined both sides of the canal. After strolling around for an hour, she sat down at a sidewalk table near a confectionery and ordered a large portion of gelato.

As she waited for her gelato, she made plans to visit Murano the next day. Maybe she could lure Lili along for that outing if she promised her unlimited time for shopping at the famous glass factories.

"Excuse me, you dropped your purse," someone beside her table suddenly said in English.

Elsa looked up and stared into the most lovely, smiling hazel eyes she had ever seen. The eyes belonged to a tall, dark-haired man who was looking down at her and holding out her purse.

"One must be careful in this area. Thieves are prying around for innocent tourists," he said.

"Thank you very much. How did you know I am one of those innocent tourists?" asked Elsa as she retrieved her purse and tried to hide her attraction.

"I overheard you ordering the gelato."

"Thank you again!"

"You are welcome. Have a good day!" he said and disappeared.

Elsa slowly licked her cone of gelato and watched people pass by. It was one of her favourite pastimes. She would pick out one person she found interesting and placed him or her into a made-up story. She would puzzle out who they were, where they came from and where they were going. Now her eyes followed a faultlessly dressed older lady carrying a small dog in her arms. She was greeted by a few people with noticeable respect.

"She is a widow," Elsa fantasized, talking quietly to herself. "Her husband was the mayor of this island community for many years. She was out walking that lap dog but picked her up when they reached the crowded street. She lives in that big, grey house with the green shutters at the end of the street. The rooms are always kept dark because she never opens up the shutters. Her room is full of ancient family paintings and antique furniture. She has tea from a delicate, china tea cup as she nibbles on sweet cookies and shares them with her little dog, who sits on her lap. She gazes at the pictures and dreams about the days when she was young and beautiful. She thinks of her handsome, loving husband and their fulfilling love life. She dreams about the house when it was full of life, full of children crying and laughing. She dries a tear or two with her lace handkerchief, and then dozes off in her old, comfortable chair."

Elsa shook her head as she wiped from her fingers the sticky gelato that had dripped down the cone. "You are an incurable romantic for a woman of your age!" she scolded herself. Asking for her bill, she paid for her gelato and then walked up and down the streets, looking into shops for presents to take home. She debated with herself about whether to buy anything for Sàndor. She finally chose a lovely, soft leather wallet and was ready to take it to the cashier when she heard the vaporetto's horn. She put the wallet back on the shelf and hurried to the platform to catch the boat. The boat was nearly full, but she managed to find an empty spot at the railing and stood there looking down at the water as the vaporetto's motor started to turn, stirring up the garbage around the boat. Someone bumped into her.

"Oh, I'm sorry," a familiar voice apologized. She turned around and looked into those hazel eyes again.

"The innocent tourist from the gelateria," he said, smiling. "How was your ice cream?"

Elsa who could never get involved in a chat with strangers, found herself drawn into a lively conversation with her hazel-eyed acquaintance.

"It was very good, thank you," she replied, turning her back on the dirty water. "I'm gelato junky who can't resist if she sees a vendor."

"Let me introduce myself. I am Tom Berontel from Vancouver."

"Hi, I'm Elsa Martos. I am from Toronto."

"Somehow I knew you were Canadian too. But you're originally from somewhere else, aren't you? Let me think … your accent is Hungarian!"

"How did you guess?"

"The Hungarians have a special accent, and I heard it long enough from my grandmother. She was born in Hungary."

"Do you speak any Hungarian?"

"Unfortunately no—just a few words which I don't dare to risk in front of a lady!"

They smiled at each other with ease and kept on talking about Burano, the weather and Venice. When Elsa noticed they had arrived at her stop and began to say goodbye, but Tom mentioned it was his stop too, so they got off together. They stood talking, both of them reluctant to part. Finally Elsa said, "I must go. It was very nice to meet you. Have a good stay in Venice."

"May I invite you for a drink?" Tom asked.

"Nooo … thank you, though! I must get back to the hotel. My friend will be worried that I got lost or kidnapped by the Venetian pirates," Elsa said, laughing. Then without thinking she blurted out, "Would you like join us for a drink later in the hotel bar?" As soon as she said it, she wanted to withdraw it. *After all*, she thought, *I do not know anything about him.*

"Gladly," Tom said, accepting the invitation like he had been waiting for it. "Which hotel are you staying at?"

"Over there!" Elsa said as she pointed behind her. "At the Danieli. Shall we say around seven?"

Tom's face showed a spark of surprise when he heard the name of the hotel, but quickly suppressed it.

"Then I'd better say goodbye now to have enough time to get changed and be presentable. Thanks and see you later!" Tom said happily.

As they shook hands, Elsa felt a strange tremor running up her spine.

She walked towards the hotel like she was walking on clouds. She scolded herself, "How can you be so taken by a stranger so fast? Maybe he is here with his wife or girlfriend. No, it cannot be, he would have mentioned it and would have asked to bring someone along. I should not let myself to be so much taken by him! May be he is just bored or just wants to have a drink in the Danieli for free and take a chance on a boring hour with an older woman. But he is so charming! And handsome too. And those eyes? I have not felt this light-headed in my whole life. Get hold of yourself, old girl. You are married and slightly over fifty! You cannot lust after an unknown man, no matter how beautiful his eyes are."

She was still arguing with herself when she entered the room. Lili was standing at the window, looking out towards the vaporetto station.

"Here you are," she said, turning from the window. "Where have you been? I was afraid you got lost or missed the last boat from a deserted island ... Hey, what has happened? You're glowing!"

"Nothing—I just had a good afternoon!" Elsa said as she kicked off her shoes and dropped down into a chair.

"There's more, I know you! Did you meet someone?"

"Well, if you must know, I did."

"Who? I hope it was a man!"

"Yes, and I invited him for a drink in the bar!"

"My, my! You're getting very adventurous in your old age! Who is he?"

"His name is Tom, and I met him in Burano. He picked up my purse from under my chair at a gelato place, and later we met again on the boat coming home. He has gorgeous hazel eyes, he's handsome and we talked a lot. He's from Vancouver, and his grandmother was Hungarian!"

"Oh yes, this is getting better by the minute," Lili said, nodding her head. "It all sounds very exiting, but is he married? What is he doing for a living?"

"I don't know, we didn't get that far. I'm sure you'll like him. I'm going to have a shower. You can interrogate him at the bar, but he is mine!"

Lili shook her head as if she could not believe the woman before her. Looked after Elsa shaking her head as she disappeared behind the bathroom, door throwing her skirt down to the floor on the way instead of folding it and carefully putting it away, as she always did. She never heard Elsa talking so frivolously and happily, "well, this guy better be something.", she told herself..

Thinking about Elsa, Tom walked to his hotel, the Cavalletto, at the other end of St., Mark's Square; the Cavalletto, thinking about Elsa. He liked her a lot. He wanted to get to know her better, and he found her attractive, intelligent and magnetic. He was surprised by his feelings because he came to Venice to be alone to deal with the aftermath bitterness of a bitter break up from a difficult relationship, which had lasted for more than five years, on and off. He was not looking for a new, short affair, or anything else, —he was glad to be free.

" It will not hurt to have a drink and a pleasant conversation," he argued with himself as he stood under the warm shower. He wanted to know more about her, and that was also unusual. It usually took a long time before he really got interested about the lives of the women's life he went out with. Stepping out of the shower, he dried himself, put on his robe and lay down on his bed, trying figure out the reason of his reactions, but he soon gave up and reached for a book. Later, he changed into a pair of grey pants, open -necked white shirt and a dark blue blazer. He was observing himself in the mirror and he liked what he saw. He was tall, well built with, just a hint of softness around his waste, lots of dark hair, tanned face and, white, a bit slightly crooked teeth. After a short deliberation, he decided against a tie or a scarf, combed his hair once more, and went out for a walk to pass the time until 7 p.m..

In the elegant hotel bar, Lili and Elsa chatted and sipped their camparis. Elsa stopped in the middle of her sentence. "Here he comes," she said.

Tom stepped up to their table, smiled at Elsa and introduced himself to Lili. He ordered a glass of wine from the waiter standing nearby and the three of them began to chat. It was easy, light conversation, and by the time they ordered a second round of drinks they were talking like old acquaintances. They then went to have dinner in a small, cozy restaurant at the edge of the canal by the Rialto Bridge. Tom wanted to pay the whole bill, but Lili and Elsa insisted on splitting it into thirds. They did not object to Tom's invitation to next have coffee and brandy on St. Mark's Square. After a while, Lili kicked Elsa under the table. She then excused herself, faking a headache and fatigue, and refused Elsa and Tom's offer to walk her back to the Danieli.

Tom and Elsa stayed on, listening to the tuxedoed band playing old waltzes. They did not talk—they just looked at each other from time to time. Elsa felt vibrations passing between them and was sure he felt the same. Tom reached for Elsa's hand, held it for a while and then lifted it up to his lips and kissed her palm. Elsa felt a surge run through her body, the kind she thought she would never experience again. She couldn't resist the urge to squeeze Tom's hand. Tom paid for the drinks and they walked hand in hand towards the Grand Canal. They stood there for a while without words, looking at the dark water, the colourfully lit gondolas gliding under the bridges and the embracing couples riding in them. Still without words they walked towards Tom's hotel.

That night changed Elsa forever. Tom made her feel like no one had before. He was a gentle, caring but passionate lover. He made Elsa come out of her shell and respond to his loving fully. She forgot her age and her wrinkles, and she felt like a newborn woman. Afterwards, they fell asleep in each other's arms as comfortably as old lovers.

∼

Lili went back to Australia, and Elsa stayed on with Tom. She called Sàndor and fabricated an excuse about wanting to finish some research for the novel she had started to write and needed stay longer in Venice and the surrounding islands.

They moved into a small apartment-hotel in the Lido, where they could have more privacy and Elsa had never been happier and more content in her life. She didn't analyze her feelings, the suddenness of the overwhelming love or the frenzy of the affair. She closed her eyes and rubbed the whole world out of her mind, living only for the present. She learned to love deeply, truly and without regret. In the process, she learned to love herself enough to free her soul from guilt and the fear of betrayal.

They were deeply in love. During the days, they wondered around on boats or on foot, and every day was a marvel. They could not get enough of each other and never ran out of subjects for conversation. Truly without any reservations, they talked about their childhoods and the happiness and sorrows in their lives.

They revisited Burano and bought a big bunch of fresh asparagus from one of the street vendors because they discovered both of them loved it. Tom made a wonderful, simple dinner once back at the apartment. He cooked the asparagus in water, threw it over some bread crumbs browned in butter and served it with a topping of Parmesan cheese. They had a bottle of cool, white wine and the world, with all its problems, disappeared around them, allowing them to exist just for each other.

In Murano, they watched the glassblowers and Elsa bought Tom a crystal elephant. Another day, they took the vaporetto to Torcello, a small island with just few dozen inhabitants. It was a long walk from the vaporetto station to the town centre, where a 16th-century chapel stood. By the time they got there, however, the chapel was closed, the square was deserted and the souvenir shops were boarded up. They sat for a while on a bench in front of the chapel, admiring the nearby old, stone cottages encircled with wildflowers. When they started heading back to the vaporetto station, the sky clouded over and a sudden downpour soaked the streets. To save themselves from getting wet, they stayed under the portico of the chapel, which was supported by stone pillars. When the rain stopped, they ran all the way to the station, but by then the last boat had left for the Lido. It looked like they would have to spend the night in the glass booth of the station when an old man appeared out of nowhere. He wore a captain's hat atop his curly, white hair and had a large pipe in his mouth. He looked as if he had just stepped out of an old photo book. He told them he was the caretaker of the island and kindly took them back to the Lido in his boat. They sat at the back of the boat in each others arms, kissing like teenagers under the full, red-faced moon.

The days were fun, and the two enjoyed them with youthful vigour. The nights were full of love and never-before-experienced pleasure through sex, fulfillment and happiness.

After a week they had to part, however. Elsa went back to her husband in Toronto, and Tom returned to Vancouver. They called each other every day, talked for hours and missed each other painfully. They stole a few weekends when Elsa's husband was away, Tom flying to Toronto or Elsa to Vancouver. A few months later when Sàndor came home after a prolonged absence, Elsa decided to ask for divorce. Her new-found love made her strong enough to deal with Sàndor's infidelity. Sàndor admitted to his affair and did not challenge it, and they parted without any hatred. Elsa got a good settlement and would receive a generous monthly alimony for as long as she stayed unmarried.

She rented a small apartment close to Tom's home in Vancouver. She wanted to keep a certain privacy for herself until they sorted things out. When she told David about the affair, he was alarmed and told his mother that she was not realistic. Tom was six years younger than her, and David could not believe it was true love on Tom's part. He had a good position in an architectural firm, but he was not rich. David was afraid that Tom was taking advantage of his mother to travel and live much better than he could afford by himself. He told her he knew about his father's affair and how much she suffered when the rumours became reality. He believed she was still vulnerable.

David could not deny, especially to her, that Tom gave her back her self-confidence. David also couldn't remember when he last saw his mother so happy, but he was afraid that if she married Tom, her alimony would stop and Tom would not be able to provide for her the lifestyle she was used to.

Elsa tried to bring the two most important men in her life together, but she failed. They just could not warm up to each other. She could see Tom knew that David was against him, and David did not try to hide it at all. This conflict was an obstacle in their otherwise cloudless relationship. Elsa loved Tom, but she didn't want to deal with the risk of losing her only son's love and respect. When David got married, Tom hoped that Elsa would free herself of the parental responsibility, and for a while their relationship was smooth and loving—they settled down into a happy togetherness. Elsa sold her apartment and moved in with Tom. She visited David and his new wife Paula for a few days from time to time. They were living in the old family home in Toronto while saving for a home of their own.

But a year later when the news came that her first grandchild was on his way,

Elsa became restless again. She was excited and happy that her wish to be a grandparent would come true much sooner than she had hoped. Before the wedding, Paula had said she didn't want to have children for awhile because she first wanted to become partner in the law firm where she worked.

Elsa felt that her place was with her family and became withdrawn and moody. Tom could not console her and was helpless to ease her suffering. Elsa flew back to Toronto two months before the baby was due, promising she'd be back soon after the birth.

It was a premature birth in the eighth month, and the newborn had breathing problems. He recovered after a week in the incubator but had to be watched carefully. Paula had complications and was forced to stay in the hospital for more than two weeks. Elsa spent long hours in the hospital, helping in any way she could. At home, she tried to comfort David, who was distressed and blamed himself for all the misfortune. By the time the baby and the mother were strong enough to come home, Elsa was emotionally drained. She felt her first priority must be her family—she felt she must stay to be with them or at least close by to give them help and support. Her overwhelming sense that her family needed her won over her love for Tom. After long, sleepless nights she made the painful decision to leave Tom. She knew that she was not strong enough to deliver her decision eye to eye, and she was also afraid to hear his voice. Instead she chose the cowardly way and wrote him a letter. It said:

My darling,

I can hardly write this letter, for my heart is aching for you! I cannot see you anymore. I love you and respect you as ever, but I no longer bear the pain of thinking that by loving you I am deserting my family. Please forgive me for being so weak. I loved and love you more than I could have ever imagined. I will never forget you. You are in my heart for ever.

Elsa.

Lili sat quietly, smoking her fourth cigarette, and when she saw the tears in her friend's eyes, she reached over and touched Elsa's hand.

" Stop the reminiscence., Let's go back to the hotel.""

""Sorry, the lake and those boats on the water reminded me of Venice."

" I thought so," said Lili.

Chapter 3

They reached the safety of their hotel just as sheets of heavy rain started moving across the lake, and they settled into their room for the night. A severe thunderstorm kept them awake, however. The thunder was deafening and the mountains echoed back every blast. The explosions, which did not seem very far off, shook the hotel. The rain kept on into the morning, but the clouds were thinning. Elsa was adamant to fulfill her plan to take the longest boat ride on Lake Como.

"But, Elsa, it's raining! Let's postpone it and drive somewhere instead," argued Lili.

"No way! You are not made from sugar—far from it—you will not melt. Besides, the rain will stop soon, and the lake and the Alps are breathtaking in any weather. You can sit inside the cabin if you want. I want to go all the way up to Colico and enjoy the scenery."

Lili gave in, and by the time they got to the ferry station the rain had stopped, the clouds were breaking up and the sun was working hard to burn them off entirely. Before boarding the boat they bought a few of the marvellous, fresh Italian buns with ham, cheese and salami at a restaurant across the pier. Once in the boat, Lili sat down at the below-deck bar and started to read the newspaper she bought at the newsstand beside the restaurant. Laughing quietly at her friend's stubbornness and leaving her there, Elsa climbed up to one of the nearly empty top decks, pulled her raincoat tighter around herself and sat down on one of the benches. The other half of the deck was occupied by a group of schoolchildren. They were running around, frolicking like ponies, shouting and laughing. Smiling, Elsa watched them. She loved children. Two boys, perhaps twelve years old, ran up to the bow of the deck, stood up on the railing and dared each other to lean out further. The teacher noticed them, pulled them off the railing and sent them below as a punishment.

The big boat was half empty, most likely due to the rain. Elsa had seen a small group of locals seated below at the bar arguing about politics. As the boat left the harbour, suddenly the surrounding mountains became more rugged and the water mysteriously darker, as if it wanted to hide secrets in its close-to-four-hundred-meter depth. The sun finally broke through completely and shined from the dark blue sky. Just a few persistent dark clouds floated on the horizon.

The boat crisscrossed the lake from one village to another, discharging and taking on passengers, both local and tourist. One of the villages, Bellagio, was the most picturesque and most-visited town on the lake. Elsa decided that on another day they would come back and spend a whole day exploring the village and its surroundings, not just run through it. She went down to the bar to lure Lili out.

"Don't just sit in this smelly hole. Come up to the deck and get some fresh air into your smoky lungs. The sun is out and the air is pleasantly warm."

"I'm hungry. I want to eat first!" resisted Lili.

"We can eat on the deck," Elsa compromised. "I'll buy two beers and we'll have a picnic under the sun. The scenery is breathtaking from the upper deck. I can't understand you—how can you sit inside? You might as well have stayed in the hotel," Elsa scolded her.

"Okay, okay, I'm coming. Don't bug me. Go and get the beers."

They sat down on the upper deck. The sights seemingly calmed Lili down, and she soon peacefully chewed on her sandwich and watched the passing shoreline.

The boat passed a small island in the middle of the lake which seemed to have been dropped there in medieval times. A stone castle stood in the center of the flower-covered island. With thick, stone walls and small, stained-glass windows, the castle had a round tower on top of which the Italian flag fluttered in the wind. Tourists piled up on the side of the boat taking pictures.

"Good business for Mr. Kodak," Lili mumbled sarcastically. Elsa thought it was mainly because she could not get close enough to the railing. The sun shone with full force, but the breeze from the lake cooled its heat.

"Put some lotion on your pale, indoor face before your nose burns off," Elsa commanded as she gave a jar of cream to Lili. "No way will I let you go inside again! Walk around the deck and take big, deep breaths to get some fresh air into your smoke-clogged lungs!"

"Yes, mother," laughed Lili and dutifully smeared some cream on her nose.

At the far north end of the lake was the village of Colico, the ferry's last stop. The boat would anchor for an hour before turning back. Elsa found Colico disappointing. An old, shabby hotel, a few shops and neglected houses lined the waterfront. Further from the water, the narrow streets were empty and bare of flowers or other plants. The mountains were far back from the village and hidden in a blue haze, making the surroundings dull.

After a short walk, Lili sat down on a bench at the shore, but Elsa kept walking around. From the first vendor she saw, she bought a large ice cream cone. Licking it, she meandered through the streets, but she could not find anything interesting. She turned around, walked back to the water's edge and sat down beside Lili.

"Can you imagine that people live their entire lives in a place like this?" asked Lili.

"It must be a very peaceful and unhurried life when the summer is over and no more tourists are swarming around. Sometimes I think it would be good for me to live in a place like this for a while. Just living from day to day, reading, writing and wandering around in the mountains," said Elsa, finishing her ice cream.

"And fall into a deep depression or die from boredom! You and your bizarre ideas! Will you ever grow out of them?" Lili shook her head and looked out over the water. She continued, "Let's walk back to the port. We have ten minutes before the boat departs. They better have coffee at the bar—after all, we are in Italy! I could kill for a good cappuccino."

At the station, a small group of tourists was waiting to get onboard. In front of the group was a woman who tripped over an anchor rope, fell to her knees and said loudly, "Bassza meg." Elsa and Lili looked at each other. That was Hungarian for "fuck." They stepped up to the woman and helped her to her feet.

Lili said to her in Hungarian, "Did you know that you only have to swear and you will find other Hungarians close by? Are you hurt?"

The woman looked at them and said with awe, "Hungarians? Small world, isn't it? No, no, I am fine. I just scraped my knee. Thank you!" She rearranged her pants, looked up and said, "Hello, I'm Margaret." She then extended her hand towards them.

Smiling politely as she shook Margaret's hand, Elsa sized the woman up. Margaret was middle aged, a little stout but tall enough to have a pleasantly round figure. Her almost-wrinkleless face indicated the beauty of her past youth. Her large, blue eyes sparkled with interest and intelligence, and her full lips suggested easy smiles and good humour. Her dark, peppered hair was cut short and cried out for a brush.

"Hi, I am Lili and this is my friend Elsa."

"Are you here from Hungary?"

"No," said Lili, "I live in Australia and Elsa lives in Canada."

"How interesting! Did you two meet here?"

"Oh no, no—we have been friends forever. We grew up and went to school together in Budapest, way back. We travel together once every year. This year we met in Milan and came up here. Where are you from?"

"Budapest. I came here to meet and spend some time with my friend who now lives in London. She got delayed and will not be here until the day after tomorrow.

"Well, I always say that the world shrank so small that I will not be surprised by anything, but this is amazing," said Lili. "Four Hungarian women living in the four corners of the universe meet at Lake Como!"

The ferry's horn sounded, so they boarded the boat and sat down, all enjoying the now-clear blue sky and the sun. They talked about the weather and the lake, and then Lili said, "I am going down to get a cappuccino. Anybody else want one?"

"Yes, please. I'll come down with you to get mine," Margaret said as she got up and opened her bag.

"Oh no, never mind. It's my treat," said Lili as she disappeared below.

Margaret and Elsa continued talking. Elsa was struck by the feeling that she knew Margaret from ages ago. She mentioned this and they tried to find some explanation for it. Was it possible that they had met somewhere in Hungary when they were kids or teens? School? Neighbourhood? They couldn't think of anything by the time Lili came back with the coffees and sat down, already chatting. The conversation was spontaneous, and they were completely at ease with each other. By the time they finished sipping their coffees, the boat docked back at Como. After disembarking, they stood on the pier.

Elsa asked Margaret, "Where are you staying?"

"In a small bed and breakfast not far from here. And you two?"

"We are at the Lakeview Hotel at the end of this street," Elsa answered. "It's about a ten-minute walk."

Elsa and Lili looked at each other. Lili then asked, "Would you like to have dinner with us? We know a good little family restaurant far from the tourist traps."

Margaret hesitated before saying, "It would be nice, but I think I should stay in tonight in case my friend calls about her arrival. Maybe the four of us can meet for a coffee or drink later this week?"

"Okay, here is the card of the hotel. You can call us. How long are you staying here?"

"About four or five days," Margaret said.

"Good, we are planning to leave in four days too," Elsa said. "Have a good evening, and please call us after your friend has arrived."

"Thank you. I enjoyed the afternoon and look forward to meeting you girls again. Good night!"

They parted ways and Margaret waved back once more before turning onto the next street. Lili looked at Elsa and asked, "What do you think?"

"I like her! She seems like a straightforward, good-humoured, down-to-earth woman. I have a feeling that she declined dinner because she was afraid of the expenses. I know Hungary has changed a lot in the last few years, but the forint still does not stand up as international currency. It takes lots of forints to buy a few dollars or even liras," Elsa said.

Lili nodded in agreement. "I wonder if she will call or just disappear," she said.

"I'm sure she will call us. I'm curious about her friend from London, aren't you?"

"Not very much," Lili said, making a face. Let's sit down here and have a drink before we decide where we are going to eat tonight."

Two days later, Margaret left a message at the hotel that her friend had arrived the previous night. The message also said it would be nice to meet at the Piazza Domo for a coffee around four in the afternoon. Elsa and Lili arrived at the square first and sat down at a confectionary's sidewalk table. It was a lovely afternoon—the sun shone from a cloudless sky, and the air was full of the sweet smell of flowers from the countless flower stalls around the piazza. An old man stood in front of one of the stalls, holding a bunch of colourful balloons. He let one balloon get away for the pleasure of the small children crowding around him. They screamed and laughed as the balloon flew higher and higher into the blue sky.

The bells in the dome tolled four when Elsa noticed Margaret coming across the square followed by a smaller woman in a long skirt. Lili waved to them and they approached the table.

"Hi, girls, this is my friend Edith from London," Margaret said.

"Hi Edith," Lili said, smiling at the woman. "I'm Lili and this is Elsa. Come sit. It's such a gorgeous afternoon!"

"Indeed it is" Edith said as she sat down beside Lili. "Especially after such a dreadful, rainy week in London. I could not get rid of the dampness in my flat. I can't get enough of this sunshine!"

"When did you arrive?"

"Yesterday afternoon. I flew to Milan and took the train from there. Margaret was waiting for me at the station. We were so happy to see each other after so many long years that I'm afraid we made a spectacle of ourselves. We were crying, jumping up and down and laughing all at once like two teenagers!"

"Did you order yet?" asked Margaret

"No, not yet. We were waiting for you two. I'm going to have a big bowl of ice cream with whipped cream on top," smiled Elsa. "I warmly recommend it."

"Do not let her corrupt you!" laughed Lili. "There are other sinful, marvellous and sweet things inside to choose from. Let's go in and pick something."

Conversation was brisk as Elsa studied the other women and watched them studying each other. The newcomer, Edith, looked older than the other three. She was carelessly dressed—her long skirt was frayed at the bottom and her shirt was rumpled, but both were made of the finest cotton material. On her feet she wore sandals made of leather straps, and she carried a large canvas bag, often dropping it on the pavement beside her chair without checking if the spot was clean enough. She gave Elsa the impression of an aged hippy. She looked at the other women through brown-framed glasses, which sat halfway down on her nose. Elsa watched Lili, who always dressed with care and would not step outside without makeup, observe Edith with disapproval she did not keep very well hidden.

Half an hour later, after having their coffees and sweets, they stood up to walk around the piazza and the surrounding streets. Lili paired with Edith, and Elsa walked with Margaret. Lili and Edith disappeared into a silk scarf shop, so Margaret and Elsa left them and went into the duomo with the next tour. They admired the famous stained-glass rose window above the gate and the many century-old hand-woven tapestries on the white and black marble walls. The light coming in through the rose window's bright colour inlets made the atmosphere of the church's long nave quite mystical. When they came out, Lili and Edith were no where to be seen, but they eventually emerged from the scarf shop, both of them carrying elegantly wrapped parcels.

"Did you buy up the shop?" asked Margaret.

"I bought four silk scarves for my friends in Sydney. They are so expensive back home and the selections are always very poor. Do you want to see? They are gorgeous. The colours are—"

"You are a shopaholic," Elsa cut in. "Scarves or china or hand bags, you always have to buy something. Would you believe," Elsa said, turning to Edith and Margaret, "that one time she spent a fortune on paper-thin china cups in France and carried the package in her hand all the way to Sydney. Once she got home, she accidentally pushed it off the table before unpacking it! Needless to say, every one broke to tiny pieces!"

"Oh, well, accidents happen. The joy was to buy them!" laughed Lili. "Edith bought two scarves too!"

"Yeah, but just two small ones for myself," admitted Edith. "I like to wear something around my neck and feel the soothing warmth of silk. I have a few but keep losing them."

"It's almost seven o'clock," Elsa said, looking at her watch with surprise. "Why don't we have dinner together? We know a nice, quiet family restaurant. Nothing fancy, but the food is good, the house wine is drinkable, the service is slow and all of it for cheap." She looked around at the others.

"Yes, why not? Let's go," they all said.

After the first litre of the drinkable house wine, their tongues loosened up and the chit-chat became intriguing. Lili was the most entertaining as she talked about men and her numerous affairs. Elsa knew Lili enjoyed being the center of the conversation and the cause of the bewilderment in Edith's and Margaret's eyes. Margaret also amused the group with funny stories about her students at the University of Budapest, where she taught English literature. Edith told stories about the many mistakes she made in her first year in London, not knowing the politically correct ways of her English neighbours. Elsa laughed out loud at her story about how Edith found out what the white coffee was. Simply coffee with milk! Elsa also loosened up and talked about her first year in Toronto, when she was penniless and living on doughnuts and milk, and about how she met her husband.

After dinner, all of them a bit tipsy, they walked back to the lake shore. In the moonlight, they said goodbye and agreed to meet at t

The next morning, Lili refused to get up.

"I am on holiday. I will not get up early for any boat ride. Bellagio will be there in the afternoon too. You go ahead—I doubt those two will be there! Boats leave every half hour. I might take a later boat and meet up with you. Or I'll be here." She then turned toward the wall and pulled the blanket up over her head.

When Elsa reached the port, Margaret was already there.

"Where is Lili?" she asked.

"And where is Edith?" Elsa answered with a question of her own.

"Well," Margaret said, "she's nursing a hangover from last night. We had a couple brandies on the top of all that wine! I left her in peace to sleep it off. What about Lili?"

"She is just lazy and did not want to get up. She might meet us in Bellagio later. Looks like it's just us. Shall we go?"

"Let's. I can hardly wait to get on that boat and see for myself how beautiful a place can be. I've read a lot about Bellagio."

They bought their tickets, looked at each other and climbed the steps to the upper deck. Somehow Elsa knew Margaret wasn't the type to stay in the ferry's bar for the whole trip.

The day was perfect for an outing. Morning mist still lingered around base of the mountains on the north side of the lake like a soft, gauze curtain. The snow-covered peaks shone like gemstones. After the boat left the bay of Como, the lake water became clean, deep and dark greenish blue, and Elsa could feel how cold the water was just by looking at it.

Elsa and Margaret did not talk much. To Elsa, the scenery was all absorbing and she felt rooted to her bench. Margaret took out her camera at one point and moved around on the deck taking pictures. She said, "I must take home a few photos to look at on rainy days. I know that a photograph is unable to give back the colour of the air, the smell of the lake and the sound of the wind, but looking at them will really help my imagination."

The boat docked at Bellagio, the most popular resort town on the lake. The town stood on the peninsula dividing the lake into two parts. The streets, shops and houses were built on the side of a small mountain. On the lakeshore was a wide, stone promenade bordered by shops, restaurants and souvenir tents.

"Let's walk around in the town first," Elsa suggested, looking at the dark clouds approaching from behind the mountains. "Looks like rain."

They left the lakeshore and walked along the steep, narrow streets. Many of the streets had countless built-in steps. Low stone houses with lots of flowers in the windows and doorways framed the streets, which were so narrow that the two of them had to walk in single file in order to let others pass by. They marvelled at the ingenuity of the flower decorations. In front of an old cottage's black door, a large, blue wooden boat was positioned up right against the wall. The seats served as shelves for many flower-filled pots and vases. It looked so unreal.

One of the streets led them to the south end of the village, where a large, yellow building stood—the Villa Melzit. Built in 1802 for the president of Italy, it now served as an elegant, five-star hotel. It was an unbelievable sight. The large building was in Empire style and was painted bright yellow. It stood majestically above a huge, beautiful park, and it was all enclosed by black, wrought-iron fencing. The garden was full of flowering azaleas and rhododendrons. A wide, yellow-gravel driveway led to the building's entrance from the beautifully contoured, double-iron gate with golden inlaid.

Elsa and Margaret stood on the road above, looking down at the azure water of the swimming pool in front of the hotel. The pool was close by the lake's edge and was surrounded by white lounge chairs, behind which grew tall, green hedges full of blooming red flowers. High, soaring palm trees stood behind the hedges. The palm trees were such a contrast to the rugged mountains' snow-covered peaks in the distance that Elsa got the sudden sensation of an enchanted land. The grounds were empty, and nothing disturbed the aura she felt around the place. The low, light grey cloud formations quickly approaching and darkening the sky made the scene somewhat subterranean as well. Elsa and Margaret were speechless for a while in fear of breaking the silence and causing the whole vista to disappear like a mirage. Fat raindrops eventually forced them to leave the scene and run into a nearby bar. They ordered coffee and some sandwiches.

"I did not realize how hungry I was," Margaret said, taking a big bite out of her sandwich.

"It's way past lunchtime. We're entitled to a rest and a few bites."

Elsa said as she looked around at the packed tables. "I thought the tourist season was over. We're lucky to have a table."

They munched on the sandwiches and sipped their coffee. The dim bar was cozy and the seats comfortable. They talked nonstop, pausing only to take bites. Margaret talked about the changes in Hungary in the last twenty years. Elsa listened with interest.

Then she said, "I haven't visited for at least six years. After my parents died, I didn't feel like going back. Before that, I visited them almost every year and noticed a few changes. I can't imagine how much has changed since then."

"You'll be surprised! Now we have giant supermarkets, Western-style shopping centers and of course all the bad things that come with all this—drug problems and crime. The number of cars has increased tremendously, and the traffic is horrible. And the pollution ... how is it in Toronto?"

"Well, it is not too bad," Elsa said, thinking fondly of her home. "There are strict rules about car mufflers and such, but on one of our infamous, humid summer days, the weathermen advise senior citizens to not venture outside for too long."

"How are you spending your days when not travelling? Do you have a family in Toronto?"

"Yes, I have a married son and a grandson. Ever since my divorce, I have lived alone and like it, no matter how much Lili pesters me about changing it."

"She is a domineering woman, isn't she?"

"That's true, but she is my best and oldest friend. We grew up together, suffered through the teenage and adolescent years together and left Hungary together. It was the irony of fate that we ended up in different corners of the world. What about you?"

"Same—I live alone and brought up two kids after my divorce. They are gone now, of course. My son lives in Germany, and my daughter lives in a small town not far from Budapest. She is unmarried but I have a granddaughter named Annie. Here, I have picture of her," Margaret said and pulled a photo out of her purse.

"She is adorable—how old is she?" Elsa asked, handing back the photo.

"Just about three, and she is so smart for her age. She is the apple of my eye!"

They talked on for a bit, but then Elsa looked at her watch.

"How fast time goes when you have a good time! Come, we have run to get the next boat. Lili will bite my head of if I'm not back for her cocktail hour. Will you join us?"

"I had better go and check on Edith first. We'll call you later, okay?"

Margaret called a few hours later, saying she had to return to Budapest the next day to substitute for a sick professor, and Edith was also going back to London.

"Too bad," Elsa said, hanging up the phone. "I really liked them. I had good time with Margaret. It's a pity that we could not spend more time with them. We hardly know anything about Edith. She was a mysterious character."

"Yeah, but I am not heartbroken," Lili said. "Let's go for dinner."

On their last day, Lili insisted on going to the Saturday market.

"Let's not," Elsa replied. "It will be crowded and probably full of junk."

"I am not going for the shopping. I just want to look around," Lili said.

"I know you—you always say that and end up with a bagful of rubbish. You'll have to buy an extra suitcase to pack it all in. When you get home you will stick the lot up in the garage to wait for your next garage sale"

"Okay, okay, smart ass. But it is fun! Let's go."

The market was crowded, and Elsa could not find a parking spot.

"Lili, you get out. I'm going to circle until I find a place to park. I'll see you over by that fountain. Don't you dare buy anything!"

Elsa was at the fountain twenty minutes later, but could not see Lili. "She could not wait for me, she went shopping," Elsa said to herself. She waited for fifteen more minutes before noticing Lili coming toward her through the crowd. Elsa waved her arms, and when Lili looked up, Elsa saw that her face was white as a sheet.

"Lili what happened?" she asked as they drew close. "Are you all right?"

"Some bastard stole my wallet out of my purse. All the money and credit cards are gone," she said, her voice tight and angry.

"Your passport?"

"No, I left it in the safe at the hotel, thank god."

"You never learn! How many times have I warned you to close your handbag and not carry too much money with you?"

"Yeah, yeah, yeah! Don't lecture me. What shall I do now?" Elsa could see her anger was fading and she was getting worried.

"I don't think it will do any good to go to the police—they most likely don't understand English! Let's go back to the hotel and call the credit card offices before someone buys a Mercedes on your Visa."

"I could think of a better way to spend our last day here," sighed Lili. "But hey, its just money and this was a great trip. Buy me one of those great-smelling sausages with hot mustard!"

Chapter 4

Lili's return trip from Milan to Sydney took her through Los Angeles, and she had to change planes there. She did not look forward to the second twelve-hour flight. She had planned a stopover in LA to spend a few days with an old friend who was once her lover for awhile. After the affair cooled off, they remained very good friends. He was married now and with his wife had visited Lili's family in Sydney a few times. Lili's husband, Michael, was not jealous of his wife's past—rather, he was kind of proud of it—and welcomed the guests. But she knew Michael was anxiously waiting for her because he had called and asked her to come home and not extend the trip. It was quite unusual for him to make such a request, so she gave in and cancelled the stopover in LA. She seldom put anybody before her own interests, but this time she felt compelled. Michael was a good husband, and he adored his slightly extreme wife.

~

Michael had been married before. She was a proper but kind of sour, dull woman who had secret side he never knew about, and after eleven years of marriage she ran away with a Bible salesman. It was a bitter divorce. He could not get over the fact that he had been cheated on. His wife had a smart divorce lawyer and got a very good settlement—three thousand dollars a month for ten years. There were no children and thus there was no fight for custody. His wife only wanted money. Michael did not contest the final ruling. He hated the entire proceedings and just wanted to be left alone. The divorce cost him plenty, regardless of the fact that he was the cheated party. After the divorce became final, they never saw each other again.

Michael was a corporate lawyer and owned his firm with four partners. He was well-known and respected by his clients. He was a mild-mannered man, seldom getting angry, and his patience was legendary even with the most unreasonable clients.

He lived alone after the divorce and led a simple life. A Filipino cleaning woman looked after his apartment. He did not like noisy gatherings and seldom accepted invitations from friends who wanted to cheer him up and probably match him with a new partner. He went out a few evenings a month to play cards with old friends. He ate a lot of junk food and noticed that his pants were getting tighter and tighter and his belly bigger. After getting comments and cryptic advice from his co-workers and speaking to his doctor, he decided to start exercising. He looked for the nearest fitness club to his office and walked into the health club Lili owned. Michael requested a private trainer, but all the male trainers were too busy to take him on, so Lili started to work with him herself. While showing him some exercises, she held his hand. Something moved in Michael with the touch of her skin, and after his second week of workouts he asked her out for dinner. Lili was nursing the sorrow of ending a hot and long love affair with a much younger man, and she was as taken by Michael's attention as he was thunder struck by her personality.

Michael had never known anyone like Lili before. Her loud and no-nonsense behaviour, her strong and stubborn opinions, her self-confidence, her love of life and her self-centredness excited him. On their second date, she told him about how many men, young and old, had been in her life so far and about how she was trying to revenge her divorce by learning to be the best lover in the world.

They moved in together after four months of dating. Michael proved to be a good lover in bed, regardless of his age. He was fifty-six years old by then, and he would say, "I'm an old car but with low mileage."

Lili was content. They bought a small but comfortable house in a good neighbourhood of Sydney overlooking one of the bays. Lili insisted on sharing the mortgage payments but putting the deed in her name. It was always important for her to have control over everything, and Michael let her. After living together for two years, they got married. Elsa came to Sydney to give the bride away. It was a nice, private ceremony with just a few friends. In the second year of their marriage, Lili sold her health clubs, became financially independent and happily settled down as a lady of leisure. Michael left early in the mornings for his office and she slept till late, walked the dog, played around on the computer and sent messages to the large number of people on her e-mail list.

If she was in the mood, she prepared dinner, and if not they went out to eat. Michael loved to show off his younger and lively (to put it mildly) wife. They had a large circle of friends, and Lili loved to play the part of the prominent lawyer's wife. They went out often and Michael was a great supporter of her shopping addiction.

Then tragedy stuck—Michael had a stroke. It affected his speech and his balance, but it could have been far worse if his co-workers had not gotten him to the hospital so quickly. After a year of physical therapy and exercises, he was able to look after himself and his speech returned. Only his balance remained defective. His left leg dragged, and he could only walk very slowly for a short distance. He became independent when he got well enough to drive, but just before Lili left for Italy he fell in the living room when alone in the house and could not get up by himself. He had to call the neighbour on his cell phone for help. This frightened him very much, and though he did not ask her, he hoped his wife would cancel her trip to stay with him.

Lili, however, would not even think about not going to Italy. It was her holiday and she was looking forward to seeing the fashion shows in Milan and the time she would spend together with Elsa. She hired live-in help for Michael.

∼

The Qantas flight from LAX to Sydney was delayed because of overcrowded runways. Lili's plane sat in its gate for more than an hour while waiting for clearance to take off. Lili, who had run through the long corridors of the LA international terminal to reach her connecting flight, was nervous and irritated. She had not had time for a smoke outside, and she was afraid that her nicotine patch would not be enough for the duration of the upcoming flight. She was so grouchy that she did not even look at the passenger in the seat next to her. In the first minutes of a flight, she usually chatted up whoever sat beside her and not long after was telling them her whole life story. The plane finally took off.

She hardly touched her dinner, which was also very unusual for her. She had no interest in the in-flight movie, so put on her eye cover and tried to sleep. She could not, however—her mind was troubled with thoughts of Michael.

She could hardly believe they had been together for more than ten years! Even just after her wedding, people gave her five years at the most to stick it out. She fooled everyone, including herself. When she met Michael, she was still devastated because of the breakup with Steven. She thought at the time he was the last and greatest love of her life, and she was not getting any younger. Her body had begun to settle into middle age. The passionate sex she had with Steve, who had the body of a Greek god and smiling, blue eyes, would never come back, and neither would the wild life she led after her divorce. She could not suppress a smile when she remembered how many times she had shocked Elsa with her escapades. Settling deeper into her seat and adjusting her eye cover to block out all light, she remembered the one with the unvisited LA friend, Brad.

∼

That year she and Elsa planned a drive down the California coast from Los Angeles to the border with Mexico or wherever the roads led them. Lili met Brad on the way to LA, in the transit bar of Hawaii's airport. She chatted him up, enchanted by his dark, dreamer's eyes and his full, sensuous lips. It turned out he was fifteen years younger than she and going to LA on the same flight. Lili managed to upgrade his seat to business class so they could sit beside each other all the way. When she met up with Elsa at the Beverly Hills Hilton Hotel, Lili announced that their drive must be postponed for a week because she was going on a bus tour across the deserts of California with a fantastic young man.

"Lili, you're out of your mind! You spent six hours with him. How do you know he's not a psycho who will cut your throat at the first possible minute and take off with your gems and wallet? No! I cannot let you go!"

"You're a chicken as always!" Lili retorted. "Nothing will happen to me. He is a lovely, boney boy with a great sex drive. I am going! You cannot stop me! This is my life! You wanted to spend some time with your girlfriend here, whom I cannot stand, so be free. All I ask is for you to drop me off at the LA bus terminal tomorrow at 2 PM."

Elsa spent the rest of the day and the next morning trying to talk Lili out of going but she could not. Elsa gave in and drove her to the terminal, but she wanted see for herself the marvellous boy.

Before they turned into the terminal, Lili said, "Stop, there he is!"

"Where?"

"There!" she said, pointing.

Elsa did not believe her. "No, not that unkempt, skinny guy sitting on the curb playing the guitar? Tell me it's not him!"

"That's him! Isn't he adorable? Stop the car and let me out!"

"No, I will not. You cannot be serious. I'll let you out at a loony house. They say here in LA there's one on every corner! I promise I'll visit you often!"

Lili opened the car door, and Elsa had to stop the car.

"You do not have guts to have adventures," Lili said as she climbed out. "See you next Tuesday!"

Elsa gave up. She said, "Okay, it's your funeral, but promise me that you are going to call every evening so I'll know you're alive!"

And what a wonderful week that was. Brad was a dreamer, and he wanted to be an artist or a musician. He was not handsome—he was too skinny—but he was full of a twenty-some-year-old's sex drive. They made love in a tent, under the stars in the desert and on the bus. They carried on long, soul-searching conversations. Lili fed him and paid the bills, but that did not amount to much because they stayed in the cheapest motels and campsites. She came back to the Beverly Hills Hilton glowing like a teenager.

"You do not know what you are missing," she lectured Elsa.

∽

The reminiscence relaxed her and she drifted off to sleep. Her dreams, however, did not give her peace. She dreamt not about Brad but of Steven. In her dream she was with him in Italy on a deserted beach. He had just made love to her and looked at her, his eyes smiling. Then he got up and said, "It was good, but I do not love you. I never did."

Then he started walking towards the sea and she screamed after him, calling him names. She then broke down and cried, got on her knees and begged him not to go. He did not look back and only walked farther and farther from the beach until his blond head was swallowed by the waves. She wanted to run after him, but some force would not allow her to move. In the next second, she was in Michael's arms, and they rocked her like mothers rock their babies. She felt liberated from her unbearable pain and held on tight to Michael's neck. Then he too disappeared and she lay on an iceberg, trying desperately to hang on. The frigid, blowing wind made her body stiff and she felt herself slipping deeper and deeper into the cold water. She woke up with a start.

"Oh, I am dreadfully sorry," apologized the stewardess standing above her. "I was pushed and spilt some water on you. I am terribly sorry." The woman tried to clean up the ice cubes and water on Lili's lap.

"Never mind," Lili said, smiling sweetly. "Would you mind letting me out?" she asked her fellow passenger in the aisle seat beside her.

Lili went to the toilette, washed her face, looked into the mirror in the harsh neon light and told herself, "It's still not too bad, but your time had passed, my dear. You should thank your lucky stars for Michael!"

At the Sydney airport, she called Michael and then got into a cab. As the taxi turned into her driveway, her front door opened. Michael stood there leaning on his cane with the dog at his feet. He had a wide, welcoming green on his face. The dog jumped up and down, greeting his mistress.

"I am home, my dear," Lili said truly from her heart.

Michael was thinner and looked older than when she had left, but otherwise he was fine. Lili told him everything about the trip and then went to bed exhausted.

After a good, long sleep she felt better. When she got up, Michael had already left for his physiotherapy, after which he would go swimming. He wouldn't be home until late afternoon.

Lili unpacked her suitcases and laid out all the presents she bought for Michael and for herself. As usual, her pile was much bigger. She made herself the customary Nescafe and thought about Elsa. She could not understand how Elsa could live alone and felt sorry that no one was waiting for her when she returned home. She really and truly loved Elsa, at least as much as her conceit allowed it. When they were young, she was the one who got all the attention—Elsa just tagged along. She never went "steady" with anybody, unlike Lili who sometimes had "steady" boyfriends every other week. Lili always told Elsa all about her dates and about who kissed better, always ranking the boys between five and ten. Elsa listened and they shared good laughs, but Elsa never really let out her deeper feelings about anyone.

In a few days her jet leg was gone, and Lili settled into her old routine, sleeping late, walking the dog, sitting in front of the computer, watching the six o'clock news and so on.

Chapter 5

Elsa paid the cabbie and gave him a generous tip because he carried her two heavy suitcases up to her door. It still felt strange for her to give the unfamiliar new address after twenty-five years of the old one. Last year, she had realized that David would never permanently move into the old family home, so after long deliberations and lengthy discussions with her son, she had decided to sell the house.

∼

David strongly supported the idea of selling.

"Look, Mom," said David, "the house is far too big for you, costly to keep up and the taxes were raised again. When you're away—and you're away a great deal—you have to worry about it and hire someone to take care of it. Sell it—the market is booming right now and you can get a good price for it. The location is excellent and it will go in no time. I know you love this house and it is full of memories for you, but think logically. You'll have enough money to buy a townhouse or condominium somewhere in the neighbourhood and some left over to invest safely. From the earnings you'll be able to travel more too!"

Elsa was very proud of her son. As young as he was, he was already a junior partner in a large law firm. She listened his advice and trusted his judgment. He was always a smart boy and had received strait "A's" in school, and after he graduated with honours from the University of Toronto, a well-known law firm in Chicago invited him to spend his probationary years with them. He met his future wife Paula there (unfortunately, as Elsa always thought). They moved back to Toronto and stayed with her for a few years but moved out as soon they were able to afford a home of their own.

This time Elsa was debating about his advice a lot. She called Lili to ask her opinion. She was against selling.

"Why would you sell your house," Lili asked, "your last asset for your old age? You have enough money for day-to-day expenses. And, as I've said a million times, if you run short your son should help you out. He is well off!"

"Lili, you should know me better than that! I would never ask for money from anyone, especially not from David (*especially since he is married*, she thought). You do not like him because you adamantly believe he was the reason for my breakup with Tom. But try to see the problem from my angle. True, I have enough money for day to day, but I panic every time an unexpected, larger bill comes. I charge them to my credit cards and these bills just seem to get larger and larger. I can seldom make a bigger payment, and I am already paying out a fortune in interest! Plus, I do not know if I can afford our trip to Italy next fall."

"I told you I'd lend you the money, interest free for as long as you need it. That cannot be an excuse!"

"It is not an excuse! The truth is, I don't see how I'd ever be able to pay you back!"

She could not convince Lili, and after a half-hour discussion, she promised her to think about it.

Well, she did think about it, long and hard, and she decided to list the house. It was hard for her to see the "for sale" sign in front of the old house she loved so much and where she had lived for so many years in happiness and sorrow. But it was far too big for her alone. She had always hoped David would live there after he got married, in which case she would remodel the third floor into her private apartment. David liked the idea—he was very close to his mother—but his wife Paula did not like the idea of having her mother-in-law so close, likely fearing Elsa's great influence on her husband. Paula told David that the old house was run down and she did not like it. She wanted a new one.

David gave in to his young wife and after the birth of their son bought a big property in the Bayview–Don Mills area. They built a big house with pool and all the modern, luxurious trimmings. It was a good half-hour drive from Elsa's house during the slow traffic hours. Though David was busy with his practice, his family led an active social life and travelled a lot, which did not leave him with much free time to spend with his mother. He dutifully called almost every day for a few-minutes' chat, but they hardly spent any time together alone—Paula made sure of it.

Every room, every piece of furniture in her family's home spoke of old memories to Elsa. The pencil marks on the door frame showing how much David had grown each year, the book-filled study where in the happier times of her marriage she used to sit before the fire while Sàndor worked at his desk, the spacious dinning room that filled with laughter and witty conversation at dinner parties, the sun-filled patio with plants and flowers, where she loved to sit with her morning coffee and the *Globe and Mail* after Sàndor and David left …

"You have to stop whining as an old sentimental fool," she told herself. "It is just a house."

She was lucky. The market was at its peak, and the house sold in two months. She decided against buying anything, as she wanted to wait until the real estate boom ran itself out. She rented a comfortable apartment in an older, three-story apartment house. Her apartment had high-ceilinged rooms, the bathrooms and the kitchen all had windows and the living room had a working fireplace. She moved in a month before she was due to meet Elsa in Milan, but she still did not see her finances clearly. The rent was more than she anticipated, and she was not sure about how well she'd be able to invest her money.

The move took a toll on her emotions, no matter how strong she tried to be. She didn't want to bother with the problems of investments and deposited the whole amount in her savings account, planning a long discussion with David after her return.

∼

The door shut behind the cabbie, who was smiling down at the wad of bills in his fist. As she looked around her apartment, she acknowledged happily that she liked her new domain and felt at home. During the trip she had often worried that she'd be disappointed and sad when she got back to her new apartment.

On her desk in the study, the mail was stacked up in orderly piles. Envelopes, flyers and magazines.

"I must call my new neighbour to thank her for looking after my mail," she said to herself, observing the neat piles on the desk.

She really did not feel like looking through them now, and she also did not feel like unpacking. She knew there would be time for all of that tomorrow, so she called David to let him know she had returned safely. No one was home, however, so she left a message and asked him not to call back that night because she was going to bed early. The only thing she wanted was a long, leisurely bath without any interruption, so she drew it, scented it with bath oil, lit a few candles and immersed herself in her deep, old-fashioned bathtub, letting her mind linger on.

∼

When Sàndor left and the divorce was finalized, she could finally be with Tom and thought she couldn't be happier. They were made for each other, knew what the other was thinking without anyone saying a word, as if they had been together for long years. Elsa loved the quiet evenings when Tom sat on the couch and she lay with her head on his lap, both of them reading. Sometimes she looked up and their eyes met, and he would bend down to kiss her forehead. She felt secure, protected, fulfilled and satisfied with her life.

Once a month she flew to Toronto to visit David in the family home and look after her bills. For a long time she could not make up her mind to move permanently to Vancouver. She was not sure that marriage would be a good solution. She loved him more than anyone after David, but deep in her heart she knew that it couldn't last forever.

Tom was more than six years younger than Elsa, and though it did not appear so at the time, once she reached her sixties it would become very noticeable. She loved him more than to just want to tie him down. She made up her mind to enjoy this love of her fall years as long she felt that Tom honestly and truly loved her. And he did love her, but the rivalry between himself and David put a strain on the relationship. Elsa often became moody as she fought her motherly instincts and her conscience. In those days, Tom never intruded and waited until Elsa was ready to bounce back. She always did, always with promises that she loved him and couldn't imagine her life without him. For a while all was well, and she was as happy and content as before.

They did discuss the problem many times.

"You are a smart, independent woman," said Tom, "and David is a married man. He doesn't need a devoted mother fussing around. It is high time to think about yourself, and us. You know I love you and want to marry you! I do not care if you loose your alimony—I can provide for both of us. Why do you torment yourself? You are not deserting your son! You are entitled to live your own life! You bought him up and gave him the education that made him ready for this world. There is nothing more you can do for him. He has his life, and you should have yours too. It doesn't mean that you love him less or won't be there for him in case of need! We are so happy and well adjusted together—we can have so many happy years! Elsa, please. Think about it!"

She did, and for a while it worked. But when David's son was born and his small family had so many difficulties, she gave in to her conscience, broke up with Tom and moved back to Toronto. She suffered terribly, and though she missed Tom more than she ever imagined, her stubborn mind overrode her heart. She wanted to be the loving, helpful grandmother who gives all her love to her grandson. But Paula never became close to her, and both of them were jealous of David's attention. Elsa felt she lost her son's affection, and Paula knew that Elsa still had influence in David's life. They had a distant and cool relationship and never warmed up to each other. Elsa never felt comfortable in her son's home, but she fought against it to be able to see her grandson. Every time she offered to baby-sit, Paula very politely but firmly rejected her. They hired a live-in nanny, and Elsa hardly had a chance to spend undisturbed quality time with her grandchild.;

∽

Her bath cooled off, and the candles burned down. With a deep sigh, Elsa got out of her tub, put on her soft, thick bathrobe and poured herself some brandy into a snifter. She sat in her favourite chair until she could barely keep her eyes open. Then she went to bed.

Over the next couple weeks, Elsa busied herself with everyday chores. She did the laundry and went shopping to make the apartment cozier. She bought drapes for the windows, a new bedspread and lots of green plants. Her grandson had grown a lot during her absence, and she almost melted when she saw him again. He smiled at her and said granny for the first time. David was very loving too, and they had a long mother-son talk in his study about how to invest the money from the sale of the house. Even Paula seemed to be warming up to her. *Of course,* Elsa thought, *she knows I am now financially independent and there is no danger of me living with them.* Elsa limited herself to two visits in a week and tried to go when Paula was not home. She gave the nanny breaks, taking the baby for walks in the park or playing with him in the nursery. She had lunch with David once every two weeks and suspected he did not tell his wife about it.

The long winter days dragged on. She kept herself occupied with writing, reading and going to the movies. The Christmas was very lonely. David took his family skiing taking the baby and the nanny too. They pushed aside however politely her offer than she would be more than happy to move in to the house and oversee the nanny.
    She refused invitations from her friends; she did not want to intrude in a family gathering no matter how close friends were. Her pride was strong ; she did not want them to feel sorry for her. She sat in her living room at the front of the fire on Christmas Eve and fought against her tears, she did not want to brake down and cry.
    She recalled her happy years with Tom, regretting for the hundredth time her decision to leave him. He did call sometimes, but he had recently taken an assignment in a remote part of Africa where

the phone lines were sparse. She did not want to call Lili because of the time difference—it was just about dawn in Australia. Elsa felt very much alone and hopeless about her life.

She pulled herself together the next morning and looked for something to occupy her mind. She found a couple dozen Hungarian books Sàndor had ordered over the years but had seldom read. Now she started to read them with interest. She dug out old photos of her youth in Budapest and was surprised by the homesickness she felt for her birthplace—it was the first time in many years.

On the last day of January, she found an envelope in her mailbox with a Hungarian stamp on it. The writing was unfamiliar, so she looked at the sender's name and address. It was from Margaret. Smiling, she opened the letter and read:

Dear Elsa,

> *I thought I would surprise you with a letter, no matter how much I hate going to the post office to mail it. I do not know if you have a computer or an e-mail address.*
>
> *I thought about you a lot in the past holiday weeks. During our trip at Lake Como somehow I felt that I had found a long-lost friend in you. I had a great time and was comfortable in your company, and I enjoyed the days we spent together. I admire your outlook of life. If you have similar sentiment for me, please write. I remember you were telling me that you are thinking about visiting your homeland after so many years. If you are still thinking about a visit, please come. I would love to show you around. I have an old but dependable VW Rabbit. It would be so much fun to drive around Hungary wherever our fancy took us. I also have a small but comfortable enough guest room (but only one bathroom) I would be more than happy offer you. I am free during the spring break, which is in the last week of March. We could do the driving around then, and after that you would have all the freedom you could want to discover Budapest again. We could talk about your adventures over dinner, while sharing a bottle of nice,*

Hungarian red wine.

Do write back. If you have an e-mail address, send me an e-mail. My address is: m.varga@axelero.hu.

All the best and hoping that you do take me up on my invitation,

Margaret

Elsa's heart started beating a little bit faster. She reread the letter again and again. Every time, her emotion became stronger and she soon decided she would take up the invitation to visit and stay with Margaret, even she could afford a room in any good hotel. She had also felt during their days together that Margaret was a long-lost friend. The thought of having someone to talk to in the evenings dismissed all need for privacy and the comforts of a hotel room with its own bathroom.

She looked at the calendar on her desk. She thought she could be ready in time to get there before Margaret's spring holiday started. It would be so lovely to drive around the Hungarian countryside she scarcely remembered. March is the beginning of spring over there, and while Toronto would still be cold, gray and miserable, she would be watching the trees get their new leaves and picking the blooming spring flowers.

She knew she must call Lili, so she picked up the phone. Before she dialled, however, she put the receiver back down. Lili did not like Margaret very much and did not hide it—she was probably jealous of Elsa's new, sudden friendship. But she couldn't go without telling Lili, especially since they had been talking a lot lately about how interesting it would be to go back to Hungary together! *I will tell her I'm going and ask her to join me later when Margaret goes back to work*, she decided. After checking the time difference on the world clock propped on her desk, she dialled Lili's number.

After many rings, Lili answered, "Hello?"

"Hi, Lili. It's Elsa."

"I can see that on my phone. Did you check your clock? You woke me up!"

"What? It must be after eleven-thirty in the morning over there! Are you sick?"

"No, no, of course not, but eleven is dawn for me. You know I like to sleep in."

"I know, but this late?"

"I was up till dawn consulting my diaries. I want to make a list in my computer about how many men I've slept with. I'm telling you it's not an easy task!"

"Are you sure your computer has enough memory for that big a job? You're crazy as usual! What's the point of it?"

"Oh, it just for my enjoyment. And to recall those good, old times! So what's up?"

"I decided to go to Hungary soon, and—"

"What?" Lili squawked before Elsa could finish. "You made a decision before letting me know you were thinking about it! Didn't we talk about going there together in a few years? Are you abounding me?"

"No, no! Of course not! I called to ask you to join me later."

"Why later?"

"Because Margaret invited me to stay with her, and I know you don't like her too much. And you would not like driving around the countryside in a small VW. You are not a nature lover and old Rabbits are certainly not comfortable for long-distance travel. I thought I would spend some time with her at her place and then later move into a hotel with you so we could explore our old hunting grounds." Elsa kept her voice as level as possible, knowing the most important thing was to keep from hurting Lili's feelings.

"Yes, that's true, but how have you become so friendly with her? Does she have a guest room with bathroom?"

"No, not with a bathroom, but she has an extra room for me. You know I liked her—we found so many things in common that day we spent in Bellagio and boating around Lake Como. I think it will be fun to stay with her. And if it's not, I always can say you are arriving sooner and move to a hotel."

Elsa thought she had succeeded in soothing her friend, but she noticed coolness in Lili's voice when she said, "Well, I'll think about it and let you know!" Then the line went dead. Elsa slowly placed the phone back on the hook.

But Elsa felt ill at ease. She reached for the phone again, but changed her mind and removed her hand from the phone.

"She always wants to get her own way with me and I obey most of the time. She'll get over her hurt pride soon. It will be great to spend time with Margaret and get to know her better. I think she is an extra ordinary character!"

Elsa sat down at her computer to write to Margaret saying she accepted the invitation and would be happy to come.

Chapter 6

Reminiscing about her trip to Italy, Margaret did not sleep much on the night before going back to work. She had enjoyed it completely and promised herself to try and save money to do it more often. She loved to travel and had never lost the urge to see things she was unable to when young. Every year she saved whatever she could in her travel folder. Something unforeseen always came up, however, and she would have to take money out of the fund to fill in the holes.

When she finally fell asleep, she dreamt about Roberto. Roberto, her first and greatest love of her young years.

They were walking in a large park somewhere, and their path led between colourful flowerbeds to a small inn. He was whispering in her ear how he would make love to her when they got into their room. He picked her up at their door, daring the possibility that someone would see them. He carried her in the room and gently dropped her on the wide, duvet-covered bed. A sudden blaring startled her, and shattered the dream.

She rolled over, stared malevolently at the alarm clock and sat up. She was grouchy all day and unforgiving to her students. They were restless for some reason and she could not get their attention. It may have been because of the poor weather, but everyone was sullen and bored. She tried her best to make Shakespeare's *Richard the Third* exciting and interesting, but she did not succeed.

After class, she argued with the dean, who was criticizing her report about one of her students. He accused Margaret of being impatient with the girl and said she should have been more understanding. The girl had personal problems with which she could not cope, and Margaret should give her more guidance. Margaret listened to him with rising anger. She knew what the girl's personal problem was—she was trying to seduce the dean (who was willing to surrender) and get better grades, but Margaret did not want to get into that kind of argument. It was common knowledge at the university that Dean Kormos let himself be seduced by pretty, young ladies. He was a handsome, tall, white-haired and admired professor of literature. He gave his lectures on poetry with passion, and he read the odes and poems with a soft, silky voice. The girls in his class were at his feet, each of them wanting to believe he read the love poem only for her. The one who was chosen from the crowd always got better marks than she deserved. I did not matter that he was married and was old enough to be their father. Margaret despised him, and not because she was a prude person. His wife was a good and old friend who suffered her husband's philandering in silence. The other reason for Margaret's dislike was that he reminded her of her own ex-husband.

When Margaret first came back to Hungary from Oxford, she applied for a position on the English literature faculty at the University of Budapest. She was desperate to get the job. She found her parents in a rundown apartment and without any money. When she had left for school, they were both professionals with important jobs. They lived well until the rise of the communist government. Though they served for a while, they could not deny their intellectual minds, questioned the goal of their work and became outcasts with a small pension. They wanted her to enjoy her time in England and kept corresponding like nothing had happened.

Margaret was not a beauty, but she was a pretty, soft-figured girl with fine, chestnut-coloured hair, beautiful, sky blue eyes and smiling lips, and she was very, very smart. She spoke five languages fluently.

In early childhood she learned German in addition to the Hungarian spoken at home, and when she was sixteen, she was sent to Moscow from the teacher's college where she studied to teach German to the talented young hopefuls of the Consomol (Young Communists) movement. She hated it there, but it was an assignment from the party that she could not refuse if she later wanted to study in London for a few years. She took Russian in high school and in a year's time became fluent in the language. She then got her chance to study in England, mostly because her father was a famous scholar whose expertise in physics was needed by the communists for the time being, and they wanted to keep him happy. Margaret was accepted at Oxford to study English literature. She had learned English from her parents—both of them spoke German and English fluently—and during her years in Oxford her English became flawless.

She got a job in London for the summer months as a nanny for the three children of an Italian diplomat. The diplomat was separated (at least that was what he let her believe), and his wife had gone back to Rome. He was a dark, handsome, middle-aged Italian male who charmed Margaret into his bed. He was her first lover and she fell deeply in love with him. She picked up Italian in no time, first to please him but later because she loved the soft, easy, flowing music of the language. The affair lasted into the early winter, and Roberto came to visit her in Oxford on the weekends. He would pick her up at her residence hall, and they would drive around the lush, green countryside and stay at intimate inns, or Margaret would take the train to London when she could borrow a girlfriend's flat for Saturday night.

Then came the bitter awakening. Roberto could no longer hide the fact that his wife had come back from Rome, where she had been looking after her sick father. Roberto wanted to keep the affair going, but Margaret was disappointed, heart broken and humiliated. She broke off with him, dragged herself though her last year, got her PhD, left London and made an oath to not fall in love again for a long, long time.

She kept her oath and withdrew from anybody who tried to get close to her. But she was lonely. Living with her parents at her age, made her edgy, desperately whishing for privacy in the small two bedroom apartment. But she could not afford anything else on her starting teacher's salary.

Làszlo Bartha was a handsome, forty-two-year-old professor of social studies and the head of the board that hired future candidates. Margaret knew he liked her fresh youth, her blue, sparkling eyes and her sharp mind, and he chose her over the other three candidates. It was rumoured that Làszlo had influential political connections in the communist party, and if he wanted to would not hesitate to expel anyone whom he did not like. So when he asked her for a date shortly after she got the position, she was afraid to refuse him outright.

She let Làszlo walk her home after classes, went to the movies with him and sometimes they sat in a small, intimate espresso café and talked for hours. Làszlo was attentive, a good talker and had a good sense of humour. He was smart, and they always found mutual interests to discuss. He was well-informed on every subject, he dressed well (through connections to the black market and the diplomats' shops) and he had money to spend. She had a good time with him and always looked forward to the next date.

As time went by, she found herself falling in love again. It was not the passion of the all-over love she felt for Roberto. She felt protected and comfortable being with Làszlo but refused to go bed with him. Làszlo saw that he could not have her without marriage, so he proposed and she accepted. Her father, who was very sick by then, was against the marriage. He warned that Làszlo was not right for her.

"Under his easy–going, humorous shell," her father said, "there is a cruel, cold ambition to cut down anybody who stands in his way."

Margaret, longing to be safe and have a family, married him anyway. It took her four years to realize that her father was right, but at that point they already had one child and the second was on its way. Margaret decided to stick it out for the children's sake.

She shut her eyes to Làszlo philandering, the affairs with young students and his merciless ways of getting to the top by unfair accusations against people who stood in his way. It was a stormy and unhappy marriage. Margaret wanted to get out when the kids were toddlers, but Làszlo was afraid that his good standing in the party would be blemished and would not divorce.

But then he had an affair with his young secretary, and the woman became pregnant. She refused to get an abortion, and in fear that this would kill all his chances of becoming the head of the department, Làszlo used his connections to get a fast divorce and blamed it on Margaret's infidelity. He threatened her, saying that if she mentioned anything about the situation he'd take away the children and also get her fired. All this happened in the darkest communist years, when black cars stopped in front of some houses in the middle of the night and the occupants were never seen again.

Margaret's mother was a daughter of small, landed gentry, and despite her standing as a respected scholar (until she started to ask questions) it was enough reason to take her away in one of those cars one day. Even though he knew of it, Làszlo would not lift a finger to save her. They took her to a small border village and forbade her to visit the capital. Margaret's father was dying and begged them to let him go with his wife, but his request was refused. He died a few months after his wife had been taken away. Margaret could not ask for help from anyone—she was sure that Làszlo would keep his threat and was terrified of loosing her children.

She had no other income beside her meagre teacher's salary and the child support Làszlo was forced by law to pay. To make ends meet, she gave private language lessons on her free days, but because she was afraid to teach at her home without having a permit, she taught in the apartment of a friend who worked during the night. Her children had to learn to look after themselves. Her daughter was eight years old and her son was six. Sometimes she ran home all the way from the streetcar stop because of a feeling that something bad happened to her children.

∾

Margaret had forgotten her umbrella in the rush of her rocky morning, and the cold, wet snow had soaked through her coat by the time she got back home. Stepping inside her door, shutting and locking it, she shook her coat to clear the raindrops from it before hanging it up in the hallway. Looking in the mirror beside the coat rack, she studied her reflection for a while. Where had those years gone? Where were the children waiting at the door for her, shouting over each other to get her attention? When her children were in college but lived at home, lots of young people sat all over the apartment on the weekends arguing about life and political changes. Where was the time her daughter announced that she was pregnant but did not want to get married, or when her son told her that he was gay?.

"You can not complain, old girl," she said to herself as she went into the kitchen to make an espresso, "you did have an eventful life! You are almost sixty—it's time to have some calmer years!"

She looked around her kitchen with a smile of satisfaction and pleasure. It had been redone, with new cabinets, new appliances and a new floor. It had been a great financial sacrifice but worth every tea-and-bread supper, the long walks instead of riding the bus to work and no theatre, opera or movies for almost a year. Her apartment was in an old tenement building in one of the better parts of Budapest, the center of downtown. After the kids moved out, she thought about selling it and buying a one-bedroom flat, but she never got around to doing anything about it.

So she stayed. She loved being in the heart of the city, where everything was just a short walk away. Every few years she would consider selling it because of the midnight noise from the three nearby bars and the parking problems, but she never went further than one advertisement in the paper. Three years prior she finally made up her mind to stay and looked around for estimates to redo her kitchen.

She ground the coffee beans, filled the small espresso machine with water and then packed the filter tightly. She wanted to have a really strong espresso before starting to work on the agenda for her classes the next day. She carried her coffee to her small desk in the living room, and while trying to make room for her cup by pushing aside piles of pads of paper, pencils, books and photographs, an opened envelope fluttered to the floor. She picked it up and saw it was from Edith and had come more than three weeks ago. She had called Edith before the holidays, which were just a few days away, to wish her a happy Christmas. She had promised to write but had not yet gotten around to it.

"I am a lazy bum," she said to herself. "Poor Edith must be wondering what happened to me! I must write to her today." The writing was okay with her, but she never had any stamps at home and hated to go to the post office. There were always lines at every window. She decided to write the letter immediately and then go mail it before the office closed. She hoped that at the last minute it would be less crowded. "Why doesn't Edith learn how to use a computer? How much easier it would be to correspond," she grumbled under her breath as she sipped her coffee and started to reread Edith's letter. It said:

Hello my dear old friend,

I survived the holidays, and I am still filled with the Italian sunshine! The weather here is lousy, raining most of the time, and the mornings are so fogged in I can hardly see a few meters ahead of me, but I close my eyes on the Tube and dream myself back to Lake Como! So, how are you doing? It was great to see you after so many long years. It's too bad we only had a week together. We could hardly cover the past years, no matter that we talked day and night. The accidental meeting with Lili and Elsa upset me at first. I felt that we were robbed of our hours together. But they turned out to be very interesting characters, especially Lili. Could you believe all those stories of her escapades? I felt that you and Elsa hit it off very well, though honestly I was jealous that you two behaved like old friends. So, I must apologize for my behaviour. I was acting like a bitch. I should have known better.

I hope you are well and your job is secure at the university. And that you do not have too many problems with your dean! You know, I think that in our age we should not be working but enjoying life and travelling often like those two. Oh well, we have to earn a living, no matter how much I hate getting up early every morning and—

Margaret put down the letter. She was not in the mood to read Edith's whining about jobs, money and friendships. She loved her friend dearly, but lately her pessimist and paranoid thinking made Margaret nervous and impatient. She was sure it started before she met Elsa, but deep down she knew that her new friendship largely contributed to her changed feelings about Edith. She put the letter on the top of the pile and promised herself that she would write a long, sweet and understanding answer.

The holidays were the usual chaos, with people coming and going all the time. Margaret cooked and baked, and it felt like the kitchen was a constant mess. Tidiness was never her best feature, and though she loved to cook for company, the cleanup was another story. Her daughter Klàri came with Annie, her three-year-old daughter, and brought her present live-in boyfriend, whom Margaret didn't like. He was far too polite and mushy—she did not trust him and worried about the future of her daughter's relationship. But that was nothing new since she constantly worried about Klàri.

Margaret adored her granddaughter, played with her and read her stories, but she had to admit she was relived when they returned to the small town where they lived, about an hour's drive away. Her son, Istvan, came home from Munich, where he worked as an interior designer for a large office complex. He was as sweet as always, he came laden with gifts for the family, and he tactfully left his life partner back in Munich. He only stayed for two days, but they had long talks after Klàri and her group retired to the guest room. Margaret had made up the living room sofa for Istvan, who refused to take over her bedroom. He was attentive and loving, and she was very happy to see that his success, being a much sought-after artist, and the money that came with it did not change his personality. Mother and son were very close to each regardless of the distance between them and only seeing each other once or twice a year.

Students and colleagues also dropped by for a glass of wine and a chat, and the holidays were over before she knew it. It was no wonder she did not find time to write to Edith, thought she did think about Elsa many times, wondering if she was spending Christmas alone or with her son. She recalled the few conversations about Elsa's daughter-in-law and understood that Elsa was not happy in the woman's company. Margaret had a sudden urge to write to Elsa instead of Edith. She did so and invited her for a visit. "I'll write Edith too," she said to herself, smoothing her conscience, "or better, I will call her." She picked up the phone. But there was no answer, Edith was not home

Chapter 7

Edith took the Tube from the market, changed at Piccadilly and got off at Hampstead Station. She walked three blocks from the station to her flat, still angry with herself for buying an antique clock at the market she couldn't afford. She loved old clocks and had a good collection of them, but this one was a rare find. A friend who knew about her passion sent her over to the seller's stall. She could not resist, and after a little bargaining she bought it. The package was quite big and heavy, and she had to put it down on the sidewalk while searching for her keys in her bottomless handbag. It took a few minutes to find them and open the street door of the house. She squeezed into the narrow hallway with the big box and climbed the steep stairway. Her home was on a quiet, tree-lined street in an old, three-story building. She had bought the third-floor flat about six years ago when her husband died in a work-related accident. His accidental life insurance was enough for the down payment.

∼

Edith and her husband met in Budapest during the Hungarian Revolution of 1956. It was love at first sight. Both of them were young, enthusiastic revolutionists, and they met at a rally in Parliament Square, marched together to the radio building and ran together for cover when the riot police began firing. That night Edith did not go home, instead following Gàbor to the rented room he shared with two friends. They talked for hours about what kind of life they would lead after the victory of the revolution.

Gàbor was studying archaeology at the University and dreamt of travelling to faraway places and making the greatest discoveries of all time. Edith was an art student in her second year and dreamt of going to Paris and becoming a great painter. Both were frustrated with the communist system, which made their dreams impossible to materialize. They were locked behind the Iron Curtain without any hope of a better future. They fought side by side with passion for the victory of the revolution that they believed would change their lives and make them free to fulfill their dreams.

In the process they fell in love with each other and their dreams. They soon found a minister in one of the small churches on the outskirts of the city and got married without letting anybody know about it.

Edith's parents lived in a small town all their lives. It was an hour's train ride from Budapest, and they visited the capital only when it was unavoidable. Edith was born late in their marriage and brought up in an old-fashioned, traditionalist way. Her father was the principal of the only high school in the town, and her mother a teacher there. Growing up, Edith hated the small town life more and more. Whenever she could, she took the train to Budapest to see a movie, go dancing or visit museums as her mood took her.

After long years of arguments with her parents, she left home for university and seldom visited them even for a few days. Her parents were very upset by Edith's outlook on life, her constantly changing cast of boyfriends and the way she dressed. She was a great disappointment to them, as they wanted their only daughter to become a teacher, get married to her high school sweetheart and settle down. Edith loved her parents, but she felt like an outsider at home. Her visits became less frequent, and she blamed her studies and the lack of free time. Her parents supported her financially as much as they could, and Edith worked nights at a department store and as a guide in a museum of visual arts on the weekends and school holidays. She shared a rented room with her girlfriend.

Gàbor was an orphan. His parents died during an air raid in WWII, and his grandmother, who died when he was seventeen, brought him up. He worked at construction sites to support himself and took as many evening classes as he could until he got his diploma.

After the wedding, Gàbor moved in with Edith. Her girlfriend was away for a month working on a commune farm as a school assignment. Throwing Molotov cocktails on the Soviet tanks and having great sex at night divided their days. When it became undeniable that the revolt was beaten and the state of affairs would remain unchanged if not get worse, they joined the other hundreds of thousands of young men and women and fled their homeland. Edith's heart was set on Paris, but Gàbor had a distant relative living in London who was willing to sponsor them, so they ended up there.

For a while they lived with his family, but the house was small and crowded and in a suburb. It took more than an hour on the train to reach the center of London. Gàbor got a job as a messenger boy, and Edith, whose English was better, found work as a draftsperson in an advertising agency. They could afford a tiny, single room in an old tenement close to SoHo. Soon they met other young Hungarians and made new English friends with whom they shared the evenings, had a pint in a cheap pub and went to meetings and discussions.

The first years flew by and they were happy. They were able to go on inexpensive trips to the Continent whenever they could scrape the money together for the trip. At first they would hitchhike from London to the Channel and then use their meagre funds to buy a two-way ticket on the ferry. From there they hitchhiked to Paris, where they stayed in the cheap student dorms. In later years when both of them had better-paying jobs, they took the train and stayed in small hotels. Edith spent days in the Louvre's paintings gallery while Gàbor wandered the archaeological floors.

She always cherished the memories of those few weeks. Their diet consisted of fresh baguettes, cheese and cheap red wine. Every day was exciting—the museums, the galleries—they never got enough of them.

Twilight Years

In the evenings they went to Montmartre and sat in one of the outdoor coffee houses, talked nonstop about the day and made plans to move to France and live there happily ever after. Later, when money was not so tight, they went to Spain and Italy to fulfill their young years of longing for travelling and never gave up their plan to live in Paris.

As time went by, however, both of them realized that their dreams would never be fulfilled. Gàbor tired desperately to get into the university to finish his studies, but he could not get a scholarship and there was never enough money for him to be able to quit his job. He worked for a small contracting firm. He worked hard and after many years became a partner. But by that time he was bitter and disappointed in life, his marriage, everything. Edith wanted to have children, but Gàbor was against it and their love soured.

Edith worked for a designer, using her talents to finish and colour the designs, and in her spare time painted landscapes and sold them at the flea market. They moved to a nice, two-bedroom flat. Edith had her paintings which she loved, but Gàbor had nothing left of his dream. He became jealous of Edith's painting and turned into a moody, bitter, grouchy and miserable man. They slowly grew apart, but they were there for each other in the fight against the hopelessness of their lives. Edith had occasional affairs but never a fulfilling one. She was looking for a soul mate, for someone to listen to her dreams, hug her and comfort her, but it never turned out that way. After her sex drive slowed down, the partners left. In the twelfth year of their marriage, a loose scaffold fell and stuck Gàbor, and two days later he died of his head injury.

At first Edith was dumbstruck. It did not matter that they hardly talked to each other—he was a part of her life. She was used to his grumbling when he read the newspaper in the evening in his old, tattered easy chair. Edith had wanted to get rid of that chair for years, but he refused to let it go. She was used to his noisy ways of making coffee in the kitchen every morning and the bang of the door when he left for work. She was used to hearing him searching for his keys outside the door every evening.

The apartment was empty and cold without him. His sour remarks when she was late and he had to wait for his dinner faded away from her mind. It took her a year to get rid of his tattered easy chair. She left his books the way he had left them on the bookshelves, his pipe on the table and his keys on the hook in the hallway. She was lonely. They did not have many friends, as in his later years Gàbor had not wanted to go out or have people over. Their old Hungarian friends were scattered around, led different lifestyles and they were not in touch with any of them. Edith had a few friends, but they were not close or intimate, rather just acquaintances to have a cup of tea with at the flea market or keep on eye on each other's stalls. There were a couple people from the designer's office with whom she could carry on conversations about politics or happenings around the world. She did occasionally invite a few people for dinner to break up the monotony of their life, but Gàbor, who had been a great host and loved to have guests around when he was young, hardly took part in the conversation. As soon as he could after dinner without being rude, he made an excuses or claimed an early start at a site the next day and disappeared. He never complained but made it clear that he was not in favour of company.

After his death, however, Edith remembered only the happy years, the love and passion, sharing their dreams and the trips in their younger years. The problems and unpleasantness faded from her mind and she became depressed.

She hoped her new, smaller flat would help bring her out of her depression, but it didn't help. Most mornings it was hard to get up, and she stayed in bed more and more or walked around the apartment in her pyjamas. She could not eat or sleep, and she started drinking excessively to get through the nights. On one especially bad day, she decided to end her life and turned on the gas oven. But when her cough became excruciating, she rushed to open the windows and the doors—she could not go through with it. This episode frightened her enough that made an oath to never try to kill herself again, and she went to a psychoanalyst for therapy. The treatment helped. She learned to live alone and started painting again, trying to express her anguish on her canvas.

When her vacation time came up, she decided to go back to Hungary to spend time with Margaret. In the years after her father died, she had been back a few times to visit her mother, and she had been back for her mother's funeral a few years ago. Those times she stayed with Margaret.

Edith and Margaret met in their university years at a fraternity party and became fast friends. Edith admired Margaret's brain and her intellect, and Margaret was fascinated by Edith's strong, opinionated views and her "who cares, I am who I am" attitude on life.

At times they would not see each other for weeks, but they shared the ups and downs of their lives and were always ready to help. They lost each other for a few years after the revolution in 1956. When six years later Edith went back to Hungary for the first time to visit her parents, she looked up Margaret. After that they kept in touch. Margaret visited Edith in London when Gàbor was working out of town, and they took the train to Scotland and booked a bus tour from Edinburgh to Portree, on the Isle of Skye.

It was a four-day tour. The first day was spent on the road. After they left the city limits of Edinburgh, they rode through wooded areas for a while, and then the scenery changed entirely. Valleys with vegetation a dozen shades of green and jagged, white rocks scattered all over. Sometimes they could not see if the shapes were rocks or sheep. Bare mountains were half-covered by black clouds, and rain pounded the mountainside while the peaks bathed in sunlight. Both of them sat wordless on the bus, and sometimes their eyes met with delight. Towards the evening they stopped at a historical castle called Eileen Donovan Castle.

The castle was located on a small island in a lake. The lake was like a mirror, and as the late afternoon sun broke through the dark clouds, it painted the lake and castle numberless hues of gray and magenta. High mountains surrounded the lake, giving a dramatic frame to the whole scene.

The two women stood on the medieval stone bridge leading to the gate. Edith took out her sketch pad and said to Margaret, "Why don't you go inside with the group to see the rooms? I want to make a few sketches before the light changes. I've never seen such a magnificent sky." She found a rock by the lake and started to work.

By the time Margaret came out, Edith had six sheets filled in her pad.

"Well, you did not miss too much," said Margaret, sitting down beside her on a rock. "Inside was a disappointment. The furniture didn't look authentic though you could see they tried, and life-size wax figures were set up in the kitchen as bakers, cooks and assistants working away with wax vegetables and meats. I hate it when they commercialize such a beauty! You were right to stay out. May I see your drawings?"

"No, don't look at them yet, these are just scribbles!" Edith said in a high-pitched voice. She tilted the pad away from Margaret's eyes. "I'll show them to you before you go back to Budapest. By that time they will be in a kind of form. Let's go—everybody is already on the bus."

They got to Portree, a small fishing village, at dark. They stayed in small bed and breakfast, and the next day they just walked around enjoying the countryside. They were in perfect harmony and at peace. When Edith stopped to draw, Margaret took out her notebook and made notes or just enjoyed the view.

They both became meditative on the topic of soul mates, maybe because of the natural beauty and pastoral settings of the Scottish landscape. They talked, exchanging the stories of their life after Edith left Budapest. She told Margaret about the hardships of emigration, their first difficulty, and their following happy years in the new country. They discussed her unfulfilled dream of becoming a well-known painter, the slowly deteriorating marriage and Gàbor's jealousy of her insignificant success in selling her landscapes at the flea market. She finally let out her despair that her life was unjustly full of failure, no matter how hard she wanted to succeed. Margaret then told Edith the story of her marriage, her divorce, the hard years after that and stories about her children. Their friendship deepened during this trip and became the close unity of two middle-aged women.

A few months after Gabor's death, the memory of that trip made Edith decide that she needed a long, heart-to-heart talk with Margaret, so she booked a flight to go be comforted by her friend.

Margaret was very understanding, but she was withdrawn. Edith sensed that she did not have Margaret's full attention. She did not realize then that she was too demanding, and wanting to spend every waking hour with her made Margaret pull further away. She was not ready to entirely give up her privacy, and Edith's rambling reminisces about the good years of her marriage and her pessimistic outlook on life as a whole made her edgy.

After this visit Margaret became a bit reserved with Edith in their communications. They did not see each other for four years, though they kept in touch with occasional letters. When Edith suggested spending their holiday together at Lake Como in Italy, Margaret was

Twilight Years

ready to go. She had a bad year behind her and many fights with her daughter about her relationships, no matter how hard Margaret tried to stay out of her life. She was ready to go away, leave all that behind and have a good time with a friend.

For a while all went well. They were happy to see each other and barely stopped talking to sleep a few hours on the first night. But after Margaret introduced Edith to Elsa and Lili, Edith felt cheated out of her rights as Margaret's soul mate. She watched bitterly as Elsa and Margaret acted as if they had always known each other. Edith felt left out. She made bitchy remarks about the two new women when she and Margaret were alone.

"They are two rich bitches who have never worked in their life. I am sure they look down on us. Just look at the way Lili dresses and the careless way she throws money around. I don't think I like them."

"But, Edith, they are not like that at all. I am sure both of them have had hardships in their lives just like us. Don't be so hard on them! I think they are interesting and intelligent women. I am glad we met."

"Well, I am not, and I am not going on the boat trip tomorrow!" said Edith with sharpness in her tone.

"Do you want me to call them in the morning and cancel it?" asked Margaret, wanting to lighten up Edith's mood.

"No, you go," Edith said, suddenly feeling sorry for being harsh. "I feel dizzy from all the red wine and all this brandy. I want to sleep it off. I would not be a good companion. Just do not wake me up in the morning."

The next day, Edith apologized to Margaret for her loose tongue and agreed to go out to dinner again with Elsa and Lili. She wanted to show her better side. But when Margaret was called back to the university she decided to leave too.

Edith placed her newly acquired clock down on the kitchen table. She sighed, and as she loosely stretched her back, she noticed the mail lying by her door. A kind neighbour must have brought it up for her. She shifted through the envelopes until one caught her eye. *Budapest*. It was from Margaret.

Long months had passed since Lake Como and since Edith's letter of apology to Margaret. This was the first response. She had been hurt, disappointed and felt sorry for herself by the lack of news and just the day before was at the point of calling Margaret. She carefully ripped open the envelope and read:

Hello my dear friend,

I am sorry to be so late with my answer, but you know me, I hate to go to the post office. I wish you would keep up with the times and get yourself a computer. I wanted to call you, but this month my budget is very tight; long distance calls were out of the question.

I hope you are well and so is everything around you. I think of you often when I step out in the mornings to the cold, wet streets. How freezing it must be for you to sit at your stall at the flea market! I hope you sell many sunny landscapes to make people feel warm and happy.

I survived the holidays with their usual chaos. I needed a few weeks to get back to normal, physically (and one more month financially). Well, I am not getting younger.

I work many hours these days, and besides my regular lessons I am substituting for a colleague who left for a year sabbatical. I can hardly wait for the spring break.

I got a letter from Elsa; she is planning to come to Budapest in the spring. She has not been back for more than six years, and she is very excited about the visit. I invited her to stay with me and offered to take her around the countryside during my spring vacation. There is a possibility that Lili will come later. Wouldn't you join us? I bet Lili will stay in a hotel and Elsa will move in with her, so I'd be very happy to have you at my place. We'll have fun and long, gossiping evenings. (I'll fill up my wine shelf.) So what do you say? Please think about it.

Love,
Margaret

Edith was upset, and her jealousy flared up again. "So," she grumbled to herself, "they are going to tour the countryside? Why didn't she invite me to join them? Why just for after? No, I will not go!" She made a ball of the letter and threw it into the wastebasket.

She was upset all the next day, so she closed her stall early and took a long walk by the canal. It was a nice day though still cold, but the smell of the approaching spring was in the air. The birds sang on the yet-bare trees, and though the afternoon sun did not give any warmth, it was shining and promising warmer days ahead.

Edith slowly relaxed, and her anger cooled off. She reminded herself that she had pushed Margaret away a couple times by her possessiveness, and she did not want to risk it again. After all, Elsa lived far away and could not be a permanent threat on Edith's own, cherished friendship with Margaret. She had been through upsetting times lately, so she decided to go to Budapest. She too needed a break.

Chapter 8

Elsa was excited for her trip to Hungary. She hadn't been back to her homeland for a number of years, since after her parents died she felt she didn't have any reason to go. Before their deaths and as they became too old to travel, she had gone on yearly visits out of duty. Her mother died eight years prior, and her father could not endure the loneliness and just gave up and died a year later. After his funeral, Elsa decided that she will not return to Hungary for a long time. Her sister and brother-in-law emigrated shortly after the funeral to join their only son in Los Angeles, where he was a well-to-do theatrical agent. Elsa kept close contact with them by mail, by phone and they visited each other at least once a year. She liked her brother-in-law and always had a good time with them.

However, a few old friends and some distant relatives were not enough reason for a trip to Hungary. She now had Margaret and her suggested trips to the countryside. Lili's reaction was bothering her, but knowing Lili, Elsa was sure she'd get past it soon enough.

Elsa called David to tell him about her trip. David was surprised that his mother had suddenly decided to go to Hungary after so many years, but he did not question her decision. He wished her a good trip and asked her to bring back a box of his favourite candy, marzipan.

"Remember, Mother, the kind grandfather used to buy me if I was a good boy when we went for a walk in the park during our visits?"

"He bought it for you even if you weren't good. It was just a promise so you would be," Elsa replied with misty eyes. She was touched by David's reminiscence. "It is so good to hear that you still remember them fondly."

"Of course I remember. I even remember the street where he used to buy it. On a narrow street somewhere close to the Danube. The street was named after a city but I've forgotten which one."

"It was called Parisi utca, and if the shop is still there I'll buy you a box and another one for Andrew. May be he'll like it too. I would like to come over next Thursday to say goodbye. Will you be home?"

"Thursday? I have a court case, but I'll try to get home early. Come around six. I cannot promise about Paula. I think she has some kind of charity meeting at her club on Thursday."

It could not be better, Elsa thought. She still did not feel at ease if Paula was around during her visits.

"That's alright. I'll call her to say goodbye before I leave. See you on Thursday." Elsa hung up the phone and then sat down to make list of things to do list before leaving. She caught herself humming, which she had not done for a long time.

The flight was too long, and Elsa could never sleep on planes. She had to wait for her connection in the crowded Frankfurt airport for more than three hours. She kept walking around the shopping area, looking for a seat and pushing the cart holding her bags. An hour later she found an empty chair and dropped into it.

"I look like hell," she told herself after taking out her hand mirror and then quickly putting it back in her purse. "I must make some effort to be presentable or else Margaret will not recognize me." Just before her flight left for Budapest, she went into a bathroom near her gate and washed her face, powdered her nose, put some lipstick on and tried to smooth her unruly hair. The flight was only one and a half hour, but she was glad to be off her feet.

Waiting for her bags in Budapest, she suddenly panicked. She had spent only a few days with Margaret at Lake Como, and now she was going to stay at her home. True, they were drawn to each other and felt like old friends, but that was then, during a holiday under the sunny skies of Italy! What if it turned out differently this time?

Margaret was waiting for her at the edge of the crowd, waving both of her arms. They greeted each other, embracing warmly but with some restraint. Elsa could tell Margaret had the same fear that the invitation could turn out to be a mistake. Driving home, they exchanged pleasantries about each other's immediate health and Elsa's flight.

Margaret drove around the block at least three times before finally finding a parking place for her small car.

"Every time I have to do this, I swear I am going to sell my apartment and move somewhere out of the city where I can have a permanent parking place. But of course I never do it. I love living here in the heart of the city too much. I'm so close to everything. There are two theatres in walking distance, lots of espressos, bars and shops. Not that I drink or shop a lot, but I do like to walk around and look at people who do so," said Margaret as she turned off the motor. They got out.

"I am afraid we have to walk one street up to get to my place. Here, let me have one of your bags."

"Have the smaller one. They are not heavy. I can manage this one—it has wheels."

The building where Margaret stopped and opened the door was an old, four-story building badly needing renovation. The elevator was a small box, which made Elsa claustrophobic. It was not an easy task to squeeze in with the suitcases. The elevator started with a big jerk, and then slowly climbed up to the top floor, groaning all the way. Elsa let out a sigh of relief when Margaret opened up the doors and they stepped into the corridor. Elsa almost felt like turning around and going to a hotel. When Margaret opened her door, however, Elsa changed her mind completely. Margaret's place was small, but it was bright, colourful and cozy.

"This is your room," Margaret said, opening a door in the hallway. "I am afraid it is not big, but I hope you'll be comfortable. The bathroom is across the hall. I cleaned up a shelf for your things. If you want to take a shower and have a nap, feel free. We can talk later or tomorrow."

"No way," Elsa said, smiling. "I'll just unpack and take a shower to feel human again. Then I'll be ready for everything."

"I'll get some food on the table and open up the wine," said Margaret as she started towards the kitchen.

"Please, don't bother cooking. I am not hungry at all. I think it will take while to get back my appetite after all that junk food they throw at you on the plane. But I can hardly wait for a glass of wine."

The two women sat at the kitchen table with the half-full bottle between them, and all of their anxiety about the visit vanished. Elsa felt close to Margaret and opened up, talking about thoughts she never felt comfortable discussing with Lili. She did feel slightly disloyal towards Lili, but it was easier to talk about such things with Margaret. Lili was a great friend, but her self-centred nature could not fully fathom the sensitivity of Elsa's soft-hearted and forgiving disposition. Elsa had learned to avoid talking about subjects that would surely meet with Lili's disapproval. She felt uneasy listening to Lili's lectures about being far too soft-hearted for her own good. It was true, but it was her nature and she could not and did not want to change and became someone she was not. Lili could never understand that giving was pure pleasure, as was loving people the way they were without judging them.

She once told Lili, "If I love someone, I love them as they are, with all their shortcomings. Everybody has a bad side and everybody is a bit crazy. Otherwise the world would be a very boring place!"

"Well, I can't be that forgiving," Lili had answered. "If someone irritates me or I don't like him or her, I let them know. You've seen me. Life is too short to waste time being nice." Lili sneered and said, "You better change at least a bit before getting ruined by your big heart."

To Margaret she was able to open up completely. By some strange wavelength they understood each other. Margaret was not as forgiving as Elsa, she judged people harder, but she was not egocentric as Lili and listened with open heart. She was ready to help and would give the shirt off her back to someone in need.

The first couple of days went by quickly. Margaret had to work for two more days, so Elsa spent the time wandering around the town to get the feel for it, to remember her childhood and to focus on her memories. The more she walked around, the more nostalgic she felt. She visited the old apartment house where she grew up. It was the same as it had been seven years ago. Nothing had changed, though the small grocery store on the street level had morphed into a food market. She didn't go inside the house, preferring to just look at it from the other side of the street. She really did not want to meet anybody who might remember her.

She recalled her last visit, when she came for her father's funeral. She could not stay in the empty rooms—they were too full of memories—and had moved to a hotel to ease up her heavy heart.

From the old house, she took the streetcar to the cemetery to pay her respects to her parents and put flowers on their graves. She stood there for a long time, simply looking at their names on the marble gravestones. They had been married for more than fifty years, they loved each other, they lived for the family and they had a good life. She knew she had caused them a great deal of pain when she left so unexpectedly, and her sister could never fill in emptiness their first born left behind, no matter how hard she tried. Elsa arranged the flowers once more.

"Rest in peace," she murmured. "I loved you both very much, and I am sorry to have caused you so much suffering." She turned away with tears in her eyes.

Before going back to Margaret's, she went to the big city market three blocks from Margaret's apartment and bought long-forgotten ingredients and food to make dinner. She had it done by the time Margaret got home. After dinner, they shared the cleaning up and talked late into the night.

On the third day, they loaded up Margaret's ancient Volkswagen and drove away from the city without any plans of where to go.

"We go wherever the Rabbit takes us," said Margaret. "But we'll start towards the north."

It was a lovely spring morning. The sun was shining and the birds were singing on the fresh, green branches. The rain from the night before had cleaned the pavements and the street smelled fresh.

Margaret drove out of the city on one of the main highways but soon left it for the side roads.

They drove through small villages where the main streets were lined with low, ancient, whitewashed houses, some of which were reed thatched. Elsa was amazed that they still existed.

"I thought you could only see these in history books."

"Then you'll be surprised," said Margaret. "By looks, these small villages have not changed a lot. The side roads are still dirt and the street wells still work. These houses have running water and electricity, but the catching up with the times is slow. As you see, there is a computer shop on the corner and TV antennae on many roofs. The problem is that the young generation doesn't want to stay. There are no industries, no high schools or any other possibilities for getting ahead. They are moving to larger towns for a better life and opportunities. The populations of these villages are shrinking dangerously and nothing has been done about it. It means the end of an area. There are quite a few 'ghost villages' around here."

They drove in silence for a while. The scenery enchanted Elsa, and she was playing her old game of making up stories to match the sights.

Two old women stood talking by a low, open garden gate. Both were dressed in dark, layered skirts, and their heads were covered with a babushka. One of them wiped her tears with a big handkerchief while the other listened and nodded. Elsa's story got as far as the crying one telling of how her daughter-in-law hurt her feelings by hardly eating anything of the birthday feast last night for her son when Margaret's voice brought her back to reality. She shuddered.

"Oh! You look like you just woke up! Are you all right?"

"Of course I am." Elsa paused, unsure of how much to tell her new friend. "I was just playing a game. I make up stories about the things I see. Isn't it stupid?"

"Not at all! Believe it or not, I used to do the same! We should exchange stories some time. But now it's getting late, and I do not like to drive after dusk. There is a place we could stay about fifteen kilometres off. It is an old tourist guesthouse—nothing fancy. They supply clean bedding, but you have to make up your own bed. The washrooms, showers, dining room, and kitchen are all common space, though of course it is clean and at this time of the year will most likely be empty. I stayed there once with someone special. I had a great time, I might tell you the story one day." She winked Margaret. "I used to go there quite often when I wanted to get away from it all."

"Sounds fine," Elsa said, smiling. "Why don't we buy some food for dinner instead of driving somewhere to eat? It would be more relaxing than a restaurant."

They stopped at a village market and bought sausages, home-cured ham, a big chunk of cheese, bread, onions, peppers, tomatoes and fruits for dessert.

"We are going to have a feast! It has been a very long time since I last tasted real Hungarian country sausage and ham," said Elsa enthusiastically as they packed the bags in the car. "Good thing I'm hungry. I think we bought enough food for a dozen. We cannot possibly eat all of this!"

"You'll be surprised what the Hungarian country air can do for your appetite! Let's go. I am hungry too."

Margaret drove into a fenced-in, sad-looking yard right next some railway tracks and stopped at the front of a long, low building. She knocked on a door that was peeling in many different colours of paint. A middle-aged man appeared at the door and looked at them with distrust, but once recognizing Margaret he changed into a jovial guesthouse keeper.

"Hello there. Good to see you again. What are you doing this godforsaken country so early in the spring?"

"Hello, Jani. I am driving with my friend around the countryside. Would you have a room for us for two nights?"

"For you, Margaret, always." They shook hands. "The place is empty and most of the rooms are not ready yet. I cleaned up a double room this morning. It has two single beds and is yours if you want it," said Jani, eyeing Elsa curiously.

"I am sure it will be fine! Jani, this is my friend Elsa, from Canada."

"Glad to meet you," said Jani, shaking Elsa's hand. "I hope you enjoy your visit here."

He showed them to the room, brought the bedding from storage, and good heartedly gave them two extra blankets while saying the nights were still chilly and there were no heaters in the rooms.

The room was Spartan. It held two single beds, and a low, slanted, water-ringed table stood between them. A half-rusted reading lamp sat on the table. A cloth rack was nailed on the wall, and naked light bulbs hung from the ceiling. But the large window facing the yard and the railway tracks was covered with white lace curtains and made the room cozy and friendly no matter how frugally it was furnished.

They unpacked the car and went to explore the kitchen. It was a large place, with a big, wooden table in the middle, a giant six-burner stove and an enormous, battered fridge on one wall. The other side was covered with padlocked cupboards. Elsa looked questioning to Margaret.

"Oh, that! Families stay here during the tourist season, and everyone gets their own locker where they can keep food and stuff. Also, every cupboard contains four plates, cutlery, and glasses that they have to account for before leaving. They can cook on the stove and use the utilities, but they have to clean up after. As I told you, this is an old tourist lodge left behind by the communist system as a 'workers haven.' It belonged to the railway workers union."

"That explains the tracks," Elsa said.

Margaret smiled. "I thought it would be an adventure for you, you spoiled Canadian lady!"

"Okay, I get your point. Let's do something about dinner—I'm starving!"

The dinning hall was a huge room with windows facing the country road they drove in on. One long table covered with faded, cracked oilcloth was surrounded with lots of different types of chairs. Margaret set up a corner of the table with plates and cutlery from their assigned cabinet. Elsa unpacked the food, cut up the fresh and crusty country bread and opened up the wine they brought from the city. Margaret lit the candle she had brought for the occasion. Chatting away, they started to eat and drink. Soon their plates were empty and only a small portion of bread, a piece of sausage and some cheese was left on the checkered linen tablecloth. The wine bottle was more than half empty.

"See, I told you we did not over shop! We ate up almost everything! I am stuffed," Margaret said, leaning back in her chair. "My pants are too tight. I have to loosen them up," she groaned, opening up her waistband and heaving a deep sigh.

Elsa reached over, filled up the glasses and lifted hers up, saying, "Cheers! You own me a story."

"Cheers. What story?"

"Remember you said that you had been here before with someone special?"

"Oh, that! Are you sure you want to hear it?"

"By all means," said Margaret eagerly.

"Okay then."

~

I may have said earlier that after my affair with the Italian Roberto, my first love, was over, I never saw him again. That was a lie.

A few years after I came home, he was sent to Budapest on official business. Somehow he tracked me down, and one afternoon as I stepped out to the street from the university after work, I bumped into him. He had been standing just outside of the gate where I could not see him from the gateway. My heart stopped for a second, but I pulled myself together and walked past him without a word. He followed me up an empty side street and begged me to talk to him. I looked around, and seeing that no one was near I stopped and told him I didn't have anything to say to him and he had better leave me alone. But my voice was full of tears, and when he touched my hand the old flame burned through my body—the one I thought was extinguished forever. He must have felt it too. "Please, Margie, please," he said to me, "I must see you!"

I was afraid that someone who knew me would see us, so I told him to meet me at the end of the number two streetcar line in an hour, at the foot of Margaret Bridge. He nodded and walked away.

You must know that this happened before the changes of the political structure. To be seen with a Western diplomat was dangerous for me just as it was for him. I was also going out occasionally with Låszlo by that time, and he was or at least wanted to be known as an important member of the communist party. Shaking and feeling sick, I walked down to the promenade on the Danube. I knew, no matter how much I wanted to deny it, I still loved Roberto and was shivering just from the memories of his hands on my body. I sat down on one of the empty benches, debating with myself.

Oh, yes! How much I wanted to see him! But it was unwise—I could loose my job, get put on the unwanted list and never teach again. After a while I gave up reasoning with myself and walked over to the streetcar stop. I let three streetcars go by before I finally boarded one. It was late afternoon, the end of the working day, and the streetcar was crowded.

I navigated myself into a corner at the end of the coach and stood with my back to the crowd, looking out the window like a kid who thinks if she doesn't see anybody she can't be seen. I waited until everyone got off at the last stop before leaving the streetcar. At once I saw him standing at the end of the platform. I walked past him and whispered, "Follow me," like in a spy movie. I led him to the bridge and started to walk towards Margaret Island. He followed only a few meters behind me. When we reached the island, I turned onto the walkway at the banks of the Danube. It was dark and only a few street lamps were lit. I stopped, he caught up with me and without a word we were in each other's arms, kissing and holding each other like we never wanted to let go. After, when we calmed down somewhat, we walked to the darkest part of the path and sat down on a bench. He told me he missed me dreadfully and could not get me out of his mind. He wanted me to go with him to his new post in Greece. He'd rent an apartment for me.

Since he was in the Foreign Service he could not divorce his wife, he told me, but soon he would retire and we'd be together forever. He begged to come with him to his hotel, where I could use the back entrance. I told him he was a naive Westerner. I was sure they kept tabs on him and we were lucky nobody followed us to the island. After many kisses and longing touches, I was ready to give in. But I couldn't go to his hotel. I had a trusted girlfriend with whom I used to go backpacking, and for the weekend coming up I could pretend I was going away with her. I told him where we could meet, but he had to find his own way there.

So, to make this long story short, I met Roberto at the end of this village, in this guesthouse, for the most wonderful two days and nights, and my poor girlfriend spent the weekend alone in an awful bed and breakfast a little ways away. It was early spring, and the place was just as empty as it is now. I gave Jani a generous tip, and he did not ask any questions. We made love in the mornings, in the afternoons and all night. We made love up on those hills on the cold grass. I must be honest with you—I was close to going with him to Greece—but I remembered my father's advice: first the head, then the heart. My mind was stronger. I knew that I was not cut out to be a mistress.

On the last night, we cried a lot, loved a lot and said goodbye. I never heard from him again. I went back to my life, dated Låszlo and listening to my head, married him. I wanted security and a family.

Elsa listened to Margaret's story with full understanding in her heart. She knew how painful could be to let go a loved one because you have to listen to your mind rather than do what your heart wants. She reached over and squeezed Margaret's hand.

Margaret drained the last of her wine. She looked over at Elsa with misty eyes and said, "This is the end of your bedtime story. Let's go to bed. Tomorrow it will be your turn."

Chapter 9

The next morning Elsa woke up early. She looked over to the other bed and saw Margaret sleeping peacefully with her head under her pillow. Not wanting to wake her friend, Elsa got up, gathered her clothing quietly and carefully left the room. She walked to the end of the long, bare, cold hallway to the showers. The water was tepid no matter how long she let it run. She was shivering when she finished and congratulated herself for bringing her warm sweater in addition to her jumper. She put both on and went outside.

In the barren garden was a large picnic table with benches around it. A plank roof overhead provided shelter for the table from sun or rain. Elsa sat down on a bench facing the railway track. The tracks were fenced in with a concrete boundary marker about two meters high on both sides. It was not a solid fence but a pattern of big, oval openings and was painted white. It did not obscure the view. The small, white house of the stationmaster stood on the other side of the tracks. The window shutters were red, and flower boxes full of early spring colours, bright yellow daffodils and blue forget-me-nots sat on the windowsills. The house stood in a yard separated from the rest of the grounds by a low, white picket fence. A few chickens scratched noisily in the dust, complaining that there was nothing to find. Three fat, white ducks waddled by them towards the one green corner of the yard where grass was growing. A large, black dog lay on a sunny spot watching all of them placidly, moving only his eyes.

It was a cool, misty morning. The sun was out but not yet strong enough to burn off the haze that was lingering on the hills.

As Elsa sat there absorbed in the sights, she felt a kind of sensation that she had been there before. The station house, the fence and the flowers all seemed familiar to her. She searched her mind and after a while realized why she felt this way.

When she was a teenager, Elsa's family spent the summer holidays at a resort by Lake Balaton. Her aunt had a house there on the top of a hill not far from the lake. To get to the beach they had to cross the railway tracks by the stationmaster's house, which looked like exactly like this one. It seemed it was only yesterday instead of more than forty-some years ago.

The memories made her smile, and a warm, tranquil feeling took over her mind and body. She remembered her father, tanned and handsome, navigating a small sailboat on the light green lake. He waved proudly to them when he managed to turn it into the wind. Her mother was seated on a chair at the end of the long, wooden pier, worrying that the boat was leaning too far over into the water, but she waved back, smiling and hiding her fear. Elsa thought about her sister as she walked back and forth on the beach showing off her first bikini and trying to get the attention of the handsome young man who was putting his kayak into the water. Those were such carefree, happy summers.

Her aunt who owned the house was much older than her mother and a big, heavyset woman with a great sense of humour. They were close knit, and ever since Elsa's mother got married and moved away from the family home, they cherished the time they could spend together. The house was always full of laughter as they mercilessly teased each other.

The sun soon burned up the mist and it day turned pleasantly warm. Elsa moved to let the sun warm her back, but kept looking at the white fence and daydreaming. The smell of fresh coffee made her turn around. Margaret was standing behind her, a big mug in both of her hands.

"Good morning, you dreamer! I saw you from the window and called down, but you didn't even move! So I made a real strong coffee to wake you up."

"You are an angel, Margaret," said Elsa, taking one of the hot mugs.

"You slept like a baby. I didn't want to wake you. What time is it?"

"Just after ten." She took a deep breath and exhaled with a sigh. "Oh, what a beautiful morning! Aren't we lucky with the weather?" said Margaret as she sat down beside Elsa. She continued, "May I, or do you want to stay alone with your thoughts? I hope they were happy."

"Yes, they were. This white barrier fence and the little house over there brought back memories of the summers my family spent with my aunt at her cottage on the shore of Lake Balaton."

"Oh, I love that lake—it is one of my favourite places. During the biggest turmoil of my life I got on the train early in the morning and went there. For hours I just sat on a pier, looking at the light green water and thinking about nothing. I took the afternoon train back with tranquility in me. Maybe we should go there next. What do you think?

"Sure! Do you have enough time to go there and spend a few days? Get a room in a hotel close to the lake? And who knows, maybe my aunt's place still exists. That would be wonderful," Elsa said with a burst of enthusiasm.

"Well, I have to go back to work for a few days next week to finish a presentation, but after that I'll have four days off again. Let's do it!" The women smiled at each other. Elsa almost slipped back into her memories of Balaton, but Margaret spoke up again, saying, "I'm hungry, what about some breakfast? After that we can scout out the countryside. There is a 16th-century chapel close by, and we can also go to Lilafured, a very fashionable summer resort, and see the historic caves. If the weather stays like this we can have lunch at one of the hotels' terraces overlooking the lake." With that, Margaret stood up and walked towards the entrance.

"What would you like for breakfast? I am starving too," asked Elsa, following her "Can I fix us some eggs and sausages in a real Hungarian style? We have some bread left over from dinner. I can warm it up to go with the eggs."

"Okay, but let me be the judge about your Hungarian style!" laughed Margaret.

In the end, Margaret had to admit that the eggs were the real Hungarian style. Elsa explained that it was her husband's favourite meal, and he had taught her to make it with painful fussiness in the first months of their marriage until she got it right.

"And beside that, it was one of the cheapest dinners after we found an old Hungarian deli where we could buy spicy sausages," smiled Elsa.

They drove off to see the medieval chapel. It was in the middle of a well-kept park and surrounded by tall, ancient trees and some ruins, but the chapel itself and one bell tower were in a good condition. The chapel was closed.

They walked around it to see if they could find someone to open it up, but there was nobody around. Giving up hope of seeing the inside, they started to walk back to the car. Just then, they noticed an old man riding towards them on a battered, rusting bicycle. He was the caretaker and sold them tickets from his pocket. With a big, rusted iron key, he opened up the thick, wooden, weather-beaten door. It squeaked loudly as if protesting their intrusion. Before stepping inside, the caretaker warned them that no photographs were allowed. He walked a few steps behind them to be sure they obey the rule.

The nave of the chapel was just as simple as the outside—bare, gray stone walls with no frescoes or small paintings of any kind. Two crumbling statues were the only decoration. The main altar was a polished, heavy wood table, and in the middle of it stood a large crucifix. Disappointed, they started to walk out.

As soon as they turned, however, the sun broke through the clouds and shone through the two narrow but tall windows above the nave. The flood of sunlight from one window fell on a confessional booth in one corner and created dark, deep shadows. In the sunrays, millions of sparkling specks of dust danced. From the other window the sun shone on the crucifix, forming a halo around it. It was a supernatural sight. Elsa and Margaret stood there until the sunshine faded away.

"It was worth it, wasn't it?" asked Elsa when they got into the car.

"Absolutely. And besides, we made the day for the old guy. I don't think he'll have many more visitors today. I gave him a nice tip. He'll have half a litre more at the pub tonight."

They drove through forested hills. The trunks of the tall trees were light brown in colour and stood strait as flagpoles. The leaves were not fully grown yet, so Elsa could see a good distance through the gaps between the tress. There was a light mist amid the tree trunks, and as the sun shone on them, they appeared to be covered with soft, fluffy velvet.

The forest ended an hour later at a small lake surrounded by old-fashioned three- and four-story hotels. The water was dark, the sky was blue, and the hills around were covered with trees in their green, early spring splendour. The sun sparkled on the surface of the lake, which was just a bit riffled by the light wind. The hotels were empty, but one of them served lunch on their open garden patio. The two women ordered the local specialty of the house, grilled trout with parsley potatoes and salad. Elsa wanted to be in solidarity with Margaret, who could only drink water because she was driving, but Margaret would not hear of it.

"You must taste the local wine," she said, signalling to the waiter. "It is a light white and goes great with the trout. I will make up for it tonight. And don't you forget tonight is your turn for a story! You'd better get ready for it!"

After a light dinner (the late and fabulous lunch still lingered in them), Elsa and Margaret sat at the end of the long table in the big, empty, semi-dark dining hall. Margaret lit a new candle and filled up their glasses while looking at Elsa questioningly.

"Am I going to hear a story from you tonight?" she asked.

"You know, all the way back I was thinking about which story from my life I should tell you. I found most of it dull and not at all noteworthy."

"Why don't you let me the judge of that? I am—"

Elsa lifted up her hand to silence Margaret.

"But, I have a story that no one knows about. Not even my mother. Lili only knows a part of it. It bothers me like a nightmare I cannot get rid of no matter how hard I try. It is still painful, and I have been bottling it up inside me for many years. I thought maybe if I share it with you it will descend to the deepest part of my mind."

"Elsa, I would love to hear it if you are sure you want to tell me. You can be sure it will stay with me forever. I would love to know you much better—I hardly know anything about your early years. I do not know why, but I feel as close to you as a sister or a lifelong friend."

Smiling, Elsa looked at Margaret and said, "Aren't we lucky to find true friendship so late in our lives?" She took a sip of her wine and then kept looking into her glass for a while in silence. Then she took a deep breath.

~

My father was a drama teacher. He wanted to be an actor, but his parents were dead-set against it and forced him to choose a "real" profession. He met my mother at the teachers' college. It was love at first sight. They got married after graduating, and I was born in the second year of their marriage. Believe it or not, I was a beautiful baby.

My sister was born three years later. I will bore you with a detailed family history some other time. I grew up to be a very pretty teenager, but I was a dreamer and withdrawn into my own world. I read a lot, made up plays and acted out the parts from the story, but it was just for me. Sometimes I let my sister play a small part too. My father saw his dreams materializing in me and encouraged me to choose acting as a profession. I finished high school in the darkest years of the communist rule, when family background, not achievements, was the main principle for getting anywhere. My father came from a humble, blue-collar worker family, and he made it to be a teacher. The system favoured him. He coached me for the admission examination (a good friend of his let him know about the application material), so I was accepted to the academy.

I was nineteen, had grown up in a sheltered, loving family, was naïve, pretty and full of hopes. I believed my father words that I had talent and if I worked hard I could be a great actress one day. I enjoyed the school, started to break out of shell slowly and loved acting. I stayed close friends with Lili, who after high school graduation went to work in a boutique. We could not see each other as frequently as before, but whenever she dragged me to parties, it would get around that I was a future actress, and I would always get more attention than her. This made her jealous since she was used to me being a girlfriend in the background. That tainted our friendship for a while.

In my second year at the acting academy, one of my teachers was a very well-known actor and the dream of many female hearts in Budapest. He was the dialog teacher. I had a good voice and could do different accents well, so he took a fancy for me. He talked to me a lot, encouraging me, asking me into his office after classes for private tutoring and making me believe that I was an exceptional talent. Soon I worshiped him and fell deeply and innocently in love with him. He was my mentor and my idol, and I fell under his spell. Believed everything he told me. I was ready to do everything he wanted me to do. I knew he was divorcing his second wife, a well-known actress, and was aware that he was at least fifteen years older than I, no matter how youthfully he acted and looked.

The first time he kissed me in his office, I just melted in his arms. He was the first to kiss me like a man. He called me into his office at every opportunity and we kissed behind the open door. We had to be very careful not to let our liaison be discovered. His kisses became more passionate, and he would fondle my breast, rubbing me against his hardened member and make me fondle it through his pants. I had never experienced anything like that. I was shaken by my own reaction—my heart was beating faster, my blood was boiling and my main desire was to please him. Soon all this was not enough.

However, we could not meet in any public place no matter how isolated it might be, and nor could we go to a hotel because his face was plastered around town on movie or theatre posters. So he borrowed a friend's apartment and promised me he wouldn't do anything I didn't want him to do. But of course I could not say no to him and he seduced me on his friend's sofa. I was a virgin, nervous and frightened, but I so wanted to please him. I could hardly keep myself from crying out loud from the pain I felt when he entered in me. He was not gentle or loving—he rushed to posses me. The fact that excited him (as I later realized) was that I was a virgin and he was the first to seduce me. He was careful enough to use condom, but he made me put it on him. He kissed me a few times, and then without any warning or foreplay he pushed himself into me, groaned, and pushed harder and harder, grinding his teeth. He bit my mouth and it was over. Afterwards, he kissed my breast a few times, murmuring how beautiful I was. Of course I did not know then that it could be any different. I had only read about sex. A few boys had kissed me on dates but I never let them go further.

The affair was my deepest secret—no one at school or at home knew about it. I went when he called, fabricating lies at home that I had to go to a workshop or had to watch a performance in one of the theatres. And I made it sure that I knew which theatre played what, who was in it and so on. I was madly in love with him and completely under his domination. He taught me how to please him. I was a good student, learned and did it all. He said he loved me and promised to make a great actress out of me. Of course I was secretly hoping that as soon as his divorce went through we'd get married. I dreamt about how we'd live together happily ever after, in our own place, and how I would furnish it. We would read plays in front of the fire and go to the theatre together. Just because of him I wanted to be a successful actress who played classic dramas on stage and starred in many movies. The summer was agony for me because he worked at a summer theatre in the country. We could only meet once or twice in two months. As my third year began, he and the school were my life.

Then one day all of it came crashing down. He missed a few classes because of working on a film, and shortly after I read that he had become sick on location and was in a hospital for two days. The first day he came back to school, I could hardly wait for my class to be over. Making sure that the hallway was empty, I ran to his office. His door was half open. I wanted to surprise him, so I quietly stepped into the room. He was not at his desk, and I heard whispering from behind the door. He was whispering the same words, phrasings and promises that he had whispered to me a year ago. I heard heavy breathing and kissing. I stood there dumbstruck. When the door moved, I turned around and fled. I heard him calling after me, but I just ran out of the building. Not looking right or left, I ran across the street. The last thing I heard was screaming and horns blowing. I don't want to be dramatic—you can see I survived without permanent bodily marks. My left arm and right leg were broken, and my shoulder was dislocated. Somehow, my spine and head escaped harm. I was in the hospital for two months and recovered at home for a year. My body healed, but my soul did not.

I fell into a deep depression, and of course everybody thought it was caused by the accident and the long recovery. There was not a minute that I did not think about my humiliation. I felt betrayed, and I just could not understand how it could have happened to me. How could I be so naïve, so innocent, so stupid? How could I not see through him, that he was just a self-centred, middle-aged male who counted every seduced student as a trophy?

I could not bring myself to tell anyone about the real reason for my depression. Lili was the exception, though I didn't tell her everything—just that I was in love with my teacher who I saw with another woman. I kept the rest deep inside me, and it weighed on my soul like a large rock. Once I tried to take too many painkillers, but it was not enough. I got only a sore throat from the stomach pump. My parents were petrified and tried everything to snap me out of it. My mother took me to my aunt's house on Lake Balaton, hoping that the place I loved would help, but it didn't. My only medication was the passing of time. Lili was a great help. She visited me almost every day, sacrificing many hours from her social life. In her no-nonsense way, she scolded me and brought back my common sense. Slowly but painfully I pulled myself together. After all, I was still young and had a healthy mind.

Of course I did not go back to the academy. I studied writing. I wanted to be a writer who could pour out her heart without giving herself away. I was cured but unhappy and couldn't trust anybody anymore. When the revolution happened, I decided to start a new life, far from my past and everybody I cared for. Lili was also ready for a change and we fled. But that is an other story for another time.

Elsa poured out the last of the wine, sharing it with Margaret. "Let's go to bed," she said, smiling tiredly. "I think I'll sleep very well tonight. Thanks for listening, Margaret!"

Margaret lifted her glass to Elsa and said, "Thank you for telling me. Just one question: did you ever see him again?"

"After the accident, he sent flowers with a 'get better soon' note to the hospital as a polite and caring teacher should, but he did not visit me. Later I heard rumours that he had been fired from school because a first-year student (who was smarter than me) reported his advances to the school board. After some time he managed to get work in movies and theatres. I took care not to see any play or movie he was in.

"Once, however, Lili got tickets for a very successful play that was sold out for months in advance. He was in it. She made me go, saying that it would be the last chapter in my affair. It would put a final end to it and delete it from my life completely. She was right! He had a small part and was awfully bad in the play. He had aged a lot. I could not understand how I could have fallen for him and almost ruined my life because of him."

They drank the wine and went to bed. Elsa fell asleep almost as soon as her head hit the pillow. She slept deeply on the narrow, bumpy bed, without any disturbing dreams.

The next morning they took their time. After a long, lingering breakfast and several cups of coffee, they accounted for the contents of the cupboard, returned the sheets, loaded the car and said goodbye to Jani with a handshake and a generous tip. Then they were back on the road towards Budapest.

Again they took to the side roads, stopping in several villages to buy fresh vegetables and fruit. It was well after six when they got home. Margaret was lucky and found a parking space not far from her apartment.

"I'll keep the car here until we go to Balaton so we don't have to carry our bags too far."

Margaret's mailbox was full, and she sorted them out at her desk.

"Look," she said suddenly, "there is letter for you from Australia!" She held up the envelope to Elsa. "And here is one for me from London, from Edith. Isn't it a coincidence that both of them wrote at the same time?"

"What is the date today?" asked Elsa, reading Lili's letter in a panic. "I am lost—I don't even know what day it is!"

Margaret looked at the calendar on her desk. "It's March 18th. Tuesday. Why?"

"Lili writes that she will be here on the 21st. She made a reservation at the Forum hotel for me too, and I should meet her there. The hotel will pick her up at the airport. We did talk about this, but she was not sure that she'd come. She was annoyed that I decided to take this trip without telling her first that she said she'd let me know. It is so like Lili to not ask first if it is convenient. She knows what she wants and she gets. What does Edith have to say?"

"She decided to come as well. She picked up a cheep flight from Gatwick and asks me if it is okay if she's here on the 24th and stays for six days." She paused, smiling happily over the letter. "It's so incredible that both wrote at almost the same time and both decided to come! I think we should wait for them and the four of us should go to Lake Balaton together. Don't you think so?"

"Well, I think it could be fun, but as I remember Edith did not like me or Lili very much. It seemed to me she was jealous of you! Am I right?"

"In a way, yes, but she is a very unbalanced soul. She can change in a second into a different person. She is very lonely in her flat in London. I am glad she is coming. The change will be good for her, just like when we went to Lake Como. I'm sure you'll learn to like her just as she will you. But I am not so sure about Lili. She did not make a secret of it that she did not like me too much." Margaret put Edith's letter in the pile of papers on her desk.

"You don't have to worry about Lili," Elsa said, laying her hand on Margaret's shoulder. "She is a good girl, and I love her dearly. As long as she feels important and in the centre of attention, she's an angel. We are going to have fun, you'll see."

That night Elsa tried to sort out her feelings. Was she happy that Lili was coming? After some serious thinking, she decided that yes, she was. They had not visited Hungary together since they left in 1956. Elsa always gave Lili a full report after her visits with her parents and even urged her to come back with her, but Lili always refused. She said she never wanted to go back. There was nobody she wanted to see, and she did not like to reminisce. Elsa wondered what made her decide to come now.

"Well, I'll know soon enough," she said to herself as she went to sleep.

Margaret was busy during the day, so Elsa wandered around the city, taking buses and streetcars but not the Metro. She wanted to see the streets and the people walking by, and she wanted to make up stories about their lives. She walked the hills on the Buda side of the city, enjoying the fresh green of the trees and the lovely vistas of the city from the different hills. She loved walking around the narrow, old streets on Castle Hill and look down on the grey Danube from Fisherman's Bastion. She found a pastry shop which sold her favourite ice cream. *I must bring Lili here,* she thought, looking at the display cases full of the most tempting cakes and sweets.

The last evening before Lili's arrival, Elsa took Margaret out to dinner at a restaurant near her apartment. It was a mild evening, warm enough to sit outside. The restaurant was on the promenade, and the Danube was just across the walkway from them. From a nearby restaurant, they overheard a four-piece band playing what they thought was blues. Elsa knew most of the songs. Her mother loved soul music—she had owned dozens of records and played them over and over again when the mood hit her.

Margaret noticed Elsa's change of mood. "Is anything bothering you?"

"Nothing at all. The blues was my mother's favourite music, and she listened to it all the time. Hearing it, I feel like a little girl again, and I miss my mother's warm smile from across the room. Isn't it silly and sentimental?"

"No. I find that as I age I reminiscence more often about my childhood, my parents, my first doll than ever before," said Margaret in a soft voice. "But we are not old yet! We have plenty of life left in us. We must make the best of it and live as we want to live."

"You sound like Lili. She is always urging me to live for myself," Elsa said, and Margaret nodded. "Speaking of Lili," Elsa continued, "I'll move to the hotel tomorrow morning, in order to be there when she arrives from the airport. I am sorry to leave you, but in a few days you'll have Edith to keep you company. Margaret, I cannot express my heartfelt thanks for those superb days we spent together, and—"

Margaret touched Elsa's hand stopping her flowing words. She said, "Do not talk as if we were saying goodbye! You are not leaving yet, just moving around the corner. It is about a ten-minute walk from the Forum Hotel to my place. I count on seeing you every day!"

"You can depend on it. You owe me at least a dozen stories, and I also have some more for you!"

Chapter 10

Elsa got out of the taxi in front of the hotel. It took longer to drive there than walk—the narrow, one-way streets were not built for autos—they were designed a few hundred years ago when horse and buggy was the mode of transportation—and were clogged with traffic. But she did not want to arrive at the hotel on foot and pulling two good-sized suitcases behind her. The cabbie shamelessly overcharged her for the short ride. Elsa did not argue. He must have been sure that this elegant lady, no matter how well she spoke Hungarian, must be a rich emigrant from somewhere in America.

The porter greeted her with courtesy and signalled the busboy to get the luggage. Elsa went to the desk to sign in and looked around, astonished.

The hotel lobby was spacious and filled with deep sofas and armchairs, a shining marble floor, crystal chandeliers and live floral arrangements. The staff wore elegantly cut uniforms, and the concierge spoke to her in flawless English. *What a change!* she thought. During her earlier visits, she spent most of her limited time with her parents and did not go anywhere else, except to visit other family members. Sometimes when she brought David along after her parents were too feeble to travel, she would show him around the city. She noticed changes then, but they didn't interest her enough to think about or look into more. She was just a visitor who happened to be born in Hungary. But now, after many years of absence, she felt differently somehow. The concierge's polite voice bought her back to the present.

He put a key on the desk and said, "Mrs. Martos, a lady who called herself 'Lili' phoned for you a few minutes ago. She said that she has just landed and will be here in about an hour. Your room is on the eighth floor facing the Danube. I hope you'll find it satisfactory. If you need anything, do not hesitate to call. We are here to serve and make your stay comfortable. Your luggage will follow you immediately."

"Thank you, I am sure I'll like it here."

The room was large and occupied a corner of the hotel. Big, picture windows overlooked the Danube and the Lanc (Chain) Bridge. On the other side of the river a road led into a tunnel under a hill. On the hillside, clog-wheel trains were moving up and down like small matchboxes, taking people up to the magnificent Royal Palace. The morning sun shone on the river as it flowed fast on its way to the faraway Black Sea. Elsa stood at the window for a long time, captivated by the view.

"How come I never noticed how beautiful this is?" she asked herself. She left the window after a while to unpack. Arranging her toiletries on the shelf in the bathroom, she took care to leave Lili enough room for her numerous jars, bottles and other beauty tools. Elsa could not stop wondering why Lili decided to come so suddenly.

She was looking forward to seeing how Lili adapted to her homeland after a decade. *What will be her reaction to this changed world?*

Elsa looked at her watch. It was after eleven o'clock, and Lili should have arrived. She called room service, ordered some coffee and sat down in front of the window, enjoying the view. "I wonder why they didn't build balconies," she said to herself. "It would be so nice to sit outside to enjoy the sun and the view."

Shortly after her coffee arrived, Elsa heard another knock on the door. She opened it, and there stood Lili, wearing an elegant, light gray designer pantsuit, a red cashmere sweater, a diamond necklace and a couple of diamond bracelets. Just beyond her, Elsa noticed the porter caving in under her three Vuitton suitcases.

"Hi, mate, it's so good to see you! How you doing?" Lili asked. They hugged many times. "I should have been here an hour ago, but the young, ambitious officer at the passport control took his time examining my Australian passport when he saw that I was born here. Then I had to wait for my luggage for more than half an hour. Mine were the last coming out on the carousel, probably because it was marked priority. Hey, but I am here!" Lili strolled in, throwing her three-hundred-dollar Italian leather handbag carelessly on the bed. The porter stumbled in behind her, placed her bags carefully on the floor and quietly accepted the bill in Lili's hand. He tipped his cap to them before exiting. "You must be surprised that I came at all! Don't play the cool cat, ask."

"As soon as you take a breath to give me a chance," laughed Elsa. "I am very happy that you came, and you're right, I can hardly wait to know why. Not that I am complaining."

"Okay, sit down because here is the news," Lili began, sitting down herself. "I didn't want to come—I was mad that you made plans with Margaret before discussing it with me. But you know I have a big heart and forgive but don't forget. Just before you left Toronto, I got a letter from Budapest. I have never corresponded with anyone here, so I was curious. It was a letter from a schoolmate of ours from high school. It took a few minutes before I could put a face to the name, but you know how clever I am. Well, to be short, it was about our forty-year high school reunion! She got my address from a very distant and old aunt of mine whom I support but never correspond with besides a short call once in a blue moon. Isn't it fantastic?"

"But if you got this letter before I left, why didn't you tell me?"

"Because I plotted this little surprise to come unexpectedly, silly!"

"Okay, let's hear the rest."

"I'm starving," Lili answered, ignoring the question. "The food on the plane wasn't bad, but breakfast was a long time ago! I am dying for a goose liver sandwich! Let's go down for lunch, and I'll tell you all about it. By the way, how is Margaret?"

"She is fine. I'll tell you about our adventures later. Let's go before you die of hunger. I have to warn you, there is no smoking in the bar or the restaurant!"

"So Hungary caught up with the Western world that fast? How do they manage it here where 90 per cent of the people smoke?"

The restaurant was just half full, and they got a table by the window overlooking the promenade and the river. Elsa watched Lili's mouth water as she studied the mile-long menu. She suddenly realized Lili would not have much trouble adjusting to the new Hungary.

"Oh, I could eat this menu from A to Z, but I'll settle for the grilled goose liver," Lili said to the waiter as soon as he approached.

"Would you like a salad with it, madam?" he asked.

"No, thank you. Too healthy for me. Just bring some dark rye bread."

The waiter dutifully smiled at her, "Certainly, madam."

Elsa ordered a cappuccino.

"What's the matter, are you on diet? How can you ignore this menu?"

"I'm not hungry. I had a big breakfast with Margaret."

"Oh, okay."

"Well, do not torture me any more—tell me about the letter!"

"Let me enjoy my lunch, about which I was fantasizing all the way here. You will last for another ten minutes," said Lili, digging in her food. She let out a few sighs while rolling her eyes. "It's heavenly!"

After lunch they went upstairs to the confectionery for a pastry. Elsa could not say no—she loved sweets too.

"So, about the letter," Lili said finally. "It was from Irèn Kàdas. Remember her? She sat behind us in the last year. She was blond, tall, wore glasses and she was smart."

"Yes, it is coming back. She was the one who always finished the math quizzes first and cheated for us. Without her help I would never have passed."

"That's the one. So she wrote that she and two other girls are organizing the fortieth reunion in May. They got numerous eager responses. It will be a lunch held on May 8th in a private room of a restaurant. They wanted me to notify you too. So consider yourself notified. I called her. Her voice sounded the same as it did forty years ago. It was ghostly. We chatted for a while and I told her that she could count on us, we'll be there! So what about it?"

"Of course it will be great, but I'm scared of it too. Forty years is a long time. It could be a great shock, but it also could be great fun."

After they finished their pastries Elsa asked, "So what do you want to do today?"

"I want to take a shower, change and then go for a walk in Vàci utca," said Lili.

They strolled up and down on Vàci utca, window shopping.

"Isn't it amazing how much this city has changed?" asked Elsa. "Look at all those designer shops. There is Yves St. Laurent, Gap, Roots and look at this Italian shoe store!"

"Yes, I can see the changes, but it still has an Eastern European flavour. Look at the people! You can pick out the locals from the tourist in a second, and not because they speak Hungarian! Their dresses are old fashioned, and the women's worn-out faces look much older than their age. This is Eastern Europe, and it will be so for many more years before they can catch up with the rest of the West!"

"Oh, don't be so critical! Of course things cannot happen fast, but the changes in the last ten years are fantastic. When I was here last, this street was unkempt and the buildings were gray and dirty and hardly anything to look at. That reminds me—let's find Parisi utca and the candy shop where they sold that marvellous marzipan! I promised David I would buy a box for him. It was his favourite when he was little. My father used to treat him with it."

"By all means. You know it is one of my favourite too," Lili said, cheering up immediately and even smiling at strangers.

They found the shop at the same place as it was so long ago. A small shop, the display cases were full of delicious chocolates in every form Elsa could imagine and many kinds of cakes. To Elsa's greatest joy, they sold ice cream too. Lili bought a big bagful of truffles and ate from the bag. Elsa licked her ice cream with a contented grin on her face as they strolled from one street to the other, window shopping.

Lili retired for her afternoon beauty sleep, and Elsa walked to the university to meet Margaret. Margaret was late, so Elsa waited around for a half an hour before she finally saw her hurrying out through the gates.

"I'm sorry I'm late, but I wanted to finish everything so I don't have to go back again for a while. Did Lili arrive?"

"Yes, and she is her old self again. She forgave me."

"Did she let you know why didn't give you any warning that she was coming?"

"You wouldn't believe it, but she came for the fortieth reunion of our high school graduating class. Of course, she knew before I left and didn't tell me, but she wanted to surprise me with the news. How typical of her!"

"Are we going to meet later and have dinner or something?"

"Oh, yes, I told her I'd bring you with me to the hotel and wake her up from her nap, no matter whether she's ready for us or not!"

"Are you sure about this? She is going to dislike me even more!"

"Don't worry about it. You suggest a real, ethnic, greasy spoon for dinner, and she'll be your friend forever."

Lili was up by the time they arrived at the hotel. She greeted Margaret with a distant, cool but friendly hello.

"Good to see you again, how was your trip?" asked Margaret. "Are you rested after that long flight?"

"I had a lovely nap. I am ready for anything," answered Lili, lighting up a smoke. "What have you two planned for this evening?"

"I know a small restaurant close to my place" said Margaret. "They serve the best wiener schnitzel with potato salad in town. Nothing fancy, it is just an eatery with good beer, and wine. The schnitzel is long, thin and cheap. But if we go there, wear something you can spare to hang out to air for a few days, because by the time we eat dinner we will smell like a boiling oil fryer."

"This is music to my ears," Lili said. "Let's go there."

"It is a block from my place. Would like to come up for a drink before dinner?" asked Margaret. "We can walk to my place from here."

"Okay, let's go," said Lili.

After a few glasses of wine and chatting about nothing, they left for dinner. The restaurant was a small, narrow room. Booths for four were built in on one side, and free-standing tables and chairs lined the other wall. The tables were covered with blue-and-white checkered tablecloths, and the waiter brought out the plates and cutlery. They ordered their meal, and to be true to tradition ordered draught beer. The schnitzel was as Margaret promised and so big it overlapped the plates. The potato salad was seasoned with just the right amount of onion and vinegar to go with the meat, and the beer foamed in the frosted jugs. The atmosphere was cozy, and Margaret and Lili became friendlier, warming up to each other.

After they finished dinner, Lili said, "I am still on Australian time, which is very early in the afternoon. Why don't we go to some bar and live it up?"

"I have a better offer," said Margaret. "Let's go back to my place. I have a good bottle of French brandy I was saving for special occasion like this one. There we can talk without shouting in each other's ears."

They went back to Margaret's place, and Margaret poured out the brandy into large snifter glasses. They sat around her coffee table in deep armchairs.

"When we were on our little tour through the countryside," said Elsa to Lili, "after dinner we told each other stories about our lives. You missed that, but here is your chance to tell us one." Lili only blinked. Elsa knew she was up to the task.

"Elsa, you know my life inside and out, and I don't think Margaret would be interested in hearing any dull stories about my life!" Lili sat forward as she spoke, and Elsa knew she was only paving the way for her performance.

"Of course I am!" said Margaret. "You are the most unusual, interesting and lively person I have ever met in my long life."

"I take that as a compliment. What kind of story would interest you?"

Margaret took a sip of her brandy before speaking. After a moment she asked, "Why did you decide to leave Hungary in 1956? I would love to hear about that very much! I know only that you two left together."

She filled up all the glasses and sat back in her chair, looking at Lili with expectation.

∼

Well, this is a question I have asked myself more than a few times, and the only convincing reasons I can come up with are the love of adventure and my restless nature. I guess the question then becomes about *which* adventure.

My parents were well off, even in the communist regime. My father had lots of money stashed away somewhere, so he did not have to work for living. He kept a job just to be on the safe side. He was never flashy or threw the money around—he was smart. My mother looked up to him as the saviour of mankind. My father was disappointed that I happened to be a girl and could not carry on his name. After me, my mother could not have any more children. My father was rigid with me, and though he never beat me, sometimes I wished he would instead of giving me his icy stares and the cold shoulder. My mother felt guilty about not being able to provide him with an heir, and so she didn't show too much affection for me. I grew up in a family where nobody was emotional, at least not with me.

When I became a teenager I rebelled against everything, regardless of cause. I started to smoke just because I was forbidden to and I drank a lot. I was lucky that in those years in Hungary it was almost impossible to get any drugs. I was bored with school, barely passed the terms and was tired of my parents' scolding me all the time and wanting to run my life. I was well looked after, I was given everything I wanted, I never had to ask for money and I was a spoiled brat materialistically. But I wanted to be free from family life as fast as I could. Having a flat of my own, even if I had the money for it, was impossible during that time. I read a lot, mostly American romance novels I picked up at the black market against my mother's objections. She was terrified that my father, who read only classics and philosophy, would find out and be furious for bringing "that trash" into his house. I read those novels and fantasized about travelling, seeing the world and meeting the prince on the white horse.

After high school, Elsa and I stayed best friends, but our lifestyle had changed. She was fanatical about her drama school, and I started to work in a boutique even on Saturdays, so we seldom spent any time together. I was frustrated, lonely and went to bed with a lot of men just for fun. Then came the revolution and the exodus to the West. I saw my chance to change my life radically, get away from my parents, and go chase after my dreams. After her accident, Elsa was also restless and dissatisfied with her life. We decided to join a group of my friends and escaped to Austria. We treated the whole thing as a big, joyful adventure. We joked and drank all the way until reality hit, when the border guards started firing at us and we had to run for our lives.

I won't bore you with the details, as I'm sure you've heard enough horror stories about those border crossings. We were lucky, however, and arrived in Vienna. The city was lit up like I had never seen before. Eyeing the stores full of the most beautiful things and admiring the well-dressed people on the streets, I was sure I had done the right thing and just had to keep my eyes open for my prince.

And believe it or not, he did materialized. I was in a coffeehouse with a group of friends, arguing about what to do next, when a tall, tanned, good-looking, elegant, middle-aged guy came up to our table. He was an Australian Hungarian and was overjoyed to hear us talking. He introduced himself as Péter Mohay and asked if he could join us. He sat down beside me. I was bored with the company, as most of them were scared of their sudden independence and kept whining about the future. I made my best effort to chat him up.

To make a long story short, we ended up in his bed. He had the body of a thirty-year-old, tanned and firm, and he was great in bed too. I said goodbye to Elsa and spent my days with him. He was charming, and he was rich. He owned a leather factory in Sydney and he was on a business trip in Austria. He was twelve years older than I was. He took me all over town and bought me everything I laid my eyes on—soon I had the wardrobe of my dreams. We dined in the best restaurants, went to the opera and to the show at the Spanish Riding School. At both places the entry ticket cost more than my monthly wages in Budapest. I enjoyed every minute of it. Before he left to go back to Sydney, he confessed that he had fallen in love with me. I was the one who was missing from his life, he said, and then he asked me to marry him. I said yes. He left to arrange my visa, but before leaving he booked me in a good hotel and left me quite a sum of money. Beside fretting about whether he'd change his mind by the time he got home, I had a great time waiting for the Australian visa.

Lili sat back for a moment and took a hearty sip of brandy. She was all smiles. Elsa could tell that Margaret was deep in the story and wanted more.

"That you did," Elsa said, taking over. "The rest of us were housed in hostels, living on the generosity of the Red Cross and trying to decide what to do with our lives. I was already homesick, and my mother called almost every day asking me to change my mind and come home. I had to admit that you did stand by me and would not let me do anything foolish like go back."

"I took you shopping—remember how we marvelled at those shops on Kertner Strasse? And we could not tear ourselves away from the supermarkets."

"And you bought chocolate by the box, caviar and champagne and we had a picnic in your hotel room. We ate the caviar on the top of the chocolate, and I was so sick the next day that I could not get up."

"Ah, the good old times!" sighted Lili.

Margaret listened to them for a while and then asked Lili, "What happened when you got to Australia? Did you get married and live happily ever after?"

"Well, *that* is an other story. Let's leave it for next time. I think I am ready for bed," Lili said, sipping off the last of her brandy. "Let's go, Elsa. Margaret, thank for your hospitality. Did you two made any plans for tomorrow?"

"We are going to play it by ear," said Margaret. "What day is the reunion going to be?"

"Day after tomorrow for lunch."

"Okay," Margaret said, walking them to the door. "Have a good night's rest and call me in the morning. I am off work for a week, so I'll be happy to drive you girls around. Though, I want to sleep in, so do not call me before nine."

"Don't worry," said Lili, "I never get up before eleven. See you tomorrow!"

When they stepped out to the street, Lili looked for a cab, but Elsa forced her to walk back to the hotel.

"It's a short walk, and you have to get some fresh air into your smoky lungs. We can walk by the Danube on the promenade. You have to see Fisherman's Bastion lit up—it's a lovely sight."

"You and your walks and sights! Okay, but I want to go up to the confectionary for a cake. I have a craving for a dobos torte."

"You are unreal! It's after eleven—no way they are open!"

"Then we order from room service. If I want something, I get it!"

"Don't I know it!" sighed Elsa.

Chapter 11

On the day of the reunion, Lili made an appointment at the beauty salon in the hotel for a facial, a manicure, hair colouring—the works.

"I have to be at my best so they can eat their heart out. Lots of them made fun of me because of my taste in fashion. You should do the same, Elsa."

"I am what I am. I don't need all that jazz. And don't overdo it. I mean, don't wear your gold and diamonds—it would just make you revolting!" Elsa said sternly.

Both of them were nervous and at the same time exited as they got into the cab to go to the reunion. The restaurant was located on Stefania Ut, a wide, tree-lined street close to the city park. The neighbourhood was well kempt, clean and housed a few of the Western embassies.

They were early, so Elsa said, "Let's get out and walk the rest of the way. I remember some of the very old photos in my grandmother's album were from this street. It was once the most elegant street in Budapest. The aristocrats used to drive their carriages up and down this street, dressed to the teeth."

"You and your stories! Okay, let's walk."

As they neared the restaurant, they noticed three ladies walking ahead of them. They looked at each other questioningly, and then stepped up to the three. They recognized Kàdas Iren immediately.

"Look," Irèn screamed, "Lili and Elsa!"

They kissed and hugged, and by that time they remembered the names of the other two. At the restaurant, a private room had been set up for the occasion with a long table decorated with flowers. Three other classmates were there already and involved in eager conversation. Greetings and hugs went all around.

Elsa did not remember most of the peoples' names, but after a while a movement of the hands or an articulation bought back the person's face with the name attached to it, just as it looked forty years ago. It felt to Elsa like she was watching a photograph develop.

Others soon arrived, alone or in a group, and a betting game started within the already seated group about who would get newcomers' names right first.

Some of them had kept in touch over the years, and some had not seen the others in forty years. Small groups formed, and happy, lively conversations, laughs and shrieks filled up the room.

"Do you remember when 'the Sergeant' made you stand by the desks for thirty minutes because she caught you reading under the table?" One woman asked Lili.

"Do I? I was furious because she confiscated my book …"

"Hey, Zsuzsa, do you remember when we sneaked out to the washroom for a smoke and got caught?"

"I never told on you …"

"Yes, I am a grandmother too. I have six grandchildren …"

"My husband died five years ago …"

"I left in '56, but I moved back because …"

"Don't say! You were married to the same guy two times?"

Everyone talked at once, and the room became as noisy as their classroom ever was before the morning bell.

Irèn stood up and banged her fork on a glass. She looked like a spinster, just as she did when she was eighteen. She was thin, her once-blonde hair was white and cut short and she wore a white ruffled shirt, a medium-long, dark skirt and low-heeled walking shoes. Her blue eyes did not sparkle as they had forty years ago, but they were still full of joy.

"Girls, girls ... may I suggest that after the meal we give four minutes for each person to tell us about the last forty years in their life? We'll do it in alphabetical order as we were in the class book."

"Hear yea, hear yea," yelled Lili. "But be honest! We don't want to hear fairy tales! There were a few among us who were masters explaining missing homework!"

The lunch was buffet style, and everybody wandered with plates in hand from one seat to another, and the forty years shrank to delusion.

"Okay, let's get started!" Irèn said, pushing her glasses to the end of her nose and opening a book on the table in front of her.

"Àdler Joli. You are the first."

A short, plump woman got up from her chair. She looked around the table with a cheery smile on her face.

"If you remember, I talked nonstop, explaining things nobody asked about, so just shoot me after four minutes.

"I am very happy to be here and see how many of us showed up after so many years! If I remember correctly, there were thirty-two of us in the class, and twenty-four turned out today! I think this is amazing! I am so happy—"

"Just the facts, Joli, or you'll run out of time!" interrupted Irèn.

"Yes, yes, I am getting there. After graduation I studied chemistry at the university. But before that I married my sweetheart, whom you must remember—he waited for me in front of the school almost every day. After I got my degree, we moved to Eger. I worked in the same pharmacy for fifteen years. In the meantime I had three children.

"After the eighties, we moved back to Budapest and I was lucky enough to get a position and later a partnership at a pharmacy downtown.

"I was not so lucky in marriage. My husband fell in love with a girl twenty years younger, left us high and dry, moved to Germany and lived happily ever after. I am retired now and have four grandchildren, all of them an apple in my eye. I love them deeply and help out whenever I can. I am happy to be healthy and try to make the best of my senior years."

Joli threw a kiss towards everybody, and said, "See how much I improved? My speech was less than four minutes!"

She got a prolonged applause.

Irèn called the next name in the book.

"Balog, Èva! It's your turn now."

A thin, tall woman stood up. Elsa did not recognize her. She looked much older than her age, and she had a humped back and a thin, wrinkled neck. She was dressed in a dark grey, old-fashioned dress, her hair was white and untidy and her eyes were unfocused.

"I can tell my story in a minute, or rather, I haven't got a story. I lived an uneventful life, never got married and I live alone. I was a bookkeeper for twenty years, and the highlight of my life was a holiday in Austria at Zelam Zee. I am lucky to have an apartment of my own. I read a lot, listen to music and try not to count as the years go by."

She sat down, staring at her plate.

There was a moment of silence before the group started to clap.

"Csolnay Erzsi," Irèn read the next name.

She was a smartly, fashionably dressed woman, her hair was coloured, her face was made up, rings sat on her manicured hands and she wore a nice pearl necklace.

"So many things happened to me in the last forty years that four minutes is hardly enough to begin," she said, looking around the table smiling, showing up a very natural-looking set of dentures.

"I will do my best to tell my story telegram style. If you are interested in the details, come see me later.

"So: I got married right after graduation to a young, up-and-coming politician who later became a minister. We lived in high society, travelled and went to parties and functions. But I got disillusioned with his politics and opened my mouth at the wrong times and places, so he dumped me and I fled to Austria. There I met my second husband, an Austrian dentist who was twenty years older than me. I went to business school in Vienna, got my degree, fell in love with my husband's assistant—a young, gorgeous guy—divorced the dentist and went with the assistant to America. I never had any children, but I became a successful business consultant and travelled all over the word. The gorgeous guy ran away with a blond Barbie and most of my money, so I moved back here after the political changes and live on my leftover account. I am so happy to see you all!" She threw kisses all around before she sat down.

She got a thunderous ovation, and Lili shouted, "That's our girl!" while clapping whistling.

Irèn looked down for the next on the list, her mouth opened to say the next name, but she looked up again. "Dalnoky Gizi died four years ago. Next is Foti Mari."

The woman who stood was overweight, her dress looked like she threw it on the wrong way and her hair was unruly, but her eyes sparkled when she got up with some difficulty from her chair.

"As you can see I still like my food, my beer and do not diet. My life is and has been a very everyday life. I got married and still live with the same man. We worked hard to have a normal life, and we put three children through university. We have four grandchildren now too—heaven bless them! I was a housewife and worked as a dressmaker at home to make ends meet. It is great to see you all and listen to your stories. I am so happy that I was able to come."

"Gàrdonyi Éva, you are next."

She was well-dressed and had a thin, long, aristocratic face and big, dark, sad eyes.

"I wish I could tell you that I had a good, happy life, but I didn't. If you remember, my father was a high-ranking officer in the army. A few years after our graduation, he was falsely accused of treachery. After a mock trial, my family was deported to a small village behind God's back, somewhere close to the Romanian border. My parents, my younger brother and I lived in one room of a thatched mud house at the end of the village. We were not allowed to do anything. My mother was a doctor, and she had to watch helplessly as the sick, undernourished children of the village, including her own, suffered from all kind of sicknesses. There was no drug store, no hospital and no doctor. She did what she could with her knowledge of natural medications. Thanks to her we didn't starve or freeze to death, because the villagers were grateful and brought food and firewood for us behind the back of the authorities.

After the political change we were allowed back into the city. I studied at the university and became a lawyer specializing in family law. I was married twice, and neither of them worked out. I have no children. I have my own firm now and try to make the best of my life."

A loud applause again erupted.

"The next is Haller Zsuzsa," said Irèn, looking over her glasses.

The woman who stood up was dressed carelessly in a big, loose pullover and a faded pair of velvet pants, and her hair was tied back with a rainbow-coloured silk shawl. On her fingers were several big, silver rings.

"After graduation I wanted to study art and went to college. But I flunked out. If you remember, studying was never my strong suit.

"So I got a job, several jobs, actually, because I never lasted long in any. I got married to a musician and travelled with him all over the country. He fled in '56, leaving me behind. I tried acting and singing and ended up in the theatre as a set designer—after all I did have some artistic talent. I am still working now and then. I'm married to a musician again, and we live happily. It's so good to see you all. If any of you want to see a play, I'd be happy to help you to get tickets. I have my connections," she said and winked at them.

Irèn looked up from her book. "I'd really like to see Ibsen's play *Nora*, but I could not get a ticket. Can you really get one?"

"Sure, what date?"

Half an hour later, the list ended with the last letter of the alphabet. There were a few who had died and a few who could not come. When it was over, everybody was in a festive mood, laughing a lot and teasing each other just like old times. Lili went to the bar and ordered ten bottles of champagne. She told the waiter to serve everybody but forbade him from telling who bought it. Elsa winked at her friend in acknowledgement when the champagne was dispersed. The hours flew by rapidly, unnoticed. When the waiter courteously reminded them that the room was booked for the evening, they reluctantly started to leave. There were the goodbyes, promises to keep in touch and plans meet again next year. Nothing proved the triumph of the reunion better than one of them who had walked in leaning on a cane, forgot it beside her chair when leaving.

"Don't even try suggesting a walk to the city park," warned Lili as she stepped outside with Elsa. "I want a taxi."

Elsa sat in the cab without talking, absorbed in the happenings of the afternoon.

The day was still pleasantly mild, and the late afternoon sun painted the windows of their hotel a dark copper. The sky was slowly loosing its colour, however, signifying the end of the afternoon. The espresso's terrace on the riverside was full, but Elsa was fast enough to notice a group ready to leave. Lili ordered a short, double espresso and a "dobos torta." Elsa had a cappuccino and ice cream.

Elsa took a deep breath from the warm spring air and looked at Lili questioningly. "You are far to quiet for your own good! What's the matter, didn't you have fun?"

"Yes, it was fun," Lili answered, "but it also made me sad and in a way shredded some of my self-confidence!"

"Lili, that's impossible. Your self-confidence is unbreakable!"

Lili waved her hand and shook her head. "Maybe so, but this was the first time that I had to admit that I am the same age as they are. Looking all those wrinkled faces and remembering how they looked forty years ago killed the image of myself I build up so carefully. I believe when I look in the mirror, dress up in youthful style and use the best and most expensive beauty products that I am not almost sixty. I made believe it was just the light when I saw the wrinkles on my face. I did not and do not want to get old! I will not surrender! I look and feel much younger than they are. I am ready to rub out this episode of my life."

"Lili, you have never been so critical of yourself! Are you mellowing, my friend?" Elsa looked at her above the rim of her cup, took a long sip, put her cup down and said seriously,

"Yes, it's true that you look much younger than your age, and I think I do too. You cannot compare us with the rest of our old class. If you look back to the years of our adolescence here, you'll realize that most of them had a much harder life than we did. They lived in a fenced-in country with no open gates to the Western world. They worked without any possibility of prospering freely. They could only have what the system let them. They lived in small, cramped apartments with their parents before they were able to get their own.

They had two weeks' holiday a year in some government-run "workers' paradise" or at some neighbouring socialist country for most of their young adult life. We left all that behind. We lived well and could do what ever we pleased. We had time and money to travel, see the world and gather knowledge to expand our brainpower. We had several bathrooms, washing machines and cars. We did not have to work after we had children. And most of the time we did not have to worry about money—our husbands took care of that. So no wonder we look younger than them. But look at the generation after us. They look just like anyone anywhere on the planet. Well dressed and confidant. They have every chance to follow their dreams no matter where it takes them!"

"I didn't ask you for a sociology lesson. I just stated my ground rules!" Lili retorted. But Elsa noted that she had not interrupted.

"I know, I'm sorry. But lately you've been getting far too worried about your age. I started to tell you that after we reached fifty, we are getting older no matter if we want to or not. There is nothing we can do about it but take it as it comes and make the best of it. Every age has its beauty. Don't sneer—it's true. If you fight against it, you'll just ruin the last part of your life. So what of the wrinkles? So what of the larger-sized pants? We have to take care of our bodies and souls the best we can and enjoy the freedom of old age!"

"Maybe you're right, but I can't take it so lightly."

"You should! You are healthy (and would be much healthier if you cut down on your smoking), you have no financial worries and you have a husband who adores you. Shall I continue?"

"No, I've heard this from you too many times already! Let's go! Are we going to meet Margaret for dinner?"

"No, her daughter is in town with her kid and staying at her place tonight."

"So, then, where are we going for dinner?"

Elsa opened her mouth, but before she could say anything a long, loud hoot from one of the cruise ships on the river filled the air.

"You know what? Let's go down to the riverbank and get on one of those cruise ships. We can have dinner there as we ride up and down the Danube. It's a lovely night, warm enough to sit on the deck."

"Let's not! The food is probably bland and made for tasteless tourists. I want to have a 'wooden-plate' tonight and listen to a gypsy band!"

The restaurant they chose, at the recommendation of the concierge (once he understood what it was they wanted), was a few blocks away from the hotel in an ancient, small, stone house. The place was called The Hundred Years, and it stood a few steps below street level. It had tiny, coloured-glass windows facing the street. The ancient wooden door held together by iron bars led into a dark foyer. A smiling waiter stood behind a table laden with many bottles of wine, and he led them to a table. The room looked rustic, the tables and chairs were carved from dark wood and native pottery and colourful hand-woven fabrics were scattered all around on the walls. In the corner of the restaurant, a gypsy band sat enjoying their recess.

The women ordered a litre of red wine and a wooden-plate for two. The wine came in a green clay jug. The waiter filled up the accompanying clay mugs, and the two friends clinked mugs.

"Here is to the past forty years," said Elsa.

As if it on command, the gypsies started playing a heartrending, softly flowing tune. Elsa saw Lili looking at her and tried to hide the tears running down her face.

"Elsa, what's the matter?" Lili asked. "Why are you diluting this already watered down wine?"

"I can not help it. Gypsy music like this always makes me cry. And the song they are playing was my father's favourite. He used to hum it off-key, I have to admit, when he was in a happy mood and working at his desk." Elsa dried her eyes on her napkin.

The bandleader noticed Elsa tears and walked up to their table, playing his violin just for her. That did not help at all, and her tears started flowing again. Lili got edgy and gave the gypsy a big tip. He left the table.

"I am not saying that I do not like this music," Lili said, glaring at the violinist's back, "but it doesn't do anything for me. I remember I hated it when I was a teenager, but lately I haven't minded listening to it. Now, I appreciate the mood and the flow of the music. Most of the songs are melancholy and soothing. I am going to buy a few tapes to take it back to Sydney with me. I have an old friend who is crazy about it."

"I've always liked it. It made me sad but gave me strength when I felt let down by life. It made it easier to deal with my problems, like when I was breaking up with Tom and moved back to Toronto. I listened to it all day long during those times."

"You are a hopeless romantic and will never grow out of it," Lili said warmly, "but I love you anyway!"

The waiter put down the wooden-plate for two in the middle of the table and refilled their mugs. Observing the plate, Lili said, "See, now that brings tears to my eyes! Look at this plate! Isn't it a gourmet's dream?"

The large, wood plate was overflowing with several kinds of grilled meat, chops, tenderloin, chicken, sausages, bacon, fried potatoes, rice, red cabbage and salad underneath. The top was decorated with red tomatoes, white mushrooms and green cucumber. It was truly a masterpiece.

"Well, let's get started. I am starving and my taste buds are jumping up and down in my throat. No more sad thoughts today—be happy!"

"Hey, that's my line!" Elsa laughed as they dug in.

They ate, drank and enjoyed the music. Elsa was relaxed and comfortable, and there was a funny warm feeling around her heart. She had not been that content for a long time.

Somehow she felt she hadn't lived all those long years in a faraway country. She felt her life during those forty years was just a figment of her imagination. This thought surprised her, since after her marriage she didn't suffer from homesickness and instead rooted down solidly in her new country and life. Why had this feeling come now? She knew that Lili wouldn't understand her thoughts and didn't feel like arguing now. After dinner, they walked back to the hotel chatting, laughing and making plans for the next day.

Margaret called them just after ten.

"I hope I didn't wake you up," she said, a bit worried, "but I have an errand to run and just wanted to know your plans for the day."

"No, no, it's fine. Lili just got up, but I have been up for hours. We didn't agree on anything, and I wanted to talk to you about our plans first. How was the visit?"

"It went well. I only had one argument with Klåri but we made up before they left. I enjoyed my granddaughter—it's amazing how much they change in a few months when they are four years old. I drove them to the bus station this morning. If you don't have any plans, I could pick you up around noon. Will that give you enough time to get ready?"

"Yeah, I'll make sure that Lili will be. If you don't see us in the lobby, come to the cafeteria. We'll be there having breakfast."

"Breakfast? This is lunchtime around here, you two spoiled brats! Okay, I'll see you later."

"So where do you want to go?" asked Margaret when she found them in the cafeteria.

"Why don't we go to Margaret Island?" suggested Elsa. "I'd love to stroll around the ruins and the rose garden. I have not been there for so many years. What do you say, Lili?"

"Fine with me, the last time I was there was, oh, about half a century ago with my first great love."

" Yes, I remember" said Elsa " You were spending so much time on the Island. At first I was wondering if you became I nature lover."

" I told you I am spending time at the pool and you were surprised that I was interested in swimming."

" You played the mystery woman for a while, before confessed that you are madly in love." Laughed Elsa and turned to Margaret " Shall we go?"

"I'll leave my car here because cars are not allowed on the island."

"You mean we have to walk?" asked Lili, terrified.

"We'll take the streetcar from the hotel and then transfer to another. It's just one stop to the entrance to the island. Coming back, we could take the bus or get a taxi at the Grand Hotel," said Margaret, reassuring Lili. "We only have to walk as much as you like."

"Okay, mates, let's go!" announced Lili as she signed the bill.

Elsa talked Lili into walking across the Margaret Bridge to the island instead of transferring to the second streetcar by promising her a fantastic dinner somewhere in Old Buda.

It was a nice, bright day. The sun was in and out of the scattered, white clouds and breeze ruffled the Danube. After they left the bridge with its heavy traffic and the suffocating smell of oil and gasoline, the air was filled with the smell of the flowering bushes and the river. The island was not busy, and only a few people walked around. Mothers pushing baby carriages, some others walking their dogs and a small group of children playing ball. The whole place was peaceful and inviting.

"I remember now!" Lili said suddenly, "This is the way to the swimming pool. Does it still exist? My already mentioned love was a goalie for a water polo team. We were both sixteen, and he was my one of my first sweethearts. He was astounding—he had a body like Michelangelo's *David*. I went to see every game he played. I loved to watch his perfect body as he dove for the ball. He was very good. He could rise up to his hips out of the deep water. And he was a good kisser too."

"I remember how smitten you were with him," said Elsa, laughing, "but he didn't last too long, did he?"

"A few months. He trained under a monster coach who forbade everything that was fun. Once there was a jazz concert here at the tennis courts. I was dying to go and made him miss an evening practice, promising that after the concert I'd walk with him on darkest road to the end of the island. The concert was great and so was the walk.

"We kissed and did some heavy necking on dark benches. His coach found out about it and made him break up with me. He did love water polo more than me."

"You very were upset that he dropped you!"

"Mostly because of my pride. But I did not mourn for long—I found his replacement fast enough. Remember that soccer player?"

"I think everybody has memories of this island, and it's still one of the favourite places of young lovers. Just look at that bench over there," said Margaret, pointing.

A couple sat on a lonely bench under a large tree, intertwined like one and dead to the world. The three women walked past them and followed the path to the rose garden. It was too early in the season yet for the roses to bloom, but there were plenty of other blooming plants. The garden was a large, oval court. Brick walkways led around the flowerbeds, and white benches were scattered around. An old couple walked slowly in front of them, hand in hand.

"Look at them! Aren't they sweet?" asked Elsa in a soft voice. "When I see that, I feel sorry for myself that I don't have anybody to walk with like that in my old age."

"How do you know they aren't at each others throats at home and sick and tired of the togetherness?" Lili asked harshly. Elsa thought it was probably because she felt the same pang that Michael was not there with her.

"Don't be so sarcastic—we know you have a soft heart somewhere deep down!" Elsa said, winking at Margaret.

They walked to the ancient ruins and the 15th-century chapel, and they went in to light a candle for the souls of their dead. Afterwards, they stopped at the Grand Hotel, where the terrace was open. The three sat under the giant, ancient maple trees, sipped coffee quietly and were deep in their own thoughts.

Margaret broke the silence.

"I'll take you to a very old restaurant tonight called, "The Old Sipos." It has been at the same place for centuries, and they are famous of their fish soup and cottage cheese noodles. It's in Buda, and we can walk there from here on the Àrpàd Bridge."

"How far?" asked Lili, sounding alarmed. "I've walked enough today for a whole month."

"About twenty minutes of easy walking. You'll see—it's worth it."

"It must be!" said Lili. "I don't want to be disappointed that I walked miles for a fish soup."

"I take the responsibility," laughed Margaret. "I'm sure you'll love it!

They did love it. The soup was full of large chunks of fish in a thick, hot, red broth with dumplings and potato bits in it to add flavour.

It was spicy and tasted wonderful. The restaurant was just half full, so they lingered over dinner, debating whether to have a second course or not.

"I can't eat another bite," said Elsa, leaning back in her chair. "I am so full I can hardly breathe!"

"You cannot leave without tasting the noodles. They are outstanding too," said Margaret. "What about you Lili?"

"Let's have a break and order the second course later. I don't think they will mind if we sit here longer. I must have the noodles," answered Lili.

"Right, take a breather," agreed Margaret. "And you know what? You still owe me the story of what happened when you arrived in Australia."

"Yes, Lili, let's hear it," nodded Elsa.

To be honest, I was terrified when the plane took off from Vienna. That was the moment when I comprehended what I had done. I was leaving my old world, Elsa and everybody else behind for a faraway country—I was off to marry a stranger about whom I knew nothing aside from that he was rich and good in bed.

But as the plane flew farther and farther, the excitement for a new life took me over. As you know, we couldn't travel anywhere from Hungary but to some of the Eastern European countries. The airports of Western Europe were all new and exciting experiences for me. The big jets, the long, many-hour flight to America, the night I spent in a hotel in Los Angeles and the stopovers in Hawaii and Fiji made me feel like I was watching myself in a movie. It was unreal to be in the places I had only heard or read about in those forbidden romance novels. I saw endless oceans. I saw palm trees and smelled the warm, humid air in Fiji. We flew over the red, barren landscape of Australia. I was afraid that all this was just a dream and I'd wake up in my bed in Budapest.

At the airport in Sydney, Péter was waiting for me. During the long flights I tried to remember his face and found I could not, so I was scared stiff that I wouldn't recognize him. But I did, and when he kissed me I felt protected and ready for everything. We could not live together because Australia was a puritan country at the time. The jailbirds who established it apparently wanted to forget the past. So Péter booked me in a hotel until we could get married. Of course we spent every night together there.

The formalities took more than two weeks. Then we got married in the city hall, and I became Mrs. Mohay. I moved into his house, which was a heaven for my eyes. The two bathrooms, the air conditioning, the gleaming white kitchen equipped with the largest refrigerator I'd ever seen, the dishwasher and the garden full of flowers. The view from the garden was magnificent. I could see the bay and the big cruise ships passing by. I walked around there stunned for the first few weeks, congratulating myself on my good fortune.

Peter introduced me all around to his few Hungarian and other friends. We had a big party in the house for this occasion. He catered it and managed everything—I didn't have to move a finger. I was on my best behaviour, smiled at every one and charmingly tried my hardest to understand a few words of the conversations. Péter was very proud of me. I was accepted in his circle, and we got invitations by the dozen. Life was good. I certainly enjoyed it. Péter hired a tutor to come to the house and teach me English.

Péter was kind and loving, but he was boring. He had dull friends whose wives were much older than me and looked at me as if I was a rare bird. I couldn't talk to them, not because of my English but because there was nothing to talk about. They were interested only in sailing, tennis or housekeeping problems. I missed my active, crazy life. I did not have any friends my age, and I missed Elsa. We wrote to each other regularly, but it was not enough.

Soon I got fed up with the blue sky, the sunshine and the always-green trees. It was interesting to go to Bondi Beach on New Year's Eve for a swim, but I found myself wishing for snow-covered pine trees instead of palm trees. I got restless and hated the monotony of the days. I hated shopping for food, I was never a gardener and it drove me crazy to sit in the house all day and wait for Péter to come home. I was not cut out to be a housewife who waits for her husband with dinner and washes and irons his shirts. I was desperately looking for ways to occupy my days and be with people. I even ventured out, carefully of course, for a few short-lived affairs.

I talked, well, to be honest *forced* Péter to let me to be a partner in his business. I had to use all my charms and powers to convince him. I said things like he was too busy and we were not spending enough time together, I wanted to learn about his business, etc. He was a conservative male and a bachelor for too long to let me into his business world. But if I want something I get it. So after long deliberation he let me look after the accounts, and later when I was familiar with the way the factory worked, he let me sit in on business meetings and handle customers. But he was hard-headed and wouldn't let me make any changes. He would not listen to my ideas, no matter how good they were—he wanted to run his business his own way.

Soon I realized that I was pregnant. It was probably the result of trying to convince him. I didn't insist on using the rubber and I was the careful one, but as it turned out I was not careful enough. That time there were no birth-control pills, and in Sydney I could not do anything about it. I never wanted to have children. Péter was overjoyed. He was in his early fifties then and very proud of himself. He spoiled me—I got everything with a blink of my eyes. I got my own car, and he hired a housekeeper to do all the housework. I lived like a spoiled, bored brat, but I was not happily looking forward to motherhood."

"What happened after the baby was born?" asked Margaret. "It didn't change you?"

"For a while, yes, but that is another story. I'm ready for the noodles—let's order them. I want mine with sour cream, bacon bits and sugar."

"Bacon and sugar? I've never heard of that. Watch the waitress face when you order it," laughed Margaret.

Chapter 12

When Margaret saw Edith coming through the customs door, she was shocked. Edith had lost lots of weight, she was a pale and had dark ring under her eyes. Margaret tried very hard no to show her anxiety, but she was not successful enough.

"I look horrible, do I?" said Edith after the two women hugged each other.

"What's the matter, are you sick?"

"It's nothing to worry about. I had a very bad month of migraines, a bad cold and so on."

"Did you see a doctor?"

"No, what for? They don't have the faintest idea why I get the headaches. They just tell me it's stress, to have plenty of rest and to not drink alcohol."

"Edith, you are not drinking again, are you?"

"Just with moderation. So at least I am able to sleep."

On the way home, Edith poured her heart out to Margaret. She had been fired from her part time job, there was a break in at her stall and she had a hard time collecting the insurance, which didn't even cover her loss es.

"And on top of everything, Allan said goodbye three weeks ago."

Margaret knew about Allan, a painter eight years younger than Edith who lived for his hope of being discovered and becoming famous. He never held onto a job because then his "creativeness would have suffered." Edith kept him—they had lived together for the past two years.

"You knew it wouldn't last when you took him in! It's better to get rid of him now than later," said Margaret, more sternly than she intended. She could never understand why Edith could not live alone for more than a year, and every time she chose the most worthless partners. She usually asked Margaret for advice but seldom followed it.

"Most important is that you came," Margaret continued more softly. "You should leave all your worries behind, have a good rest and we'll have a good time with Elsa and Lili. The day after tomorrow, all four of us will take a trip around Balaton."

"I don't know if I am able to go. I would just ruin your days and spoil the trip with my miserable mood. Why don't you stay with me and let those two go. I sure they can afford to rent a car. I need you for myself!"

Margaret forced herself to stay unruffled, and they did not talk until Edith unpacked and they were sitting at the kitchen table having tea and cookies. Edith calmed down and asked for forgiveness.

"I'm sorry, I know I was out of line. I shouldn't have come! But I needed your shoulder to cry on."

"You know you can always cry on my shoulder—I am here for you. I have the next day just for you. We can talk and I'm sure you'll feel better. We'll take a long walk in the hills like we did in Scotland. Remember? It will do you good."

"Thanks, Margaret. Would you have some vodka or rum? My migraine is acting up again. I must go to bed and sleep it off."

Margaret took out a more than half-full bottle of vodka and wanted to pour some in a glass, but Edith took the bottle from her hand and headed towards the guest room.

"I'll be good as new tomorrow, my charming old self, I promise," she said as she winked and shut the door. Margaret looked at the closed door for a long time. She felt sorry and worried for Edith, and her seventh sense told her that there was much more behind Edith's depression than she was letting on.

Margaret cleaned up the kitchen before she sat down at her desk to work on her papers. After a short while, she quietly opened the guest room door to check on Edith. Edith was sleeping on her side in the fetal position, and the bottle was empty on the night table.

They spent the next day together, walking the hills of Buda and lunching in one of the small restaurants atop Svab hegy and overlooking the city and the Danube. Margaret tried to carry on conversations, but Edith was withdrawn and inattentive. She played with her food, pushing it around on her plate, but she did drink two glasses of wine. They sat there in silence for a while enjoying the warmth of the May sun.

Later, when walking back down the hill, Edith opened up and talked.

"I am lost," she began. "I don't know who I am anymore. I walk around in a haze, making myself do what I must do, but I feel my life isn't worth a penny. I soon will be sixty years old and have nothing to look forward to. I have nobody to belong to me, to love me or for me to love. The last months with Allan were hell! We fought a lot, mainly because of money, screaming at each other and slamming doors. My downstairs neighbour wanted to call the cops on us. I was relieved when Allan left, but a week later I wanted him back and was devastated when he refused. Of course he sacked up with a much younger, rich art student who didn't know that he is a crook.

"I've not painted for months now. I just sit and stare at the empty canvas if I even have the strength to set it up. I go to the market and sit in my stall, not caring if I sell or not or if somebody likes my work or not. I close up early but hate to go home, so I wander around London on foot or get on the Tube and ride from one end of the line to the other.

"My head is full of thousands of swirling thoughts, and I can't make any sense out of them. At home I go to bed but can't sleep. If I do sleep, I have strange, frightening dreams, and when I wake up my head is pounding like a steam hammer. So I have a stiff drink to knock myself out. Margaret, what am I to do?"

"I think you need professional help. Why don't you look up the good doctor who helped you through your husband's death? You are heading for a full nervous breakdown, and a cry on my shoulder can't bring you out of it."

"I thought about it, but he is very expensive and my health insurance doesn't cover it. As you know, I am not exactly rolling in money," Edith said resentfully.

"Then find someone less expensive. I'm sure your family doctor can refer you to one who will be covered by your insurance. Edith, you must before it's too late!"

"I'll look into it when I get home, I promise. But that's enough of my misery for now. Let's talk about what we are doing. Are we meeting the two rich bitches today?"

"No, I wanted to spend the whole day with you alone. We can call them tomorrow morning. I told them I'd call before picking them up at the hotel."

"Where are we going?"

"We'll just follow the road around Lake Balaton and stop wherever we feel like it. It will be fun, you'll see. Those two are easygoing and funny. You need good company to cheer you up."

Edith was on her best behaviour. She sat beside Lili in the back seat and listened to the never-ending stories of her escapades when she was young. Her stories were funny, and she told them with gusto, full of life and like they happened yesterday. They stopped for lunch at a roadside restaurant. A little while after lunch it started to rain, so they decided to stop at the next town to bunk down for the day. Margaret was looking for a bed and breakfast, but Elsa would not let her.

"Look, all of you are my guests—I insist on it. Let's go to a lakeside hotel and get two rooms overlooking the lake. This time of the year it can't be any problem. Let's spoil ourselves, have a good dinner and good wine. We deserve it!"

They stopped in Balatonfoldvàr, a large resort town on the south side of the lake.

"I know a nice hotel, if it still exists," said Margaret. "Let's find out."

She turned off the main road and soon stopped in front of a square, five-story, gray building.

"Here we are! Just as I remember it—the same ugly, drab building. But the rooms overlook the lake and are comfortable enough. I was here when it was a government-run establishment for the outstanding workers of the party. My ex was treated like a king because of his position. I hope I do not run into anyone who remembers me."

The reception desk was empty, and the room was dark, unfriendly looking, filled with oversized, stiff-looking armchairs and large paintings left over by the socialist realist artists.

"This place gives me the chills. I feel I've stepped back fifty years," said Lili. "But let us live dangerously and get the rooms if anybody ever shows up at the desk."

A young man wearing a smart uniform suddenly appeared from the door behind the desk.

"Can I help you?" he asked in accented English.

"Yes, you can," said Lili with the charming smile she saved for any young man. "But you can speak Hungarian. We understand it."

"How nice, thank you. Would like to see the rooms?" He continued the sentence in Hungarian, eyeing Lili's thick, gold-and-diamond-decorated necklace.

The hotel was almost empty, but a German tourist group had just started marching in single file from a long bus in the parking lot, shaking hats and umbrellas.

"Nice view! Look at the lake!" said Elsa, opening the windows wide to let in the scent of the spring rain. "It is just as light green as I remember it. My family used to spend the summer holidays on the other side of the lake. You must remember my large, good-humoured aunt. You stayed with us there often."

"I remember that your aunt did not like me too much! I was far too wild for her liking, and she was afraid I would spoil her innocent niece! The view is fine, but look at this room! Like a cheap, roadside motel on Route 66! But as I saw, the rates are much higher!"

"Stop criticizing! It's really not bad. It is clean, and the bathroom is big and full of towels. Look, we have a small fridge too!"

"There is nothing in the fridge but a few sad-looking bags of chips. I'm hungry. Let's call Margaret and go somewhere to eat. I don't feel like eating here."

Margaret recalled a small restaurant somewhere close by, and they set out to find it. She drove around for a while in the rain before suddenly making a sharp left turn and stopping at a low, stone building with a reed-thatched roof.

"Now that's what I call ethnic!" yelled Lili. "Is it a restaurant?"

"It was about twenty-some years ago," said Margaret. "Let's see if it still is."

It was. A fire burned in the white-crested, open earthenware oven where a young man was working. He put flattened, round dough on a large, round paddle with a long handle and pushed it into the oven.

Lili shrieked with pleasure, "Don't tell me he is baking långos! This has been on my wish list ever since the war when I spent the winter months in a small village with my father's cousins. There was no variation in food and just enough to eat, but they had plenty of flour. As I remember, it takes only flour and water to make långos! Oh, Margaret, I'll be in your debt forever for this!"

They found an empty table close to the oven and settled down. The proprietor was a smiling, friendly older man with small, dark, dancing eyes under his bushy eyebrows. He was holding large menu books in his big hands.

"We don't need those," said Lili, giving her friendliest smile to the man. "We would like to have four of those, right girls?" Lili pointed to the earthen oven.

"What would you like on the top?" the man asked. "Sour cream, cheese, fried bacon?"

"Everything!" they said like a choir. "And some of your red house wine," said Margaret.

The flat bread was hot and smelled and tasted wonderful with all the toppings. For a while everybody was busy eating, emitting a few ohhhhs and ahhhs. After they finished the first portion they ordered one more, and by then their tongues were loosened and the chatting beg an.

Edith was quiet throughout. She could not let herself go enough to take part in the chatting and laughing. She felt like an outsider in that happy group, and she eyed her companions one by one. Margaret was relaxed and laughing, and her face was glowing from the heat of the oven and the wine. Edith felt a jealous pang in her heart. She wanted to demand how she could be happy, knowing very well how unhappy and miserable her friend was!

How can she relate to those two? She has nothing in common with them. She knew both of them had easy lives, family, money and no heartbreaks. She looked at Lili, who was telling a joke and acting it out like a comedian onstage. And the wealth on her fingers alone—one of the rings had such a large diamond that Edith figured the price of it would be enough for her to live on for a year! Lili's soft, angora sweater must have cost a fortune too. And Elsa, while she did not wear any jewellery, her pants and silk scarf screamed of well-being.

"Edith, you are too quiet!" Elsa said suddenly, interrupting her thoughts. "Is anything the matter? Are you not feeling well? You look tired. Edith?"

"Oh, what? No, I am okay, just a bit tired. I'm ready for bed, aren't you all?"

"Hey, it's only half past eight!" Lili protested. "You can't be sleepy! The fun is just beginning! Whose turn is it to tell a story from her life? We have not heard one from you, Edith!"

"What story?"

"We've been telling each other stories of our life on some evenings, stories from the innermost corners of our pasts," explained Margaret. "Not made up stories but real ones. Elsa and Lili already told two, and I had my turn also. Now it's your turn—don't disappoint us!"

"I am afraid I have to. I am not in the mood for anything like that. There was nothing in my life what would interest you! It was full of misery and nothing worthwhile talking about. I would rather listen to your stories. I am sure they are very interesting. Both of you lead a stimulating life with all that travelling," said Edith, looking at Elsa and Lili with poorly hidden bitterness in her voice.

"We also had our problems, ups and downs, pains and joys," Elsa said. "I think it is gratifying to talk about all those painful or happy stories from our life, especially at our age. We see things differently now, and talking about long-hidden pain will lighten our souls." She paused. "You should try it, Edith."

"Maybe I will, but not tonight. Rain check, okay? You three just stay. I want to walk back to the hotel. It can't be more than a ten-minute walk and all of it downhill. And it's not raining anymore! I need to air out my head."

"You can't go alone, it's almost dark. You'll get lost. Wait for a half an hour and all of us will go!" said Margaret soothingly. She could feel the despair in Edith's tone.

"Thanks, Margaret, but I really need to walk alone. See you later at the hotel," said Edith as she stood up, picked up her coat and walked out without saying anything more.

Edith walked with her head down, not looking right or left, just following the pavement under her feet. The rain had stopped, and the air was full of the late spring mist and the smell of fresh foliage. When she looked up, she found herself at the railway station. She crossed the tracks and kept walking towards the lake. She arrived at the lakeshore and stepped onto a wide, tree-lined walkway. The hundred-year-old trees looked ready to open up their full green splendour for the summer. It was semi-dark, and just a few old-fashioned gaslights on top of iron rods blinked between the trees. The twilight, intertwining with the yellow gaslight, danced on the smooth surface of the water.

Edith stopped close to the lake. A solitary sailboat glided soundless towards the green light marking the entrance to the harbour. Watching the boat approaching its mooring, she walked out to the end of the pier and sat down on a concrete barrier. She pulled her coat tighter about her shoulders and felt cold, miserable and empty. No way was she going to talk to them about her miserable life. It would not enlighten her. For the most part, she did not even let herself remember anything of her early youth and the later years' mistakes and pain. She did not want their pity—let them play their stupid reminiscing games—she could deal with her life alone.

The sailboat docked in its berth. The sailor tied up the ropes with some difficulty. The ropes must have been wet, slippery and cold. He checked all the ropes, closed the cabin door securely, and jumped out on the pier without making any noise with his soft, rubber-soled sneakers. He looked up after lighting a cigarette and he noticed the dark figure sitting on the barrier. He hesitated for a few seconds and approached the solitary figure.

"Hello there," a voice suddenly said from behind her. "Nice evening, isn't it?"

Edith was stunned by the human voice and looked up with a haunted look.

"Oh, I am sorry! I didn't want to frighten you, forgive me!"

"Its okay, you didn't. I was just looking at the lake. It is so mysteriously dark that it looks like it never wants to be lit up again!"

"But it will be a beautiful light green again before the sun gets up on the horizon. It can't be helped."

"Yes, like many things in life."

The sailor sensed Edith's mood, and asking, "May I?" sat down beside her and offered her a cigarette. Edith took one and he gave her a light. For a while, they sat side by side, smoking in silence.

Then Edith asked, "You are the one who just came in on a boat? I watched it. It sailed so quietly and smoothly like a dream."

"I love sailing. It has been my life since I retired and don't have to work for a living. I take every opportunity to take the boat out—even in the rain."

Edith looked over the man beside her as a draw on his cigarette lit up his face. It was a weather-beaten, suntanned face with hard lines around his mouth. His dark eyes looked back at her with frankness.

"May I introduced myself? My name is Antal," he said, offering his hand. Edith took it. His handshake was firm and strong.

"Hi, I am Edith. Do you live around here?"

"Now on weekends only, but I spend the summers here. I live on my boat. I was on my way to get a drink and something to eat. My food box is empty after a long day of sailing."

"Do you really live on your boat? How exciting. I always wanted to do that when I was a young girl, and I dreamt about sailing for days and days to some faraway place. But of course it never happened."

"How about making your dream come true? Would you like sail with me tomorrow?"

Edith was taken aback and moved farther from Antal. He laughed.

"How stupid I am!" he said. "We just met! Don't be afraid, I am not a stalker who lures good-looking woman onto my boat. You must be cold sitting here. Why don't we go and have a drink so we can take a closer look and see if we like each other or not at all. No hard feelings if we don't—we just say goodbye after a warm-up drink. How about it?"

Edith hesitated but then there was no good reason why not. She said, "Well, that sounds harmless enough. Let's go."

Antal took her to the small bar in the railway station.

"I'm sorry, but it's too early in the season and nothing else is open around here. What would you like?"

Edith's heart was set on a double shot of vodka straight, but she asked for a glass of white wine.

They sat in a booth nursing their drinks and talked. In the dim light of the bar, Antal looked raggedly handsome, and she guessed him in his late fifties. He talked with ease, intelligence and good humour. They talked about sailing and life in general but nothing personal. Edith slowly warmed up, felt relaxed and her gloomy mood changed into light expectation. He ordered a second round, and this time Edith gave in to her craving and changed to vodka. Antal drank beer with a whisky chaser.

"Oh, look at the time!" Edith said after a while. "I must get back to the hotel. My girlfriends must be worried. I left them at a restaurant to walk back alone to get rid of a headache."

"Have you?" asked Antal, winking at her. "Which hotel are you staying in?"

"I don't know the name. The big ugly one on the shore," Edith said, giggling. The double vodka was taking effect.

"I will walk you home."

At the darkened hotel entrance, they shook hands. Antal did not make a move to do otherwise, but Edith moved up closer and kissed his cheek.

"I'll be waiting for you at my boat tomorrow morning around ten," he said and kissed her lightly on the lips. Then he turned around and disappeared into the darkness.

Edith looked after him for a long time, and she knew that if he had asked her to go with him she would have gone without any hesitation. But he did not.

His loss, or rather mine, she thought. She wanted a warm body beside her tonight. She told herself she was getting old, wishing for a warm body and not for sex. She didn't feel like going in and facing Margaret's questions and wanted to stay out for a while, but she noticed Margaret pacing the empty lobby. She drew a deep breath and went inside.

"Edith, where were you? I was worried sick and ready to call the police!"

"Come on, Margaret, I am a grown woman. What could happen to me? I walked for a while and sat down by the harbour looking at the lake. It was lovely night, everything smelled so fresh after the rain. I lost sense of the time! I am sorry to worry you! Where are the others?"

"Probably asleep. I did not let them know that you were not in. Are you ready for bed?"

"You know, I ..." she almost revealed the meeting with Antal but stopped herself. "Yes, I think so. Let's go up."

Chapter 13

The breakfast buffet table was laden with all kinds of cold cuts, cheeses, eggs in many forms and at least half a dozen kinds of bread. Lili came back to their table with a plate so full that she could hardly keep food from falling to the floor.

"I'll diet at home," she said with a happy sigh. She sat down and lowered her plate carefully to the table.

Edith had already finished her breakfast and was on her second cup of coffee. She looked deep into her cup as if trying to see something there.

"A dollar for your thoughts," said Elsa. "You look like you are far away from here. Did you sleep well? We didn't hear you coming in last night."

Edith just nodded her head and kept looking into her cup.

"So, what are we going to do? Are we staying or do we move on?" asked Margaret.

"Let's go and stop again where we fancy," said Elsa. "You know, I would like to stop and spend some time at my childhood haven on the other side of the lake, but before that let's spend a day at the thermal bath I've read so much about. What do you think, girls?" she asked, looking around the table.

"Fine with me, let's go!" said Margaret and Lili simultaneously.

Edith looked up from her cup. "I am not going with you!"

The other three looked at her with open mouths.

"What do you mean, not coming with us? Do you want to go home?" asked Margaret abruptly.

"No, I am not going home. I met someone and I am going sailing for a few days."

"Sailing? What are you talking about? What boat, with whom and how come?" The questions were flying around the table.

"That someone is a man?" asked Lili, winking at Edith.

"Yes, he is in his late fifties, handsome and nice. Did I satisfy your curiosity?"

"No, you did not!" Margaret said harshly. "You did not say anything about it last night when you came in, and it could not happen in your dreams!"

"I am sorry, Margaret. Last night I wasn't sure if I wanted to do it. I decided at just this minute. Last night I met him at the marina, we started to talk and then we had a drink at a bar. He is really very nice and quite safe. I feel I need some change and challenge in my life—you can explain why to Elsa and Lili. I will meet you on the other side of the lake two days from now at the marina in Fured."

Edith got up from the table, but before she left she put her hand on Margaret's shoulder. Squeezing it, she said, "I am sorry, don't worry, I have to do it, I'll be okay." Then she left.

The three other women looked at each other in disbelief.

"Well, that's a surprise! I've never heard of anything like that! What do you make of it, Margaret?" Elsa asked.

"As I said before, she's had very difficult times lately. She is unbalanced and I am worried sick about her, but I cannot run her life. She is a mature woman. I only hope this adventure will turn out to be good for her. Let her be and hope for her safe return …" Margaret stopped in the middle of her sentence. "At least she should have told us his name or the name of the sailboat! I'll go after her and try to talk some sense into her."

Margaret went into the hall, but she missed the first open elevator and had to wait for the second one. By the time she got to their room Edith was gone.

Edith packed her bag quickly, as she knew Margaret would come after her and she did not want to be questioned. She checked her purse for her passport and money and then rushed out of the hotel. It was well after ten when she reached the pier. At the end of it, she saw Antal sitting on the barrier.

"I almost gave up on you," he said with a grin, "but somehow I was sure you'd come. It is a lovely day for sailing. The sun is shining and the wind is just right for a leisurely run. Come aboard!"

He took her bag and helped her to step over the railing and into the boat. The boat was twenty-five feet long, the cabin part was blue, the body was white and it had two small portholes.

Edith looked around inside the cabin. It was small but professionally set up and everything had its secure place. It was clean, the table shone and the bench behind it was upholstered with a warm-looking brown material. Towards the bow was a tiny kitchen with a hot plate and a propane refrigerator. On the table was a small bunch of spring tulips.

"Well, how do you like it? Does it look as it did in your dream?" asked Antal as he put down Edith's bag on the end of the bench. "It's not big," he continued, "but it can sleep three and behind that small door is a chemical toilet—all the comforts of home. There's no shower, so I wash in the lake. In the early summer that can be a freezing chore!"

"Oh, this looks like heaven," said Edith, looking out a porthole to the light green water. "You were right, the water looks emerald green again, and it is breathtaking." She felt unperturbed, as if she had been on this boat for years already. She looked at Antal and said, "Are you sure you want to take me with you? "

"Of course I'm sure. I liked you the first minute I sat down beside you on the pier. I was lonely, and I sensed that you were too. We are going to have a great time!"

He got busy preparing the boat for sailing. He unhooked the ropes, started the fifteen-horsepower outboard motor and then steered the boat out of its mooring and through the harbour to the open water. Then he cut the motor and pulled the main sail up the mast, and as soon as the wind got into the sail, he pulled up the jib too and steered the boat into the wind. Once he secured the ropes, he sat down beside the steering wheel. The boat glided on top of the small waves, hardly making a sound.

They sat there for a while before Antal asked, "Where to?"

"I told my friends I'd meet them the day after tomorrow at the marina in Balatonfüred. Is that okay?"

"Perfect. We'll just sail to the end of the lake today, moor at Keszthely, have a great dinner at one of the best restaurants in town and spend the night on the boat. The bow the bed is comfortable enough, and I'll sleep on the bench. I have a good collection of CDs and a few bottles of wine. But if you'd rather go to a hotel I will be not offended. Tomorrow we'll sail on to Tihany—it is a beautiful place to walk around—and later head up to Balatonfüred. The weather forecast is good. We're supposed to have warm, sunny days with a slight chance of rain tomorrow evening. We are going to have fun. Leave every sad thought behind." Antal put an arm around Edith's shoulder. "So, where are you from and what are you doing here?"

Edith opened up and told her life story to Antal.

She told him about Gábor, her marriage and the hard times they had. But she wanted to impress Antal and left out that she was poor and had to struggle for living. She told him that she lived in London and was an artist, a painter. She had her own apartment and a small studio. She came to spend some time with an old friend, but the visit didn't turn out the way she had wanted, so she jumped at the offer to go sailing and fulfill her childhood dream of living on a boat for a few days.

As she talked, she didn't even notice that she moved closer and closer to Antal and felt secure with his arm around her shoulder. Antal let her talk without interruption. He tried to be eagerly interested and not let it show that he was bored with the marriage details, but when he learned that Edith was from England and a painter, his interest sparked up.

"So you have been living in London ever since 1956? And travelled a lot in Europe! I have always wanted to do that, but my wish never materialized—something always came up to prevent me from travelling. I wanted to flee after the revolution too, but my mother was very sick and I just could not leave her. When she died, things were changing here politically and my desire to leave was not so strong. Also I was in love with my first wife who did not want to leave, so I stayed. My marriage lasted for only six years. We had no children, but we did have a bitter, ugly divorce. Later, I got interested in computer technology, left my job at an accountant's office, took courses and became a computer geek. It was just the beginning of the computer business here, and there were not too many people who had my kind of credentials. I made a lot of money. Bought this boat and learned to sail. I became a good sailor and even won a few trophies here on this lake. I am semi-retired now and comfortably off to live the life I want. I had a few love affairs but did not want to get trapped in marriage again. I wanted to stay free. But freedom sometimes turns into loneliness. I am glad I stopped to talk to you last night. You are interesting, intelligent and a lovely woman, I enjoy your company."

"I feel the same way about you!" she said lovingly as she looked into his eyes.

Antal tightened his arm around Edith's shoulder, smiling at her. Edith felt relaxed and protected like never before. He was so comforting as he listened to her story with great interest. She was fantasizing that after sailing they would stay together, make love and maybe he'd follow her to London and they'd live there happily. They sat side by side without talking for a while.

∼

The lake's colour changed from light green to a darker shade as the sun climbed higher in the deep blue sky. The only sound was the smooth swells of the waves hitting the bow of the boat. A number of gulls followed them for a while, hoping for some handout. The shores were hidden in a white haze, which was occasionally broken up with glitter when the sun shone on a window of one of the taller buildings. From somewhere in the far distance, a ferry blew its horn as it started to cross the lake.

Antal turned to Edith, gestured at the wheel and said, "You take care of it for a few minutes. It's easy. Just hold it straight. The wind is light and nothing will happen. I am going below to make a morning drink for us. You must taste my Bloody Mary."

"Isn't it too early for a drink?" asked Edith.

"No, we'll live it up today. I am the master of Bloody Mary s. I'm sure you'll like it," he said as he went down into the cabin.

He closed the cabin door half way and looked around for Edith's purse. It was on the bench beside her duffle bag. He glanced up and saw Edith obediently holding the wheel and looking straight ahead. He opened her purse and looked inside. Taking out the British passport, he checked the name and the photograph and then looked inside the wallet, where he counted more than two hundred pounds and some forints. Two hundred pounds was a lot of money if converted into forints. He was satisfied, so he carefully put everything back where it was and started to mix the drinks. With a tall drink in each hand, he went up to the deck and handed one to Edith.

"Hmm ... strong and spicy. Just the way I like it, cheers," Edith said. She looked into Antal's eyes and he felt something click. Antal put his glass down, reached for Edith's and put that one down too. He pulled her face toward his and kissed her gently on the mouth. She responded and they engaged in a long but gentle kiss.

"Well, that was nice," said Antal, smiling at Edith and giving back her glass. "We should do it more often. But now I have to steer the boat before we hit the shore."

The hours passed leisurely with talking, drinking, more gentle kisses and long, comfortable silences. Early in the afternoon, Antal said, "I'm getting hungry and a bit tipsy from the Bloody Marys. We'll have to dock somewhere to get some food. A few miles up there is a roadside deli where we can get something. Not anything elaborate but bread, sausages and stuff." Edith nodded, so he guided the boat into a small harbour and tied it up at a neglected dock.

"I'll come with you," Edith said, "and let me pay for the food. After all, I pushed myself on you!"

"Okay, you buy the food, I buy the wine and it's a deal!"

Back on the boat, Edith set up the table and Antal opened the wine. Edith ate sparingly and Antal with gusto. They drank one and a half bottles of wine.

"Do you want to sail on? Are you sure you're not drunk?" asked Edith.

"I'm fine—not even tipsy" he said and started to undo the ropes with unbalanced steps. He looked back to see Edith watching him. She seemed slightly drunk and had not eaten much. He turned his attention back to his task. The fresh air cleared his head a little, and once he had freed his boat, he sat at the wheel. Edith sat beside him. Antal put his hand over Edith's and caressed it gently.

"You know what? Let's moor close to the shore further up. A little snooze before going on might be a good idea."

He sailed into a sheltered cove, threw the anchor about two hundred meters from the shore and then guided Edith down into the cabin. He pulled out the day bed, unbuttoned his shirt and pulled down his pants. He had a nice body, lean and firm, for a man in his late fifties. Edith, as if it was the most natural thing in the world, took off her sweater and stepped out of her pants. They looked at each other for a while, and both liked what they saw. Antal pulled Edith by the hand down beside him on the bed. He felt Edith melt in his arms. Antal was an experienced lover, and he slowly explored her body, first kissing her breast, her face and her neck. When Edith started to moan, Antal made love to her slowly with the experience of his age. She had tears in her eyes which Antal kissed away. When it was over, he turned on his side. Before he went to sleep, he felt Edith curl up to his back with a deep sigh.

It was already dark when they woke up. They decided to spend the night there and continue sailing early in the morning, they went up and sat on the deck watching the moon come up in the clear, dark sky.

"I am so glad I came. Thank you, Antal!"

"The pleasure is mine. You are a great girl! We are so lucky to have bumped into each other, aren't we? Let's just see where these next few days lead us. I like to believe we'll have many more of the same!"

"Yes, just enjoy!"

"I have a bottle of French brandy hidden down below—got it from an old friend of mine. Let's go down. It's getting chilly up here," Antal said, offering his hand to Edith.

"To be honest, my head is still spinning a bit," laughed Edith.

"But a good brandy sounds just right to finish a magnificent day," said Antal as he kissed Edith's nose.

He poured the brandy into two large snifters, lit a couple of candles on the table, turned on the propane heater to ward off the chill of the night and put on a CD of love songs from the sixties. He sat down beside Edith, kissed her softly, said "Cheers to us" and drank.

They finished half of the brandy while stroking each other and then crawled into the bed. Too smashed to make love, they both fell asleep immediately. Some time later, Edith woke up smelling smoke. She looked at the table where the candles burned with low, yellow flames. She thought about blowing them out, but she was too dizzy to get up. Turned onto her other side and went back to sleep.

∼

The sun came up and lit the dawn's gray sky. Dense mist covered the surface of the lake. The seagulls were waking up and took off from the railing of a blue and white sailboat. In the silence, their wings made a lot of noise as they flew. At the shore, a solitary fisherman pushed a small dinghy into the water, jumped in and started to paddle out onto the lake.

He noticed the moored sailboat and thought nothing of it. He figured it was just some crazy city folks anchoring for the night too early in the spring. But he could not help his curiosity and steered his dinghy close to the sailboat. There were no sounds, and the boat was rocking gently on the quiet lake. The fisherman stopped for a few seconds but then resumed his paddling towards open water. Suddenly, he noticed smoke coming out from the cracks of the cabin door. He pulled his boat up and shouted, "Hello, anybody there? Hello … hello …"

There was not a sound from inside, so he climbed over the railing, still shouting, "Hello … hellooooo …" He waited for a while, not knowing what to do. Should he go to shore and call somebody, or see for himself if there was something wrong? His instincts told him to open the door immediately. It was not locked, so he opened it and had to step back. An acrid smell poured out from the cabin. He took a deep breath and went inside. In the semi-darkness, he saw two motionless bodies on the bed.

Chapter 14

Lili was bored. She did not like the hotel, she did not like the town and she hated the thermal bath. It was crowded with old people. It was too hot and smelled of rotten eggs inside the building, and the naturally warm water of the lake outside was murky and dirty looking. The purple water lilies were nice though and covered large part of the surface.

She had read that this was the second-largest natural hot water lake in the world, but it didn't make a favourable impression on her at all. She sat on one of the outside benches watching Elsa and Margaret as they swam slowly around and later hung on a rusted iron rail talking. Suddenly she felt homesick for the blue water of Sydney Bay, the cloudless sky, the palm trees and, yes, Michael. She had called him last night and sensed the loneliness in his voice, no matter how much he wanted to sound cheerful. He said he was well, and his days were full with the therapy programs, his computer and reading. He told her she should enjoy herself and not worry about him, he was doing fine. She wanted to believe all this, but it didn't work.

"I have to cut this trip short and go back. What am I doing here anyway? I do not belong here at all," she grumbled. "I don't have any desire to recall my childhood and my youth. No, there was nothing happy and exciting in it! I just hated those years, I did not like my parents (peace on their ashes) and I lived the better part of my life—the wiser part—on the other side of the world. I'll never come back again!"

She sat and watched an old couple as they helped each other down the green, slimy and narrow steps into the water. The sight didn't cheer her up but more made her more depressed.

Lili glanced back at the other two and saw they were watching her from their perch on the railing. She alternated between ungraciously thinking they looked old too and not wanting to even look at her own hands for fear of seeing wrinkles.

"I think she is very unhappy. She doesn't like this place, I can see it on her face," said Elsa, "and because I know her well, I know there is something else is bothering her too."

The other two swam towards her and asked if she liked their plan of starting out now and spending the night at Tihany.

"Yes, that would be great. This place is giving me the shivers. So many old people around, and I hate this smell!"

When they got to Tihany, the sky was clouding over and promising rain. That didn't lift Lili's spirits, but during the walk through the little shops in the old village and up to the top of the hill, she came back to her old self.

"You know, this place is lovely!" she exclaimed. "I love the view from high up here. That old church is like a supreme ruler of the lake, it's so majestic! And the echo was really fun! Look at the lake! I never saw a lake with this green hue. Lakes are usually blue or gray, not light green. Look at the sailboats! Maybe Edith is on one of them and having a great time with her handsome sailor!"

"I hope so!" sighed Margaret. "Let's go and find a place to stay. There was a very fine hotel in the valley. Maybe it's still there. But it is very expensive, I'm afraid!"

"Never mind that," Lili said. "In dollars it's still cheap, and I am the hostess. Just hope they have free rooms!"

"Oh, I am sure they do. Not that many rich people are running around nowadays! My only worry is how to find the way leading to it," said Margaret.

She drove them down the winding road on the side of the mountain, after a few wrong turns they stopped at the front of a grand building.

"This is a hotel?" asked Elsa in wonder.

"Yes, it is now, but it was built as a summer residence for the last Habsburg-Hungarian archduke. After him the Hungarian governor used it, and in the war when the Germans occupied Hungary, it was a retreat for high-ranking officers. Then after the war, it became the property of the working class as did everything else, but it was only used by the leaders of the party. After the political change, it was privatized and now it's a hotel for rich Hungarians and tourists."

"Well, that was an interesting history lesson," said Lili. "Let's see if we can get rooms."

The hotel was open. The entrance hall was three stories high, had a marble floor and beautiful, antique furniture was scattered around. A circular grand stairway between two white columns led up to the rooms. They got lake view rooms, and even Lili was satisfied with them. Flower boxes lined the windows and balconies, full of the early flowering red and white geraniums, which were in great contrast with the light green colour of the lake. The huge park around the building was in perfect order, with century-old trees and a well-cut lawn. All this gave a feeling of well-being and a calming ambiance. They decided to eat in the hotel's dining room instead of driving back to town in the rain to search for Lili's "ethnic diner." The food was excellent, the service was good and elegant white linen and silver cutlery covered the tables. The menu and the wine list were exclusive.

"I am sorry Edith missed all this. I am sure she would have enjoyed it," said Margaret with a sigh, "but her loss!"

"I think she is enjoying sailing and her companion much more than sitting here with three other woman," Lili said, winking to the others. "Do you think she'll tell us about it?"

"I don't think so—she can be very secretive about her affairs. Maybe because I hardly ever agreed with the live-ins she used to keep. We'll see her tomorrow in any case. May I sign the bill?"

"No way!" said Lili and Elsa together.

"Lili will sign it," Elsa continued, "and she and I will do our accounting after this trip. You are our guest, and you have been driving us around, thank you!"

"Let's go to the bar for a nightcap," Lili said, rising from the table. "Who is telling us a bedtime story to night?"

"You promised us the continuation of your life story after your baby was born, right?" asked Margaret.

"I'm not sure you really want to hear it tonight. It is a sad story, gloomy like the weather outside. Why don't we leave it for some other night? Why don't you tell us a story, Margaret? I haven't heard any of yours yet."

"Fair is fair," agreed Elsa, "Let's hear yours tonight!"

They sat deep in the comfortable, velvet armchairs and ordered three cognacs. Once the drinks had been served, Lili and Elsa looked at Margaret with expectation.

"Well, all right. I can't promise it will be interesting or uplifting, but here it goes."

∼

As Elsa already heard, I got married mostly for convenience. I loved Làszlo, but not in a passionate way. I wanted security and a family. My other reason was that I hoped he'd help my parents who had lost their good standing with the government. He was an influential and high-ranking member of the communist party. Boy! I couldn't have been more wrong.

The first year of our marriage was good. We enjoyed each other's company, had good sex, worked at the same place, had lots of friends and went out often. True, I hated all those big party receptions at the university, but I did my best to support his goal of becoming the head of the faculty. After two years I got pregnant, and our first baby, a girl, was born. That was in the early sixties. The terror of the fifties had loosened up a bit, but it was still there.

He was disappointed that I did not deliver him a son, but we were still young and hoped that the second one would be a boy. In the meantime, my father became sick and my mother lost her job. She was falsely accused of giving out secret information to a non-classified government office. It didn't help her case that she was born into a small, noble landowner family, which was not a factor if she did not ask questions and did what she was told. Her knowledge in her field of science was very important to the government. When she later fell out of grace, it was just a matter of time getting her extradition papers. It did not matter that she was an internationally known scientist, her parents were long time dead and their land was converted a long time ago into a communal farm.

My father called me in despair, asking for help, and his influential son-in-law refused him. I begged—I got down on my knees and promised I'd do anything he wanted of me. Then I threatened that I'd disclose his black-market activities and his corruption. He just laughed at me and said I couldn't do that, because then he would take away my baby and accuse me of being an alcoholic and not responsible enough to bring up a child for the better future of a socialist society. I knew he would do it and would get away with it. He wanted to be the head of the university and later the minister of culture. He told me he would not risk his standing in the party and the future of his career by lifting a finger for an old fool and his wife. I knew he would get rid of me and take away my baby if I tried anything.

My mother was deported. My father wanted to go with her but was refused. He died not long after. My mother lived in a small village close to the Russian border in a hut without proper heating or enough food. She died a year after she was taken there. I was not allowed to visit her or look after her funeral. I was devastated—I hated my husband with passion. I refused to sleep in the same room with him, we didn't speak to each other and I lived in constant fear. My life was unbearable. Only my baby kept me from committing suicide or killing my husband. One night he came home drunk and forced himself on me. I could not scream because of the neighbours. He was stronger than me, and also the alcohol gave him extra strength.

The result was a second baby, my son. During the pregnancy, I was terrified that he was conceived when his father was stinking drunk, but he survived and was a healthy baby.

My husband and I continued to live together as strangers, but to the outside world we looked like a well-situated family with a husband and father who was on his way up the official and political ladder. It was hell! I knew that one little mistake on my part and I would loose my job and my children. Of course he enjoyed his power and terrorized me. One day when the children were three and five years old, a friend of mine called my office at the university, saying that the director (my husband) sent a truck to our apartment and was moving furniture out.

The children were in daycare and nobody was home. By the time I got there, everything was gone but the children's beds and the furniture that was built in. To cut this ugly story short, he got a young secretary pregnant who refused to end the pregnancy. She wanted the well-paid director hooked. He was a coward and didn't want to face me. He left the children with me. He got visiting rights, of course, but hardly ever saw them and paid just as much support as the court made him. The judge was a friend of his waiting for favours, so he ordered the minimum payments possible under the law. My husband then transferred himself to another faculty in a different building.

Fortunately, he saw to it that I would keep on working as before, because if he made me lose my job, he would have had to pay more child support. I tried to do my best to bring up and educate my children. It was hard but somehow I managed to do it!"

Margaret took a last sip from her cognac and looked at the other two. They had listened to her without interruption.

"Well, he was a dirty bastard and that's for sure. Couldn't you ruin him some way? What is he doing now?" asked Lili. "I would hire an assassin to shoot him like a dog."

"He and his wife fled during the revolution. There were too many people who wanted revenge for his doings, so he ran. I haven't heard about him since. My kids hardly remember him."

Elsa just sat quietly, and Lili saw there were tears in her eyes.

"You had a very hard life. I don't think I could do what you did."

"Well, I am sure if you had to you could have, but fortunately you didn't. Let's go up to bed and hope it's a nice, sunny day tomorrow. After all, my story didn't lift our spirits up. I am sure Lili's would have been more lightening!"

"Don't put your money on it!" said Lili.

In their room after they said goodnight to Margaret, Lili asked Elsa, "Do you believe that someone could be as cruel as Margaret's husband was? I remember hearing stories about the "terror," the black cars and the people who were taken away during the fifties and sixties, but I always thought those stories were made up just to petrify the people. Remember our classmate's story at the reunion about her and her family's years in a godforsaken village? I see now it must have been true—this was the second time we heard about it. If I think about my father now, I don't know how he continued to exist with all his money in that regime! He must have been very clever. Sometimes I wonder what happened to his fortune after he died. My mother outlived him by a few years, but she never corresponded with me. They disowned me after I left. Too bad I'll never know."

"I can't think of anything more horrible than being forced to live with someone whom I hate, despise and am afraid of," said Elsa.

"Maybe she was not strong enough to stand up for herself. There must have been a way to step over him! Maybe she was just too good, too soft or used the kids as a defence for not doing so!"

"You can only think like that because you didn't have a child to bring up. You have not experienced the feeling of give your whole self for him or her if necessary!"

"Maybe so!"

That night, Lili had a terrible nightmare. She dreamt about her baby. Her baby boy, a memory she had almost successfully forced out of her life.

She dreamt that she held her baby in her arms while a dark figure appeared from nowhere. The figure wanted to take the baby from her, so she fought with all her strength and wanted to scream, but her throat closed up and not a sound came out. She bit the hand of the attacker and could taste blood in her mouth. But the bloody hands took the baby from her arms anyway, and she found herself all alone in the nursery. She ran into the bedroom where her husband slept and shook him, but his body was cold, and as she shook him harder the body started to disintegrate into a pulpy mess.

She woke up drenched in cold sweat. It took a while before she realized where she was. Elsa was sleeping in the other bed and breathing regularly. Lili got up, put her robe on, stepped out onto the balcony and lit a cigarette. Smoking, she looked at the dark, quiet lake. The sky had cleared up and the new moon was high in the sky. She heard tiny waves licking the shore. As she stood there, her eyes suddenly filled with tears, and for the first time in her life she let her emotions take over. She cried silently, deeply from her heart for her baby. In her mind she saw the small grave in the cemetery in Sydney, a white marble stone with golden letters. She saw it now so clearly. She could feel the cool marble under her hands. She never visited the grave after the funeral—she wanted to wipe out Mark and that part of her life forever.

"Mark ... lived two months," she said aloud.

Chapter 15

The flashing lights and blaring siren of the ambulance stopped as it pulled up in front of the small hospital in Balatonföldvàr. The attendants pulled out two stretchers and rushed them to the emergency room. The doctor was already there—he had been called away from his breakfast table. He listened with his stethoscope for any sign of life in both bodies. The man was dead. He removed the oxygen mask from the face. He detected faint heartbeat from the woman, so he started to work on her, signalling the nurse to cover the body of the man.

After the ambulance left, the police searched the boat and found a woman's shoulder bag and in it a British passport. They couldn't find any identification for the man.

"Call the marina in Balatonföldvàr," the sergeant said to his man. "They must know the name of the owner of this boat. Then take this bag to the hospital and give it to the administrator. Try to ask a question or two. I'll hold onto the passport and try to find out some information about this woman. How can people be so careless as to leave a propane heater on with closed windows and go to sleep?" The other officer just shook his head. "Report back to me about these people. I hope they pull through."

"Yes, sergeant," saluted the policeman as he started the patrol car.

After breakfast, Lili paid the hotel bill and the three women got in the car to continue their trip around the north side of Lake Balaton. Just before they turned onto the highway, they saw a police car speed up to the entrance of the hotel. Two policemen got out of the car and rushed inside.

"Maybe we just missed some excitement, like the arrest of a Hungarian drug lord," said Lili. "I remember seeing an elegant, white-haired man eating alone at dinner, but at the next table sat two large men in dark suits."

"You read too many detective stories," laughed Elsa. "There is no such thing in Hungary as drug lord. Or is there, Margaret?"

"Well, Western civilization is getting here very fast. You never know, maybe Lili is right and we'll read about it in the papers tomorrow." She pulled the car into the road and began to accelerate. "Let me know if you want to look around as we are heading towards Balatonfüred. I'm happy to stop anytime. We have plenty of time to meet Edith at the marina by early afternoon. It is not that far."

The road was a single-lane highway, but there was hardly any traffic and Margaret could easily pass the slow trucks. They stopped once at a roadside souvenir stall, where Lili bought a hand-woven table cover that she "could not live without" for the table in the entrance hall of her house.

It was just after noon when they reached Balatonfüred.

"I don't think Edith is here yet," Lili said as they walked out of the parking lot where they left Margaret's car. "Let's have lunch at one of those sausage stalls. I love grilled sausages with horseradish and fresh bread!"

"Yes, and I'm sure you love swallowing Tums tablets by the dozen. Don't say I didn't warn you!" noted Elsa.

"I don't care, I must eat one! Just breathe in that smell! I can't leave it," said Lili on *her way to the stall. "Aren't you two coming? Come on, don't be such picky old ladies!"

After lunch, they walked out to the dock and looked at the sailboats, hoping to find Edith and her sailor. It was already late afternoon, but

Edith was nowhere. Margaret was worried, but Elsa said, "Maybe she's having such a good time that she decided to stay longer."

"No, it's impossible," Margaret said. "She is not very reliable, but she would not do that to me. I'll go back to the car and get out the pullovers. The sun is going down soon and it will be chilly. You two stay here and watch out for her."

When Margaret reached her car, she saw two policemen standing beside it.

"Good afternoon, madam. Is this your car?" the younger one asked politely.

"Yes, it is. Is there any trouble? Did I park illegally?"

"No, not at all. Did you stay at the Lake Shore Hotel in Balatonföldvàr two days ago?"

Margaret's heart sank. "Yes," she answered, "why?"

"We traced your license plate number from the hotel registration. And we just missed you at Tihany. I am sorry, but we have rather bad news for you." He showed her Edith's passport and said, "Was this woman in your company with two others?"

Margaret could not say a word. She just nodded.

"She is in serious condition at the hospital in Balatonföldvàr. She has carbon monoxide poisoning, and the man who was with her died of the same."

Margaret grabbed hold of the officer's arm, feeling as if she was going to faint. The officer led her to a nearby bench, and the other one ran to one of the stalls and brought her back a glass of water.

"Are you all right?"

Margaret swallowed some water and pulled herself together. "Thank you, yes," she said, shaking her head. She stood up, fighting the dizziness she felt. "I just have to let my other friends know, and then I am going to the hospital."

"We'll drive you there if you wish."

"No, thank you, but I would like to follow you. Let me go call to my friends."

Elsa and Lili were sitting on the railing of the dock when they saw Margaret hurrying towards them, her face ashen.

"Margaret! What's the matter? What happened?"

"Edith is in the hospital at Balatonföldvàr in serious condition. I have to go to her right away. I'll explain everything later. I have to hurry—do you want to stay here?"

"No, we are going with you!" they said in union. Without asking any questions, they followed Margaret to the car.

It was after ten when they got to the hospital. Margaret was led away to see Edith, and the other two sat down to wait. Far too dumbfounded to talk, they just sat motionless.

Margaret showed up an hour later. They looked at her and didn't like what they saw. Her eyes were red, her mouth was trembling and her face was as white as a sheet.

"She'll live, but they don't yet know the extent of the damage or how her brain survived the lack of oxygen for such a long time. She is not conscious. I am going to stay, but please go to the hotel. It is late. I'll talk to you in the morning. By then I hope I'll know more."

"Don't you want us to stay here with you? We hate to leave you here alone."

"No, believe me—it's better if you leave. I'll come as soon as I can tomorrow."

Margaret kissed both of them on their cheeks and disappeared down a corridor.

Lili and Elsa looked at each other and found their voice for the first time since they arrived.

"I can't imagine what happened! Where is the sailor? Did the boat burn down or what? What a tragedy! I am astonished! I can't believe it! It is like a bad B movie! What shall we do?"

"Right now we can't do anything. Let's go get a taxi, find the hotel and wait for Margaret tomorrow morning," said Elsa in a firm voice.

After an unsettled night, Elsa and Lili went to the reception hall of the hotel. Neither of them had any appetite for breakfast, so they just ordered some coffee and sat facing the entrance door. It was after ten o'clock when they saw Margaret driving up. Both rushed to her wordless but with thousands of questions in their minds. Margaret's face was ashen with dark circles under her eyes.

"Maybe it will be best if you go up and have a rest before we talk," Elsa said, embracing her. "You look like you didn't sleep at all last night. Would you like to eat something? You must be starving!"

"No, we have to talk now. I have to get back to the hospital soon. I just want a strong coffee."

"How is Edith?"

"She regained consciousness for a few minutes early this morning. I think she knew who I was because she wanted to talk. I saw it in her eyes. But we don't know the damage to her head yet."

"Margaret, what happened? How much do you know?"

"The police gave me the report. The portable propane heater in the cabin of the sailboat was left on overnight, as were some candles on the table. The blood work showed that both of them were drunk when they fell asleep. The portholes were closed and the exhaust duct was not cleaned after winter storage—there were some traces of a bird's nest blocking it. Also, the candle's wax warmed up the plastic tabletop and when one of the candles burned down, it started to melt the plastic. Fortunately there was not enough oxygen for the flames and it just smoked. Otherwise the boat would have blown up. A man who was going fishing in the early hours saw the smoke coming out from the cabin, pulled the bodies out to the deck and called the police. It was not soon enough for Edith's partner. He died of carbon monoxide poisoning. The police didn't know his name yet when I left the hospital."

Lili and Elsa sat there frozen for a long time. Then Elsa asked, "What's going to happen to Edith? What did the doctors say?"

"This is a small hospital, so they are going to take her to Budapest as soon as possible. The only thing they can do here is administer hyperbolic oxygen, which means that she gets pure, 100 per cent oxygen with controlled pressure for sixty or ninety minutes. The increased oxygen can reach bone and tissue that is not normally accessible to red blood cells, and this way the red blood cells carry more oxygen through the whole body. After the treatment they will know more. They don't know how long Edith and the man were breathing the carbon monoxide, but it was long enough for the man to die from it."

"What are you going to do? Does Edith have someone in London who has to be notified? Any relatives? If she has to stay in the hospital, does she have insurance coverage for it?" asked Lili.

"She has some kind of insurance because I told her to get some before she came here, but I don't know what it will cover. She has a few friends in London, but I just can't think about that yet. I am going with her in the ambulance—I have to ask you to drive my car back to Budapest. How long are you two going to stay there?"

"I have to go back in two days. I can't stay any longer," said Lili.

"I'll stay until you know what's going to happen with Edith. I'll call my son and let him know that I am fine but delayed in my return. I don't have anything important to take care of back home," said Elsa.

"That will be great. Thank you both for your support. We can meet later tonight or tomorrow morning at your hotel in Budapest. Elsa, I'm sorry we could not visit your childhood summer place! I have to go back to the hospital now. She might have recovered full consciousness, and I have to be there. I hope you can drive manual!"

"Don't worry, I learned to drive on one. We'll wait for you at the hotel."

Margaret handed the car keys to Elsa and left.

Elsa looked at Lili and said, "I think we'd better get going. Let's pay the bill and get our things into the car."

They drove back to Budapest without incident. The roads were as clearly marked as on any other European highway. Elsa gave the car key to the porter so he could park the car and then the two women went up to their room.

They hadn't talked too much during the trip, as Lili was busy looking at the map and supervising Elsa's driving. They also just hadn't felt like chatting.

Once in their room, they were able to unwind, start a conversation and talk about their thoughts during the drive.

"What did you mean that you have to leave in two days? I thought the plan was that you were going to stay until the 26th and we would fly out together. Today is only the 20th."

"Look, Elsa, I'll be honest with you as always. I don't feel comfortable here. I have a feeling that I am closed in and can't move freely. No, no, let me finish," Lili said, raising hand as Elsa opened her mouth. "I know that those times of people following you or watching your every step are over. But I just can't be myself here. I do like Margaret. It's not her or Edith. This trip could have been fun, but I am a stranger here without any links. The reunion was fun but it upset me too much. I shouldn't have come! Yes, the hills over there are very nice, as is the Castle, the Danube and so on. I admire the scenery just like at any other place, but it doesn't stir any emotion in my soul.

"I don't know how you can be so attached to this world of our past! It was so long ago! It was okay, but that's all. We made our lives elsewhere, and it was and is a very good life. We couldn't have that here. I thought your roots here dried up long ago just as mine did, but watching you, I see you more relaxed and happier than during any of our other trips together.

"Well, you were usually relaxed and happy, but somehow your present mood is different than it was elsewhere. After a few weeks you would be missing your son and later your grandson and were more than happy to return to your old habitat. That's what I cannot sense now. What happened? Finally overcame that overbearing culpability feeling of yours? I'm sure it won't last. After a while you'll be itching to go home to your apartment and your life, just as I am now."

Elsa was silent for a long time.

"Well, maybe you are right," she said finally. "I don't know why, but I feel at home here. I know I am sentimental and nostalgic, but being here brings back all my happy memories of my family and my childhood. Up till my horrible university accident, I was content with my life here. I had my dreams, and I was on my way to fulfilling them. When it was so ruthlessly destructed, I didn't see any other way out than to leave with you."

"I know all this, but you were happy in Canada. You didn't suffer much from homesickness and visited your parents often, but not once did you stay longer than was necessary. So why now?"

"Honestly, I don't know! You could be right that after a while I will run back to my other life, but not yet."

"I hope you are not even thinking about moving back here!"

"No! I could never live that far from David and Andrew!"

"Okay," Lili said, and some tension seemed to leave her shoulders. "Let's talk about Edith. I hope she'll recover. If not, I don't know what Margaret will do with her! As I see it, Edith leans on her heavily!"

"I am afraid of that too. Knowing Margaret, I don't think she'll be able to send Edith back to London before she reasonably recovers."

"I hope you are not planning to stay until then. It's not your problem after all."

"I'll stay for a while until things straighten out. I have to give some support to Margaret—she is such a good person. And after all, I don't have any urgent business to take care of at home. David can look after my bills, and I am sure he wouldn't mind looking around in my apartment occasionally."

"Well, my dear, it's your life. I wish you would come with me. We could stop over in Paris, walk around Montmartre and sit in those lovely bistros. Just think about it!"

"I thought you had to hurry home!"

"I do, but a few days in Paris wouldn't do any harm. Michael will be fine to wait for me a bit longer."

"No, Lili, you should go home. I know you worry about Michael. You cannot hide it from me, I know you much better that that! I noticed your mood shifted, but I didn't want to bring it up."

"Okay, mate, I'm going the day after tomorrow. I'll call the airlines to change my dates. I hope it can be done on such short notice!"

That night Margaret called to say they were in the hospital in Budapest. Edith woke up from her coma, recognised Margaret, also asked about her partner whom she called Antal. But they could not tell her the truth. When she left Edith was sleeping. The next day she had to go through lots of tests.

"I am going home," Margaret said, her voice sounding exhausted. "I am dead tired and I have to get some sleep. I'll call tomorrow morning."

Chapter 16

The British Airways VIP lounge at London Heathrow was like a quiet island in the middle of a stormy sea. Lili sank gratefully into one of the comfortable couches, gripping a cup of coffee. It had taken her more than an hour to get to this terminal from the one where the Malev from Budapest landed. She hated this airport, and she always tried to avoid it by choosing a different route if she could, but when she changed her ticket to an earlier date, Heathrow was the only option. So she took it.

Budapest-London-Los Angeles-Sydney. She ran the cities over in her head, wondering offhand how many times she had been to each. The Malev plane had parked in a far corner of the airfield, and the bus took more than twenty minutes to reach the terminal building. She was astounded to see the countless giant jets parking at the gates and lining up on the runways. Hundreds of cargo carts full of suitcases were scattered around the planes and looked abandoned, as if they had been left there forever. She had wondered how it was possible to sort them out and put them where they belonged.

Construction was going on as well, and detours through mile-long corridors took Lili from one airline to the other. The loudspeakers blasted gate numbers, and people from every race she could imagine were running towards their destinations. The waiting rooms were crowded, people slept on the floor and on chairs, babies were crying, toddlers were running around and mothers were screaming in many languages. It was a real madhouse.

"I am a lucky woman to be able to afford the business class, but hey, I deserve it!" Lili told herself. She called Michael after checking the time in Sydney on the international clocks and told him she was on her way. Michael did not sound too well, but he said he was just tired after an exhausting therapy session.

She had two hours to wait for her connection. She looked around for someone interesting enough to start up a conversation with. The lounge was half full. She saw a few middle-aged businessmen busy with their laptops and one or two women reading, but nobody seemed interesting enough to make an effort at being friendly. Lili finished her coffee and started to read the Hungarian version of *Elle*, which she picked up at the airport before boarding. As she leafed through the pages without too much interest, she felt someone watching her. She looked up and met the eyes of a man who sat opposite her, drinking what seemed like a whisky (that early!). He smiled and asked her in Hungarian, "Did you enjoy your visit to Budapest?"

Lili was taken aback. She usually assumed that by her appearance no one could guess that she was Hungarian. With the magazine in her hand, she supposed it would be easy to guess.

"Yes, I did."

"I hope I didn't offend you by accosting you. I saw you on the flight from Budapest and heard you talk to the stewardess in Hungarian. I sat in the row behind you. I was thinking that this exclusively dressed lady with those fabulous diamonds must be one of our long-lost compatriots. Am I right?"

"Yes, you are. I was back visiting after many years living in Australia—for my forty-year high school reunion."

"Then you must have been very young when you finished high school," said the man, smiling at her.

"That was a flattering remark, thank you."

Lili's spirits picked up as usual when someone, especially a man, paid her compliments. They started to chatter. She interviewed him thoroughly about his life, as was her custom. How old was he, was he married, did he have any children, what was he doing, where was he going and so on.

He was a businessman from the new breed of smart, adventurous Hungarians who realized the opportunities available shortly after the political change well before most others did. He made a lot of money when the rules and the laws were still loose and murky for private enterprises. He presently owned a large, export-import firm and was going to Los Angeles for business meetings. He spoke perfect English and German. His name was Tivadar Botas, he was married and had two children—fourteen and sixteen years old. He was well dressed with casual elegance in gray pants, a blue, open-necked shirt and a brown, small-checkered blazer. They talked away the time until their flight was called.

The business class was not full, and the aisle seat beside Lili in first row remained unoccupied. Tivadar sat in the aisle seat in third row, and before the stewards started to serve snacks, Tivadar asked Lili if he could join her. She agreed, and they sipped champagne and talked. Lili told him that she had been the owner of a few health clubs in Sydney but she sold them years ago. She was looking after her husband, who was not invalid but limited in his activities.

Tivadar seemed to listen with great interest, asked polite questions and looked very impressed when she talked about her business past.

Lili liked him. He was good conversationalist, had intelligent opinions about everything, and looked directly into her eyes when talking. His dark eyes didn't wonder all over the place. Mainly, she liked how he looked at her with openly sincere respect. When the stewardess had cleared away the trays from their snacks, Lili said, "Now I will take a nap. I had to get up at dawn to be at the airport on time. I will never understand why one has to be there three hours before departure when one has a ticket and a seat number already. Maybe we could talk again at dinner time."

"I would like it very much. Enjoy your nap," said Tivadar and went back to his seat.

Lili eased her chair to the most comfortable position possible, pulled down the window shade, put on her eyeshade and tried to sleep.

"How nice to be appreciated," she told herself. "I've missed this more than I thought. He is an intelligent, nice-looking guy. He must be in his late fifties. I can see I impressed him. Well, yes, before I was simply looking for sex, but now that's past and I am pleased just with admiration."

She was smiling as she remembered Brat, the young lover with whom she fled to the California deserts after picking him up on the plane between Sydney and Los Angeles. Those were the days—it was so nice while it lasted! With a smile on her lips, she drifted off to sleep.

Waking slowly to the low, constant drone of the plane's engines, Lili realized she was thirsty. She waved to the stewardess and asked for a glass of water. Before she could take a sip, Tivadar appeared in the aisle.

"Did you have a nice nap?" he asked. "Good dreams I hope?" Lili signalled him to sit down.

"Yes, it was refreshing. What did you do?"

"I went over my papers, preparing for my meetings in LA. I am nervous because I am hoping to find investors to buy shares in my company when I go public on the Hungarian stock exchange. I don't want to sell more than 40 per cent of the shares, but I am not sure I can afford to stay in control. I have plans which unfortunately extend beyond my financial capability. I did manage to get a few people interested in Los Angeles the last time I was there, but not enough to reach my goal. So I have a few difficult days ahead of me. But I don't want to bore you with business problems. I am sorry I mentioned it!"

"Just tell me, I am interested. How big is your firm? What are you importing and exporting?"

"I started out with a small vinery and then expanded it to all kinds of alcohol, like the Hungarian pàlinka and special wines. Later, I ventured into other kinds of food products—goose liver, red paprika and so on. Now I have large vineries and packing plants all over Hungary. I have a permanent workforce of about sixty people, and my head office is in Budapest. We do everything from processing to exporting, and we export to many countries. We import a few products like sardines and frozen seafood. The operations are getting too complex for a private company and for me to run it alone. So, I am planning to go public on the Hungarian stock exchange. If I can persuade people in LA to buy in, I'll have the backing I need to be trustworthy enough to get some more shareholders."

"Goose liver? I love it! I ate myself silly during my stay. And also all the other food we can't get in Australia! Why don't you export there too?"

"I tried, but the rules are far too stringent for food products, and I don't have any connections. Maybe you could give me hints or … do you know someone approachable?" "I know a few business men. My first husband had a leather factory in Sydney, and I worked with him looking after customer relations and the accounting department. I really would like to help you, but Australians are very tight-fisted and are usually skeptical about new, European businessmen if they do not have sufficient capital."

"I don't want to overwhelm you," Tivadar said, leaning closer, "but I just had an idea. You are a smart businesswoman with years of experience in Sydney. What would you say if I offered you a partnership? How would 15 per cent of the shares and a director's chair on the board sound? You would be a representative of the company and an organizer for an Australian outlet."

Lili didn't let her face show any surprise or shock. She had sat in on far too many meetings and bargaining sessions in the past. She knew that most of the deals didn't happen in the boardrooms but in restaurants, at parties or by casual, private conversations.

"And what would be the price? How much do I have to invest?"

Calmly, Tivadar replied, "Not more than fifty thousand U.S. dollars. And I guarantee that your return would double in a few years."

Lili was expecting a much bigger amount. Fifty thousand was an easily affordable risk for a change in her life, well worth it to be important and busy again, rule over people, meet new faces and be challenged.

"That is certainly a very fast twist in our conversation," Lili noted, smiling. "Look, they are just starting to serve dinner. Let's enjoy it and talk about this later."

"Of course. I am sorry to be so abrupt with this, but somehow I had a feeling that I was doing the right thing, and I always follow my instincts."

"So do I," Lili said, lifting her champagne glass. "Cheers!"

During the five-course dinner, they chatted about everything but business.

When their after-dinner brandy arrived, Lili turned to Tivadar and said, "Go back to your seat. We have two more hours to LA, and I am going to think about your offer. I promise I'll give you an answer before we land. We can carry on from there."

Tivadar stood up, and in gallant European fashion kissed Lili's hand.

"Thank you. I hope you know that no matter what your answer will be I still admire you and look up to you."

Lili leaned back in her seat and looked out the window. She watched the endless blue of the horizon. There were no clouds above, hazy nothingness below. It seemed the plane. to just hang in the air, going nowhere, but Lili's mind was busy.

She tried to analyze what happened. She got an offer from a stranger, a Hungarian, to invest in a business she didn't know anything about at all. He seemed honest enough and full of energy, but she knew she couldn't form a judgment after a few hours of conversation. She also knew that she liked him mainly because he admired her and looked at her with respect. It was true that she was bored with her life, with the endless comfort, laziness, watching the news on TV and sending and getting stupid, little e-mail jokes. The landmark of sixty years was hovering above her, and she was terrified of the future ahead. Michael was getting very old, and he was not active any more in mind or body. She loved him but had to admit that his slow immobility made her uptight and bitter. Maybe this business would be an opportunity to shake herself up. Didn't she consider herself much younger than her years? She had so much energy left! She shouldn't just lay back and watch her life as it slowly passed. Michael would understand that she needed a change in her life. She could look after him just the same as before, and if his condition got worse they could always hire a nurse or someone to help out.

The more she thought about it, the more excited she got. The money was not an object, she had more than enough. She had invested her capital very well, and one of the buildings where her club had been was still hers. She now rented it out to a new business, and that annually brought in as much as she was asked to invest. She usually reinvested this income anyway so she wouldn't miss it. She has other sources of income as well, but she couldn't let herself be taken as an old, foolish, rich woman who fell for warm smiles and compliments. She had to play hard to get.

When the captain announced that he was starting the descent and estimated their arrival at about forty minutes, Lili called Tivadar over.

"Look, this all came far too fast," she said sternly. "I have to think about it more. All I can tell you is that I am interested. You have to send me the documents of your finances, your company's history and its official worth. Let me know how the meetings go in LA. My husband was a corporate lawyer, so we'll look over the papers. In the meantime, I will look around Sydney for possibilities for the business, talk to people and see if it's feasible. Here is my card. Keep in touch with e-mail."

The seat belt sign came on. Tivadar did not show his disappointment. Lili wondered if he thought the deal was in the bag. He smiled at Lili and said, "Well, of course you are right. I didn't except a final answer without proving that I am not a charlatan but an honest businessman with dependable resources behind me. I'll collect all the documents and mail them to you, and if I may, I'll call you from LA after my meeting. My best regards to your husband, and have a good flight to Sydney." He kissed her hand once more and went back to his seat.

Lili felt washed out. The early morning wake up call, the waiting and the long flights took their toll. She did not even bother taking her mirror out to fix her face before landing in Sydney.

She called Michael when she landed and took a taxi home. As always, Michael was waiting for her at the open door with the dog at his feet. The dog jumped and yelped as he should and Michael was smiling, but Lili was shocked by his appearance. He had lost weight, he was pale and he leaned heavily on his cane.

Lili would not sit down for home coming sweets and drink Michael had ordered for them. She said, "Michael, I am dead tired. I can't even talk. I just have to go to bed. Can we talk tomorrow, please?"

Still smiling, Michael kissed her forehead.

"Of course, my dear. I understand. I am home all day tomorrow, so we'll have plenty of time to talk. I don't have any therapy scheduled for three days."

Lili was far too tired to ask why he did not have therapy. She took a shower and fell into bed.

The next day, Lili got up well after 11 AM. Michael was sitting in front of his computer and checking his papers on the stock market. Lili went to him and kissed the top of his head.

"So how were you, my darling, during my absence? You didn't cheat on me I hope, you handsome devil?"

Michael's face lit up. He liked Lili teasing him and looked up to his wife with adoration.

"My dear, you know how devoted I am to you. I always let the opportunities pass, no matter how tempting they are. I hope you did the same?"

Lili sat down on the sofa and patted the seat beside her. Michael rose from his computer chair and sat down on the sofa.

"Well, I had a tempting offer from a handsome Hungarian on the plane between London and LA."

"You did? I have always known that your charms were irresistible! Are you going to tell me about it?" smiled Michael.

"He was a Hungarian businessman. We started to talk, and he told me about his business …"

She told Michael about Tivadar's offer to be the representative of his products in Sydney and to buy into his business.

Michael listened to Lili attentively, but she saw a flicker in his eye when she mentioned how much money was to be invested.

"The whole thing sounds like a sham to me," Michael said when she had finished. "You don't know anything about him, and he doesn't know anything about you! How could he approach you with such a serious offer? I think he took you for a rich woman and tried to get your interest with well-thought-out phrases and sweet compliments about your looks!"

Lily looked at him, annoyed and angry. "Michael, don't take me as a fool!" she exclaimed. "I am not a woman who gets smitten by compliments! I am a businesswoman, and I might add a good one. I think it could be an opportunity for me to get involved in business again. He'll send me the results of his meetings from LA and also his company's official history. You and I could look it over, research it and then decide if it is an honest offer or a sham. I would like to get into some action. I am bored with doing nothing!"

∼

Michael didn't say anything for a while. He knew his wife well enough to know that right then it was better to remain silent. He did sense that Lili was bored with her life beside a disabled husband, missing being with people and missing the feeling of command. She didn't like to be tied down, not even by her husband. He knew she needed the freedom to be responsible for no one but herself. Deep down in his guts, he was afraid that one day Lili would leave him.

Not long before, he had read a book and could not forget the few lines that caught his eyes:

> With a woman there is always the sense that they are loaning themselves to you. You have to remember that they could go anytime and if a man is smart, he never forgets that.

Remembering those lines, he said simply, "Of course, you are right. Sorry, dear. When do you think you'll get the papers? Do you want me to look through them?"

"Yes, and I'll consider your opinion before I decide," Lili said kindly. "I am going to make some coffee," she continued, standing up. "Would you like some?"

"Yes, thank you. I'll come to the patio and you can tell me all about your trip and the reunion. I can hardly wait to hear everything that happened."

Chapter 17

After Lili left for the airport, Elsa went back to sleep. She was very tired, as the last couple of days had drained away all of her energy. The loud ringing of the phone jolted her from a deep sleep, and it took a few seconds to find the phone beside her bed.

"Hello," she said in sleepy voice.

"Oh, Elsa, I am sorry to wake you up!" she heard Margaret apologizing.

"What time is it?"

"It's after eleven."

"Oh my god! It's that late?" The shock woke her. "I went back to bed after Lili left with the intention of getting up at nine and taking a shower! It is high time to get up! How are you? How is Edith?"

"I am fine—a bit tired. Edith pulled through and there is no excessive damage to her brain, but it will take awhile for her to get back to normal and remember everything. She needs a lot of undisturbed rest. The doctor sent me home, and there's really nothing more I can do for her right now. I am going to take a hot bath and go to bed for a few hours. I've hardly slept for two days. How are you doing?"

"I am okay. I'll pull myself together and take a long walk to get my head straightened out."

"Look, Elsa, why don't you move back to my place? It is a waste of money to stay alone in that expensive hotel, even if it's much more comfortable than here. And to be honest, I could use a friend around. Edith will not be released from the hospital for at least a week. When her time gets closer, we can think about what to do."

"Are you sure? I'll be glad to stay with you and have long talks in the evenings! What about if I get your car from the garage here after four this afternoon and drive it to your place with my bags? You'll be up by then?"

"Definitely. All I need is a long, hot shower and a bit of shut-eye to be normal again, at least as normal as I can be. I hope you find a parking place close enough. See you after four."

"Great, I'll be there. And I want to take you out to dinner at a nice place, so don't even think about cooking!"

Elsa ordered some coffee and toast from room service and then called the desk to prepare her bill.

The receptionist told her that it had been already taken care of up to today and the only extras would be the room service. Elsa let the receptionist know that she was checking out and asked her to arrange for her luggage to be picked up in an hour and kept in storage until the afternoon, when she would come back to collect it.

After drinking her coffee, she started to pack. By one o'clock, she was ready to go for her walk. She thought about calling David, but it was still too early in Toronto. He'd be up, but she didn't want to call him at his home. The last thing she felt like doing was chatting with her daughter-in-law, no matter how nice it would be to hear Andrew's voice too. She decided to call his office later. When the porter arrived, she went downstairs with him and her luggage and then left the hotel. It was a cool, cloudy afternoon, and she was glad she wore her jacket over her turtleneck. Without any plan, she started to walk toward Erzsèbet Bridge on the promenade. She didn't go all the way to the bridge, however, crossing instead the small park at the end of it and going into the church at the foot of the bridge. It was old and neglected, and the inside was dark, cold and depressing. A few old women were scattered around the wooden pews, fingering their rosaries as they knelt in the worn, shiny rows.

She didn't stay, but she put a few forints into the collection box and walked back out into the fresh spring air. Taking a deep breath, she turned towards Ferenciek Square. She didn't visit the old church there but kept walking on Kossuth Lajos Street towards the national museum on Museum Avenue.

She planned to spend some time at the museum, but somehow when she got to the corner where she should have turned right, her feet made her walk straight ahead on Ràkoczi Avenue. In five minutes she was standing in front of the Academy of Performing Arts. The memories flooded her brain.

How happy she was here! A young, enthusiastic and pretty actress to be filled with hopes, dreams and deeply in love. And how all ended so cruelly in a few short minutes. How many times had she wondered what would have become of her if that car hadn't hit her? Most likely, she would have recovered from her first great disappointment in love and continued her studies. Maybe she could have become a great, famous actress with fans cheering at her feet. She would have found her real love of life again and lived happily ever after. And when her acting years were over, she could have become a drama teacher like her father and help young, aspiring actors fulfill their dreams.

"You are a hopeless, sentimental old fool! What happened happened, and you can't change any of that!" she scolded herself.

Crossing the street carefully at the traffic light, she went into the big bookstore on the other side of the street to browse around. She wanted to find some Hungarian children's books in English with lots of coloured pictures to take home to Andrew and get him interested in the old stories. She found two really nice ones, and she could not let pass an English version of her favourite novel by Màrai Sàndor, *Embers*. Tucking away her purchases, she started back to the hotel to make her call to David.

On the way, she kept a look out for a nice restaurant where she could take Margaret for dinner. She didn't like anything she saw and decided she'd leave it up to Margaret. She knew the restaurants much better anyway.

From the hotel, she made her call to Toronto. Luckily, she caught David as he just stepped into his office.

"Mother, is there a problem? Are you all right?" he asked worriedly.

"Of course I'm okay. Why are you so worried?"

"You never call me at the office!"

"Nothing is wrong, but because of the time difference I could not make the call any other time. Look, David, I am going to move out of the hotel today and into my friend Margaret's place. And I'm going to stay a week or two longer here. I didn't see everything I wanted since Lili was not in the mood for outings. She went back today because she was worried about Michael. Would you please look into my place a few times to check my mail and pay my urgent bills?"

"Gladly, mother. I'm happy you're having a good time."

"How are Andrew and Paula?"

"They are well. Andrew started going to a nursery for half the day and seems to enjoy being with children his own age. You'll see how grown up he is already. He knows lots of rhymes and songs and is very proud of himself."

"I miss him and all of you a lot. I already mailed some marzipan for you two! Thanks, David. I'll see you in two weeks. Kiss the family for me."

"I will, Mother. Have a good time and take care of yourself!"

Elsa felt a bit guilty for not telling David the real reason of her extended stay and for the extra two weeks she'd not see Andrew, but she shook it off, collected the car and her luggage and drove to Margaret's apartment.

Margaret looked better, but she still had dark circles under her eyes.

"Did you have a good rest?" asked Elsa after they greeted each other affectionately.

"Yes, but I couldn't sleep. I was worrying about far too many things. I just rested on the bed for a few hours."

"What you need is a good dinner in a nice restaurant and a couple of glasses of wine. Let me put my things away and let's go out. Do you have a favourite place?"

"Well, if you don't mind eating Greek instead of Hungarian, there is a nice place not far from here and they have a terrace too. The street is noisy and it's not as nice as the promenade, but it is next to the Danube."

"Greek it is. Let's go."

It was too cold to sit outside, so they choose an inside table by one of the windows. The place was nicely decorated like a Greek village inn—walls painted blue and white, large, plastic evergreens in the corners, wooden steps leading to the upstairs rooms and false beams. It was a bit tacky but very friendly.

Elsa didn't want to pressure Margaret with questions and decided to wait until Margaret was ready to talk. After the waiter cleared away their dinner plates and they were waiting for coffee, Margaret opened up.

"I honestly don't know what to do! Edith will pull through—that is for sure now. She is still a bit dazed, but she'll recover fully. It will be a slow process, and I will have to keep her with me until she is ready to go back to London. She has nobody else to look after her."

"But, Margaret, you have your job, your life. She just can't expect you turn all of it upside down because of her! She must have friends in London who can help her out!"

"She has a few, but she is not well enough to think about it. She is very distressed by the death of her sailor."

"Did you find out anything about him?"

"Oh, yes," Margaret said, and the way she said it made Elsa think she was in for a good one. "The police found his file. He owned the boat but nothing else. He was an aged drifter, living off everyone he could catch. His name was Antal Takàcs—no fixed address or profession. He was married before, and his ex-wife lives in Germany and paid him an allowance every month. Lots of people around Lake Balaton knew him, and he was well liked. He was charming and good looking. He had a talent for convincing people that he was well off, had no worries on this earth and was free to sail as long as he liked. During the winters, he shacked up in a friend's old wine cellar somewhere on the north side of the lake. He got his room and board free in exchange for guarding his friend's winery equipment. I think he was intending to go to London and live off Edith for a while. We'll never know what kind of stories Edith told him about her life in London. She always exaggerated her situation to everyone but me. I know her far too well for that. She was darn lucky this time to not pay for it. She must have fallen for him hard, because the first question she asked when she came to was, "Where is Antal?" She kept asking for him too."

"How much does she know now?"

"The doctor said we should tell her a part of the truth, so today I told her he died of the poisoning. But I will let her find out by herself who he really was. Once she heard he was dead, she became hysterical, saying that she killed Antal, she was the one to blame and she wanted to die too. They sedated her again. She'll sleep deeply and without any dreams tonight. How she'll cope with it later has to be seen. That's why I have to keep her with me until she is emotionally strong enough to go home. She did try to commit suicide once some time ago. She is not a stable person."

"How long will they keep her in the hospital?"

"Maybe a week for neurological observation. She'll also get a few more treatments to boost her red blood cell count. After that, she'll have to stay with me. I can get a week off from work—my colleague is back from sabbatical and will take over my classes. After that we'll see."

"Margaret, I am ready to stay for longer, and I would like help in any way I can. I don't want to offend you, but I can help financially as well."

"Thank you, Elsa. I need your support. I let you know if I need money too."

"Can I come to the hospital with you tomorrow?"

"I would wait for a few more days until we see how she'll settle down."

After Elsa and Margaret had breakfast together, Margaret left to do her chores at the school and then go to Edith in the hospital. Elsa didn't feel like wandering around alone, so she signed up for a sightseeing tour. It was very disappointing. The two-decked bus first took them to the old city. The guide, a young, pretty but finicky woman, walked the group around the castle district, explaining the history of the old buildings and churches in a kind of dreary tone. After that she ushered everyone into the numerous souvenir shops. She looked at Elsa disapprovingly because she stayed outside to study the statue in the middle of Trinity Square. Later, they went to see the big, new, Western-style shopping centers growing up in and around the city like mushrooms after rain. They could have been anywhere in the world.

They next got a mediocre, hurried lunch in a third-class restaurant near the city park. After a fast walk around Hero's Square, where the guide didn't give them enough time to admire the magnificent statues, the bus drove through the park, past the zoo and the circus and at three they were deposited in front of the travel bureau.

Elsa was irritated and walked off without tipping the guide. "Well, that was a waste of time and money," Elsa said to herself. "Why did I do it? I can walk leisurely around many of the places I really want to see. What gave me this stupid idea?"

She crossed the square near the travel bureau and walked to Vörösmarthy Square. The outdoor cafés were crowded with people having their afternoon espressos and enjoying the warm, spring rays of sun. It seemed nobody worked in the afternoon. On her way through the square, Elsa passed an open bookstall. She stopped and browsed through the table until she found a book about Lake Balaton. As she leafed through the pages, she got an idea.

After dinner, she told Margaret that if she was going to be busy all the next day, then she would take the morning train to visit her childhood summer place by Lake Balaton and be back in the afternoon. Elsa had checked the train schedules, and there was an outgoing train at 8 AM. An afternoon train could get her back in town by 6 PM.

Margaret nodded and said, "I am very sorry we can't do this together. I hope you find everything there as you remember. I'll pick you up at the station at six."

Elsa sat in the train compartment looking out the window as the city passed by. She was amazed at how big it had become. The suburbs were endless—it took more than half an hour to reach the open fields. The stations followed each other rapidly, and the distances between them were short. As the train passed the station which she remembered Lake Balaton could be seen just after, her heartbeat sped up. At the first glimpse of the lake, she felt the same excitement she did as a child. She remembered how she and her sister would glue themselves to the window and fight for the best position for seeing the lake. They wouldn't move until they reached their destination.

Another half an hour and she was there. Elsa stood on the platform for a long time. The station hadn't changed at all. The station house was still painted white, and green vines covered its walls. The benches beside the single-rail track were painted red and were peeling just as they had in the past. After the train left, she could see the lake and the stationmaster's little, white house with red shutters and flowers on the windowsills. Further down the road on the other side of the tracks was the gate to the beach, thought it was half hidden by the dense reeds covering the shoreline. She decided to first go up the hill to find her aunt's old house. After that she'd go to the beach.

A steep, dirt road led up to the highway, and after crossing it she found the old, stone steps leading up the hill. The wobbly, crumbled stones were familiar to her, but the surroundings were not.

In her youth there were hardly any buildings beside the stairs except for a small hotel and one house further up in the forest of giant pines. The hotel was still there, but it had been rebuilt. It was now a somewhat uncongenial-looking grey building with small windows. Before, it was white stucco, the windows were covered by wooden shutters with green trim and the small balconies overlooking the lake were full of flowers. She spotted the other old building also, and it was just as it had been. The plaster was peeling and the roof was in bad need of repair. Elsa remembered the old lady who owned it and her white poodle. The dog was always yelping when somebody passed the house, and the lady seemed to be endlessly working in her flower garden, never giving up hope that one day her garden would bloom in the red, dry soil. She always wore a big, straw hat, a green cloak and rubber booths no matter how hot the day was.

Buildings now lined both sides of the steps. Some small, some large, and all fenced in with closed gates. A few of them were tastefully built and others were cheap patchwork. The further she climbed, the more disappointed she became. The forest had been thinned out, and at the end of the steps the road was now paved and the buildings were denser. She arrived at the spot where the road turned and ended in a small square. She recalled that there used to be only a manual well for drinking water. The well was still there, but it was fenced in as a memorial. Behind it, a new, big hotel took away the view of her aunt's house, which was further up the hill. Elsa stopped and sat down beside the well. She was afraid to go any further. She was afraid of seeing some tasteless thing where once had been her aunt's small, wooden cottage in the middle of a large garden and surrounded by a beautiful wrought-iron fence.

"How could I hope that nothing had changed during so many years? Time did not stop here when I left!" She took a deep breath, stood up and walked around the well towards the steep street that led to the top of the hill where the cottage was. She closed her eyes before turning onto the street, and she kept her eyes on the pavement as she went up the hill.

When the street levelled out, she forced herself to look up. She couldn't believe her eyes. The cottage still stood in the middle of the garden, with the same silly-looking, pointed rooftop and painted the same ugly dark yellow colour with green trim. The veranda was glassed in with small glass patterns, and a few of the glass plates were still missing. The fence was rusted, but it was the same fence. The gate was shut, and the old-fashioned latch was broken, just as many years before.

The garden looked the same too—dried-out, red dirt. Her aunt had never had a green thumb and didn't like gardening. A few sad-looking vines covered an iron-frame arbour in the corner of the garden.

As if in a movie, she felt she was stepping back into the past. She saw her aunt, wearing the dark loose shift she always wore (because she believed it made her look thinner and smaller), coming out of the cottage carrying a big plate of sandwiches. Elsa's mother followed her aunt with napkins and cutlery to set the table. They laughed, teasing each other in good humour.

Her aunt's much thinner and smaller husband, who was a blacksmith and who had built the fence, sat in the arbour at the table, puffing on his pipe with a wine jug the front of him. Elsa's father appeared from behind the house with his camera around his neck. He was an ardent amateur photographer, and he used to wait patiently for endless hours to take pictures of birds. Somehow, his pictures were out of focus most of the time, and Elsa's uncle teased him mercilessly because of it.

Those were the best summers of her childhood. She could never forget them, and she treasured highly those old, faded, out-of-focus photographs of the birds and the family. Just a look at them could make her smile. She felt tears in her eyes now, however, and she tried to blink them away. She heard the cottage door open, and a woman about her age came out.

"Can I help you?" the woman asked. "Are you lost?"

"No, I'm not. I'm sorry I've been staring at this place for such a long time, but this was my aunt's house and I spent many summers here when I was a child."

The woman came to the gate and looked at her closely.

"No, it can't be! Are you Elsa?"

"Yes, I am. But—"

Before Elsa could say anything more, the woman opened the gate, ran out and embraced Elsa tightly, crushing the air in her lungs.

"I can't believe it! Where did you come from? Where were you?" The woman paused, let go of Elsa and stepped back. "Oh, how stupid I am! You don't have the faintest idea who I am, do you?"

Elsa shook her head.

"I am your second cousin's wife. We inherited the place after your aunt died. I recognized you from the old photo albums in the cottage. Your aunt was very fond of you and was devastated when she heard that you left and were living in Canada. Your parents and your sister spent a few days with her every summer and brought letters and photographs from you. Are you alone? Where is your husband? How is your son? I talked your mother a few times a year before she died, God bless her soul, and I really liked your father. What handsome man he was! Come in, come in. Let me give you some tea or coffee. What are you doing here? How long are you staying?"

Elsa could hardly open her mouth. Her suddenly found, bubbling relative of a sort had floored her. Finally, she caught the woman taking a breath and said, "I still live in Canada. I'm just visiting a girlfriend of mine in Budapest, and I took the train out here today to look around my favourite childhood place. I'm going back with the train in half hour," she lied. She didn't want to stay and talk for long.

"Oh, what a pity. Your cousin, my husband, will be out in the hills working in the vineyard till dark. Are you sure you have to go back? Why not stay and have dinner with us? You remember him, don't you? He spent time here too when you were kids. I believe he was called, "Shorty" because of his height. And he is still kind of short." The woman, who was not especially tall herself, gave a big laugh.

Elsa tried to remember and recalled vaguely a freckle-faced, chubby boy who was a bully and chased her around the garden with a big, green frog in his hand.

"Yes, of course I remember, and I am sorry I can't stay. I promised my friend I'd be back with the early train, and she will worry if I don't show up. Maybe when I visit again we can talk longer. It was so nice to see you. Say hello to Shorty for me."

"Can't you stay for just an hour? You must eat something—it is way past lunchtime."

"I ate at the restaurant beside the station," she lied again. "Thank you!"

"At Miko's? He has been a highway robber ever since this place became so popular with tourists. I hope he didn't poison you."

"Oh, I had a good enough lunch. And I am still alive. But I must go now. I want to walk around before my train leaves. Thank you," Elsa said. Very quickly, she kissed the woman on both cheeks and walked out of the garden before the woman was able to offer to go with her. When she shut the gate behind herself, she could still hear the woman talking.

"Phew, that was close," she sighed when she was at a safe distance. She really wasn't in the mood to chitchat with a so-called relative and answer thousands of questions. She was angry—because of the woman, she could not stay there and reminisce. She would have liked to walk around in the garden and look in the house, but she wanted to do it alone. True, she felt guilty and figured the woman would say she was a stuck-up Canadian woman who thought she was better than anybody here. *Well, let her think it. At least she'll have something to talk about for a long time.*

Elsa walked towards the station the same way she had walked so many times when going to the beach. Her good mood was ruined, and she was devastated to see that her enchanting forests and meadows had changed into a suburban holiday retreat. She was debating in her mind whether to visit the beach or not—it also could be a depressing sight. But it was too early for the train, so she walked on. She crossed the highway again and headed towards the shore, passing the restaurant she had lied about. She was hungry, so she went in to eat something.

The restaurant was the same as she remembered, and that cheered her up a bit. She sat down at a table on the terrace which overlooked the railway tracks and the entrance to the beach. The dining room was empty and didn't look very clean. To be on the safe side, (and remembering the chatty woman) she asked for a pogàcsa and ordered a beer. The pogàcsa was surprisingly tasty, still warm from the oven and made of dough with bacon bits in it. She asked for a second.

Her hopes a little higher after her meal, Elsa walked across the tracks at the level-crossing barrier and down to the shore.

The beach hadn't changed. It was deserted so early in the season, but the gate was open and a man was cleaning the grounds. He looked at Elsa questioningly as she approached.

"The beach is closed," he said.

"I just would like to look around for a little while. Would you mind?"

The man shrugged his shoulders and said, "There is nothing to see, but go ahead if you want to. But be careful. The far side of the dock is rotted out, so don't go there."

"Thank you, I'll look out for it."

She walked down to the water's edge and sat on the low, stone wall between the sand and the water. A rusted steel ladder attached to the crumbling wall led down to the shallow water. From the middle of the sandy beach, a long, narrow, wooden dock led out into the water, where widened out and formed a larger platform. Even further out, about fifty meters from the dock, a round, floating, wooden stage bobbed on the waves. It was covered with an ugly blue indoor-outdoor rug. It was just naked planks in Elsa's childhood, and she remembered how slippery it became with kids jumping on and off. They called that stage "monkey island," and it was her favourite place because only the older kids who were strong swimmers could play there. Her mother, who never learned to swim, sat on the dock and worriedly kept an eye on her until she swam back to the dock. Elsa was a good swimmer. She didn't remember when she learned to swim—she just took to the water like a duck. Her father was very proud of her when she beat all the kids in a race out to "monkey island."

Suddenly a deep sadness filled her heart. She missed her parents and realized she had never gotten over feeling guilty for leaving them. She helped them financially, of course, as soon as she and Sàndor had established themselves—Sàndor was a good provider. Elsa looked out over the water and listened to the whispering reeds as her mind turned to Sàndor, who had been a solid rock in her life in Canada for many years. But just as quickly, she stopped her flow of thoughts. She didn't want to think about him. He was a closed chapter in her life, just as Tom was.

Elsa got up and slowly walked toward the long dock. She noticed that the old boathouse was still standing in the reeds, so she walked over. It was abandoned, planks were missing and the landing was underwater. How she liked to play around it with her sister, frightening their mother with the long water snakes they caught and put around their necks! It was here when a boy kissed her for the first time in her life. She was fifteen and he was sixteen, very grown up, a good swimmer and very handsome. All her girlfriends envied her because he was the heartthrob of that summer. She thought hard but could not recall his name.

She walked along the beach for a while longer, and then it was time to catch the train. The caretaker still looked at her strangely, probably wondering what a well-dressed lady would be doing walking around that ugly, empty beach. She thanked him as she passed.

Elsa walked back to the station and sat down on one of the peeling benches. She was happy, now, that she came. The trip made her feel content and at peace with her life. She had made mistakes and had regrets during the past years, but she survived, had her family and had friends who loved her. She knew she was lucky to have memories to warm up her heart for the rest of her life.

The train whistled and pulled into the station. She found an empty compartment and watched the stationmaster in his red hat as he waved his disk, signalling the train's engineer that all was clear. The train jerked and slowly pulled out of the station. Elsa moved so she could see the lake until it disappeared. After a bend, some trees and a hill hid the light green expanse, so she leaned back in her seat, shut her eyes and dreamt about her childhood.

Chapter 18

Edith stared at the ceiling, feeling very wobbly, weak and distressed. It was just yesterday that she was able to collect her thoughts and remember what had happened in the last week.

She recalled the meeting with Antal, the sailing, the lovemaking and how happy and relaxed she had felt after so many bad years. She remembered the last evening, the dinner in the cabin, the wine and the brandy. They were so drunk they passed out on the bed. The smell of the burning candles came back to her too, as did the memory of wanting to blow them out but being too dizzy to get up. After that everything blacked out.

The next thing she remembered was being in a small, white room with some kind of device on her nose and mouth and a man in a white coat beside her bed. Margaret stood on the other side, holding her hand and calling her name. She desperately tried to ask where she was and what happened, but she could not, and then the darkness came again, as if she was in a hole in the ground. Next she felt she was being lifted up out of a car that smelled of disinfectant. She taken and placed on a motionless place. She did not know how long all this lasted. An hour, a day, a week? When she woke up the last time, she was in this room and Margaret was dozing beside her bed in a chair. She wanted to sit up, but she was unsteady. Margaret had woken up and caught her by her shoulders.

"Edith, are you all right? Do you know who I am? Do you know where you are?"

"Of course I know you, why? And why am I here? Is this a hospital? What happened? Oh, I feel lousy," she said, holding her head with both of her hands, "like after a whole week of a drinking party! Where is Antal?"

"Edith, you had an accident on the boat."

"What kind of an accident?"

"Shhh ... don't talk now. I am going to get the doctor."

"But where is Antal? Is he here too? Is he okay?"

"Later, Edith. The doctor must see you now. He'll let you know everything, but first he has to do a few tests."

Margaret left and came back with a small, round, bald man in a white coat. He stood by the bed and smiled down at Edith.

"So you came around after all! We were afraid for a while that we'd lose you!"

"What do you mean, lose me? I was going to die? Why?"

"What are the last episodes you remember?"

Edith told him about Antal, the sailing boat, the wine and the candles.

"Very good, and after? Nothing?"

"Just a few fractions about drifting in a dark space, waking up once and seeing Margaret holding my hand."

"Do you have a headache? Is your vision clear now?"

"Yes, I have a dull pressure in my head and I am seeing coloured rings, but otherwise I am just weak and tired. What's the matter with me?"

"You had been exposed to a large amount of carbon monoxide, and your system wasn't getting enough oxygen to function properly. We were afraid that your brain cells were permanently damaged by it, but it seems you are fine. You are one lucky woman! Tomorrow we have to take a few tests, and if they work out fine you can leave the hospital in about a week. But you'll need a lot of rest to get your strength back."

"I asked so many times—what happened to my companion, Antal? Is he here too? Is he okay?"

The doctor looked at Margaret and said, "We have to tell her."

"Tell me what?"

"Edith, your companion was not as lucky as you. He died of the carbon monoxide poisoning—he had a weak heart."

"No, it can't be! No! No! He didn't die! Tell me he didn't!"

"I am very sorry, but he did. They couldn't save his life. He was dead when the ambulance arrived at the hospital in Balatonföldvàr."

Edith started to scream, jumped up from the bed, tore at her hair, tried to run out of the room and kept shouting, "I killed him! It was my fault, I drank a lot! I didn't blow out the candles ... I killed him ... I killed him!"

Margaret and the doctor held her until the nurse came in and helped put her back to bed, still screaming and kicking. The doctor gave her a shot. Soon she was asleep, but her body quivered from time to time.

The doctor looked at Margaret again, saying, "I'm sorry, but I had to tell her the truth now. If we waited until she recovered further, and kept her hoping to see Antal again, the truth would be a new shock to her system and lengthen her recovery. It's better this way. We'll keep her under close observation and give her medium doses of Valium. Tomorrow you can try to talk to her about him if she wants to. It will take a while for her to get over this tragic accident. Is she a stable person?"

"I'm afraid not. She tried to commit suicide once, but didn't do it at the last minute. She had a few very hard years after her husband died in a work-related accident. And as you know, she lives in London and has to go back sooner or later. What do you think, doctor? How long will it be until she's able to live on her own?"

"Hard to say. She is physically strong, so let's hope she'll be okay in a month's time. Is she staying with you after her release?"

"Yes, she came to visit me. We are old friends. She has no relatives here or in London. She lives alone. I'll be happy to take care of her for the time being, but I have a full-time job at the university. I can take a week off, but after that I must get back to work."

"Well, after a week she'll be fine alone during the day. She mostly needs a lot of rest. Maybe she'll be able to go back to London in two weeks. Come and see me tomorrow before you go to see her, and by then I'll know more about her condition."

The next morning, Edith awoke from a sixteen-hour sleep. A nurse looked into the room, and seeing that Edith was awake, stepped in and smiled at her.

"How are you doing this morning? It's time for a shower. Let me help you to get up."

"I can get up by myself, thank you, and I want to take a shower alone! I don't need any help!" Edith said, ill-tempered. She sat up and pushed the helping hand away. She stood up too fast, her legs gave out and she fell back onto the bed. Her head was spinning, and she couldn't stand up again.

The nurse paid no attention to her bad mood, helped her to get up and walked her to the shower. Again ignoring Edith's arguments, the nurse pulled off Edith's hospital gown, stood her in the stall, opened the faucets and stayed there until Edith finished washing herself. Afterwards, she put the towel around Edith, helped her dry off, walked her back to her room and deposited her on the bed. As the nurse left, Edith thanked her quietly.

She felt better and stronger, but her head was still hurting. She shifted to a more comfortable position and closed her eyes, trying to go back to sleep. As she started to drift into the dream world, everything suddenly came back. Antal was dead! Antal, the gentle, sweet and handsome lover she had known for only two days. But it felt like she had known him forever! He made her feel loved and gave her hope that she'd be happy after so many lonely and troubled years. At long last she had found the man for whom she was longing and trying to find. She was sure that he was the one who would take care of her, and maybe they'd be together for a lifetime.

He was so sweet, patient and caring when she told him her life story! She felt tears welling in her eyes. Then she became angry and bitter. Why had all this happened to her? Why was life punishing her so mercilessly? She never got what she wanted and nothing good ever happened to her. Those few exciting years, when she met and married Gàbor and lived freely in London, were great but didn't last long. Not one of her dreams had become a reality. Life was unfair to her and never gave her the opportunity to prove her talent in her art—she had to sell what she could at the flea market! She believed that she was a talented painter and that she should be famous and rich by now.

Her plan to retire somewhere in the south of France in a comfortable villa where she had no worries and could spend the rest of her life painting with Antal by her side were shattered. Why couldn't she live in Paris, the city of her dreams? How wonderful it would be to set up her easel under a bridge on the Seine and paint her emotions on the canvas. Why was life so brutally unjust to her? She felt sorry for herself and sobbed until the tears streamed down her face. And then she panicked. What was she going to do now? She had to go home to London, to her miserable life and empty apartment. Her days would return to struggling with the bills, looking for part-time jobs, freezing at the market and silently listening as ignorant people judged her work. She felt lost in a long, dark tunnel with no light leading a way out. She shut her eyes and drifted back to sleep. She dreamt about Paris.

Margaret went into Edith's room after seeing the doctor, who told her that Edith had seemingly pulled herself together and accepted the fact that Antal's death was no more than a tragic accident. Her physical health was fine, the blood test came back normal and her head was clear. He would keep her in the hospital for two more days, and then she'd be released. He gave his card to Margaret and said to call him if she needed any help. Margaret thanked him, and as per Hungarian custom, discreetly put a white, unmarked envelope on his desk with "gratitude money" in it. He just nodded and put it in his desk drawer.

Edith was dozing. Her face had healthier colour and looked relaxed. When she woke and saw Margaret standing beside her bed, she started to cry.

Margaret sat down on her bed, put her arms around Edith and said quietly, "It's all right to cry. Let it all out, you'll feel better."

"I'll never feel better again," Edith said through her tears. "I am a murderer, I let him die! I didn't get up and blow the candles out! He made me so happy! He promised to come with me to London and take care of me!" Edith's sobs took over again, and Margaret ached for her friend because she knew Antal's promises were far from the truth.

"He was well off," Edith said, sniffling, "we could have lived happily in London or Paris or anywhere!. And now he is dead because of me!"

"Edith, it was an accident—you can't blame yourself for it," Margaret said sternly. "The police told me that the cabin's exhaust pipe was not cleaned properly after the winter, and the cabin didn't get enough fresh air. You were lucky, but he had a weak heart and could not survive that long without oxygen."

"I should have gotten up, blown the candles out and opened the porthole! But I was drunk and could not! Oh! I loved him so much!"

"How could you? You only knew him for two days. You didn't even know who he was!"

Edith said impatiently, "It was love, you have to believe me! I'd never felt like that before and he said the same. I am sure he meant it. He was so sincere, so caring and so full of love! That was my last chance for happiness. I am close to sixty, and I will never love again! I'll have to live alone and be lonely for the rest of my life! I hope it won't be long! Why didn't I die too?"

Margaret just couldn't tell her the truth about Antal. She didn't have the heart to do it, and Edith probably wouldn't believe her anyway. Margaret thought it would be better to let her have a memory of a beautiful love affair that ended tragically at the height of happiness. Edith rambled on until she tired out and lay back on the pillow.

Wanting to change the subject of the conversation, Margaret said, "Lili went back to Australia three days ago, but she sends you her love and best wishes."

Edith made a face as if to say, "Who cares?" but she asked, "And Elsa?"

"She is staying with me for the time being and offered to help financially if you need it …"

"How considerate of her," Edith said bitterly, "but I still have some cash in my purse and money in my bank account in London. I don't need her help, thank you. How long is she staying with you? I can't fly back to London for a while. Where will I stay?"

"Don't worry, she's leaving soon to go home to Toronto. You can stay with me for as long as you need."

Edith's eyes became softer and she took hold of Margaret hand. All trace of bitterness and anger gone from her voice, she said, "Thank you. What would I do without you? You are such a good friend. You are always there when I need you! How can I ever repay you?"

"There is nothing to repay. This is what friends are for. Just get better soon, keep the good memories and let the bad ones fade away. Think about how lucky you are. You could be a just a brainless body. What happened happened, and nobody can change it."

"It is easier to say I want to be dead instead of lucky! I don't have any reason to live."

"How could you say that? You are healthy, you have a home and your talent, you'll paint lots of good pictures and in time you'll meet someone else. You should never give up!"

"I wish I could be as strong as you are, Margaret! But I am not."

"Please, Edith, try! You are tired now—I'll leave you to have a good rest. I am going to the railway station to pick up Elsa. This morning she went to Balaton to visit her childhood summer place."

Margaret kissed Edith's forehead. As she walked out the door, she said over her shoulder, "I'll be back tomorrow morning. By then we should know when are you are going to be released. Have a good rest and a peaceful night!"

Chapter 19

Margaret took the subway to South Railway Station. It was much easier than driving because the subway line ended at the station and from there it was just a short walk up to the tracks. Parking was always a great problem in the city, and traffic jams were frequent at any time of the day. During the last couple of years, the number of cars on the streets had multiplied by hundreds. Budapest, just like any other old European city, was not built for cars.

On the way to the station, she thought about Edith. She was very sorry for her and wanted to help any way she could. But she knew that Edith would absolutely depend upon her and she'd never be free from responsibilities regarding her. Edith would suffocate her with her dependence. Margaret couldn't and didn't want to turn her life upside down for her friend, no matter how much she cared and was sorry for her.

Edith was a middle-aged woman. She had to be able to take care of herself. Margaret decided that she'd keep her in the apartment for a week and then make it clear she had to go back to London and rebuild her life alone. Maybe if Edith didn't feel so sorry for herself and complain so much about her past and present life she would have a better chance of starting a new chapter. But Edith had a tendency to play the martyr and wanted to be pitied by everyone.

"I'll have to give her another heart-to-heart talk after a few days and try to pour some strength into her." Margaret sighed, got off the subway and walked up the steps to the platform. She was on time. The train from Lake Balaton was just arriving on track six. She waited at the end of the platform, watching passengers getting off and hurrying towards the exit. She noticed Elsa at once and waved to her. Elsa's face was blank, but as soon as she noticed Margaret, she smiled and her eyes lit up.

"How good of you to come and meet me!" said Elsa, embracing Margaret. "You shouldn't have bothered—I could have found my way home. You must be dead tired."

"Oh, I am, but I wanted to come. By the look of you, I'd say you didn't find what you expected. Am I right?"

"Unfortunately, yes! But on the other hand, I'm happy I went. I found some of my happy memories again, and now I can treasure them for ever."

On the way home, Elsa told Margaret about the changes that had taken place, the unexpected meeting with a distant relative who almost ruined her day, the unchanged beach and her reminiscence there.

"You know, Margaret, I realized something else too. It is high time for me to grow up and not get overly sentimental about recollections of my childhood and youth. Maybe it is because I am in my late middle age, but I've never before been so sentimental about my past life here in Hungary. The time has come for me to go home to my real and present life and stop these emotional flights before I become traumatized by it."

"Don't go yet," Margaret pleaded. "Stay for an other week. I need your support with my problems with Edith."

"Of course I'll stay as long as you need me, or at least until this situation is resolved."

"If ever…" groaned Margaret. She said, "I took the Metro here. Would you like to walk for a while?"

They walked to the park across from the station. It was a large park and well maintained. Children were playing in the playgrounds, people were walking their dogs and couples wandered around dreamily, hand in hand on the paths. The air was full of the sweet smell of lilacs, and many big bushes lined the main path down the middle of the park.

The sun had already disappeared behind the tall buildings, and its dark red glow made the narrow streets between the buildings sparkle. It was pleasant, warm, late spring evening. The two women walked in silence for a while. They went through the park and reached the maze of old, narrow streets beyond it.

"Where shall we go?" asked Margaret. "Do you want to go across the Lànc Bridge or the Erzsèbet Bridge? If you've had enough of walking, we can get on the bus. The bus stop is just over there." She pointed across the street.

"I don't mind walking all the way home. It is such a lovely evening! Let's walk over the Lànc Bridge—I think it is one of the most beautiful bridges in the world. Do you know that the engineer, I think his name was Clark Adams, built a smaller one just like it in a small town not far from London?"

"Yes, I saw it when I was visiting Edith. We drove up there once."

They crossed the bridge, admiring the stone lions standing guard on both sides of the bridge. They stopped in the middle of the bridge, looked down for a while into the dark, rushing river underneath and then walked towards Margaret place.

At home they relaxed, sipping coffee until Margaret said, "I don't know too much about your marriage. You told me the story about Tom, but I would love to hear about your husband too. Would you mind talking about him?"

"No, not at all. I was thinking about him today, actually. We became friends after the sourness of the divorce eased up in both of us."

"Let's go into the living room," Margaret said, rising and walking out of the kitchen. "The easy chairs are much more comfortable."

I left in '56 because I felt I had to get away from my old life and build a new one somewhere else in order to free myself of the painful years prior. After Lili left for Australia, I stayed with the rest of the group. Three of us—all girls—applied for Canadian immigration. We got them and ended up in Toronto. At first we lived in the basement of one of the girl's relatives. The Hungarians were old-time immigrants and very helpful, and soon I got a job at a Hungarian newspaper as a column writer, editor and supervisor all in one. It was a two-man operation, and one of them was too old to work. My salary was small, and even though the owner later gave me a raise, it was still much less than the job deserved, especially since I had to take over the advertising department too. That meant I had to go out to collect fees and also sign up new clients. I did it to the best of my ability, but I hated it. I felt easygoing on the stage, but I was so shy when collecting money or talking people into signing up for advertisements. I was not happy. Many times I wondered why I left. I missed my family and my home. I had no close friends, Lili lived far away and the letters didn't substitute for her in person. I had little money and struggled with a minimal existence.

Many times I was ready to pack up and go home, but my pride held me back. I could not run away from the life that I had chosen for myself so selfishly and because of which I caused so much pain to my loved ones. I didn't like having roommates, so when I made more money I rented a room from an old Hungarian woman who ran a rooming house and also provided cheap food.

I kept in touch with my old roommates and we went out together a few times, but I had little time for myself. During the day I roamed the city trying to get advertisers, and in the evenings I wrote and edited the columns for the paper. I was lonely and fought daily against the danger of an approaching depression.

One day, one of the girls called and invited me to a party. I didn't want to go, but I made myself do it. It was a gathering of the new, young immigrants, and we argued about our present life, the politics and the news from home while drinking cheap wine and beer. We all sat on the floor of the small, bare apartment. Beside me sat a young man. He was thin, tall and dressed in an old, bulky sweater and shiny pants. He had dark brown hair, serious-looking brown eyes and nice, full lips. We started to talk. He was intelligent, had a dry, almost cynical humour and drank only soda water. When the party started to break up, he walked me home. We talked all the way.

I learned that he was a student on scholarship at the university's math department. On the evenings and weekends, he worked in one of the Hungarian restaurants as a cleaner, dishwasher and occasional waiter. He was lonely, just like me. It was a long walk home, and we parted as friends. He called me the next day for a date, so we went to the restaurant where he worked, because there he got free food from the leftovers.

After the first date we met frequently, whenever we could manage to find free time. We walked a lot because it was the cheapest entertainment. We walked in the parks, on the shores of Lake Ontario and on the streets of downtown. When we got cold and tired, we shared one hot chocolate—two were too expensive. Slowly, we fell in love. It was the kind of love two lonely people who need each other share. To save money, we moved together to a small apartment, and after a six months we got married.

He was gentle and not demanding when we made love, and I felt very comfortable with him. When he graduated and got his credentials, he got a job with a life insurance agency. By then I was running the newspaper because the other owner had retired too. I became a full-fledged manager, with good pay and bonuses for the advertisements. When I became pregnant in the third year of our marriage, Sàndor was making enough money for all of us. I happily quit my job, and we put a down payment on a small house with a nice garden. David was born. He was a healthy, lovely baby, and we were happy and content with our life.

I did some writing and took as many evening refresher courses in English as I could. Life was good. The company where Sàndor worked started to grow and he grew with it. He got better and higher positions, and by the time David was in high school, Sàndor was the vice president. We lived in a big, beautiful house in one of the high-class neighbourhoods and entertained often, which was a must with Sàndor's position. I learned to be a gracious hostess. I was the "lady of the house" and had a cleaning woman come daily. After I did the chores of a mother and wife, I was free to do whatever I wished. My parents visited us every three years, and I visited them in between. They were satisfied to see my happy family life and material well-being.

Sàndor was a great provider. We loved and respected each other."

∼

"Were you really that content or was there some regret behind this idyllic life?" asked Margaret when Elsa finished her story.

"After a while I would sometime get restless and want to expand my horizons. That's when I started travelling with Lili. David was at the university, Sàndor travelled a lot and I was not needed at home. Money was not an object for either of us, so we went to places that were just dreams in our youths, like Egypt, China, all over Europe and so on. After David moved out and Sàndor was away more and more for longer periods of time, I got lonely. There was gossip that Sàndor was travelling with his young secretary. I didn't believe this rumour, but I could not dismiss it. That was during the time I went to Italy with Lili and met Tom in Venice. That affair was the best part of my life in every way." Elsa sighed and got up.

"Let's go to bed. You have to get up early tomorrow. I would like to come with you to visit Edith if you think it's okay."

"Sure, why don't we meet at the university around twelve, grab lunch somewhere and then go to the hospital."

Margaret could not fall asleep for a long time. She was thinking about her unfortunate marriage and fantasizing about how different her life would have turned out if she gave in and followed Roberto as his mistress. Where could Roberto be now? He must be around seventy-five years old if he was still alive. Maybe they would have lived in Italy in a small fishing village, somewhere above the blue sea in a stone house. They'd tend the flowers beds and the olive trees and not have a care in the world. No children to cause problems and pain—just the two of them. She fell asleep with smile on her lips and dreamt on.

Lying in bed, Elsa mused over the old times when David was little and she walked him to school, holding his hand. She thought about the comfort and warmth of the house, the laughter and happiness around the dinner table and when after dinner Sàndor kissed her forehead and whispered, "Thank you." Why did it have to end? She searched her memory as she had so many times before, trying to find where she went wrong, why she could not keep her husband after David left home.Could it be that she leaned on him too heavily because she felt useless and was lonely? That question brought her to thinking about Tom and their incredible love for each other—why did she let him go?

Lili's voice rang in her ears, saying, "You are too conscientious for your own good, and you always count yourself second."

Perhaps she was right, Elsa thought before drifting off to sleep.

Chapter 20

Edith was not happy to see Elsa, and she didn't even try to hide it. Elsa said a few things, but Edith answered her questions with annoyed coolness.

After a short while, Elsa said, "I am sure that you two have many things to discuss." She stood up. "I hope you feel much better soon, Edith. Goodbye. I'll go to the cafeteria and wait for you, Margaret. Please don't rush, stay as long as you like. I bought a book to read."

"Why did you bring her?" Edith asked Margaret nastily as soon as Elsa was out of the room. "I am not in the mood for visitors!"

"Edith, you should at least have the civility to be well-mannered. I thought you'd welcome a new face beside your bed. Elsa was worried about you and thought she might cheer you up a bit with a chitchat. Also, she wanted to personally offer you her help!"

"Well, I don't need her help, and I am not up to any chitchat. I want to get out of here! I hate this place!"

"Did you see the doctor this morning?"

"Yes, he was in for one and a half minutes, took my pulse and said I am fine and can leave the day after tomorrow. But I don't want to wait that long. I want to leave now!"

"He must have a reason for wanting you to stay for another two days."

"I feel fine, my headache is gone and I walked in the corridors without any difficulties. And that sour-faced nurse let me take my shower alone. So I don't see why I should stay here any longer. Please have me signed out!"

Margaret saw that there was no point in arguing with her, so she stood up and said, "All right, I'll go to the office and try."

The doctor who had the authority to sign her out had already left for the day, and the head nurse on duty told Margaret that Edith had to stay until the next morning. If the doctor signed her out, she could leave, but only under her own legal responsibility.

Edith fumed when Margaret told her the news, but she saw that she had to wait another day.

Margaret sat down beside her bed again and wanted to talk about future plans. She asked Edith if she could call someone in London to let them know that she'd not be going home as was planned.

"Margaret, please not now. I promise to think it over tonight and tomorrow after I leave this horrible hospital. We'll discuss it at your place. And besides, you don't have time for all that now—your friend is waiting for you!" Edith said mockingly, "You'd better hurry!"

Margaret found Elsa in the cafeteria, sipping coffee and reading. She sat down across from her and let out a deep groan.

"She was that bad?" asked Elsa.

"She didn't want to talk about what she will do, or even when. She sent me away saying that she'd think about it tonight and we'd talk tomorrow. I really don't know what I am going to do with her!"

"When is she leaving the hospital?"

"She is supposed to stay until the day after tomorrow, but she wants to sign herself out on her own responsibility tomorrow morning. What am I going to do?"

"Don't worry about me, Margaret. I'll go back to the hotel for a few days, and I'll go home next week. She might be more relaxed and agreeable outside of the hospital, and you might be able to reason with her better."

"I hope so. But I hate to see you move out. I was looking forward to a few more days together."

"Well, you don't have to be with her all the time. We can meet when she is resting. Yes, it would be much better if I could stay with you, but we shouldn't aggravate Edith more than necessary. I think it's better if I disappear from her sight. I wonder why she hates me. It can't be just jealousy because of our friendship. There must be more."

"She was rude. She is in a stage when she blames the whole world for her misfortune, and you were the closest target. She is just unpredictable."

The next morning after Margaret arranged her one-week leave from teaching, she went back to the hospital. Elsa stayed behind, and they agreed the she would move back to the hotel before Margaret returned with Edith.

Margaret got to the hospital a few minutes after eleven. There was nobody at the nurse's station, so she went straight to Edith's room. The room was empty, the bed was stripped and a woman was washing the floor.

"Where is the patient who was here?" she asked the woman.

The woman shrugged her shoulders and said, "I don't know."

Margaret went back to the nurse's station. She was not worried and just thought Edith had gotten impatient and didn't want to wait in the room. Margaret figured she was waiting for her in the cafeteria. A middle-aged nurse now sat at the desk.

"Would you know where my friend from room 205 is? I came to pick her up."

The nurse looked at her, asked her name, handed her a letter and said, "She signed herself out and left more than an hour ago. She asked me to give you this letter."

"What do you mean? She left the hospital?"

"Yes, I walked her to the exit as per policy. She got in a taxi and left. Are you all right?" asked the nurse, watching Margaret's face.

"Yes, thank you."

She sat down in the lobby and gathered her strength. Then she opened the letter.

My Dear Friend,

I had a long night to think about my situation. I realized that I couldn't stay and be a burden to you. I am well and must look after myself. I had my passport and my return ticket with me in my bag, and I decided to fly home today. Please do not come after me to the airport and do not worry about me. I will not do anything foolish, I promise. I'll take care of myself. I will call you in a few days from London and ask you to send my suitcase over. Thanks for everything, and please don't be angry with me.

Edith

Margaret couldn't help but feel relived of the responsibilities, but knowing Edith, she knew that the sudden change of mind must cover a lot of things. Margaret was hurt and angry that Edith didn't wait for her and just left like a thief after a successful robbery. She was worried that Edith's state of mind was not yet vigorous enough to cope with life alone. She decided to go out to the airport and talk some sense into her, but then she realized Edith could be on the plane to London by now—there was a flight almost every hour. All she could do was wait for Edith's call.

She called her place to see if Elsa was still there.

"Don't move out, please stay," she said when Elsa answered. "Edith checked out early this morning and is on her way to London. I'll be home soon and tell you everything. Please stay."

Elsa was waiting for her in front of her apartment building.

"What happened? She just left without calling you?"

"Yes, she left me this letter and went to the airport," said Margaret, passing the letter to Elsa. Elsa read the letter on the way up to the apartment.

"I don't understand her," Margaret said as she opened her apartment door. "One minute she is a helpless, whining woman and the next minute she is making her own decisions without any regard for the people who care for her."

"You think she'll be all right?" Elsa asked.

"I don't know, but there is nothing I can do for her anymore. I'll try to call her tonight." She shook her head and sat in an armchair. She smiled suddenly and said, "But now I have a whole week off work. Why don't we go somewhere? It would do a lot of good for both of us after all this mess! Could you stay for another week?"

"Gladly! Where should we go?"

"What about Vienna? It's just a hundred and sixty kilometres away. We can stay in a bed and breakfast, listen to Strauss waltzes at the park, eat real wiener schnitzel and drink real Bavarian beer!"

"You could not have had a better idea, Margaret! I have not stayed in Vienna for thirty years. I just travelled through a few times since. I don't have good memories of that place either—I was lonely, miserable, without any money and with plenty of doubts about my life. I think now I can look at it differently. We could go and visit all those places that I could not see back then because of the lack of funds. I did go to Schönbrunn Palace, but I didn't have money for the ticket so I could only walk around outside and admire the surrounding park. Oh, how I longed to see the Lipizzaner horses doing the ballet!"

"Well, we can do it all. Let me check the train schedule. Then we can pack and be on our way!"

Edith had to pay full price for a one-way ticket because her original low fare didn't allow any changes and she was two days late for her scheduled return. Fortunately she had a credit card to charge the ticket on. The check-in girl looked at her with suspicion when she said she had no luggage to check. She passed through the security gate, where her purse was searched attentively, and hardly had enough time to get to the gate before boarding closed.

When the jet engines started to roar and the plane moved to the end of the runway in preparation for takeoff, Edith closed her eyes and leaned back in her seat. She was sure she had done the right thing. She had to look after herself and put her life together alone. She could prove she was able to do so!

Her head suddenly started to hurt, and coloured rings danced behind her closed eyelids. The hammering of an approaching migraine began. She reached into her handbag and took out the little sack full of sleeping pills she had saved while in the hospital. Not bothering to ask for water, swallowed two of them. Soon she was half asleep, and the pain was dulled down but definitely still there.

She was dazed when the plane landed at Heathrow. Her hands shook all the way home, and it took some time until she found the right key and could put it into the lock. Inside, she unhooked the phone, peeled her clothing off and drew a hot bath. In the kitchen cabinet she found a half bottle of vodka behind the dinner plates, poured a generous portion into a glass without ice and lay down in the tub. As she sipped the vodka, the hot water relaxed her body, her mind became engulfed in a pink haze and she felt herself floating without any thoughts.

As the water cooled down, she came to feeling cold. Her glass was empty. She got out of the tub, put on her robe, poured another full glass of vodka, searched for the little bag of the sleeping pills, took three with a big gulp of vodka and fell into bed.

She woke up the next dawn from a deep, dreamless sleep. At first she didn't know where she was and looked around the semi-dark room wondering. She felt weak but comfortably warm and relaxed.

After a while, she forced herself to get up. Her legs were unsteady, and she had to support herself on the walls while she searched for her robe. Then she stood in the middle of her living room, trying to get everything in focus. Finally she was able to open the windows. She took a deep breath of the late May dawn air. Birds were waking up in the nest on the tree just outside her window and cleaning their bodies with their beaks as they waited for the sun rise above the horizon. When it did, they flew off in search of food.

The memories of the past few weeks suddenly flooded her brain, but they arrived without the nagging pain or self-pity—it was just simple memories. She felt to some extent that she had freed herself from the past.

Her body was light, and her head was clear. She waited at the window until the rising sun painted the sky above the trees a deep orange and the dewdrops on the trees reflected a rainbow of colours. The birds twittered loudly as the darted about. From the street below came the early morning sounds of cars starting, the newspaper boy's bicycle and the bumps as the papers he threw landed on doorsteps. She took one more deep breath of the fresh air and then turned away from the window. The room was a mess. Her clothing all over the floor, her handbag half open under a chair and an empty glass overturned by the side of her bed. She observed the scene with self-disgust.

No, this can't go on anymore, she thought. She would change. After all, she was a strong-willed, intelligent woman. She was convinced that she had been saved from death as a challenge to do better than she ever had before. Yes, she would! She didn't need anybody. She would do it all alone and prove that she was worth saving! She felt some regret because she left Margaret without saying goodbye, but she knew Elsa would help her to get over it. She pressed her lips together at the thought. They probably did not mind at all that she left them alone. Before her thoughts become gloomy again and made her fall back into self-pity, she lifted her head up towards the sky and said out loud, "I'll show them, yes I will. Yes I will!

She cleaned up the place, took a cool shower, made a strong cup of coffee, found some dry biscuits in the cupboards, sat down in the kitchen beside the open window and looked at the brightening blue sky for a long time while sipping her coffee. By the time she finished her coffee, she knew what she was going to do. She dressed and went out. With sure, energetic steps, she walked down her street to the business section of the main street and stepped into the real-estate office on the second corner.

A young girl sat behind a desk drinking coffee and eating a bun. She looked up with surprise—it was too early in the morning for a customer walk in without an appointment.

"Good morning," she asked. "Can I help you?"

"I hope so," said Edith in a firm voice as she sat down in front of the girl's desk.

Chapter 21

Elsa and Margaret took the early train and arrived in Vienna just after ten o'clock in the morning. They each carried one small case only, so they decided on walking to look for a clean bed and breakfast to stay in for a few days. Westbanhoff railway station was located close to the center of the town. They walked down Mariahilfer Strasse towards the old town. Elsa looked around with amazement.

Her memories told her that this street was wide and lined with century-old, stylish buildings on both sides. They were still there, but how much everything had changed! Modern chain stores, like Roots, Zara and Tommy Hilfiger, thrust their big windows into the street, and oversized, colour posters of advertisements covered the façades of the lovely old buildings. The street had lost its old European charm. The small shops with friendly owner-operators were gone. No appetizing deli windows (but plenty of fast food places), and no flower stall on every corner.

After a twenty-minute walk, they found a pleasant-looking bed and breakfast place, but they were shocked by the price the landlady asked for a night. Margaret talked to her in flawless German, but when Elsa asked Margaret in Hungarian what the landlady had said, the landlady looked at them with a wide smile and switched to Hungarian.

"Why didn't you tell me that you are Hungarians? I always have a special price for my countrymen! Many of them stay here often, though I never advertise. They hear about me by word of mouth. I give them a special price and the best rooms. You two can have the largest room in the house with a private bath."

The price was much less than the first time, so they thanked her and went up to the first floor to look at the room. It was nice but not very bright, and it was stuffed with old-fashioned furniture, big, velvet armchairs and a table with legs that ended in lion's paws. The table was topped with a white lace tablecloth. The large double bed was covered with a brocade blanket, and porcelain figurines and vases were all over the place. It was a room from the last century's faded splendour of the middle-class. It was spotless but had a musty smell of the old furniture.

"What do you think?" asked Margaret.

"It is friendly, but I cannot sleep in a double bed with you. Let's ask her if she has a room with two single beds."

As soon as Elsa spoke, the woman stepped in the open door.

"I have one room with two beds, but it is on the third floor and we don't have an elevator. It is the only room on that floor. The bathroom is private, but it is at the end of the hallway."

They inspected the room. It was smaller but homier. The ceiling was slanted, and the space was sparely furnished with two beds, two armchairs and a small table. Two small windows cut deep into the roof looked out onto the street. Elsa and Margaret looked at each other and then paid for the room for two days in advance.

"But we might stay longer, if it's okay with you," said Margaret.

"You can stay as long as you like. There is nothing interesting going on here this time of the year. I don't have any reservations," the woman started to walk away but then stopped. "I serve breakfast from eight to nine-thirty. You have to come down to the dinning room—I don't have room service." The landlady said. She stood around as if hoping for some chatting, but when it didn't happen she reluctantly left the room.

Elsa looked out to the street. It was a narrow and lined by two three-story, old houses. There was a canvas stall on the corner selling ham, cheese and other Austrian specialties.

"Well *this* is the Vienna I remember," Elsa said. Turning back to Margaret, she asked, "So what are we going to do now?"

"Let's unpack and then walk. I'm getting hungry. Let's just follow our noses and find a small restaurant with big wiener schnitzel and potato salad."

"Yes, let's," agreed Elsa heartily. "You know, I remember a place down a side street close to the Stephan Kirche where I ate sometimes with Lili when we had enough money to share one big schnitzel. The proprietor patronized poor Hungarian refugees, gave us giant schnitzel that was plenty for both of us and never charged us for the emptied breadbasket. I hope I can find this. It was ages ago."

They consulted their map and started out towards the church. Walking around the plaza at the church, Elsa screamed, "This is the street for sure. We have to go through that old courtyard first. The restaurant will be on the left side of the street." She started to run ahead. And there it was. The glassed-in patio and long, wooden tables looked just as they had so many years ago. Elsa could not stop smiling when they entered the restaurant. It was not full, and they sat down at a long, empty table.

"You should let Lili know about your success—she'll be proud of you!" said Margaret, laughing. They didn't look at the menu and ordered the schnitzels and beer at once.

"You know, Elsa, you should record all of your memories. Did you write a diary during your emigration or before?"

"Yes, I did, but not regularly. Just marked down some important-looking dates and happenings. Why?"

"You told me that you took classes and workshops in writing and wanted to write, but so far you haven't. Why not?"

"I don't know. I've thought about it many times, and I even took computer classes to learn to use the WordStar program. I bought a laptop, a printer and paper for it too. I started to write, but somehow the story never materialized. There were so many books, fiction and nonfiction, about those years that I thought my story and the stories I could write would be boring and interesting to no one. I have a manuscript a couple dozen pages long put away somewhere. Perhaps when I get back I will consider it seriously and discipline myself to write every day."

"I think you should. Every life has a story, and every life is different. Everybody looks at it from different angles and with different convictions. I am sure you would do a great job! I will bug you with my letters to do it!"

"It's a deal! I promise to start writing seriously!"

The schnitzel came and it was beautiful, large, thin, rightly coated with breadcrumbs and fried to a golden brown.

After lunch, they walked around the streets, wanting to find the Freud Museum—the original apartment of Dr. Sigmund Freud. They kept consulting the street map, but they still got lost on the many ring avenues that framed the town in large circles. Finally, they gave up and flagged a taxi.

They to the museum a half hour before it closed. It was a dark, solemn-looking place, and in the consultation room was the famous couch. Shelves were cramped with books, and dark furniture overcrowded the rooms. On a large, mahogany desk, the doctor's steel-rimmed glasses and some other personal articles lay in apparent disarray. The exhibit gave the impression that Dr. Freud had left the room just a few minutes before and not a half a century ago when he escaped from the Nazis before they overran Austria.

"I can't help thinking about Edith," sighed Margaret when they left Freud's office. "I hope she finds a good psychiatrist who helps her overcome her problems. I tried to call her before we left, but there was no answer. I am seriously worried about her. I feel responsible for her. After all, I invited her to that trip."

"Oh, Margaret, don't agonize over it. You are not responsible for anything. You didn't send her sailing and you did your best to help her. Leaving was her own decision. You couldn't do anything to stop her."

"Yes, I know, but knowing her I am afraid she is doing something immature, like committing suicide!"

Elsa was quiet as they walked away from the museum. She glanced at the map, hoping to find the way to Strauss Park, where J. Strauss's statue stood playing his violin, and you could listen to live concerts of his music in front of an open pavilion.

It took them a good hour to get to the park. They sat down on an empty bench, being very proud of the distance they had covered. The sweet music of the Vienna Waltz filled the air. For a while they were occupied with their own thoughts, and then Elsa turned to Margaret.

"I just had an idea. We are in Vienna, about two hours from London by plane. I am sure the Austrians have the cheap flight programs too. Why don't you fly there to see Edith?"

"Elsa, same-day plane tickets are always far too expensive, and besides, I don't know if Edith would appreciate it if I showed up."

"Look, I am coming with you and I'll buy the tickets. No, don't argue. I think you should put your mind at ease. Don't carry this problem with you and spoil your days. If we can't get her on the phone tonight, we are going to fly there and see what the trouble is. I am worried about her too."

They tried to call Edith late into the night, but the phone just kept ringing. After more arguments about plane tickets, Margaret gave in with the condition that she was going to pay Elsa back as soon as she could get the money together. There were no free seats the next day, so they booked a flight for the day after. They called Edith again, but her phone just kept ringing without response.

They spent the next day walking around Vienna. Elsa tried to find the espressos and hostels where she spent the days in 1956 until she left for Canada. The Spanish Riding School had no performance that day, so instead they took the afternoon train out to Schönbrunn, the palace of Emperor Frank Joseph and his wife Elisabeth. They signed up for the inside tour and walked through many rooms furnished with golden grandeur. But after the fifth one, the excessive gold, the chandeliers, the official dining room with table settings for forty people (each with six cutlery, five crystal glasses and three golden plates on the top of each other) and the overt opulence became boring and overwhelming. They looked at each other and then skipped the rest of the tour. At the next possible exit, they left the castle.

"It is an experience to see how the nobility lived in the last century, but it was enough for me," said Elsa when they sat down in the famous garden, where colourful flowers were blooming and the trees and shrubs were trimmed into painfully strait lines.

"I remember when I came here with Lili in 1956 while she was waiting for her visa to Australia. She wanted to take this tour—she had her boyfriend's money—but I didn't want to go. I was in a very solemn mood, so she gave in and we just walked around here. I remember there was a man-made lake with a giant statue park around it. I was just as taken by those shaped trees and bushes then as I am now. How many gardeners work on them, I wonder?"

"Do you want to look for that statue park?" asked Margaret.

"No, lets take the train back. It is getting late. We have to get up early morning for that redeye flight to London."

At the bed and breakfast, they said goodbye to their landlady and promised to spread the good words about her establishment. They said they were leaving very early in the morning and didn't want to disturb her. She was sorry to see them go and said she'd hoped they would have helped to balance her books in the off-season.

They landed at Heathrow after nine in the morning. Because they had no checked luggage, they were almost the first to get through passport control. Margaret led the way to the Tube.

Elsa had been to London a few times with Lili, but they never took the Tube. Lili always insisted on a taxi or a limo to take them to and from the hotel they stayed at.

"I hope you know where we are going," said Elsa. "I am always completely lost in subways—I loose all sense of direction."

"Trust me, I know. I've ridden the Tube many times before, and it doesn't change. They transferred to the Piccadilly line and then got off at Hampstead station.

Whenever Elsa looked at Margaret, her friend seemed very nervous and worried. When they reached the street where Edith lived, Margaret stopped. Elsa gently pushed her forward.

"It will be okay, don't worry. She is fine and getting on with her life. Which house is she in?"

"The fifth one down the street. You are right, let's go. No matter what we find it will help to stop my nightmares about her."

She walked ahead and then once again stopped suddenly.

"There is a for-sale sign in front of her house," she said slowly. "It says, 'third floor flat,' and that one is hers! Why would she move?" asked Margaret, alarmed. They rang Edith's apartment and waited. They rang again, but still nothing happened.

By now Margaret was shaking.

"She could be out shopping or she could be at her stall at the market," Elsa suggested.

"The market opens early in the afternoon only on weekdays. She couldn't be there, but she might be out shopping. Let's wait for a bit."

They walked up and down the street for almost an hour. There was no sign of Edith.

Then two women stopped at the house. One of them opened the door with a key and walked in, leaving the door open.

"Let's ask them. Maybe they know her and they would tell us where she is," said Margaret as she went into the hallway.

The hallway was empty. The sounds of voices led them up to the third floor.

"This is Edith's place," said Margaret, and she went in without knocking.

The two women looked at her with surprise. One of them, who had some folders in her hand, said, "Can I help you?"

"I am sorry to barge in like this," Margaret said, standing in the door, "but I am looking for my friend who lives here, and I saw you two go into her apartment. Would you know where I can I find her?"

The woman with the folder looked at her. "Are you related to Edith Kalmàr?"

"No, but I am her old friend from Hungary. I am Margaret."

"I don't think I can give out any information about her. You are not related and I've never seen you before."

"Please, I came all the way just to see if she was all right after her accident in Hungary. She hasn't answered her phone for days, and I am more than worried. This is our mutual friend Elsa," Margaret said, pointing to Elsa. "Please tell me where I can find her."

The woman finally introduced herself, likely giving in to the sincerity in Margaret's voice.

"I am Susan. I work for the real estate agency your friend listed her flat with days ago. I believe she has left for Paris, France. She didn't leave any forwarding address and said she'd be in touch with us. She didn't say when she is coming back. I am sorry, but that's all I know." She gestured to the woman beside her and said, "This lady is a client of mine and I am showing her around the place."

Margaret could not utter a word. She just looked at Susan numbly, so Elsa stepped in, asking, "She didn't leave a forwarding address? That's very unusual. How can you sell her place without her being here?"

"As I said, she told us she would be in touch. We will hold the offers until she calls us."

"You mean she is not coming back at all?"

"I don't know that, but she authorized us to do the banking in case of a sale."

"Do you know if she has a lawyer? She must have one or else she can't make a sale."

"Our firm has several and we'll do all the necessary papers. She said she would let us know her address there as soon as possible. Yes, I know this is very unusual, but we serve our clients by their wishes."

"Thank you for the information," Margaret said. "I really appreciate it. Will you please tell her when she calls that I was here and am very worried about her? Please ask her to call me as soon as possible. Here is my card—tell her to call collect."

"Yes, I will, and I hope she calls you. I am sure she is fine," said the agent as she turned back to her client.

Elsa and Margaret walked away silently and stopped at the first coffeehouse and sat down. Margaret was shaking. She looked very angry and at the same time relieved.

"I can't get over this," she exploded. "Did you hear anything like that? She did all this in a week! Move to Paris? How will she make a living? She doesn't know a soul, and her French is not good enough for her to get along alone! She must be out of her mind! I know about her fascination for Paris—she talked constantly about how much she would like to live there, but she could never afford it! She was sure that Paris was the only place where she could paint her masterpiece and become famous! Why did she go so suddenly? Without letting me know! She must know that I worry about her! She just left like she did from the hospital, but this time she didn't even write a letter! She is not emotionally ready to start a new life in a strange place! Not to mention her financial situation! What can I do?"

"Nothing," said Elsa, trying calm her friend. "Edith is an independent woman. It is very shocking that she left you twice without a word, but as you said she is an unstable person. You cannot be responsible for her actions. She left by her own will. Nobody forced her. Try to push her out of your mind, or at least don't carry her on your conscience. It is her life. If she doesn't want to be found, it is her business. You should get back to your own life and stop worrying about her. She doesn't deserve it."

There was a long silence. Margaret just stared into her cup. To Elsa, she looked like a fortune teller trying to see the future in tea leaves. She almost smiled.

Margaret looked up and said, "Edith is an unfortunate soul who always wanted to be somebody she was not. Nobody can live with that approach to life without being forlorn and depressed. We have to realize who we are, accept it and make the best of it. You are right. I should try not to have her on my conscience."

"Well, it looks like we've finished our business here. What shall we do now? Do you want to stay for a day and walk around, or should we go back to the airport, get the first flight to Vienna and the first train to Budapest?" asked Elsa.

"I am not in the mood to be a tourist, and I've been here before. Let's go back. And Elsa, thank you very much for your support and company. Without you I couldn't have put this situation behind me."

"What are friends for? Let's get on the Tube."

Elsa stayed with Margaret for a few more days, but when it was time for Margaret to go back to work, Elsa was ready to go home.

"Margaret, I had a wonderful time with you. It was great even with all those ups and downs. I hope we can do it again—maybe in Toronto? I would love to have you! You never been in that part of the globe, have you?"

"No, and I really would like to see your home. I have never even been out of Europe. Maybe one day I'll come. It was so comforting to have you with me in those awful days I had with Edith. I'm sorry to see you go, but I understand you have your own life and a family."

The two friends said their tearful goodbyes, promising to see each other soon and keep in close contact by e-mail or phone.

Elsa would not let Margaret drive her to the airport. She always dreaded those last hours when there was nothing more to say, when two people just look at each other and try to find topics for conversation. After Margaret left for the university, Elsa called a taxi.

She checked in and went through security to her gate. She found an empty row of chairs and took out her book, but her head was much too full with thoughts to pay attention to it. She put the book away, leaned back in the chair and closed her eyes, and in her mind she was already in Toronto, kissing her son and grandson.

Chapter 22

As a few weeks went by, Lili gave up on her Hungarian. He was a swindler after all, she decided. Too bad—the project had sounded interesting.

Then at the end of the fourth week, the mailman delivered a big, registered package marked "personal" from Budapest. Lili signed the receipt and took the package to her study.

Michael was at his physiotherapist, and after that he would go swimming, so she didn't expect him for lunch. It was the day when he would meet a few old friends of his by the pool and talk about good old times. She was free until the early afternoon, and she took the dog out for a short walk so she wouldn't have to worry about him later. She wanted to go through all the papers before Michael got home. If she thought it was a sham, she wouldn't show it to him and just destroy the papers. She didn't want to hear, "I thought so, didn't I?"

An elegant leather folder contained the full history of company. A carefully drawn colour graphic presentation of the growth followed. Then came photographs of the machinery and the warehouse filled with merchandise. The warehouse was in the suburbs of Budapest, and the office was located in the business district downtown. The photographs showed several nicely furnished offices, numerous computers and desks with well-dressed and content-looking employees behind them. It all looked impressive. Also in the package were the minutes of the LA meeting, stating that Tivadar had succeeded in selling 35 per cent of his company to two U.S. businessmen for a large sum of money. He remained the owner of the other 65 per cent. There was also an official letter with a well-designed, eye-catching logo of the company on the top, and it was on good–quality, light grey stationery.

Dear Madam,

Following up our conversation during our flight to LA, I am sending you the promised documents. I hope you'll find them satisfactory. Anxiously waiting your answer,

Yours truly,
Tivadar Boda, president

In the same folder there was another letter, this one written by hand.

Dear Lili,

It took me some time to get all the necessary documents together. Please forgive me for the long delay. I think about you very often, and I hope we can meet again soon.

As you can see, my meetings went well. The two men who bought into the company are of Hungarian descent, but they are second generation and are about 35 and 40 years old with very successful businesses behind them. One lives in and operates out of Texas, the other from LA. If you want to get in touch with them, you'll find their full name and phone number in the folder.

As I said, I am offering you 15 per cent of the shares and a seat on the board as the company representative in Sydney (and hopefully later in many more places in Australia) for $50,000 U.S.

I hope you find everything satisfactory and get back to me in the near future about your decision. If you are interested in my offer, I would be happy to visit you in Sydney to talk about everything personally.

Also, I could look around to feel the place out. I have had some hard months behind me. I am looking forward to an almost business-less holiday.

My best wishes to you and your husband,

Yours truly,
Tivadar

Lili removed the personal letter from the pile and put it in her desk drawer. The rest of the documents she put back in the package and left on her desk—she'd go through them again tonight after Michael went to bed. Then she would decide how to present the whole package to him.

She liked the idea of Tivadar's visit. It would be a nice change in her dull days to show him around and have a reason to dress up and go back to her old haunts. She hadn't done any of that since Michael got sick.

"Well, I'll sleep on it and decide. As Scarlet O'Hara said, 'I'll think about it tomorrow.'"

She heard Michael's car in the driveway and went out to greet him.

"How was your lunch with those old chums of yours? Did you guys watch the girls pass by and sigh?"

"We could not sit outside because it was far too hot, so we just looked at them through the window," smiled Michael as he gave Lili a kiss. "And how is your day so far?"

"Oh, the usual. I tidied up, took the dog out for a walk, paid some of the bills and made a few phone calls. Michael, I don't feel like cooking tonight. Can we go to that Spanish place where they serve that perfectly roasted suckling pig?"

She noticed a slight frown on Michael's face, but it only lasted for a second. He said, "I am a bit tired from the exercises and swimming. I'd like to have a nap first if you don't mind. Don't you think it is too hot to go out?"

"Michael, we drive an air-conditioned car, and the restaurant is also air-conditioned! I feel like going out today. After your rest you'll feel better. I'll get you up in an hour. Have a good nap," said Lili. Relieved that he had agreed to go out, she kissed him on the forehead.

During dinner, she didn't mention the package from Hungary. They talked about their plans, or rather *Lili's* plans to remodel the house to make it more comfortable and give both of them more privacy.

"I don't know why you want to enlarge the living room," Michael said. "It is big enough. Maybe we can just rearrange the furniture or get new pieces if you like."

"But, Michael, it's so gloomy. We don't have enough light! It is not a big deal. We just extend the walls out onto the patio and put in large picture windows. It will be much more homey. And we can buy the big TV set you wanted and didn't have enough room for before."

"Maybe, but you know how I hate the inconvenience of having workmen around for weeks. And the noise and—"

"Don't be such a sissy," Lili interrupted. "It will take about a week, and during the day you can go to your fitness club while I look after the workmen."

"Well, let me think about it. How much would it cost? You know my stocks are not looking the best. I know it is just temporary, but one can never know how long "temporary" means in the stock market's terms."

"I'll pay half the cost. Your share will not be more than six thousand, and you can afford that!"

Lili saw that Michael didn't want to agree too fast. He said, "Okay, I'll think about it."

"But not too long, because the rains will come soon and that will make the work last much longer."

Lili saw that her decision was right to let the news of the package rest for a while. Maybe she wouldn't even show him tomorrow—he could be very difficult when he was in one of his "money worry" moods.

After Michael went to bed, she looked over the documents again very carefully and liked what she saw. Maybe it looked a bit too good, but she pushed that thought away from her mind. After all, hadn't she just come back from Hungary where she heard from everyone about how private business was booming and there was still lots of room for new enterprises? She saw how much life had improved there and how many new hotels opened in the last few years.

"I'll sleep on it, "she told herself.

She dreamt that she was sitting at the head of a big conference table. The people around the table all looked at her with admiration.

When she got up in the morning, Michael had already left for his fitness club.

Lili loved the mornings when she was alone. She made herself a coffee and sat out on the patio. Looking around, she thought, "Yes, I want to have that work done, and I will."

She looked at her watch, and after checking her "world clock," she called Elsa. Elsa picked up on the third ring.

"Hi, Lili, I knew it was you. How are things?"

"It is probably too early in morning for me to answer that question, but everything's okay. Guess what? I got those papers from Hungary."

"And you had given up on it! How do you like what you got? What do you think?"

"It looks very good. It is a dependable company—I have all the papers, charts and photos. He sold 35 per cent to some and is waiting to go public. I think I'll jump on the bandwagon."

"What did Michael say?"

"I haven't shown him the papers yet."

"You mean you decided without his opinion? You can't do that. After all, he is a lawyer and he is your husband."

"I know that. I will talk with him about it, but you know him. He is very cautious with investments and very conservative. I am afraid he will advise me against it because he'll be worried that I am going to be too busy to look after him. But I am so bored with my nothing-to-do life! I must get into something or I'll go crazy."

"Lili, please think it over carefully. There is a big sum of money involved and I know you can afford it, but don't decide until you talk it over with Michael."

"You are just as worrisome as he is! Okay, I'll talk it over with him, but my mind is made up. Also, I am going to invite my future partner to Sydney so we can finish up the deal here. He wrote me a very nice letter, where he said he is thinking about me a lot."

"Are you sure you are not just taken in by his charms? It's been a long time since you had any admirers around!"

"Come on, Elsa, you should know me better. This is strictly business!"

"I am afraid I know you better than you know yourself. Please don't do anything foolish."

"Okay, okay. How is your family?"

They talked for ten minutes more about everything, and Lili promised to call and tell Elsa how things turned out. Before she hung up, she asked, "How is Margaret? And what happened with Edith? Did she hear from her yet?"

"Margaret is fine—she is back teaching. Edith finally called her from Paris, but Margaret could not get any facts out of her. Edith only said that as soon as she settled down she'd call."

"I must say she, I mean Edith, is a strange one. Say hi to Margaret for me if you talk or write to her. I call you in a few days. Be good, but not too god—that is too boring." And then she hung up.

The dog ran to the door, barking happily. Michael came in.

"You're early!" Lili said. "What happened? Was it a short treatment?"

"I am not feeling too well. Maybe the suckling pig didn't agree with me. I didn't even work out. I think I'll take some Pepto-Bismol and go to bed. Would you cancel my physiotherapist?"

"Sure, anything else? I don't feel anything from dinner last night!"

"Well, we know that you Hungarians have stomachs made of steel! You can digest a whole pig and not just a piece of it. Are you staying in?"

"No, I have to go shopping at the market. I'll switch on the answering machine so you don't have to pick up the phone. Would you like anything special from the market?"

"Only some Ben and Jerry's chocolate ice cream if they have it."

"You can't be too sick if you're craving ice cream! It is just an off-day. See you later."

During the drive and in the supermarket, Lili's mind was on Tivadar's offer. She thought about it hard. True, it was not chicken feed she had to put up, but she could afford it, and it was her own money. The more she thought about it, the more excited she became. She already saw the products she'd import on the shelves of the supermarket, busy days, ordering people around and being a boss. She was going to prove to Tivadar that she doesn't just look like a smart businesswoman but she actually was one. After all, she was not even sixty and still ready for everything. In the afternoon she'd talk to Michael, and, yes, she'd invite Tivadar to Sydney!

The house was quiet when she got home. Too quiet. She became alarmed and rushed into the bedroom. Michael lay on the floor beside the bed, hardly breathing. He opened his mouth as if to say something, but no sound came out. Lili put a pillow under his head, ran to the phone and dialled 911. After the quick call, she rushed back to the bedroom and put blanket over Michael. Sitting down beside him, she stroked his face and whispered comforting words.

Ten minutes later, she heard the ambulance's siren. The paramedics hooked Michael up to life support, assured Lili that Michael was going to make it and then rushed him out to the ambulance. Lili got in too and sat beside Michael holding his hand. Once at the hospital, they took Michael away. Lili heard one of the nurses say, "It looks like a stroke." She then instructed Lili to sit down in the waiting room and told her she'd come back as soon as she could.

Lili's mind was numb. Sitting on the hard plastic chair, the only thing she could think about was the melting ice cream she left on the kitchen counter.

Chapter 23

Edith sat in a bistro on the Boulevard De Strassbourg, close to the Gare de l'Est, eating a still-warm croissant and drinking coffee from a large bowl in true Parisian style. She sat erect, but her mind was full of fear. It had been a week ago since she got off the train in Paris. From there she went searching for an affordable hotel while pulling her suitcase behind her. She vaguely remembered the street and a small hotel close to the station where she stayed with Gábor on their occasional visits. The streets around the station were full of hotels, but most of them were remodelled and too expensive for her. She couldn't afford the sixty-euro charge per day. After walking for a while, she found the small, rundown hotel a couple of streets behind the station. The plaster on the façade was peeling, the windows were small and dirty and the reception desk was in a dark, little alcove. The sullen clerk asked for her passport and a credit card and gave her a key without asking if she wanted to see the room first. The room was tiny and without a telephone or TV, but it had a small bathroom with a shower. The room's one window looked out over the rooftops across the street. It was clean, bright and most importantly affordable.

For the first two days, she just walked around getting the feeling of the city and not thinking about anything. She was content to be in the place of her dreams, free to go wherever her mood took her. One day she walked down the Boulevard De Strassbourg, continued on the Boulevard De Sebastopol, crossed the Rue de Rivoli and sat down on the stone bench of the bridge watching the sightseeing boats cruise the river before walking to the Ile de la Cité. She didn't go in the Sainte Chapelle to admire the breathtaking Gothic church and the 1,134 stained-glass windows because she had to watch her money. She did take the Metro to the Sacre Coeur one day, and she walked up the hill to avoid paying for a ticket for the cable car. She spent hours at the "painters' square" where many artists tried to sell their work and drew portraits of tourists. She breathed in the smell of garlic from the small restaurants with grumbling stomach, but she ate only croissants at the cheapest stalls. She visited the Louvre's giant glass pyramid and the new shops under it. She longed to go in and lose herself in the rooms of the famous masters for the whole day, but the ticket was too expensive. Maybe she would go on Sunday when all the museums were free.

She consoled herself with her unceasing dreams that she'd paint her masterpiece, be famous and never again have to worry about making a living. By the fourth day, her confidence began to fade and the worries took over. And then came the panic.

Paris was not the same as it was years ago when she romped through the streets and parks and spent days in the museums. In the evenings she would meet with Gábor at the Latin Quarters in their favourite little restaurant, eating escargots in garlic butter with fresh baguettes, drinking the cheap house wine and talking nonstop about their days. Everybody seemed so much friendlier then too. Nobody frowned at them because they spoke bad, accented French. Some even were taken in by their efforts.

Now, no one had smiled at her or wanted to be helpful when she was looking for some place. True, she was a much younger, good-looking woman then, who looked at the world trustfully with stars in her eyes.

What had she done? She left her only asset, her flat, in the hands of a real estate company she didn't know anything about. She gave them free rein to handle the sale if she agreed to the selling price. She authorized their lawyer to handle the paperwork and transfer the money to her bank after the deductible fees. She had cleared out her savings and left only about two hundred pounds in her checking account. The money she brought with her wouldn't last for more than two months, no matter how frugally she planned to live. She had a few friends in London, but here she didn't know a soul! Her French was so-so—good enough to get around and not get cheated. She only brought one suitcase and a portfolio of her paintings. In the case of a sale, the rest of her personal belongings would be stored by the real estate agency until she asked for them.

She desperately needed the suitcase full of clothing that she left at Margaret's apartment and knew she must call her soon. Margaret was probably be out of her mind with worry, and Edith knew it was not fair to conceal her whereabouts from her friend.

She calmed herself. After all, she had done what she always wanted, and all without taking anybody's advice or help. She wanted to be free of her old life and start a new one. That could only be done the way she did it—fast and without hesitation. She was going to prove that she was an able woman who could against life's disappointments. The apartment would sell, and she'd have enough money to live for a few years. She knew that at her age it would be impossible to find any kind of work. But then again, she didn't want to work. She wanted to live for her art, fulfill her dreams and find an agent and a gallery to represent her. She'd paint all the heartache and dreams and tragedies of her life on the canvas. She would paint and paint good! She was going to be a known painter making a living from her art.

Yes, she knew that was what she wanted, but how would she start? She had to search for a gallery and show them her portfolio and the notices from her first show, which a friend in London had arranged for her years ago. Times had changed and so had the public's approach to painting, but she knew there was room for her kind of work—the old school never went out of style. She would not give up her dream. No, not this time! She would go for it! She knew that it might take a long time, and she tried to silence the rising worries about what would happen if her money ran out. She couldn't go back to London. There was nothing left for her there.

"I will do it!" she promised herself and then turned her face to the sun.

She paid for her breakfast and walked back to the hotel. On the way, she bought a fresh baguette, some cheese and two bottles of the cheapest wine. She reached out for a bottle of brandy but restrained herself and didn't take it. She also bought a paper and an art magazine.

In her room, she carefully marked up what she had spent on the food and started to read the paper. But she could not get Margaret out of her mind. She felt very bad about the way she had treated her.

"I must apologize and ask her to forgive me. After all, she is the only person I can count on!"

Edith went down to the reception desk where there was a pay phone. The clerk gave her coins, and she dialled Margaret's number. It was Saturday morning—she hoped Margaret was home. The phone kept ringing for a long time, but there was no answer. Disappointed, Edith hung up. She went back to her room and continued to read the paper, but she could not concentrate. Looking at the black rooftop across the street, she could see a few pigeons sitting peacefully and cooing in the sun. She became unsteady and her head started to pound, a sure sign of an approaching migraine. She took some painkillers and went to bed.

Margaret got home from her shopping just after noon. She checked her phone to see if anyone had called. She didn't have an answering service, but the phone registered callers' numbers. There was one from her daughter and one long-distance call, but she didn't recognize the area code. It bothered her, and she wanted to know where the call came from. Maybe it was Edith.

She went looking for the phone book, but she couldn't find it. After a while she remembered she had thrown it out because the big book took up so much room on her already cluttered shelves, and she rarely used it. She called the directory, and they told he it was a Paris code number. Margaret was sure it could only be Edith. She called the number.

The call connected and a bored man's voice answered, "Hotel La Isly."

In flawless French, Margaret asked for Edith. The clerk told her there was no phone in her room and he couldn't go up to call her, but she could leave a message for him to pass on when the guest came down. Margaret started to argue, but the clerk just said, "Sorry" and hung up. Margaret was relieved that at least she knew where Edith was. Hopefully she'd call again.

Margaret checked the clock and saw that it was early morning in Toronto—she'd have to wait to call Elsa with the news about Edith. And maybe Edith would call back in the meantime and then she would know more.

The phone rang a few hours later, and Margaret picked up the phone on the first ring.

"Edith?" she almost shouted. "Where are you? Are you all right? What did you do? I was so worried that I went to London with Elsa, and the real estate woman who was in your flat told me you are in Paris! How—"

Edith cut in, "Margaret, I am grateful for your concern, but please do not worry about me. I am okay, but right now I'm recovering from a bad migraine and I can't talk. I just wanted you to know that I am fine. I promise I'll call you tomorrow and tell you everything. Please don't be angry with me, everything is in order. Please? I'll call you tomorrow night and we can talk."

"Well, okay, at least now I know where you are! Please call as soon as you can. Call collect if you have to, but call!"

"I promise I'll call tomorrow night after eight. Are you going to be home?"

"Yes! I'll wait for your call as long as I have to. Take care. Are you sure you okay?"

Edith stood by phone for a few minutes and then went up to her room.

She looked for her pills, found them and wanted to open the wine, but she stopped herself and put the bottle down. When she decided to start her new life, she made an oath to not take her migraine medication with alcohol. She had to be strong and depend on the drug only. But then the pounding became stronger and the pain worsened. She could not restrain herself, opened the wine and drank half of it from the bottle. She swallowed two of her migraine pills, and after a short hesitation she took a sleeping pill too, chasing it down with more wine. She put a wet towel on her forehead, but before she lay down on her bed, she finished the bottle of wine. Closing her eyes and waiting for the floating feeling and merciful darkness, Edith let her mind wander. Soon she was sobbing, feeling very sorry for herself and cursing life for her hardship. Sleep didn't come. She got up, opened the second bottle of wine, took a long gulp with another sleeping pill and soon felt her body relaxing. Her sobbing ceased, and she slept.

She dreamt of her mother. She was crying in a garden, but it changed into a cemetery with many broken headstones all over. One of the broken stones started to move, and her father came out from behind with her mother. The two of them went to a new-looking headstone, and Edith saw her name on it. She started towards her parents to comfort them and tell them it was all a mistake—she was alive and well—but her parents could not see her. She started to cry and ask their forgiveness for being an ungrateful daughter, but the earth opened under her and she felt herself falling faster and faster into a dark hole. She wanted to scream, but no sound came out, wanted to grab onto something to stop the falling but couldn't get hold of anything. Finally, a big scream broke from her throat.

She woke up to her own scream, jumped out of bed and hit herself on the night table beside her bed. She sat on the floor for a while and slowly came to her senses. Her head was still pounding, and her nightshirt was soaked in sweat. She got up with some difficulty, went to the bathroom, washed her face, got rid of the wet nightshirt, put a towel around her body and went back to bed. She felt dead tired and unable to get up again. Looking at her watch, she saw it was after ten in the morning.

"I am going to rest for awhile and then go out for coffee," she told herself as she fell into a deep sleep.

When she woke up again she felt calm. Stretching her body, she looked out the window. It was raining and the raindrops ran down on the glassin little, curving streams. The sky was dark grey, and she could see a few lights on in the windows across the street. It was now after seven o'clock in the evening. She wanted to turn over and rest a bit more, but then she remembered her promise to call Margaret. She suddenly felt famished and knew she had to eat something. She still had the sour taste of the wine and the pills in her mouth. She got up, threw something on and went out to the small bistro close to the hotel. After eating, she felt much better and strong enough to make the call to Margaret.

"Hello, Margaret," she said after the call went through. "I'm sorry to call later than I promised, but I went out to eat and service was slow. It took me an hour just to get my very simple order of veal and fries."

"That's okay, I wasn't planning to go out tonight. It is miserable here—raining and grey"

"It's raining here too."

There was a long silence. Neither of them knew how to start the conversation.

Finally Margaret said, "Edith, what happened with you? Why did you decided to go to Paris so suddenly and leave everything behind? How are you planning to live? What are you going to do? Just, what the hell are you doing?"

"Margaret, I'm starting a completely new life! I needed the change. I was standing still with nowhere to go. I've always wanted to live in Paris, so I want to start my new life here."

"Yes, I can understand that, but how could you do it without organizing your affairs first? As far as I know, your French is not that good, you don't know anybody there and you don't know how much you'll get for your flat. How do you know what kind of a place you can afford there? What happened with your stall? Did you leave everything behind? I can go on and on. I think it was a very foolish thing to run off like that. You had plenty of the time to think and make sensible decisions about changing your life."

"Margaret, if I started to think about it, I would never go ahead with it, and I would be just as miserable for the rest of my life. I had to do it. Can't you understand?"

"No, I can't! You are an intelligent, middle-aged woman. You can't run around like an ignorant teenager! Do you have any plans for what you are going to do for a living? The money, whatever you have, won't last forever! In London at least you had roots and a small business."

"Don't you understand? I hated my life there! I had to get out!"

"You could go to Paris without giving up everything. You could rent out your place for a few months or a year, and if you liked your life in Paris you could move there permanently. Please think about it. Call the agency and cancel the sale! Stay in Paris for a few weeks or as long as you can afford it, look around, see if it is what you really want and then make your move. What will happen if you fall into one of your depressions there? You are not quite well yet!"

"I am, and I don't want to listen to your anxiety anymore! I know you care about me, but I'll live my life as I want and face the consequences! It is my life!"

Edith could tell she had stunned Margaret with her harsh tone. She wished for a moment that she were completely sober, but she knew her words were spoken from her heart.

"Well, do it your way," Margaret said huffily, "but if you need anything you know where I am!"

After hanging up the phone, Edith went up to her room. Fuming, she walked circles in her room. How dare Margaret tell her what to do? On what authority could she tell her that she was wrong? How could she butt into her life? She didn't need mothering! She was perfectly able to look after herself! She would show Margaret and the rest of the world that she was a smart woman!

Edith put on her coat and went out. She walked around a bit, and feeling the chill taking over her body, she dropped into a bar and ordered a Calvados. The bar was half-empty as it was too early yet for the night crowd. A few older men sat at one table playing cards, and a woman about Edith's age sat at the other end of the bar. When Edith ordered a second Calvados, the woman came over and said, "Hello, you are English, aren't you?"

Edith looked at the woman more closely. Her unmistakable British accent gave away her roots, and she was a few years younger than Edith by her looks, well dressed and just a bit pallid. She had makeup on, but it was not very well applied. She looked at Edith with dark, sparkling eyes.

"Yes, I am."

"Are you visiting?"

Edith was happy to have someone to talk to, so she told the woman that she came from London and was planning to live in Paris.

After a few minutes, the woman introduced herself as Barb Clark. They ordered a third drink, left the barstools and sat down at a table.

The Calvados made Edith feel warm inside, and Barb's attention as she listened to Edith's story made her fall into her old habit of colouring up her life.

"You're a painter?" asked Barb, impressed. "You exhibited your work in London and sold most of them last year? That's fascinating! What kind of paintings you do?"

"Mostly landscapes. Sometimes I do portraits, but those I only do for previous arrangements. I have been to Paris several times. I love the atmosphere of this city. I decided to retire here and just paint when the mood strikes me."

"Where are you staying? Did you find a place yet?"

"No, I am in a small hotel where I stayed a few times when I was young. It was fine then, but I must say I don't like it so much now and am in the process of finding some other accommodation until I can get myself a permanent place."

Barb looked at her for a while without speaking and then with a friendly smile said, "What a coincidence! I don't want to push myself on you, but I am presently looking for a roommate who'll share the rent with me. I have an apartment. It is a small place, but it has two bedrooms. My old roommate left for a job in the south of France. She will not be back for more than six months, which would leave you plenty of time to look for a suitable place."

Edith's mind told her this was coming too fast and she shouldn't agree, but she was lonely in her stingy hotel room with nobody to talk to.

"Where is your place?"

"Just around the corner, on Rue Lucien Sampaix and the banks of Canal St. Martin. It is a nice, quiet street. The apartment is on the top floor of an old, five-story house. But we have the usual shoebox-sized elevator, so when it's working I don't have to climb all those steps. It is cozy, with a living room, bathroom and kitchen aside from the two bedrooms. There is enough space for two people to be comfortable. My roommate only took her personal belongings and left her furniture. She pays a fraction of her share of the rent for that. I don't want to move, so I am stuck paying the full rent. You could pay her full share and we could make arrangements for other expenses."

"Well, this sounds very tempting. I am interested. What are you doing here in Paris?"

"I have been living here for more than two years. I teach English in a private girls' school, and I work most days from ten in the morning until three in the afternoon. I don't like to be alone and I could use a woman's company like yours! I am dying to have someone around who speaks intelligent English! I've collected a few nice friends during the past two years to whom I could introduce you. They are French, but it would be a big help to you for getting familiar with the language. What do you say? Do you want to come over to inspect the place?"

Edith didn't want to be too eager to except the offer, so she looked at her watch and said, "It is too late now. Why don't we meet here again tomorrow after you finish working? I'll come over then."

"Deal. I'll be here after four. What about one more drink? My treat, but this time you should try absinthe, the real French drink. Have you had it before?"

"No, I've only heard about it. They say it is a very dangerous drink and can get you mad drunk."

"True, but one won't hurt," said Barb as she signalled the bartender for two. "You must have a taste of it. Otherwise, you can never claim to be Parisian!" she said, laughing.

After they said their goodbyes, Edith walked back to her hotel. Her head was spinning and she could hardly keep her balance. When she got into her room, she realized that she was very hungry. She was too tipsy to go out again, so she chewed on the half-dry baguette and the cheese, rinsed it down with the leftover wine and went to bed.

She thought about how nice it would be to have a human being around to socialize and go out with. She liked Barb, and before she fell asleep she decided that she was going to take her offer. She could always move out if it didn't work out!

Barb, who had been following Edith at a safe distance, walked into the hotel lobby and asked the porter about the lady who had just walked in. When the concierge said he couldn't give out any information about their guests, Barb put ten euros down on his desk. The man told her Edith's name and that even though she had an English passport, she was born in Hungary and paid for her room with a valid Visa card. He also mentioned that she had only one suitcase and a portfolio case. Barb thanked the man and walked away.

Chapter 24

"It's not a good idea to take Andrew to the park, Elsa," Paula said. Paula had come home unexpectedly early while Elsa was over visiting her grandson for the customary one day a week. She had wanted to take him to the park and treat him with an ice cream. "There is a flu virus going around, and I don't want him to get it from the other kids there."

"Okay, then we will just walk over to Baskin Robbins to get an ice cream. I promised him we'd go."

"But Elsa, he just got over a sore throat, didn't the nanny tell you? He can't have ice ream! Maybe some other time."

Elsa was taken aback, she but didn't say a word. She went back to Andrew's room and played with him until Paula called him for dinner, though it was far too early for his dinnertime.

"I'm sorry, but I have to meet David at his office. We're taking an important client of his out for dinner. I came home early to supervise Andrew's supper. I can't really rely on the nanny, no matter how trustworthy she is. She would let Andrew get away with anything, like not eating his vegetables and having two portions of dessert. Would you like to stay? I'm sorry but this meeting is very important for both of us."

"Yes, I'll stay. Why don't you go and get ready. I'll make sure Andrew eats everything he should. I'm sorry I couldn't meet David—I was hoping to see him too," said Elsa.

Paula's lips tightened, but she had smiled when she said, "I'll tell him and I'm sure he'll call you tomorrow. Andrew, be a good boy and don't tire Grandma out. I'll come back in later and give you a kiss." And she left.

Elsa stayed until Andrew had his bath and the nanny put him to bed. She read him a bedtime story and then left. Her heart was aching because she felt like an unwanted visitor in her son's house. Paula had always been jealous of David, and now she was just as jealous of Andrew and used every possible chance to keep Elsa away from them. She knew that Elsa still had a strong influence on David no matter how much she wanted to end it, and she obviously didn't want the same to happen with Andrew.

Elsa tried everything possible to convince Paula that she just loves her family and doesn't want to interfere with their lives. She always tried to be affectionate towards Paula, hoping that their relationship improved. Elsa knew that Paula was a smart woman and would not try to turn David against her, but she was clever enough to keep Elsa a safe distance from her husband and son without them noticing anything.

Elsa was bitter. She have given up so much in her life for her son. She wanted to be needed so badly that in the end she had become the needy one!

"And there is nobody else to blame but myself," she said at the first red traffic light as she wiped the tears from her eyes.

Elsa let herself in to her apartment and looked around as she always did, waiting for the comforting feeling she got when stepping into her home. But her heart was heavy and even that could not cheer her up. She made herself a cup of tea and sat on her balcony with a book to get her mind off her sorrow. It didn't work.

She couldn't shut out her thoughts. She read the lines in the book but they meant nothing. She gave up, put the book down and as always when she was in distress, her mind wandered to the past—to Tom.

Why had she given him up? If she could, she would change everything back to how it was. The quiet evenings in Vancouver, looking at the water from Tom's bay window and watching the lights come up on the bridge and in other houses. How much she liked to read there as she waited for him. And when he did arrive from the office, the room lit up and became even warmer. It was a nest for two people who loved and trusted each other. Tom always bought some flowers for the dinner table on his way home. They could talk endlessly after dinner because they knew each other inside out and knew what the other was thinking. Why was it that Tom hadn't fought harder for her when he got her letter about not coming back? Perhaps it was because he knew that no matter how much they loved each other, he couldn't make her happy if her relationship with her son suffered because of him. And she herself was melodramatic enough to think that her presence in her son's life was very much needed! What a bitter awakening! She was not needed at all! Her son led his own life and seemed to be happily married. Sure, he was affectionate and loving toward his mother, but he had his own family to spend his emotions and love on first of all. She felt alone and useless.

Sàndor had married his mistress a long time ago. He was retired now and lived in Florida. Elsa and he had remained friends and talked a few times in a year, and when Sàndor came to Toronto to visit David and Andrew or to celebrate Christmas or some birthday, she was invited to family dinner too. Sàndor's second wife was an intelligent, nice woman, and they never felt ill at ease with each other.

She wondered how Tom was doing now. She hadn't heard from him for quite a while. He used to call her now and then, and they always had a long conversation, both of them feeling the same ache for each other. She knew that he was in Africa somewhere it was difficult to call from, and yes, she missed his voice and his person terribly. Oh, what she would give if they could go back to the way they were! She shook her head to get rid of that hopeless wish, stood up and went to take a shower.

"I can only blame myself," she said again. "I am a sentimental, over-conscientious, old woman!"

After stepping out of the shower, she looked at her naked body in the mirror and gave her image a sad smile.

"Well, not so old yet—I am still a woman!"

Her body ached for Tom's caressing hand, his warm kisses on her neck and his body entangled with hers. She closed her eyes—she didn't want to look at her body anymore. It became a throbbing shield for her emotions. She threw herself on the bed, embraced her pillow and cried.

She did her chores during the days, and in the evenings she tried to fulfill the promise she gave to Margaret. After she came back from Budapest, she had dug up her old notebooks and photographs and started to put her thoughts on paper. Sometimes she didn't notice the hours ticking away as she sat at her desk, her fingers flying across the computer keys. There were other days, however, when she could not write a word, and despite her struggles her mind stayed empty. Those times made her lose courage and stop writing for days or even weeks. But after a while she would just start again. She hoped that by writing out her feelings and thoughts she'd become a more objective individual, get to know herself much better and deal with her life accordingly.

The phone rang. Elsa sniffed and wiped the tears from her cheeks before answering.

"Hi, Elsa, I was thinking about you! I always say I love to be alone, but after two days I just can't cope with it. I have to talk to people."

"Hi, Lili. I wanted to call you yesterday, but it was too early over there, and when I came home it was too late. How is Michael?"

"He is still in the hospital. The doctors said it was a mini stroke and he'll recover soon. Hopefully there will not be any after-effects. They also warned that the same thing could happen again. He is coming home in a few days. How are you?"

"I'm fine. I had a "feeling sorry for myself" evening, but it is over now. I am good as new!"

"Problems with your darling daughter-in-law?"

"Nothing new, just the usual bickering, but sometimes I can't take it calmly."

"Well, you should, you know her. I can never understand why you live alone in your ivory tower. You should go out and find somebody!"

"Your old storyline again! I told you I am too old to change my ways. I can't imagine having somebody beside me."

"How about Tom? Have you ever thought about him?"

"He is far away, and it is an old story."

"Yes, but I can't see why it can't be a new one again. When did he call you last?"

"About a month ago. He was in Africa. I haven't heard from him since."

"But Elsa, be honest and tell me—if he materialized at your door, would you send him away?"

"I don't fantasize about that!" she lied. "Tell me what's happening with your big business deal!"

"Obviously, I can't talk it over with Michael for a while, but I am thinking about it, and I still want Tivadar to come to Sydney and go over everything in person. I've decided to wait on a decision until Michael recovers fully, which I hope will be soon. To tell you the truth, I am not looking forward to that period—I'll be chained down in the house. I think I'll hire a nurse or somebody for a few hours each day so I can get out."

"Lili, don't do anything hasty no matter how bored you are!"

"Okay, you over-precautious woman, I promise! What did you hear from Margaret? Did Edith show up?"

"It's just as I told you last time. She called Margaret from Paris and said she was going to call later and tell her everything because she had a bad migraine at the time and didn't want to talk. She is holed up in some cheap hotel there."

"You know, I do admire her guts!"

"I think she was a fool to put her place on the market and move without doing any kind of research or thinking about her future."

"There you go again, you'll never change. You have to chew things over so many times before you decide on something! But the one you didn't do it, it became the best time of your life! Think about that!"

"Okay, okay. Let me know how Michael is doing and take care of yourself. And don't smoke too much, you sound like Louis Armstrong!"

The talk with Lili made Elsa wonder. It was true that she never let herself seriously think about what she would do if Tom appeared in her life again. She yearned for him, and she did occasionally dream about their lovemaking and then wake up feeling empty. But maybe she was just hanging on and nursing the good memories. She knew people were inclined to remembering the good and letting the bad fade away.

By now Tom could have found someone and be living happily somewhere in Africa! But her heart refused to believe it.

"Why I am whining like a lovesick schoolgirl? He was the love of my life, I ended it because I wanted to end it so there is no reason to dwell over it."

She brooded for a while longer and then opened up her laptop and started to write. Soon she was absorbed in her work. The ringing of the phone brought her back to the present.

"Hello, Mother, how are you?" David's voice asked. "I am sorry I missed you the other day and didn't call yesterday, but so many things are going on in the office that I hardly have enough time to eat."

"Is that a good sign or a bad sign? In any case, you work too hard! You should take a holiday somewhere with no newspapers or TV—just the blue sea and warm sand. You do overwork yourself. It is dangerous for your health, no matter how young you are!"

"Mother, I am over forty. That's not young anymore!"

"Then it should teach you that life is running fast and you have to take time out to enjoy it! Anyway, you didn't call me for my motherly advice. What's new?"

"I want to ask you to have dinner with me on Thursday. Just you and me at your favourite restaurant—I have to talk to you! No, don't get alarmed, it's nothing bad. Are you going to be free?"

"Yes, of course! But what is it? Can't you give me a hint now?"

"No way! You have to wait until Thursday! I'll pick you up just after seven. Bye, Mom!"

Elsa set to wondering. David hadn't sounded at all worried or troubled but rather cheerful. What could have happened? It must be something very important because he didn't invite her for lunch, and it was just for the two of them. What would Paula say? *Well, I'll know all about it in a few days*, she thought.

Now that she had lost her mood for writing, she looked in the TV guide, checking if there was something worthwhile to watch, but she didn't find anything. She decided to go out for a walk to the park before her dinner. The park was busy in the early evening hour.

People were walking their dogs, and a number of dog owners were standing in a circle, discussing training secrets with their fellow dog walkers and showing off their pets' obedience. There were nannies and young mothers pushing strollers, and the little kids in the sandbox and on the swings were screaming because they didn't want to go home yet. Mothers pleaded with them, saying it was time to start dinner. Older couples walked slowly hand in hand. Groups of teenagers talked and laughed while sitting on the grass. It seemed to Elsa that she was the only one alone! She shook her head, pushing away the sad thoughts. Why should she feel sorry for herself? She was healthy, and she could do whatever she pleased. If she wanted to travel, she just had to lock her apartment and go. There was nobody to hold her back or be worried for. She had friends to share her thoughts and feelings with. True, she had no partner to hold and comfort her when she felt the need for a warm body beside her, someone who could remind her that she was still a living woman.

"You can't have everything, just count your blessings!" she reminded herself.

Her thoughts went back to David and any possible reason for a dinner with just the two of them. Surely it was not problem in his marriage. They seemed happy together. They adored Andrew, made lots of money and had a lovely, big house. Elsa always thought it was far too big and modern to be a cozy home, but they were nicely settled in it. Perhaps there was a new baby on the way? That couldn't be, because then Paula should be there too to break the happy news! After a while she gave up guessing and walked home.

She didn't feel like cooking, so she called the Chinese takeout and ordered dinner. As usual, got lost in the menu and ordered too many dishes—she'd eat Chinese for a week. She set her table, lit a candle, opened up a bottle of good red wine and put on her favourite CD, one of Frank Sinatra's. "Going My Way" came on and she made believe that she couldn't be more satisfied with her life.

On Thursday evening, she dressed with care and waited for David. He was on time as usual.

"Mother, you look great! You can easily renounce a dozen years of your age!"

"Thank you, you sweet liar! Where are we going?"

"I made reservation at the old favourite of yours—the Barbarian Steak House."

"Is it still there? I think it's been at least twenty years ago since I last had dinner there. Your father and I were regulars. He loved their rib eye steak, but I liked their "fried apple with ice cream" dessert the most. Are they at the same location on Elm Street?"

"Yes, let's go. I am famished. I didn't have time for lunch—just a donut and coffee at my desk."

The restaurant had lost some of its old charm and seemed much smaller and darker than Elsa remembered, but she was happy to be there again.

They ordered dinner and Elsa looked at David expectantly. "Are you going tell me why we are here or do I have to pry it out of you?" she asked.

"Mother, I got an offer from the firm which I couldn't refuse," David said, taking a deep breath. "As I told you before, we are expanding into international law. We have offices in the U.S. and some in Europe, and now we are going to open a branch in South America. I was offered an important position there, thanks to your hammering on me to learn more than two languages."

Elsa almost choked on her excellent tender steak.

"South America? Where in South America?'

"Buenos Aires."

"David, that is at the other end of the globe! Are you going to take it? How long do you have to stay there? Are you going to move there?"

"Mother, one question at a time. Yes, I am going to take it. Well, I already signed the papers. That important dinner the other night was with the head of my firm. I made the decision together with Paula, of course. My income will be tripled for the first two years with all the expense allowances, and after that I'll have shares in the firm and bonuses if I do a good job. And yes, of course we have to move there. I signed a six-year contract."

"But, David, when did all this start? It could not have happened in the last weeks."

"No, I've known and negotiated about it for more than four months. But I didn't want to upset you before it became positive."

Elsa was deeply hurt. She knew at once that Paula was behind it. She was afraid Elsa's influence would make David hesitate to take the offer.

David looked at her mother and reached for her hand over the table.

"See, you are upset! I didn't want you to worry for four months about what's going to be. Buenos Aires is not at the end of the word—you can be there in nine hours. It is a civilized, modern town with safe drinking water, concerts, operas, theatres and so on. You'll come to visit and stay with us during the miserable winter months in Toronto. The firm rented us a lovely, big penthouse apartment on the most exclusive avenue in the city. And it has several guest rooms. This move doesn't mean that we are cut off from each other!"

Elsa was struggling to withhold her tears.

"Yes, but I won't get to take part in Andrew's growing up years. He'll forget me. I'll be just a faraway grandma who sends birthday gifts!"

"That will not happen. We will always be in touch on the phone and e-mail. There is a new technology that even lets us see each other on the computer. You'll be able to read bedtime stories to him!"

Elsa was silent for a long time, fighting with her tears.

"Mother, you must understand that this is great opportunity to establish our family's future! I could retire as a rich man by the time I am sixty. And besides that, this is a very honourable challenge for me! I have to make the sacrifice of moving far away from you, but it will be only by measurable distance and not by heart. You know I love you and admire you! I am sorry to cause you this heartache!"

Elsa was afraid to ask the next question, but she did. "Did you discuss this with your father?"

The answer came as she expected it.

"Yes, I visited him last month, and we talked it over. He was very supportive and excited about the whole thing!"

Elsa's heart dulled with pain. David discussed everything with Sàndor but only let her know when the decision was already made. He didn't trust her unselfishness! She felt overlooked and let down by her son, who was the most important person in her life. She managed a smile, but she couldn't avoid her tears.

"David, I am proud of you. This is a great step up in your carrier. To bad that it had to happen this way, but it is your life and I can't interfere. I don't have the right to do so. I can't lie and promise you that it will be painless for me to live so far from you and my only grandson, but I'll be all right. And I hope and wish from the bottom of my heart that everything will turn out the best for you!"

"That's my mother! You are wonderful! I love you dearly! As soon as we settle down, I'll send you airplane tickets so you can see where we live. Maybe you can talk Lili into coming also."

"When are you moving?"

"I'll go on the 26th, and Paula and Andrew will follow me as soon as I get the place ready for them. The apartment is furnished, so we'll just take our personal belongings and buy whatever we need there. The firm will foot the bill. We will store the furniture and rent out our house. I am not going to sell it because I intend on living here later."

"That's only ten days from now!"

"Yes, I know. We are going to give a big farewell party at the house next week and of course you are invited. You'll come, won't you?"

That night Elsa couldn't sleep. She lit a fire in the fireplace and sat in front of it for most of the night. She could now fully understand the agony her parents felt when she left them so suddenly. If their pain was just half of it what she currently felt, it must have been devastating.

"You can't get away with your guilt without atonement in life. You have to pay for it sooner or later," she said to herself mournfully. She thought about Andrew's little hands in her own, his wide-open eyes when she read him bedtime stories, his welcoming smile when he ran out to greet her, the warmth of his little body on her lap ... she'd be deprived of all this in just a few weeks. Andrew would grow up far from her, and soon she would become nothing else than a distant relative in his life, no matter how often she was able to visit them.

The darkness of the night slowly gave away to the greyness of the dawn. The sky turned lighter, promising a new day. Elsa's fire went out, and the small chunks of the glowing embers lit Elsa's face and made her tears look like dark rubies as they rolled slowly down her cheeks. Elsa looked at the faint glow of the embers for a long time and felt that her life had just lost its last glow. With a deep sigh, she got up from her chair and went to bed.

Chapter 25

Margaret didn't hear from Edith for more than a week. Finally, when she could not hold out any longer, she called the hotel. The concierge told her that Madam Edith Kalmar checked out four days ago. No, she didn't leave any new address behind.

Margaret decided to give up on her. After all, she had done everything she could and offered her help and support, but if she didn't need it then so be it. She had to forget about Edith. She was not worth worrying about—she had ceased acting like a friend.

A few days later, there was a letter in her mailbox addressed in Edith's handwriting. She almost threw it out without reading it, wanting to forget the whole affair, but she couldn't. Back in her apartment, she made her customary thick espresso and sat down at her cluttered desk, still debating whether she should or shouldn't read the letter? If she opened it she would have to respond to it. She should send it back unopened to make Edith understand that she doesn't want to be in her confidence anymore. Their friendship was finished.

"Oh, what the hell," she said and reached for her letter opener.

Margaret,

Please forgive me and read my letter. I know I behaved unforgettably rude and horrid. I don't deserve you as a friend. Your friendship was the only fixed point in my miserable life. You always let me cry on your shoulder, gave me advice and stood by me even when I acted against it.

Please forgive my behaviour and read my letter.

As I told you, I wanted to start a completely new life. I knew if I stayed in my old environment I would never be able to get out of my desolation. I knew I should discuss it with you or at least call you about my decision. There is no excuse for not doing so, but I was afraid that your logical advice would make me uncertain and afraid to act. So I did it alone.

I am sorry about my conduct when I called, but I was just getting over a very bad migraine, I was lonely and I felt sorry for myself. But now I can tell you that my self-pity and doubts are over. I have become a new person. At last!

I moved out of the hotel and moved in with a newfound friend, a remarkable woman who understands me and helped me settle down here. She is English and she is teaching English in a private girls' school. She has a two-bedroom place. I rent one of the bedrooms and we share the food expenses. Her name is Barb Clark, she is a few years younger than I am and a lively, easygoing person full of humour and laughter—just what I need in my life right now. She has lived here for more than two years and knows quite a few people. She will help me to look for a gallery which might be interested in my work. She insists on speaking French and she is very unyielding about it. It is possible that she could get me a part-time job at her school as an art teacher as soon as my French is suitable.

Dear Margaret, I am content and happy to be here, a feeling I haven't had for a very long time! Please don't worry about me.

I let the real estate people know my address. So far there are no offers for my place, but they can call me if they get one. I'll go back to finalize everything (I am absolutely sure that I want to live here) and bring over whatever I need for my new home. As hot as the real estate market in London is nowadays, I'll probably sell well and have enough money for a new home here and to live on with the help of a teaching job and hopefully painting.

I'll have to ask you to send over my suitcase to the address below. I'll mail you a money order for the expenses, so please let me know how much it was.

Please, dear friend, answer my letter and let me know that you did forgive me.

Barb has a computer, and since I know you hate to go to the post office, the e-mail address is below as well. Please write. I'll always treasure your friendship.

Thank you for everything,

Edith

Margaret put down Edith's letter feeling relieved, but she could not help thinking that all this sounded far too cheerful to be real—it was not in Edith's character. But it was real and the drastic change was actually what she needed to survive her depressions and migraines. Maybe she was on the right track and even stopped drinking!

"I hope that her new friendship will last and that Barb is an honest person and going to be a true friend," she thought as she put the letter on top of her computer. "True friendship can happen a short time, just like it happened with Elsa and me."

She turned on the computer to write Elsa with the news about Edith.

The summer recess was coming soon, and Margaret was making plans for her two months off. Regarding her bank account, she couldn't go anywhere far. Of course she'd spend a week with her daughter and granddaughter, Annie, whom she didn't see as much as she would have liked. She was planning to bring her to her place and let her daughter have a week or so for herself.

Lately, Klàri sounded tired and overworked, so it would be good for her to be free. She would entertain Annie, who was a smart little girl and interested in everything. There were so many things to do, like the zoo, the puppet theatre, the circus and the walks on Castle Hill. They could drive to Lake Balaton for a few days and stay in a guesthouse somewhere close to a nice, safe beach.

After that, Margaret decided she would fly to Munich for a visit with her son, who sent her a round-trip ticket every summer. She was looking forward to being with him—the last time they were together was at Christmas. They did talk on the phone every week, but to be with him was a treat. He was very close to her, much closer than Klàri.

Margaret often did soul searching about this but could never find the real reason. She brought them up with the same amount of love and motherly care, and she never favoured or gave advantage to either of them. Nevertheless, they turned out differently in their relationship with her. It could be because Klàri inherited more of her father's self-absorption and behaviour. Margaret had hoped that the birth of her granddaughter would bring them closer, but the circumstances of her pregnancy (she was not married and the father took off as soon as he learned about the baby) was a constant obstruction.

Klàri had stayed with Margaret for a few months after the baby was born. Margaret did everything she could to help, but Klàri had different ideas about how to bring up a baby. The apartment was too small, the baby cried a lot at night and both of them were tired and irritated. When an opportunity came up employment outside of Budapest, Klàri took it and they moved there. Esztergom was only an hour by bus, and Margaret tried to visit them almost every Sunday. She missed them at first but had to admit that it was good to be on her own again. Later, when Klàri met her man and they moved in together, her visits were less frequent. Margaret didn't like him, and timed her visits for when Klàri's partner was away. That happened often, as he was a technical advisor in the Toyota plant there and was sent out to dealerships all over Hungary.

Margaret's son, Istvàn, was a quiet, warm-hearted artist who loved his job and was very good at it. He was in the process of leaving his employment and setting up a private business. He had become a well-known interior designer and felt he was ready to strike out on his own. His long-time partner was a writer who wrote mystery novels and sometimes made enough money from them to live on. He was

German, tall, blond and good looking. They were soul brothers and had lived together for six years now. Margaret got along fine with him. He was very considerate and went to visit his sister, who lived outside of Munich, whenever Margaret came to stay. Istvàn told Margaret that he had already rented a showroom and an office, and she was enthusiastic to see it. She liked Munich—the old town and the beer halls where she would go with Istvàn to drink beer at the long tables and sing with the locals.

And the rest of the summer? There would be many projects, like having the bathroom repainted, reorganizing her closets and throwing out old clothing. Her closets were so full of old, unused things that she had to open them carefully so the contents wouldn't spill onto the floor. But first of all she would go on a strict diet—all her skirts and pants were too tight.

With a deep sigh, she got up from her desk and stood at the window. The street below was busy. Early tourist groups were walking in and out of the souvenir shops, and street vendors were selling postcards and ice cream. She thought about Edith again. Edith's sudden change still bothered her, though she knew she should feel liberated from all the responsibilities she felt for her. Edith had a new life, and Margaret had no major part in it. Edith had a new friend, a new shoulder to cry on if she had to. She should be happy for her and wish her the best of luck in her new life. But why *couldn't* she be happy for her? Maybe because she knew Edith far too well to believe that everything had suddenly turned out so rosy. She recalled the fiasco with Antal and how Edith had fallen under his spell in a very short time, fell in love with him in two days and blindly believed everything he told her.

"No use brooding over her. I need some fresh air and exercise," she told herself and went out for a walk.

She walked down to the esplanade by the Danube, and after a short hesitation crossed Lånc Bridge over to the other side. It was a lovely June afternoon. Once on the other side of the bridge, she sat on the steps leading to the riverbank and watched the rapidly flowing water for a long time. The river was so peaceful and eternal that after a while her worries floated away with it, her spirits rose and she felt light on her feet. She decided to walk up the numerous steps to the top of Castle Hill.

"After all, I must start exercising seriously if I want to get back into my old pants without any discomfort," she encouraged herself. She walked slowly, but she had to stop a few times to catch her breath. She had to admit that she was sadly out of shape.

When she reached the first bench at the Fisherman's Bastion, she gratefully flopped down.

"I should do this more often before I go to Munich so I'll be able to keep up with Istvàn on those long, mountain passes he likes to go to so much," she muttered herself.

She sat there, content, relaxed and thinking about Istvàn. Her soul smiled, and as she closed her eyes, the smile slowly took over her lips and let the time slip by.

Suddenly, as if lightening had hit her, she picked up her head. Someone was talking to her in Italian. It was a male voice. Her heart started to beat faster and she was afraid to open her eyes. When she finally looked up, there was nobody beside her. Two men had just passed by her bench talking loudly in Italian—tourists.

Margaret was shaken. How could that happen? It was so many years ago! She had wiped out the last memories a long time ago. She hardly ever thought of Roberto anymore! True, in the last months she had talked about him to Elsa, but it was just a reminiscence of her youth and nothing else. If that was true, how could a few Italian words have such an affect on her? She got up from the bench and walked to the bus stop. She didn't feel strong enough anymore for all those steps.

On the way home, she thought about Roberto. What became of him? He was most likely fat—he liked his pasta and wine just as much as his women.

"Oh, what's the use. I should stop thinking about him and let him fade away into the past for good! I should make plans for Annie's visit instead!"

When she got home to her empty apartment, she could not shake off the feeling of loneliness. She thought about calling Elsa, but she had to watch her budget with the summer visits coming up.

She made herself a sandwich and sat down at her desk to draw up a plan for Annie's visit. It was after nine when the phone rang. She hesitated to pick it up since nobody ever called her in the evenings, but her curiosity over took her.

"Hello?" she said.

"Hi, Margaret."

"Elsa! What a surprise! Is something wrong?" she asked, hearing Elsa's muffled voice.

"Sorry to frighten you, but I must talk to someone or I'll suffocate myself!"

"Elsa, what happened?"

"David is going to move to South America for six years! I just can't bear this news alone."

She then told Margaret the whole story of David's promotion and how much she was offended by the fact that he let her know only when the decision was made.

"Do you think I'm over reacting?" asked Elsa with shaking voice. "Please tell me that I am."

Margaret thought for a while and then said, "No, I don't think so. They should have discussed it with you when they started the process, but it's possible that David didn't want to burden you with worries before it became final."

"Yes, that's what he told me, but he discussed it with his father months before and asked for his advice. I just know that Paula was the one who told him not to talk about it with me because I might influence him with my reaction to the idea of my son and grandson living so far away from me! I am devastated. I'll be as much alone here as a drop of water in the desert!"

"Elsa, I believe it was painfully shocking news for you, but you have to get over it. You are a strong, smart, independent woman. David has to live his own life, and you have to cut the umbilical cord at last. You should have had your own life without him for a long time already! He will always love you and you can always count on him—that's for sure! And you know there are no distances anymore. The word has shrunk and become incredible small!"

Elsa was quiet on the other end of the line.

"Elsa, are you there? Please talk to me."

"Yes, I am here and you are right. I had to hear you to tell me what I knew anyway, but my oversensitive emotions took over my brain.

Thanks, Margaret, for being so frank with me! I didn't even ask you how you are—I just started to whine. So how are you? School will be finished soon. Are you going anywhere for vacation?"

Margaret told Elsa about her plans with Annie, her visit to Istvàn and her determination to lose weight and get in shape. They talked about Lili's business plans and Edith's new life.

Suddenly, Elsa stopped mid-sentence and said, "Hey, I just got an idea. Why don't you come and visit me? Even with all your plans, you still have plenty of time for one more visit. Your closets can wait! It would do a lot of good for both of us. You have never been to this part of the globe, and your company could help me get over David's leaving. Please, Margaret."

"Elsa, it would be fantastic, but it is impossible. I can't afford such a trip. Maybe next year."

"Look, it will be my treat. After all, I was your guest for such a long time! I am going to send you a ticket—just let me know the dates. We'll have so much fun, and maybe Lili will drop over for a while too."

"I can't except your generosity, it wouldn't be right. I would like to see your world, but I have to wait until I can afford the ticket on my own. Then I will happily take you up on your hospitality."

"Please, please, Margaret, don't be such a stranger! You would be doing me a great favour if you came. The tickets don't cost much. I have lots of flying points and I can get it for almost nothing. Please come."

"I'll have to think about it. What if I send you an e-mail next week?"

"Okay, but please, please say yes!"

Chapter 26

The apartment Edith shared with Barb was small but cozy, and since her room opened onto the other end of the hallway from Barb's room, she had her privacy. The windows looked out towards the channel and a small park on the far side. They agreed that she would pay two hundred euros per month toward the rent and they'd split up the food shopping. One week it would be Barb's turn to fill up the refrigerator, and the next week Edith would do the shopping. They both looked after their own personal needs like shampoo, soap and so on. They also bought their own liquors aside from the three bottles of wine per week which were included with the grocery shopping.

Soon they settled down to a routine. Barb left every morning at nine and returned after four pm. Edith tidied up read the paper, looked up small galleries, but could not gather enough courage to ask for appointment in any of them. She read the papers and listened to the radio, watched TV to improve her French. She spent lots of time in the museums on Sundays. On weekdays she walked in the parks and sat at the outdoor tables of a small bar at the "Painter's square watching the artist work and they mostly unsuccessful attempt to sell. The evenings they were together with Barb went to the movies and afterward for a drink somewhere The one drink usually turned out to be three, sometimes four. They had great soul searching conversations. Barb brought out all the frustration from Edith's soul with her devoted attention. She cried with her hearing the story of Antal, and made funny comments to cheer Edith up. She introduced Edith to few people in her favourite bars. Somehow it was always Edith who paid the bills. Barb left her purse at home, or she just ran out of cash and so on. A month later Edith discovered that she had little money left, not even enough to pay het share of the rent for the next month.

She called the real-estate agent if there was any interest for the flat. The agent told her
that there was one but they could not come up with the down payment. But she had a client who would rent the flat as it is and sign up for a two-year lease. Edith decided to go home to close up her life there for good. She assured Barb that she'll pay her share as soon as she comes back and gave her all the money what was left after she bought the train ticket.

Edith opened the door to her flat and stepped in with mixed feelings and looked around at her familiar things. Her favourite armchair in front of the window where she used to sit and daydream, the tiny, cozy balcony off her bedroom where she put her easel to paint in the mornings when the sun started to shine. Her small kitchen, where the window opened to the west and she used to have her tea while watching the sun go down. But those feelings were not strong enough to change her mind.

"I want to live in Paris. I made up my mind and that's final. I will not hesitate and chicken out just because of some stupid sentimentality for old junk."

She called the agent and asked for a meeting. In the meantime, she went to her bank and looked over her account. It was in very bad shape. She desperately needed money to be able live in Paris, so she had agreed to rent her flat for a lower amount than she had hoped for. She called a moving company to have them pack her personal belongings and paid the bills with the first month's rent payment. She sold a few items from the flat and was lucky to get a nice sum for part of her clock collection. She kept her favourite pieces and sent them to storage with the rest of her personal belongings. She'd have them sent after her later. More than a dozen of her paintings packed by the moving company were to be sent with the first shipment of her things. She filled two suitcases with clothing she thought she would need to take immediately and then visited her friend at the market and offered her, her stall for the rest of the season free. After that there was only one thing left to do—go to the cemetery. She stood at Gabor's headstone and read his name on it many times, as if to engrave it in her heart forever. She couldn't think about anything, her mind was blank. Finally she just patted the gravestone and said, "Goodbye, Gabor. I am finally doing what we dreamed about together, but I am doing it alone."

On the train going back, she felt liberated. She had done it! Her old life was behind her, and she was ready to start the new one in the autumn of her life.

A few days after of her return, Barb suggested they throw a party to celebrate the beginning of her new life and to get to know new people. Barb invited more than a dozen various friends of hers. They set up a bar in the kitchen, pushed the living room furniture aside and threw pillows on the floor. Edith had a great time. Everybody accepted her and said her French was charming, so she eased up and was able to chat without being embarrassed by her accent.

It was a mixed group, mostly men between forty and sixty and a few artist-looking women about her age. There was one man who kept looking at her, noticing her empty glass and offering to fill it up. They started to talk. He was of medium height, just a bit taller than her, had a slightly balding head, dark intelligent eyes and light ebony skin.

He introduced himself as Jamal and said, "Would you mind if we talked in your language? It will be good for me to brush up on my English—it was a long time ago that I lived in England."

"I don't mind it at all, it would be a relief. I'm very tired from all the chatting in French—I have to concentrate on every word! Your English is very good, much better than my French. When did you live in England?"

"At least eight years ago. I was working for a French firm there. How long have you lived here?"

"Just about a month. I always dreamt about living in Paris and finally my dream materialized. I am staying with Barb temporarily until I find a suitable place of my own."

"It must be nice to effectuate your dream. Congratulations!"

"Oh, yes it is. I was waiting for this for long years. Are you a Parisian?

"Well, yes and no. I was born in Hammamet, Tunisia. It is a lovely resort town about sixty-four kilometres from Tunis. My father owned a carpet factory there. After I finished my basic schooling, he sent me to the Sorbonne to get educated and after that take over his business. But I am afraid I wasn't interested making and selling carpets. I was interested in art. I ended up as an art dealer and moved to Paris permanently. My father was very much disappointed and actually disowned me."

"Really! Do you have a gallery?"

"Yes, but just a small one on the Rue de Seine. I have a warehouse for the dealership. Barb told me that you are a painter. Is that so?"

"Yes, I am. I had a few exhibits in England. "

"Wonderful, what galleries?"

"I'm sure you never heard of them, they were very small."

"I would like to see your work. Would you like to show it to me?"

"I'd love to, but my things haven't arrived from London yet. Could I get touch with you later?"

"Yes, but why don't we meet before and get to know each other better? Are you free Thursday for dinner?"

Edith was pleasantly surprised. "Yes, I think so. It would be a pleasure."

"I'll pick you up at eight then. I have to say good night now, but I look forward to seeing you. It was really nice to talk to you."

Jamal bowed his head and then moved over to Barb. Edith followed him with her eyes. He talked to Barb for a few minutes, but since his back was turned to Edith, she could not follow their conversation.

The party went on for hours, and the last guest staggered out as dawn broke. Edith and Barb were so exhausted that as soon as the door closed behind him, they fell into their beds, leaving the clean up for the next day.

Edith was happy, and as always she started to build sand castles about her good fortune. He was so polite and nice looking. He was an art dealer. Even his skin colour excited her. She fantasized about his body, which had seemed to be lean and muscular under his well-cut suit.

I must ask Barb about him tomorrow, Edith thought, and then hoped he was not married or lived with a woman—or with men. She had read lots of stories about Arabic men.

When she fell asleep, she dreamt that she was standing at the railing of a boat on the Seine with Jamal. He looked at her with adoration and pulled her close.

Both Edith and Barb slept the better part of Sunday away and got up late in the afternoon.

"I saw you talking to Jamal," Barb said as the started to clean up the apartment. "How did you like him? He was very taken with you, he told me so!"

"Really? I liked him too. How long have you known him? He told me that he is an art dealer and has a gallery here in the city."

"I invited him because of you! I met him at a party in the first year I lived here. Yes, he is an art dealer, and a very successful one I must add. He makes lots of money. He is, I think, around sixty years old now and half retired. He spends lots of time in Tunis where his family runs many businesses, but he keeps a permanent home here too. I was involved with him for a while, but it didn't work out, so we are just friends now."

"Is he married?"

"He was twice but divorced both times. He says his biggest defeat in life is that he has no son—just two daughters from his second marriage. He is still a lady's man, so be careful you don't get taken by his charm! Or at least don't count on a serious relationship. He is just good for some pleasant nights and evenings!"

"He asked me about my painting and wants to take me out for dinner. Do you think I should go?"

"By all means. He is a gentleman, and who knows, if he likes your work he might give you an exhibition."

"My things won't be here for at least another week or two. But I do think it would be nice to have dinner with him."

"Yes, that's for sure. And he could be the break you need and have been waiting for so long," said Barb. Then she looked Edith over from head to toe. "We have to get you a new dress, though. You must look your best. I know a boutique where the owner is our age and very good at choosing the right things. She is a friend of a friend and will give us a discount too. I'll call her and we can go to see her on Tuesday. What do you say?"

"Oh, Barb, what would I do without you?" Edith said, but she shook her head. Thanks, darling, but I have to watch my money. I have a limited income for a while, and I can't be extravagant."

"You don't have to spend a lot of money in Paris to be fashionable and elegant! It is time for you to live for yourself!" said Barb and she kissed Edith on her cheeks. "And now let's finish up this mess and go out for dinner!"

Edith bought herself a lovely, long, many-coloured silk skirt, a red blouse, a black, woven vest, a necklace made from big brown beads and a new pair of earrings. Barb and the saleslady encouraged her to buy a new pair of shoes, so she chose a low-heeled pump. Looking herself in the mirror, she hardly believed the person in the mirror is she.

"Now we just have to do something about your hair," Barb said.

"I don't want to cut it. I like my hair long."

"Okay, just a trim then. And have it coloured. You will look years younger."

So Edith ended up spending half of what she got for her apartment in London each month.

"Well, this will last me forever, and I really needed a new look to go with my new life!" she consoled herself. "I'll spend much less next month!"

Barb scolded her, saying, "Don't fret, you deserve it. When was the last time you spent money on yourself? Life is for living. You look lovely—you can easily take off ten years from your age!"

"You look beautiful!" said Jamal when he picked her up on Thursday evening. His remark made her light on her feet and happy in her soul. He took her to a small but popular bistro walking distance from her apartment. The owner knew him and served them with the utmost attention. The food was excellent, as was the wine. During dinner they talked about themselves. Fuelled by the good wine and the cocktail before dinner, Edith fell in to her old habit of expanding on the truth.

She believed the story she told to Jamal—she was an independent, well-off woman living off her income from several investments and the income of her rented apartment in London. She just wanted to paint when she felt like it and live in Paris. She told the story of her youth in Hungary, promoting her parents to estate owners and herself to a society girl who got married for love against her parent's wishes and eloped to England. There they lived happily until her husband died in a car accident in the tenth year of their marriage.

Jamal spoke about his birthplace, the small resort town of Hammamet on the shores of the Mediterranean. He described the white sandy beaches, the crystal-clear blue sea, the fishermen's colourful boats, the restaurants, the food stalls and the relaxed atmosphere.

"Unfortunately the modern times caught up with my town. There are hardly any deserted beaches left, and since the big hotels and fashionable discos were built, tourist mobs are everywhere. But it is still beautiful and the sea is clean. The Gulf of Hammamet shelters many kilometers of sandy beaches, and here and there you still can find a secluded spot for a midnight nude swim in the cool, sparkling water. I should not complain about the tourist trade. My brother joined my father's business and worked for him until my father's death. Afterwards, my brother invested in new developments and now he is one of the richest men in Tunis. And because I was smart enough to join him in his escapades, I became well off too. I don't have to worry if I don't sell enough artwork! When I am tired of the hustle of the big city, I fly home and just laze under the sun."

"Do you have a place there?"

"Yes, I have a house at the edge of the town overlooking the sea. Below it I have a private beach just for myself. I would love to invite you one day!"

"Oh, I would really like that. Even after living in London for so many years, I never lost my cravings for blue sky and sunshine!"

"Would you like a Calvados?" asked Jamal.

Edith forced herself to say no.

"No, thank you. I don't want to mix it with that excellent wine. Maybe next time."

Jamal paid the bill and they started to walk back towards Edith's place. It was a balmy summer night, the sky was dark and the starts were sparkling.

Jamal took Edith's arm, adjusted his steps to hers and they walked very close to each other without talking. At the door of the building, Edith hesitated about what to do. Invite him in for a nightcap? But she knew that Barb was home and decided not to. She took her arm away and said, "Thank you for a wonderful evening. I enjoyed myself very much."

"So did I," he said. "You are a very interesting woman, and I would like to know you better. May I call you next week?"

"I'll look forward to it. I hope that in a few weeks my things will be here and I'll be able to show my work to you."

"We'll have plenty of opportunities to talk about your work."

He kissed Edith on both cheeks. She glanced over her shoulder as she stepped into the elevator and saw him give her a friendly smile. Then the lift took her up.

Barb was waiting for her in the living room.

"I am dying to hear about your evening! Did he make a pass at you?"

"No, he was a perfect gentleman. We talked during dinner about our lives and almost nothing else. He did hold my hand for once or twice, but he didn't go any further. And he only kissed my cheeks when we said goodbye. I don't know if he liked me as a woman! I think he is very sexy and I am a bit disappointed."

"Don't be, I know him! We only slept together after our fifth date. He was okay in bed, but far too complicated a soul for me. After a while, he bored me to death so we just remained friends and see each other only occasionally. If you get some flowers tomorrow thanking for you the evening, that will be his next step and mean that he likes you! But as I said, don't except a cozy, long relationship. He is not the type."

The next morning there was a delivery for Edith. It was an elegant flower arrangement with a note attached.

Thank you for the lovely evening.

Jamal

Chapter 27

Lili was waiting for Tivadar on the Sydney airport's arrival floor.

She was excited and looking forward to the change in her boring life. Michael was home from the hospital, but he needed constant care. He was afraid to walk even in the house, his balance got worse and he fell a few times while going to the bathroom. Lili couldn't help him up alone and had to call the neighbour for help. They hired a nurse to look after him during the day so Lili could have a little time to herself. It was very expensive and the insurance didn't cover the full cost. Michael was worried about the expenses, but Lili put her foot down.

"Michael, don't make a fuss about it! You have enough money for the rest of your life no matter how the stock market performs. If it starts to go down, you can sell and invest in something dependable that will bring enough interest to cover your expenses. And I don't need to inherit from you—I have my own money. So what's the worry? You have to understand that I can't look after you alone. We must have help!"

After a week or two he confessed that he felt much safer and relaxed with the nurse around.

The flight from LA touched down, and Lili watched closely as the passengers came out from the customs office.

Tivadar was in the last group out, and he waved to Lili with a wide grin on his face.

"So good to see you! You look wonderful! I can see that Sydney treats you well!" he said. First they shook hands, but then Tivadar pulled Lili closer and kissed her face.

"Sorry, but I had to do that. I am so happy to be here!"

"I'm happy to see you again too!" As they waited for the porter to pack Tivadar's suitcases on the cart, Lili told him that she had checked him into a hotel not far from her house.

"I am sorry to put you up in a hotel, but my husband is not good enough condition for a live-in guest. He needs his privacy and undisturbed rest."

"I am so sorry about your husband. Of course I'll be fine in a hotel, but I insist on paying for it!"

"Let's not argue about that now. The hotel is just a few bus stops to my house, but there are also taxis, of course. I think I'll take you to your hotel. You must be dead tired after that long flight. Did you stop over in LA for a few days?"

"No, I was in a hurry to get here. I might do it on the way back if I can set up a few meetings with my new business partners."

Tivadar was impressed with Lili's brand-new BMW sport coupe.

"Woo, this is a nice car! And what a comfortable ride!"

"Oh, I bought it two months ago. Traded in my big American car, which I hated to drive and park. I am very pleased with this one." The car pulled smoothly into a hotel parking lot. "Here we are at the hotel. It is a small one but very comfortable. It was recommended to me by one of my girlfriends who visits here often." Tivadar signed in, and the porter took his luggage.

"So, I'll say goodbye for now," Lili said, stepping back toward her car. "Have a good rest, and I'll pick you up around seven to take you out for dinner. It will be only me. Michael is not well enough to go out at night, but I'm sure you two will get the chance to get acquainted over the next few days. He is looking forward to meeting you. Here is my number, and if you need anything, just call. See you later."

Tivadar watched Lili go through the revolving door and get into her car. He waved to her and walked towards the elevator. But then he changed his mind and went to the public phone in the corridor. He didn't want to call from his room because it would be recorded on his bill.

He dialled an LA number.

"Hi, it's me," he said when the call was answered. "She is nice and friendly, and she checked me into a hotel. I'll give you the number, but call me only in an emergency. I'll get in touch with you from time to time to let you know how I succeed. You must stick to the story we rehearsed in case she calls you. Don't screw up! I think this will be a piece of cake."

He went to his room, unpacked, took a shower, called down to the desk for a wakeup call at 6 PM and went to bed.

∼

Lili felt great. She liked Tivadar, and he seemed more handsome than she remembered. It would be so nice to have a new face around, even if only for a few days. She was distressed by Michael's condition, but she felt she had the right to live her own life and have some fun.

When Lili got home, she found Michael in a bad mood. He was sitting on the patio and didn't ask if her guest had arrived. He just mumbled something under his breath when Lili kissed him and then turned back to his newspaper. When Michael was well enough to listen, Lili had told him as much as she wanted about the dealings with Tivadar. Michael was definitely against the whole project, including Tivadar's visit.

"If you invite him here, you commit yourself. You don't need such an expensive adventure. If you are so bored with your life now and want to do some kind of business, do what you know something about. Open a new fitness club or an office for customer relations. You don't know anything about the import-export business. The procedures for shipping here are very complicated, overbearing and frustrating. It takes years and lots of money before you can actually bring products in. Then you have to sell it to get your investment back. Only years later, if you are lucky, can you think about making any profit. Why do you want take on such a big headache? You can lose your money in no time!"

Lili argued that the visit would not commit her to anything—she just wanted to know Tivadar better. After all, it was only a few hours they spent together on the plane. She was a good judge of character, and if she was not satisfied there would be no deal, no matter how much she wanted a new challenge to prove herself as an able businesswoman.

Now she wanted to soften Michael up because she felt bad about going against his advice. On the way home she picked up some Ben and Jerry's ice cream and his favourite cookies. She took a platter of the treats out to the patio.

"Well," she said to Michael, "he is here and very happy to be here. I left him to have a rest, and this evening I'll take him out to dinner. If you feel better tomorrow, we can all have dinner together here. What do you say?"

Mellowed by the ice cream and cookies, Michael said, "We'll see."

Lili dressed with great care. She looked elegant in a beige shantung pantsuit and a green silk blouse, which bought out the colour of her brown eyes. She had a matching green handbag and shoes. She fixed up her face and her eyes, and she made her eyelashes longer. A diamond necklace and matching earrings were her finishing touch.

When she looked in the mirror for the last time before leaving, she threw a kiss to her image and said, "You look gorgeous." And when she saw Tivadar's face looking at her as she stopped in front of the hotel, she was sure that the mirror's image didn't lie.

She took him to an elegant restaurant in the harbour.

"Let me order for you," she said. "I know the menu here inside and out. Do you like seafood? I know it's late to ask this, but this is one of the best seafood restaurants. They serve other kinds of food too, and I can recommend almost all of them."

"I love seafood. As you know, at home, the fish is always frozen and never fresh. And where else you can eat fresh seafood if not in Sydney at a seaside restaurant? Yes, please order. I like everything."

Lili ordered, and they talked about Tivadar's trip until the food came.

"I've never had such fantastic oysters in my life! Thank you very much for bringing me here. I just love them!" Tivadar said, smiling happily. A little juice trickled down his chin, but Lili let it go without saying anything.

"If you like oysters, we will take the ferry across the harbour to Manly one day. On Manly Esplanade, eateries are lined up side by side and offer oysters and other seafood in every imaginable form. Deep-fried, breaded, smoked … all made from the day's catch. They serve it in a paper box with a fantastic hot sauce, and you can sit on a bench by the sea to eat."

"By all means—that sounds wonderful. I am ready to try it!"

During dinner, Lili asked Tivadar about his family. Tivadar was quiet for a while and hung his head. Then with a deep sigh, he said, "Well, I am on the verge of a divorce. My wife fell in love with a co-worker of hers and wants out."

"Oh, I am very sorry to hear that! How do you feel about it? Or is that a stupid question?"

"No, not at all. In the last four years we have drifted apart. I was very busy building up my business, and I neglected my family life, I must confess. But I provided them with a very good life, well above the standard. The kids went to expensive schools, and though my wife kept her job, she only worked because she wanted to. I must say that after twenty years of marriage, the whole situation is very painful for me. That's why I jumped at your offer for this visit. I decided to leave all my worries behind me. My trusted manager is looking after the business so I can escape to this faraway land."

He looked deeply into Lili's eyes and continued in a softer voice, "Also, I really wanted to see you again. And not just because of your success in business—as a woman too. Sorry to be so blunt, but I wanted to get that off my chest."

Lili felt warm all over. It was such a long time ago that a man looked at her as a woman and talked to her in an affectionate voice. But she didn't want to give herself away.

"Thank you. That was a nice thing to say!"

"I meant it from the bottom of my heart. It was not just a compliment!"

He picked up Lili's hand and kissed it.

She squeezed his hand and then quickly pulled hers back so as not to show capitulation. She said, "I think we should leave all the serious business discussions for tomorrow. Let's just enjoy this lovely evening. We'll meet after breakfast and then talk business only. How long are you planning to stay?"

"I am hoping for ten days. I would like to go around a bit on this island at the bottom of the globe to see what life is like here. Who knows if I'll have a chance to come here again? I was hoping for your help in organizing some kind of a trip—would you?"

After dinner, Lili drove Tivadar around downtown and then to the Harbour Bridge and the Opera House. She parked the car there, and they walked around the building. It was warm, a half moon shone in the dark sky between thousands of blinking stars and the air smelled fresh and salty. After walking around, they sat down on a bench by the water.

"What an absolutely wonderful evening this is. I can't thank you enough for having me! If not for you, I would never have seen this part of the world!"

Tivadar put his arm around Lili's shoulder and pulled her closer.

But Lili thought, *Let him wait.*

"Look at the time," she said, "it is terribly late! You must be exhausted! I'll drive you back to the hotel. Have a good, long sleep tonight and call me when you feel rested and ready to talk business."

At the hotel, Tivadar asked her to come up to the room for a nightcap, but Lili said no, she had to go home, even though she wished to go up with him.

"But I'll see you in the morning, and I'll make myself free for the entire day so after we talk business I can show you around some more. Good night, Tivadar. I am glad you came." She kissed his cheek, and before she pulled back, he took hold of her head and kissed her lightly on the mouth.

"You are a sexy woman, you know?" he said and jumped out of the car. He waved until Lili drove off.

Lili was pleased and congratulated herself. She drove around slowly before heading home in order to have time to analyze her feelings in private. She discovered that she still had her magnetism to attract men—she could still get what she wanted. In the last few years she had thought age caught up with her and was not interested in sex anymore. But she was not an old woman yet and could possibly teach Tivadar a trick or two.

Michael was fast asleep when she got home. She kissed his forehead and went into her own bedroom. She went to sleep with a smile on her face.

The next morning, Michael asked her how was dinner was and what they talked about.

"We didn't talk business. He was still a bit zombie from jet leg. But I'll go to see him after breakfast and get down to serious talk. I will just listen. Don't you worry, I'll not commit myself to any deals, I promise!"

Lili arrived at the hotel after ten and found Tivadar in the coffee shop having his breakfast. He waived to her, and she sat down at his table.

Tivadar kissed her hand and asked, "Would you like something? Can I order for you?"

"No, thanks, I had breakfast with Michael already."

"How is he this morning?"

"He is well, thanks, but not quite his old self yet. Why didn't you order room service, it is much more comfortable to have breakfast in the room."

"I wanted to give the staff a chance to clean up before you came."

"But we can have our meeting in one of the conference rooms of the hotel. I should have told you that."

"I didn't think about that, but it will be much more private in my room. I have a suite with a nice living room. Do you mind? Knowing myself, I would have to run back and forth for misplaced documents." He sipped his coffee and looked over the rim at Lili. "You certainly look fresh and lovely this morning."

Lili smiled at him and said, "Thank you for the compliment. Shall we go?"

The suite was clean, bright and friendly. A coffee thermos and all the trimmings were nicely arranged on a tray on the sideboard.

"Before we start to get down to business, let me give you a present as a token of my admiration for you," Tivadar said. He then led Lili to the bedroom. She barely held in a gasp when she saw the gifts arranged before her. There was a beautiful Herendi vase, a large polished hand carved wood box filled with goose liver tins and attractive, small linen bags of the famous Hungarian red paprika.

"Oh, Tivadar you shouldn't have! But I am glad you did. I adore this vase—I've always admired Herendi china. And all those goodies, thank you, thank you!"

She kissed him on the cheek only, but she did it in a way that let him know she wouldn't mind more. Tivadar got the message, pulled her close and kissed her neck. When Lili responded with a little moan, he kissed her on the lips. Then they looked each other and started the serious kissing.

Lili was playing with him, and she withdrew.

"No, I shouldn't do this, let's stop."

"Why? You are enjoying this—I can feel it. I want you. I want to go to bed with you and you want it too!" said Tivadar. He tightened his arms around Lili, kissed her deeply and long and then let her pull away, but only so far that he could caress her breast and her buttocks and kiss her neck and between her breasts. Lili wanted to play it cool, but her blood was boiling she could not control herself any longer. She caved in, closed her eyes and thought about Steven as Tivadar led her to the bed.

He was a good lover, and he serviced Lili very well. He kissed her while whispering how beautiful she was, and he was eager to please her. He slowly brought Lili close to her climax with a long, loving foreplay, and then he entered her and moved the way Lili wanted it. Lili was in seventh heaven—she didn't think about Steven anymore and gave herself entirely to the pleasure of sex.

They stayed in bed, Tivadar opened up the champagne and a tin of the goose liver, and they had a picnic lunch in bed. Afterwards, they made love again, and the second time it was even better.

They got down to business after all their passions were spent. Lili tried to clear her head, but she didn't entirely succeed. The fact that she could still arouse and rule a man to serve her the way she wanted made her lose her coolness and started to look at Tivadar as a lover, not just as a sex object. They didn't bother to dress, just putting on the hotel's soft, comfortable robes as they sat down to look over the papers. Tivadar presented the documents with gusto and took time out to caress Lili's neck and hand and kiss her ears.

"Tivadar, let's get serious. We have to concentrate on business if we want to make a deal!"

"I can't get over you! I am over sixty and it has been years since I was able to make love twice in a short time! You bought out the tiger in me. You are a fantastic, sexy, beautiful woman. I am at your feet! But you are right, let's get down to business." There was not much new in the documents aside from the income figures for the past month and the proceedings about going public with the company.

Lili closed the portfolio and moved her chair farther from Tivadar.

"Look," she said, "I did some serious research about opening a business here. And I can't say it is promising. It will be a very long, expensive and complicated process to not just get started but even to approach it. It would involve a wide range of dealings with the federal, state and local government. They are especially picky with food businesses. If we get through there, next we have to apply for ABN, register for GST, which is 10 per cent of the sale TFN and pay at the Australian Business Register. You have to guarantee a fifty-thousand-dollar turnover. We have to register with the Australian Securities and Investment Commission in order to be recognized as an Australian company ..." Lili paused, seeing Tivadar's suddenly long face. "Shall I continue?"

"I never dreamt that it could be so difficult. I see now that it would be a great risk to undertake all this before we know that our product will sell. I should have conducted a survey before I came here, but I was so eager to be here that I neglected to do so. I can't imagine what just the lawyer's fee would go up to. Let me think. "

He stood up and went to the window, looking out to the street below. Lili got herself a cup of coffee and waited.

Tivadar turned back from the window and sat down beside Lili.

"Here is what I can offer. I think that to start the proceedings here before I am secured as a public company in Hungary would be a big mistake. We have to wait to expand to Australia. But, I can still offer you the board membership without it. You buy fifty thousand dollars worth of shares and get 10 per cent of the company. As a board member, you will receive a fee of about a thousand dollars a month. You'll sit on the board, you can vote and you come to every meeting on the company's expense. We'll have meetings here and all over the globe, and this will justify our being together. I don't want to lose you. I think I am falling in love with you. No, don't say anything now! I know you are committed to your husband, but life is short! Let's enjoy it."

Lili was suddenly speechless, which didn't happen often. When she pulled herself together, she said, "Let me go through the documents again before I make up my mind, okay?" Lili looked at her watch and began gathering up the papers.

"Oh, my, look at the time! It's already four o'clock! I have to call Michael. I told him I would be back by 2 PM to give him lunch! I hope the nurse was smart enough to do it!"

She made the call, and satisfied that Michael got his lunch and was having a nap, turned to Tivadar.

"Let's go. I'll give you a tour of the town."

Tivadar opened up his robe and then Lili's.

"Not just jet! Look, I have something else in my mind. You bought the stallion out of me!"

Chapter 28

David had left two weeks ago. The parting was traumatic for Elsa. He had come up to Elsa's apartment, saying it would be a more private way to say goodbye. He didn't want her to accompany him to the airport.

Elsa decided to be as strong then as she was at his farewell party. There, her heart ached but she forced her eyes to smile. She was talkative, graciously received the congratulations for her son's success from friends and family members. It was a lavish party, attended by at least sixty of the closest friends and business associates and catered by one of the best catering companies in Toronto. The food was excellent, the French champagne abundant and the people elegantly dressed. It was a black-tie affair. Paula looked radiant in her light green designer gown, and David was handsome in his tuxedo.

Watching the striking couple as they circulated between the guests, Elsa was proud, but that didn't diminish the pain in her heart. She did convince herself, however, that the change was a great step forward in David's career and she had to and would deal with it. On the way home, she had to stop the car a few times to clear her eyes of tears. At home she sat in front of her fireplace all night, feeling abandoned and miserable.

This mood lasted for a long time. After David left, Elsa visited Andrew as often as she could, mainly whenever Paula was away from the house (Elsa had paid the nanny to give her Paula's schedule and call her when the coast was clear). Paula was very busy, so her visits with her grandson were very satisfying, but the partings became more and more painful to her because she knew that the time for the final kiss and embrace was imminent.

On the day of their departure, they exchanged goodbyes over the phone. Elsa could hardly speak no matter how hard she tried to be nonchalant and chatty. David called her the next day to say that they arrived safely and Andrew was very good during the long flight. He slept most of the way. He liked his new room, and most of his favourite toys were already there. He was getting to know his new nanny, a lovely, young girl who was fluent in both English and Spanish. David was sure his son would pick up the second language in no time. The family had started to settle in, they had lots to do, and he'd call again in a few days and they would chat longer. Before he hung up, he asked in a worried tone, "Mom, are you okay? Do you eat and sleep well? Please take care of yourself."

For a few weeks, Elsa lived for those phone calls. She was afraid to leave the apartment in case they called at an unusual time. David, who knew his mother well, later set up the day and time when he'd call. Only then could Elsa relax and go about her chores, but the emptiness in her heart stayed on.

She did call and talk to Lili a few times, but Lili was too aloof to give her full attention to Elsa—she was busy spending time with Tivadar. She promised that after Tivadar left she would call and they would have a long chat. She promised she'd have plenty of news. Finishing their chat in a whisper so Michael wouldn't hear, Lili said, "He is great." Elsa couldn't help smiling and told herself, "That's the old Lili, all right," but she was ashamed because she felt jealous.

At the end of July and after a few pleading phone calls, Margaret accepted Elsa's invitation and agreed to a visit. However, it was not before getting into a second argument over the ticket, because in the high season only business class was available. Elsa ensured Margaret that her flying points and just a small amount was needed for the necessary upgrade, so she finally agreed to come. Elsa was looking forward to her friend's visit. Her bouts of loneliness still troubled her, she couldn't sleep well and she was weary during the days. She hoped that Margaret's visit would perk her up.

She lovingly arranged her guest room for her friend's arrival, collected many brochures from CAA for planning the trips they would make and made a reservation at a resort hotel on North Bay for two days. She looked up the train schedules and made plans to visit Montreal and Ottawa. She wanted to show Margaret as much as she could of Canada during the three short weeks Margaret was able to stay.

Lili called her a week before Margaret's arrival.

"I'm sorry I was so short with you in the last weeks, but now I am alone at home. I can talk. Are you sitting? I had the best week of my life—lots of wonderful sex!"

"Congratulations, but how could you pull it off with Michael around? Wasn't he suspicious of your comings and goings with a strange man?"

"Oh, you know Michael. He was happy that he didn't have to accompany me to restaurants or movies. He liked Tivadar ... well, sort of. At least he was friendly enough when I brought him home for dinner. And besides, he thinks I am too old now for sex escapades. But, Elsa, I am not!"

"As always, I am impressed with your abilities! I don't even think about sex anymore."

"Believe me, you should! We are in an age when we can let ourselves go—no nervousness, no restrictions and knowing that this could be our last big fling, enjoy it fully. We don't have to worry about relationships, agonizing over love or the future of this affair. He said he is in love with me, but I am sure it will pass and we'll part as friends until the next time we meet!"

"What do you mean, 'until next time'? Are you going to carry on with him? How and why? Isn't he going back to Hungary?"

"Yes, he is, but we'll do business together and meet under the cover of board meetings. It will last as long as it will, but right now I feel like a thirty-year-old."

"You sound like one too. I'm afraid you'll get carried away, fall in love with him and suffer terribly in the end. Shall I mention Steven?"

"Oh, come on, mate. I am older and wiser, and I don't make the same mistake twice. And besides, Tivadar is not younger than I am, and his body … let's just say it's far from a Greek god's!"

"What about the business? How will it go?"

"We are not going after the export business to Australia—it would be far too complicated and costly. But I am going to buy 10 per cent of the shares of his company and become a voting board member."

"For how much?"

"We agreed on sixty thousand U.S."

"But wasn't it fifty at first?"

"Yes, but that wouldn't give me enough shares to be a voting board member."

"Did you talk it over with Michael?"

"Not fully, just a few details. Of course he didn't like it, but it is my money, and I can do whatever I want. I know that it is a good investment—it will come handy when I feel like travelling around Europe. I won't have to use my Australian account. Michael was not strong enough to argue with me. I think he stopped arguing just to end the visit."

"So, he couldn't stand Tivadar, could he?"

"Okay! I kept them apart. They met only twice. They were polite and cool towards each other. I was relived when the dinners were over. The first time, I called a cab to take Tivadar back to the hotel, but the next time I drove him home and was rewarded with fast but wonderful sex."

"I don't understand how you can do it!"

"Elsa, as you know, Michael and I haven't slept together for over four years! He knows I am a vivacious woman. He would understand."

"I doubt it, but it is your game."

"Well, I am not going to tell him. Tivadar will leave soon—"

Elsa cut in, saying, "Sixty thousand dollars richer! It's amazing how much you are willing to pay for sex."

"That was an ugly remark from a best friend, and I resent it! Goodbye!"

Elsa felt bad as soon as she said the last sentence. She wanted to take it back, but it was too late. She called back immediately.

"Lili, I am sorry, really sorry. I don't know what came over me! You know I love you. You are my best friend and I wouldn't hurt you for anything! Please forget my last sentence. You know that I always worry about you when you get into your 'it's just sex' adventures! Some of them ended painfully and you suffered."

"Oh, all right, I forgive you! When will Margaret arrive?"

"In two days. I'm sorry you can't be with us! I'll call you before we go on a trip. Enjoy your adventure! Peace?"

"Yep, I will. And peace."

Elsa did the last little chores in the guest room, bought flowers and wrote a welcome note, and then she left for the airport to pick Margaret up. The flight was on time, and Margaret was in the first group coming out of customs. She looked good, having lost some weight, and she sported a becoming haircut and wore a well-cut pantsuit. The two friends embraced happily.

"Margaret, you look wonderful, at least ten years younger! What happened with you? Are you in love?"

"Ha, ha, that would be the day! Of course not! Thanks for the business class ticket. I've never travelled in such a comfort. I am not tired at all! As for my weight, I was serious about exercising."

They were pushing the cart towards the exit when the second group of travellers came out of customs. A tall, white-haired man strode away from the group and stopped beside them.

"I would just like to say goodbye again," he said "it was nice to talk with you."

"Yes, it was," Margaret agreed, smiling. "Have a good visit with you grandchildren. Oh, this is my friend Elsa. Elsa, this is Mr. Jànos Horvàth. He sat beside me on the plane."

"Hello, nice to meet you in person," Jànos said. "I heard a lot about you during the flight."

"Hello, nice to meet you too."

Jànos turned to Margaret again and said, "Goodbye. See you on the way home." Then he smiled at Elsa, bowed his head, looked around, waved to a young couple in the crowd and hurried towards them.

"Well! Who was that?" asked Elsa once Jànos was out of earshot. "He seemed to be quite taken with you!"

"Just a fellow traveller. We talked a lot during the flight. It helped pass the time."

"Is he married?"

"Oh, Elsa, you sound like a matchmaker! No, he is a widower. He is a retired chemical engineer, his son lives here and he came for a family visit. As it happens, we are going to fly back on the same flight. He is a nice, intelligent man. We chatted a lot. That's all!"

"Well, if I were you, I would want to know him better."

"Look who's talking? Did you start to chat up, as Lili used to say, someone on a long flight lately?"

Margaret looked around with great interest during the drive home. Elsa took the Gardiner Expressway regardless of the fact that it took longer. The skyscrapers, the CN Tower, Lake Ontario and the parks by the lakeshore gave a better impression to someone seeing the city for the first time than the other route, which mostly concrete and suburbs. It was early afternoon, the mild wind from the lake blew away the smog and everything looked clean and fresh.

"How beautiful this is! Those skyscrapers! And this lake looks like a sea—no boundaries! And those sailboats! Oh, Elsa, I am so happy to be here! Thank you!"

"Don't thank me. You can't imagine how happy you made me when you agreed to visit!"

Margaret was similarly enchanted by Elsa's apartment.

"Elsa, this place is so welcoming and warm. You must be happy here!"

"Yes, I am. I love it! Is your room comfortable enough? The bathroom is all yours. I use the one upstairs even when I am alone because I don't like to take showers in the tub. Upstairs I have a full shower."

"Oh, it is more than I need! Come and talk to me while I unpack."

Elsa sat on the bed and watched Margaret as she unpacked her suitcase and placed items in the bureau in the room.

She took out a leather-bound book and gave it to Elsa.

"What is this? Margaret, I told you not to bring me anything!"

"Well, just open it."

It was a photo album full of photographs from Lake Como and the Budapest visit.

"Margaret, you are unbelievable! This is so thoughtful! What a present! Thank you very much."

As she turned the pages of the album, her smile widened.

Margaret had finished her unpacking and was checking the side pockets of her suitcase when she pulled out a Hungarian newspaper.

"Look, Elsa, I read this paper on the plane. I remember what you told me about Lili's adventure. I hope this is not the man she hooked up with."

Elsa read the article with growing alarm. There was a picture of a man at the bottom of the page. Elsa had never seen Lili's new love interest, but she had mentioned his name was Tivadar. Under photo, the name "Tivadar Boda" was written. The article was about a swindler group that sold fabricated shares in companies in Hungary and the U.S. They had cheated people out of many thousands of dollars. The leader, Tivadar Boda, had left Hungary and the police were looking for him. Elsa could not believe her eyes.

"No, this can't be. It will kill Lili!"

"You mean this is him?"

"I don't know—I've never seen him—but Lili told me his name is Tivadar.

Please tell me that there are many Tivadars in Hungary! What can I do? If I call her and he is not the one, Lili will never forgive me. I was very stern with her about that affair in our last conversation and it hurt her feelings." She looked at the clock and then said, "I can't call now, it is the middle of the night in Sydney. Oh, what shall I do? I hope she didn't give him the money yet!"

"You mean Lili fell for this sham? She gave him money? How much?"

"Sixty thousand dollars!"

"Oh my God, that's a lot of money! Is she that rich?"

Elsa was lost in her thoughts.

"I will call when it's morning there. There is nothing I can do right now. Let's hope that nothing can happen during the night!"

Chapter 29

Jamal took Edith out twice before her belongings arrived from London. He was courteous and gallant. They ate in select restaurants, and they had long talks about art and about life in Paris. Before dinner on their second evening together, he took her to visit a small gallery owned by one of his friends. Jamal introduced Edith as an artist friend from London whom he would represent in the near future. Edith was jubilant and felt important, and she looked up to Jamal with admiration. However, she was not so positive about showing her work to Jamal. After all, she had lied about her shows in London. But during the wait, she built up enough self-confidence to feel secure in believing that her long-time dream would come true and her paintings would hang in a gallery.

After the visit to the gallery, Jamal took Edith to dinner on the sightseeing boat on the Seine.

"This is a real tourist trap, but one has to do it once," Jamal said as they boarded. "The food is so-so, but the view, like this balmy, summer evening, is unforgettable." He stood very close to Edith at the railing as the boat slipped away from the pier at the foot of the Eiffel Tower. Edith remembered her dream and saw her wish come true. She nestled closer to Jamal. He didn't react and just led her to their table. He ordered drinks first.

The boat slowly moved down the Seine, the searchlights were turned on and off to illuminate couples embracing on the banks and the voices of Edith Piaf and Yves Montand wafted from the speakers. Edith saluted Jamal with her drink.

"Thank you! This is so lovely and brings back so many memories from the years when I visited here with my husband. We were so happy and young!"

"You are not old yet—you have a great life ahead of you!" said Jamal, lifting up his drink and smiling at her. "What did you hear from London about your shipment?"

"They told me that everything was packed and sent as we agreed and most likely got held up at the customs office here. I called them, but they said they hadn't received it from London yet. I really don't know what's happening. I am worried that it got lost on the way or went to some other place by mistake!"

"Oh, don't worry, I am sure you'll get it soon! Let's enjoy the evening. You look lovely tonight, Edith!" said Jamal as he patted her hand over the table. Edith shivered at his touch and was hungry for more. She wanted to be kissed, cradled and taken to bed.

She asked for one more drink before dinner to gather courage for the seduction. The dinner was the same fare as in every tourist trap, but the wine, which Jamal carefully selected from the wine list, was excellent and relaxed Edith completely. She forgot about her worries regarding her paintings, and she found she had one wish only—to go to bed with him. After disembarking, she put her arm through his, squeezed his hand and said, "Why don't we go to your place for a nightcap?"

Jamal looked at her and smiled. "Are you sure?" he asked.

"Oh yes, let's!"

The next morning when she got home, there was a note from Barb on the kitchen table. As she walked to her room, Edith read aloud, "Well, I guess you seduced him! I hope you had a good time! See you tonight." Edith laughed and threw the note away.

Edith took a leisurely bath and recalled the night with Jamal, which was disappointing. Jamal was a dispassionate lover and didn't give very much—he just let himself be loved. The lovemaking was short, and afterwards he went to sleep. He didn't even wake up when Edith left in the morning. Edith's feelings were hurt, but she made an excuse for him.

"It was the first time. It will be much better the second time. I am sure there will be second time because I still want him."

Jamal didn't call, but early in the afternoon a flower arrangement came with a note.

Edith read, "I am sorry, but I had to for leave to Tunisia suddenly because of some business problems. I enjoyed our night together. Hoping to see you again after my return, sincerely, Jamal."

"Sincerely! I slept with him, at least he could sign, 'fondly.'" fumed Edith.

When Barb came home that night Edith related the whole evening to her.

"What do you think?" she asked when she finished her story.

"As I warned you, that's Jamal. He is not a European male, no matter how much he wants to be. His ancestors used females as slaves for their own pleasure, and this bestowal will never leave his genes. He was the same with me, though it did get better after a few more times. But he was never a really passionate or loving lover."

"You think he will call me when he gets back? Did he really go away or it is just an excuse?"

"I'm sure he'll call. I can tell he likes you, but just don't except too much. He'll keep his promise about your show, so just play the game. If he calls, go."

The next day, Edith got a notice from the customs office that her things had arrived. She went in and signed the many official forms and paid the fees. With Barb's help, she found a storage place to use until she got her own place. She selected ten of her paintings and had them delivered to the apartment at a time when she knew Barb would be away. Edith put them in the back of her closet and covered the pile with a big sheet. She wanted to study them before showing them to anybody. She was sure that she was a talented, good painter, but people in London hadn't understood or valued her work. But now that she had a possibility to be judged by experts, she temporarily lost her courage again. To build up her confidence, she studied her paintings every day when Barb was at work. Yes, she ensured her mind, she was an artist whose work deserved attention.

But still she didn't show any of the paintings to Barb and only told her that she could see them after she made her selection for a show. By the time Jamal got back, she had fully regained her self-confidence. He took her out to dinner and afterwards they went to his apartment. He made love to her, told her he had missed her and was more affectionate than the first time. Edith relaxed, and as usual she made mountains out of Jamal's lovemaking and his words. She was sure that he was in love with her, even if he hadn't said anything like that. She fantasized that her talent would overwhelm him and he'd arrange an exhibition for her with champagne, and where people would marvel about her work. After, he'd take her to his house in Hammamet by the sea, where she'd paint and be happy and loved with no worries about the future.

A few days later, she told him that her paintings had arrived and she would like to show them to him. They agreed on a date for Jamal to come up to the apartment during the day, when the light was good for looking at her work.

On the day when Jamal was due to visit, Edith set up her paintings in her room, carefully selecting the light sources. When Jamal arrived, he asked her to leave him alone with the paintings so he could observe them undisturbed. Then he'd come back the same evening and they'd talk about them. She agreed and left.

She then went to the same boutique Barb had taken her and bought a new dress for the opening she was sure would happen. She wanted to pay with her credit card, but the computer rejected it. She could not understand why, as she had paid her minimum the previous month. Maybe her payment was delayed in the mail and the bank didn't get it on time. She felt humiliated, but the saleswoman told her not to worry—she'd put the dress on hold until she straightened things out. Edith paid a cash deposit on the dress, and because it was still early, she went to the Jardin des Tuileries and walked around trying to calm the butterflies in her stomach.

She crossed the Grand Palais and sat down for a coffee on the Avenue De Champs-Elysees, and to relax her nerves she had a couple of Calvados. It was after four when she got home. The lift was out of service as usual, so she walked up the stairs. She opened the apartment door quietly and stood in the hall to be sure that Jamal was gone. The door of her room was halfway open. She heard Barb's voice and just as she was about to say hello, she heard Jamal's voice too. She froze and listened.

"Those are daubs, not worth a cent! Like a kid's paint-by-numbers! Barb, how could you ask me to get involved with her? I have to think about my reputation!"

"Sorry, Jamal, I knew she had a muddled mind, but I didn't see her work. She talked a lot about her shows in London and her portrait orders. I thought it would be worth it to get into her confidence. I did check out her story about her flat in London—it was true and she always had money to pay the bills. I was hoping we could get a load of money out of her before—"

Edith ran out and slammed the door of the apartment. She was in shock. She started to shake and felt on the verge of fainting. Edith was out of the building and blindly running down the street by the time she heard Barb and Jamal calling after her. She ran until she was out of breath, and then she collapsed on a bench in a small park. She didn't know where she was, how far she had run from the apartment or in what direction. She was still in shock and could hardly breathe. She heaved suddenly and vomited all over the bench, barely missing her shoes. She wanted to die and disappear forever.

She didn't know if she passed out or just fell to sleep, but when she came back to her senses, the sky was dark and light drizzle wet her face. She was cold but could not stand up. A few people passed her by, looking at her strangely, but nobody asked her if she was okay or needed help. Finally, she managed to stand up and with staggering steps walk towards the first lit window on the street. It was a small, neighbourhood bar full of cigarette smoke and noise. She checked her purse on her shoulder and ordered an Absinthe, poured in the water and watched as the water changed the contents of the glass to light green as if it was the most important thing in her life. Then she drank it fast and ordered one more.

The strong drink warmed up her insides, and she was finally able to think. As soon as she recalled what had happened, she lost control, became hysterical, banged her fist on the table and screamed in English and Hungarian. The bar became silent and everybody looked at her, but she could not stop. Finally the bartender went to her table, forcefully lifted her up from the chair and pushed her out into the street. The cool, night air cleared her head, and she slowly calmed down. She knew that she couldn't go back to the apartment to face Barb, who had betrayed her and taken advantage of her unsuspecting good faith in their friendship. She looked around for a cheap hotel, and she knew that in Paris there were several on every side street. She found a very rundown one where they did not ask any questions after seeing her state of being and after she paid the few euros. She was given a hole of a room. Its window opened onto the airshaft in the back of the building. She did not bother to undress and dropped down on top of the questionably clean and smelly bed.

The new, devastating collapse of her dream world shook her to the bottom of her soul. She was beaten again by the unfairness of life. Why was she so unfortunate? When everything was going well and smoothly, and when she believed that she was on top of her world, all came crashing down on her again and again and again. Her short happiness in marriage, her countless unfaithful lovers and the tragedy with Antal, dear Antal … and now this! Just when she was ready to start a new life and was full of determination to make her dreams come true. And how happy and hopeful she was for a few sunny months!

It didn't occur to Edith to look deep down in her soul and search for the reasons within herself. She was still convinced that she was a woman pursued by fate no matter how hard she tried to beat it. She cried, she sobbed and she cursed. When she was half asleep from exhaustion, she only thought of getting revenge, even if it cost her life.

She awoke the next morning with a splitting headache. She wanted to go back to sleep, but she got hold of herself and cleared her head enough to think about what to do. She had to go back to the apartment to collect her personal things, like her passport and the money she kept in a book in her desk drawer. She had to assume they knew that she had overheard them.

Edith got to her feet. Barb had to go to work and couldn't miss a day, so just then was the best time to go to the apartment. Edith had her own key, and she doubted there had been enough time for Barb to change the lock. She decided she was going to demolish her place, break everything she could get her hands on. Afterward, she would get her things and disappear. Unfortunately, she could not do anything about the bastard Jamal now. She was afraid to go to his place, and besides, she didn't have a key to get in. But she promised herself she'd find a way to revenge him too.

She went to the chipped, rusted, cold-water sink in her hotel room, washed her face, combed her hair and tried to tidy up her clothing. Checking the secret side pocket of her purse, she was relieved to find a bit of money, which had been intended for buying a bottle of champagne and some cheese for the night when Jamal was supposed to come back to talk about her show. She left the hotel and went looking for the Metro station. When she found it and looked at the route she had to take to get back to the apartment, she was amazed at how far she had run the night before. It was after ten in the morning when she sneaked through the apartment house door so the concierge wouldn't see her and quietly walked up the steps. She stood at the apartment door, listening for any noise from inside. All was quiet. She carefully inserted her key, turned it and the door opened smoothly. To make it sure that Barb was not in, she closed the door with a small bang, called out "Barb?" and stood quietly for a few minutes. The place was empty.

In her room, she opened her desk drawer to get out her wallet which held the extra credit card she kept for emergencies. The wallet was empty! And there were only a few small notes left in the hiding place in the book beside her bed. Her few pieces of jewellery were missing too. She looked into her closet. Her things were there, but the canvasses were missing. She threw everything out onto the floor, looking for the bankcard in her suit pocket. She had left it there the last time she went to the bank machine to get cash for groceries. The card was there. Of course, without the code Barb wouldn't be able to use it.

Edith's brain suddenly flooded with red fog. She ran into Barb's room and with fury demolished the place. She broke vases and glasses, tore up the bedding, the books and her clothing. Most of her energy was spent before she reached the kitchen, which was lucky because that kind of noise would have alerted the neighbours across the corridor.

She piled her things in her suitcase and left the apartment. She got out unnoticed and flagged the next free taxi. She told the cabbie to take her to the railway station. On the way she counted the money in her purse and realized she did not have enough for the one-way railway ticket. Maybe it was enough for the bus. She told the driver, to take her to the bus terminal and bought her ticket for the next bus. She had two hours to wait. She sat down on a bench, closed her eyes and said, "Now what?"

Paris had lost its impact on her. She was beaten and humiliated in the city of her dreams. She couldn't live there. She had to go back to London, defeated and full of bitterness, to where she still had her own place even if it was rented out. Maybe her friend at the market would let her stay with her until she could arrange to break the lease in some way. She'd have to start from scratch, because she was sure that Barb would get everything out of the storage facility in Paris which she so "selflessly" arranged.

"But to hell with her. I damn her, and if there is justice in this lousy world, she'll end up in the gutter somewhere," she assured herself. She sat in the waiting room for a long time lost in thought. Then her mind eased up.

"I know what to do. I'll call Margaret from London and tell her that I didn't like Paris after all. I didn't like the French people, and I changed my mind and came back to London. But I'd like to go to Budapest and stay with her for a while until my apartment is free! I'm sure she'll take me in. She was always a good friend no matter how impossible I was."

During the long hours on the bus, she was again building castles in the air about how good it would be to visit with Margaret, cry on her shoulder and tell her everything that had happened—in her own way, of course.

She was dead tired. Before she could fall back into the dark, depressing thoughts, the humming of the motor and the motion of the bus lolled her to sleep.

Chapter 30

Lili was in heaven. After so many long years, she had a lover again! A lover whom she could control and a relationship she could enjoy without committing anything of herself. Well, beside the money. But so what? She could afford it, and it gave her power to be part of a business adventure. Tivadar was so smart and so good in bed!

They sneaked away for two days, and she told Michael that they were looking for business connections in Melbourne. Before they left, Lili gave a money order to Tivadar for thirty thousand dollars to deposit into his company's LA bank. She then told him he'd get the other half when she received the papers of the shares. She sensed Tivadar was disappointed about not getting the full amount, but he didn't really show it.

They flew to the Barrier Reef and stayed in a remote but exclusive hotel (many hundreds of dollars a night). They spent the days swimming, snorkelling and lazing on the white, sandy beach. They drank cocktails and champagne, ate seafood and made love. Lili felt her years melting away, and she was again the same young woman who had romped across the beaches of Greece with Steven. She didn't ever want to wake up from this illusion, but the trip had to end and they flew back to Sydney.

When they returned, Michael didn't ask a question—he just listened to the stories Lili made up about their meetings with different companies. He was still against the whole adventure, but seeing Lili's enthusiasm and her suddenly happier self, he kept his mistrust and apprehension to himself. He knew that in the past few years he had not been the kind of partner Lili needed, and he felt grateful for her love and kind consideration. It didn't occur to him that more than the business challenge had caused her personality change. He knew about her escapades in her younger years and was sure that now, over sixty, she was over that part of her life and sex was not important to her anymore.

The two times he had met with Tivadar was enough for Michael to form an opinion. He didn't like his appearance or his overdone politeness, and he didn't trust him at all. But he knew that he couldn't do more than fully express his points against the whole deal. His mind was not at ease about the future, and he could hardly wait for Tivadar to leave, hoping that with his departure the deal would fade away. He didn't know about the money, as Lili had chosen not to mention anything about the changes in the deal.

He watched his wife as she looked herself over in the mirror in the hallway, petted her hair in place and turned to him. She asked, "Are you sure you don't want to come? Tivadar is leaving tomorrow morning, and it would be nice of you to say goodbye. I'll wait till you change."

"No, thank you, my dear. I am a bit off today. I'll go to bed early and let the nurse go. You have a good time. Say goodbye for me, please."

"Well, if that's what you want. But please don't send the nurse away before you are safely in bed. I don't want to find you on the floor. I will not be late."

"Don't hurry home, dear, I'll be fine," said Michael. Lili kissed him on both cheeks, patted the dog at his feet and left.

Lili was puzzled by Michael's dislike for Tivadar, but on the other hand she was relieved that there would only be two for the farewell dinner.

Tivadar was waiting for her in the hotel lobby. When he saw that Lili came alone, a wide grin spread over his face.

"Lili, let's skip dinner! Let's go up to my room instead."

"No way, we have to have dinner. Michael knows the restaurant where I made the reservation, so we must show up. Let's go!"

During dinner they talked about their plans and about where and when they could have the next "board meeting." After they were served the coffee, Tivadar got hold of Lili's hand, looked deep into her eyes and kissed her hand.

"Lili, why don't you give me the other half of the money we agreed on? It would speed up the happenings and we would be able to meet again sooner … or don't you trust me? Don't hurt my feelings!"

"My money is tied down in bonds and trusts," Lili replied. "It will take time to cash the other half. That's all."

"Oh, I understand it now! But could you hurry it up so we can meet very soon? Please, please? You are the most remarkable businesswoman I have ever met! And may I add the sexiest? Let's leave and have a goodbye in my room!"

Lili paid the bill, and on the way to the hotel Tivadar kissed her hand on the wheel, her neck and slid his hand up and down on her thighs. Lili got aroused, and the thought that it would be the last for a long time made it even more exiting. She parked and went up the elevator alone after Tivadar. He was waiting for her at the door. He pulled her in and covered her with kisses.

"Lili, I'll miss you terribly! I never thought that I would meet at my age with a woman whose touch could turn me on as if I were a young man! You are unbelievable—you gave me back my youth for these unforgettable days! We must meet very soon again!"

Talking rapidly, he took off Lili's dress, kissed her all over and led her to the bed, where he undressed her completely. He then undressed himself (silently saying thanks for the Viagra he took before dinner) and stood beside the bed proudly showing his full erection before falling onto Lili. He was in a great form, bringing Lili to climax two times before he collapsed on top of her. Lili dressed hurriedly.

"Look at the time—it's almost midnight! I must hurry home in case Michael is still up. Sometimes he reads late into the night or wakes up after just a few hours and reads till dawn. I don't want to be unreasonably late. I'll pick you up and take you to the airport in time, around 11:30 AM. I think. Good night, my vigorous lover!"

She kissed Tivadar, who was still lying in bed, on the lips.

"Have a good night, see you in the morning!"

After Lili left, Tivadar packed his bags and went to bed. Before he fell asleep, he felt sure that Lili would bring the money the next day. After all, he had worked hard for it.

It was not yet six o'clock in the morning when the phone rang beside his bed. Half asleep, he reached out, picked up the phone and said, "Hello …"

Before he could say anything more, a well-known voice said on the other end, "Tivadar, get out fast, now…"

As he listened to the caller, Tivadar's face got whiter and whiter, and without another word he put down the phone, dressed in a hurry, picked up his suitcases and headed for the elevator.

Driving home, Lili thought that this past week was worth more than a few years of her life and the money. She was still a woman—a sexy woman and not a burnt-out, old shell. No matter if the shell was a bit baggy and wrinkled. The fire was still there.

Michael was asleep, and he didn't move when she pulled his blanket up to his chin. She took a long shower and fell asleep. The next morning, she woke up with her alarm at 10:30. Michael was on the patio reading the paper.

"Good morning, dear," he asked. "Did you have a good time?"

"Yes, we had a great dinner. Too bad you didn't come—you would have enjoyed it too. How was your evening? Did the nurse do everything she was suppose to? Did you eat your dinner? Sid you sleep well?"

"Yes on all counts," said Michael as he kissed Lili's cheek. "By the way, Elsa called you around ten this morning. I told her that you were still asleep and would call her back later."

"Why did she call so early? She knows I am not myself before 11 AM. I'll just have my coffee and call her back. I'm in a hurry because I promised to drive Tivadar to the airport at 11:30."

"He could take a taxi or a limo to the airport. Why do you have to drive him all the way and drive back? He does speak English. He can look after himself," Michael muttered behind his paper. Lili chose not to respond. She made herself some fresh coffee and went into the study to call Elsa.

"Hi, Elsa. What's up? I'm up now and fresh as a daisy."

"Lili, I don't know how to tell you this."

"What? Is something wrong? Are you all right? You don't sound yourself! What's the matter?"

"Okay, I'll be short, but I think you should sit down. Margaret arrived yesterday—"

Lili cut in, saying, "I know that. Has something happened to her?"

"No, no … please listen, Lili. She read an article in the Hungarian newspaper on the plane. It was about a certain Tivadar Boda and his company of swindlers who have cheated people out of many thousands of dollars by selling false shares in companies. The Hungarian police are looking for him, and they already arrested two of his accomplices … Lili are you still there?"

Lili sat frozen to her chair. Her mind went blank, and she could only tighten her hand on the phone.

"Lili, is his name Boda? Is it he? Did you give him any money yet?"

Lili shook herself and stood up from the chair. "Elsa, I'll call you back later. I must run."

"But, Lili, are you all right? Where are you going?"

"I'll call you later. I am okay."

She jumped into her pants and a shirt and ran out of the house without a word for the dumbfounded Michael. With screeching tires, she backed out of the garage and sped down the road. She left the car at the entrance of the hotel and ignored the concierge, who waved at her, as she took the elevator to Tivadar's room. There were no signs of him or his suitcases. She ran back down to the reception desk.

"Are you looking for Mr. Boda, madam? I wanted to tell you before you got into the elevator—he left in a great hurry early this morning. He said that some family emergency had come up and he had to leave immediately. He said he'd call you from the airport, and he said you'd take care of the bill. I have the credit card number with which you made the reservation, and I remember you said Mr. Boda was your guest. I hope it's all right?"

He came out from behind the counter, alarmed by Lili's suddenly white face and furious eyes.

"Madam, are you all right? Would you sit down or like a glass of water?" He pulled up a chair for her and signalled to the busboy.

Lili got hold of herself and refused the chair and the water. She said, "I am fine, thank you. Let me sign the bill."

She went back to her car and drove slowly, her body still shaking, to the park at the seashore. She parked the car there but didn't get out. She took a cigarette out of her purse, lit it, closed her eyes and leaned back in the seat, smoking. The salty, fresh air from the sea and the cigarette slowly helped her to calm down, and after a while she could think rationally.

"Well, I did it again! Blinded by flirting and sex. I was used—he made a monkey out of me. How could I be such a fool as to not see through him? Me, the smart businesswoman? Michael had a good nose not to trust him. But he seemed so sincere, and he was so clever he made me believe that he was in love with me. He made me believe that I am a sexy and desirable woman who can make a man fall in love with her! How could I be so blind to let myself be led by my nose like a dumb ass! I am a fool, an old fool who fell into a smart swindler's trap. At least I was smart enough not to give him all the money. But this is just a small comfort for my self-esteem—my pride will be shattered for a long time to come."

She finished her cigarette and felt a bit better. She decided not to say anything to Michael. Hopefully Tivadar's story would not make the international press or the Sydney papers so he would never know how his wife was taken for a ride. The money was from her account, and Michael had no cosigning privileges on it. She knew that it was hopeless to try to catch Tivadar. He was probably on a plane to somewhere to South America with all the money he had charmed out of fools like her. Besides, she wanted to keep the whole affair exclusively for herself. She wouldn't let anybody laugh at her. She would tell Elsa that for the time being she didn't want to talk about it and she'd let her know the whole story some time later. She knew she could trust her best friend's discretion.

"And, damn it, Elsa was right after all! I paid dearly for my lust. But never, never again! I will act my age—well, almost my real age—and stop throwing my money around at any charming lover boy. But to be honest, if I forget my pride I enjoy every minute of it."

Chapter 31

Elsa and Margaret had a great time. Elsa took Margaret for tours around the town and showed her all the interesting sights. The CN tower impressed Margaret, and Elsa was planning to have lunch in the slowly revolving restaurant. The weather was clear and Elsa told Margaret they would have a panoramic view of Lake Ontario, the American shore and even the mist over Niagara Falls, but Margaret didn't want to go up. Elsa tried to convince her friend that it would be worth the wait in line (which wasn't very long), but Margaret remained adamant and eventually confessed that she would get so claustrophobic up there that she wouldn't move away from the wall. So Elsa took her to the harbour instead and they boarded a sightseeing boat. The boat slowly circled around the islands and the view was superb. The city skyscrapers reflected the sunrays, and the windows looked like they were on fire.

"Elsa, this is a beautiful city. Look at that sight! And this lake, and the parks full of trees and flowers … and how clean! No wonder you like living here!"

"Well, I didn't show you the rough part of the city. I want you to have pleasant memories of this trip. It's enough if you know that not everything that shines is gold. We have our share of homeless people, crime and shantytowns, as does every other big city in the world. Tomorrow we'll drive up north to the cottage country and tour around just like we did in Hungary, but you'll see things you can't found anywhere in Europe. The immense open spaces, the thousands of lakes and bays ... for miles and miles there is nothing aside from just water, rocks and trees. And after we come back we'll take the train to Montreal and Ottawa for a couple of days. After that I'll take you Niagara Falls—you can't go home without seeing the seventh wonder of the world. I planned it so that if we'd like to stay longer somewhere, we can do it without rushing. Niagara is only an hour and a half away, an easy day trip even if we drive on the country roads. We can do that part one or two days before you are due to leave."

"I can hardly wait to see the North Country. I looked up Canada on the Internet before I came. I read its history, and I was more than impressed by it."

They had dinner at home, and afterwards they sat on the terrace sipping wine and talking with long, comfortable silences between their sentences. They listened to the hundreds of birds on the surrounding giant, old trees as they settled down for the night.

"What do you know about Edith?" asked Elsa.

"It's been a while since I've had any news from her. Her last letter was cheerful. She liked her new friend and the place, and she had met a man who is an art dealer and promised to arrange an exhibit for her if he liked her work. She was waiting for her things to arrive from London."

"That's great news. You think she will settle down finally and try to be happy?"

"I hope so, but knowing her I'm not too optimistic. She is very emotional. She can be high up in the pink clouds singing happy songs one minute, and the next minute she is down, back in a deep depression."

"Do you like her paintings?"

"Some of her earlier works were really good, but I haven't seen any recent ones. I don't know if she's worked at all in the last few years. I hope she'll have her dream come true and have an exhibition in Paris. That would make her very happy and content, at least for a while. You know, if somebody well-known in her type of art saw any chance to make money by promoting her, it would be great. After all, the promotion is the key to a success. Rich people tend to trust well-known art dealers because they don't understand art." Margaret paused. "Well, I wish her luck. She rented out her London flat and lives on the income from it. I'll definitely call her after I get home. What have you heard from Lili?"

"She was very short and to the point. That, yes, Tivadar was the crook but didn't cost her too much money. She didn't want to talk about it yet and would appreciate it if I just forgot the whole thing until the next time we get together. So I will. But I know her, and judging from the sound of her voice, she is badly shaken and very, very furious about the whole affair. I might visit her in Sydney when the weather gets cold and miserable here."

Margaret was quiet for a long time.

"What are you thinking? A penny for your thoughts!" Elsa said, smiling at her friend.

"I was thinking about you!"

"What about me?"

"I can see that you have a good life here and a lovely home in a beautiful city. But ever since your family moved to South America, you have been lonely, and I think a bit depressed too. Why don't you move back to Hungary? You said you felt at home there."

"Tell you the truth," Elsa replied, "I was thinking about that too. I don't think I could move there permanently—I lived my adult life here and have my roots in this earth, but my roots in Hungary didn't die off either. What I was thinking was to spend a few month there every year. I have nothing and nobody here to tie me down, and I wouldn't really be any further from David and Andrew there."

"Elsa, that would be wonderful! Maybe you could buy or rent a good apartment close to mine and we could spend lots of time together. We get along so well, and both of us are lonely most of the time."

"Yes, I was thinking about that too. We could be a part of each other's life but also have our privacy and freedom. I even made some calculations, and I think I could afford to buy something. The difference in cost of living might even end up saving me money in the end. But I have to think about it a little more before I decide. And you have more than ten days to talk me into it! Now let's go in and pack our bags so we can leave right after breakfast and after the morning rush hour."

They left the city and were on the highway just after ten the next morning. The scenery was not very interesting until they left Barrie, one hundred kilometres north of Toronto. The hills were suddenly covered with tall pines mixed with the white trunks of birch trees. The summer flowers were blooming on the fields and in the small valleys. Margaret was impressed.

"Such an open country. Where are the villages or towns? Are there any?"

"Oh yes, plenty, but they are well off this highway. When we get closer to the Muskoka Lake District, it will change. I thought I would drive up to Gravenhurst and have lunch there in one of the lakeside restaurants. After that we can take the scenic route over to Georgian Bay."

They found a charming rustic restaurant which promised home-cooked meals. The patio looked over the lake, the sun was shining and a light summer breeze cooled the air. Margaret was enchanted.

"What a colour combination! Dark blue lake, light blue sky and all the hues of greens! I must take a few pictures. Do we have time to walk around?"

"We have all the time on the world—we are not in a hurry. We could stay in Parry Sound for the night. And you know what, tomorrow we'll take the thirty-thousand-island boat ride."

"'Thirty thousand island'? I don't believe it! Is it just a name?"

"Believe it or not, there are that many and more islands and bays. You'll enjoy it! Let's walk and so you can take your pictures."

They walked around for more than an hour, and it was the middle of the afternoon when they started out towards Parry Sound. The road was as scenic as Elsa promised, with giant rock formations, tall pine trees, bays and inlets. They drove through small summer resort towns. Around the lakes were colourful cottages, and sailing boats gliding on the lakes. Here and there a motorboat dragged a water-skier behind. After they left the resorts, nothing again for many kilometres interrupted the views of lakes, rocks and trees.

The whole scene was as tranquil as a painting. Elsa drove slowly, and both of them quietly observed the beauty of nature. It was dusk when they got to Parry Sound, and Elsa drove around the town and the harbour. It was busy with people, as it was the height of the holiday season. They decided to stay in one of the lakeside lodges outside of town, and since it was a warm evening, they went for a dip in the lake. Margaret couldn't believe how smooth and silky the water was.

The next day after breakfast, they took the cruise among the islands. It was a big ship and the morning tour was not crowded, so they walked around as much as they wished all over the decks. While Margaret was taking pictures, Elsa walked to the front of the ship and looked down at the lower deck to where a few people were standing. In the middle by the railing stood a familiar figure—a man. Elsa could only see his back, but his pose and the way his hands held the railing suddenly made her dizzy. Her heart missed a few beats and then started to beat fast.

"No, it can't be," she told herself. "It's just a hallucination." She turned around and went back where Margaret sat, putting a new roll of film into her camera.

"I should have bought more ..." Margaret began, but then she looked up at Elsa.

"Elsa, what's the matter with you?" she asked, alarmed. "Are you sick? You face is white as a sheet!"

Elsa sat down beside her and for a few seconds didn't say a word. "Nothing really," she said finally. "I saw a man on the lower deck, and for a few crazy moments I thought that he was Tom. But that's utterly impossible, isn't it?"

"Did you wait for him to turn around?"

"No, I was afraid to!"

Margaret pulled Elsa up from the bench and said, "Let's go back. You can't leave it just like this—you are almost in shock! You have to make sure it's not him, or you will forever wonder, no matter how impossible it seems."

They went back to the spot where Elsa stood before.

"See that tall, thin man standing at the railing? His back looks just like Tom's. But it can't be him. The last time I heard from him, he was in Africa."

The man at the railing must have felt them staring at his back, because he turned around and looked up at them. Elsa stopped breathing and stood motionless, looking at the man below them. He also stood frozen, looking up at Elsa. It was Tom. Elsa left the railing and sat down on the nearest bench, shaking like a leaf.

"It's him," she whispered.

Margaret just stood there, but as Tom appeared at the top of the stairs and started coming towards them, Margaret discreetly moved to the other side of the deck. Elsa met her eyes and smiled weakly. Then Tom was there.

Elsa looked up at the man who stood in front of her. Thousand of questions ran through her head, but when she opened her mouth to speak, no sound came out. They looked at each other for a long time, wordless and motionless, then at the same time they moved together. Elsa's head rested on Tom's shoulder, and Tom's arms encircled Elsa tightly, still without words. Elsa's tears started to flow, and she freed herself from Tom's arms.

"Why didn't you let me know that you were back?" she asked, but just then she noticed with a shock how thin and sick Tom looked. He had lost a lot of weight, his eyes were cloudy, his face shrunken and his colour was rather gray.

"Tom what's happened to you? Are you sick?"

Gently holding her hands, Tom led Elsa to an empty bench.

"Please, dearest, later! Let's not talk about me. I will tell you the whole story some other time. I came here to have a rest, fresh air and peace. Not in my wildest dream could I imagine meeting you here! Are you on holiday? Alone?"

Elsa was still shocked by Tom sudden appearance and hurt about the accidental meeting. She swallowed hard, forced a smile and said, "I brought a friend of mine, who is visiting me, for a trip up here."

"The lady who stood beside you? She isn't Lili, is she?"

"No, she's Margaret—a dear, new friend."

"Where are you staying?"

"At a lodge by the lake. And you?"

"I am at the Country Inn on the other side of town."

They again fell wordless for a long time and just looked at each other while holding hands. Both of them were hesitant to speak and unsure about the other. They didn't realize the boat had docked. Margaret walked over to them.

"Hello, I am Margaret, Elsa's friend. I'm sorry to interrupt, but we docked and we have to leave."

"Oh, I'm sorry. Margaret, this is Tom."

"Hello, Tom. I've heard a lot about you from Elsa. How nice to meet you!"

They shook hands and the three of them walked down the plank. At the pier, they hesitated. Elsa still felt dazed.

After a few minutes of stressed silence, Tom looked at Elsa and asked, "Would you have time tomorrow afternoon for a drink or a cup of coffee and a long talk?"

Elsa knew they were planning to leave the next morning, but when she looked at Margaret, her friend's eyes said, "Say yes."

"Yes, I think so. Shall we meet around three over at that restaurant's patio?"

"That would be wonderful, thank you, Elsa. See you tomorrow. Ladies, have a nice day."

He turned around and left. Elsa watched him go and didn't move until Margaret put her arm around her shoulders and said quietly, "Let's go, Elsa."

They walked towards the car in deep silence. Before starting the car, Elsa leaned back in her seat, sobbed and let her tears flow freely.

"What happened with him, why didn't he call me when he came back? Why? I always sensed the love in his voice when he called me from Africa. Or I was just fooling myself because I wanted to believe it? He doesn't love me anymore! Not that I can blame him, I ran away! And why? To be alone and miserable in my old age! Never in my life was I so happy and content than during the years we were together! Oh, Margaret, you know how many times I've regretted that decision of mine! I was sentimental and stupid enough to believe that I was needed to hold the family together and I couldn't be selfish with living my own life. And look at me now! They are in South America and I am left to be on my own on the other side of the world!"

Margaret put a tissue box in Elsa's lap.

"Elsa, don't torment yourself. At least wait until you talk to him and know the reason why he didn't tell you he was back. I am not an expert, but by the way he looked at you I'd say he is still in love with you. Let's go back to the lodge. It is early enough to have a swim and laze on the beach. Put the dark thoughts behind you—you won't gain anything but a sleepless night. Try not to think about it. You'll know everything tomorrow!"

Elsa tried, but she couldn't get Tom out of her mind. They were sitting on the beach after dinner and she said, "Lili used to ask me what I would do if Tom materialized at my door. I always lied and said I never thought about it because it could never happen. But I think about it often and I always get to the conclusion that, yes, I still love him and I would be happy to get him back," she said and then paused. Grief welled up again. "He did not want to be back! Otherwise why didn't he call me, why did we have to run into each other accidentally?"

"Please, Elsa, let it rest. You'll know everything tomorrow."

"Yes. I guess you are right. But what are you going to do tomorrow afternoon?

I hate to leave you all alone."

"Don't be silly. I have a good book and I can just laze around here and read leisurely, which I could never do back home—it is a rare luxury for me! You go and stay for as long as you like. I just hope you'll be happier when you come back."

Somehow Elsa got through the morning hours. She went for a long swim in the lake, lay on the beach on the sun and closed her eyes and tried not to think. But she could not get rid of the many bitter thoughts running through her head.

She dressed carefully right after lunch and told Margaret that she'd go for a drive before the meeting and left. She drove to a secluded spot off the road and sat on a rock, wanting to calm down as much as possible before seeing Tom again.

She sat motionless for a long time. The beauty of nature helped relaxed her. She watched as a hawk circled in the dark blue sky, coming down lower and lower watching out for prey. The white seagulls dove into the water and fought for food, making a big racket. She watched the bees buzzing around a bunch of wild flowers and a small frog hopping towards a muddy pond. When she stood up to go back to the car, she was calm, but when she got to the restaurant and saw Tom sitting at a table, her heart began to beat as fast as a young girl's who is going on her first date. Tom noticed her immediately and hurried out to the parking lot to meet her. Both of them were unsure what to do—kiss, hug or shake hands. Tom took hold of Elsa's hand and led her to the table. They sat silently for a few minutes. When the waitress came to take their order, the silence was broken. After she left, Tom looked at Elsa and she was shocked to see tears in his eyes.

"Oh, how many times I've dreamt of this moment!" Tom said. "Forming the sentences in my head, what I'd say when I saw you again at last! Elsa, there was not one day that I didn't think about you, and here I am speechless when it finally happens! You must know ... you must feel that I still love you! I am ready to beg you and do everything that's possible or impossible to get you back! You must love me too! Tell me, am I right?"

"Yes, Tom, I love you! But if you felt like you say, why didn't you let me know? Why didn't you call me when you got back from Africa? When did you get back?"

"Two months ago."

"Two months? And we had to meet accidentally? Tom, how could you ..." Elsa was shaken, and she couldn't say any more.

Tom reached for her hands and kissed her palms one after the other. "Elsa, I couldn't."

"But why, if you love me? And if you felt that I love you still, what could hold you back?"

Tom looked at her with loving eyes, and held her hand tighter. "You asked me yesterday if I am sick. Well, I am."

Elsa looked at him with fear and wanted to ask a question, but Tom gently put his finger on her mouth.

"No, don't ask anything. Let me tell you my story."

∼

As you know, I was sent or rather volunteered to take a job in Africa. I volunteered because I was unhappy without you, because I knew that you were not happy either and because I could not see a way out of this misery. I didn't want to interfere with the life you choose for yourself, so I went, hoping that I'd get over you in a country that I had always wanted to see. My boss was a dreamer with connections to a few very rich oilmen in Arabia who owned a huge portion of the Atlantic coastline in Mauritania, one of the poorest countries of North Africa. My boss convinced these men that a tourist resort along the coast would boost the economy of the country and also make them a lot of money. He asked me to do research on the project because of my knowledge of Saharan architecture.

He warned me that it was the third world. The capital, Nouakchott, is the largest city in the Sahara, but there is only a small section of rich settlements in the midst of very large slums and widespread poverty. There was no good hotel, no transportation but driving yourself on almost impossibly rough roads and malaria was a serious health hazard.

Without thinking, I said I would go. I got all the necessary shots, a big box of different pills, first aid kits and a book on how to prevent afflictions. As it turned out, all of that wasn't enough. I had to travel on the coast and deeper inside to the fertile belt along the Senegal river, where there were oases with old settlements and forts. On one of my trips, the jeep broke down. My guide left on foot for the next habitat to bring help. I had supplies but not enough. I had a small tent, but my mosquito nets had been stolen at the last stop. I got sick, my pills ran out and malaria over took me. I was hardly alive when my guide returned three days later with a jeep and took me back to Nouakchott. That city was not the best place to be sick. To cut the story short, my firm arranged to flew me to London through Malaga—it was almost thirteen hours of flying. I was running a high fever and drifting in and out of consciousness. I ended up at the hospital of tropical diseases in London. There I stayed for three weeks until they got me well enough to transfer me to the Toronto General, where they worked on me some more. The problem was that I wasn't treated in time and also that the food I had there was not sufficient for keeping my immune system strong enough to fight the parasites. But now I have recovered most of my health, and the doctors sent me on a holiday to have a break from the treatments."

∽

Elsa listened to Tom's story with anxiety in her heart.

"But you can be cured for sure? Oh, Tom, why didn't you let me know that you were in Toronto in a hospital? You don't know anybody there. Or do you?"

"No, Elsa, not anybody. But how could I call you and have you see the state I was in? Many times during my fever delirium I dreamt that you were sitting beside my bed, holding my hand, but I just couldn't call you and put such a burden on your shoulders. But during my long recovery I decided I was going to get in touch with you when I was cured and not before."

"How are you now? Are you still on medication? Do you have to go back to the hospital?"

"Yes, I have to. This is just a tryout leave. If I can manage to look after myself, taking those pills every day will let me survive. They will run some more tests and then, hopefully, discharge me."

"Do you still have the same apartment in Vancouver?"

"No, I gave it up before I went to Africa, because I wasn't sure where I wanted to live after. Now that you've heard my story, am I forgiven for not to calling you?"

"No, you are not! You should have called me and let me take care of you, but your pride was stronger and beat me out! The most important thing now is to get you well again. Please, Tom, let me help you. I was miserable without you. I missed you and regretted my decision to leave you a million times—"

Tom kissed Elsa's hand again and finished the sentence for her, "But your pride was in the way."

"Yes, that's true, and because of both of our stubbornness, we've lost so many years of happiness! Oh, Tom, do you think we can make up for it?" asked Elsa with tears in her eyes. "Can you forgive me?"

"Darling, there is nothing to forgive. You did what you did because you felt it was the only way you could live with yourself in peace. I had to accept that."

They looked at each other with so much love that it hurt. Tom stood up, paid the bill and they walked out to the lakeshore with their arms around each other. Elsa felt through Tom's light linen jacket how thin his arms were, and her heart went out to him. Before they reached an empty bench, Tom started to shake. His face was sweating when he sat down. Alarmed, Elsa took off her scarf and started to wipe his face gently. Tom took out a pill box and swallowed a few pills.

"I'll be okay in a few minutes. Don't worry, darling."

Elsa sat beside him. Suddenly strong and determined, she got hold of Tom's shoulders. "Tom, look at me! I want you to stay with me. I want to take care of you. We could beat this together."

"No, Elsa, I can't do that now. I must be sure that I will be able to recover. I have to go back to the hospital for more tests. After that we will talk about it. Please, you must understand. I promise I'll call you as soon as I know the results. Now that I've found you I don't want to lose you again! I love you just as much as I did during our happy years together, but I must know what my chances are for getting healthy again."

Elsa was quiet for a while. She wanted to argue, but she knew Tom better than to try it.

"At least let me drive you back to Toronto tomorrow morning."

"No, thank you. You came with your friend for a trip, and you should go ahead with your plans. I'll go back on the bus tomorrow. Really, dearest, don't worry about me. If the doctors let me leave the hospital, I must be able to look after myself."

"You are just as stubborn as you ever were," said Elsa, kissing his cheeks, "but at least let me drive you to the hotel."

"Your wish is granted, lady! But forget about tucking me in."

They held each other tightly for a long time before Tom got out of the car. He wouldn't kiss her on the lips, just her eyes and forehead.

"I'll call you after the tests are done, no matter what the results. I love you!"

He turned back at the entrance, threw a kiss and then disappeared behind the door.

Elsa drove back to the lodge and found Margaret in one of the hammocks in the shade, asleep with an open book on her stomach. She didn't want to wake her, so she found an empty chair nearby and sat down. She was happy to have Tom back in her life, but she was sad because of the crazy circumstances. Without any doubts, she knew that she wanted to have him and take care of him no matter how his sickness turned around. She loved him and wanted to make up for those lonely years, all those empty evenings both of them had because of her oversensitive, naive conscience towards her family. She would not let him out of her sight again.

Margaret stirred, and Elsa looked over at her. When she sighted Elsa, she jumped out of the hammock.

"Elsa, what happened? Did you rush back? Tell me everything—but only if you want to!"

"Let's go down to the water's edge," said Elsa, pointing to two empty chairs there.

She told Margaret to the last sentence what had happened during the few hours she spent with Tom. Margaret listened to her without interruption.

"That is a heartbreaking story! When will you know the results of the tests?"

"Most likely by next week. He'll be back in the Toronto hospital tomorrow."

"Elsa, I have a suggestion. Let's go back to Toronto tomorrow—I don't think you are in the mood for driving around. What I saw was breathtaking, and the scenery further north is probably almost the same. I am lucky to have seen so much of this beautiful country already. I am satisfied with that."

"But, Margaret, we are not even halfway through our planned trip! I don't feel right about turning back now! Who knows if you can come again."

"You never know how many times I might just show up on your doorstep, now that I know the way," joked Margaret. Then, suddenly serious, she continued, "Elsa, I know you. Your heart will be in Toronto with Tom all the way! Let's just go tomorrow, and maybe you can drive a different route and I'll see many more wonders of this countryside. But let's go tomorrow morning. And Elsa, let's just forget about Montreal and Ottawa. I would not feel comfortable going there knowing that you have much more important things to do!"

"Margaret, you are the most understanding person I've ever known! Thank you! But at least let's go out for a nice dinner. I can't offer any first class restaurant in Parry Sound … no, wait. I have an idea!"

She stood up and went to the reception desk, talked to the young girl there and came back smiling.

"Okay, go and bring down a jacket. We are on our way to Frying Pan Island Fish Restaurant, which is about a half-hour boat ride from here. It is a big, flat rock of an island at the edge of the open water. We'll ride around many smaller and larger islands, and you'll see century-old cottages. They are from the times when people came up with steamboats from the city because there were no roads at all. They moved up, bringing servants and supplies for the whole summer.

You must see those historic islands and those big, old-fashioned, wood cottages with the screened in verandas all around. The restaurant is just a simple country diner right on the water's edge, but the fish dishes are always good and you'll enjoy the boat ride. One of the beach boys will take us out. Now you can see a bit more of this part of the country and how these people lived, and I will not feel so bad dragging you home so soon. And tomorrow we'll drive back to Toronto, and I'll find out at Toronto General Hospital where Tom is. I will not wait until he calls me."

Chapter 32

Edith banged down the phone with fury and ran out of the rooming house. She was distressed and enraged. Margaret was not answering her phone and hadn't called her back for five days now. Where was she? Where was Margaret now when she needed her so desperately? Edith had been back in London for almost a month, but she didn't call Margaret at first. She hesitated, not wanting to confess her failure—she was not ready for that yet.

Everything went badly. The tenant would not give up his lease. Her old stall had been rented out to an artist who wasn't willing to share it. She couldn't find the friend to whom she had given away the paintings she left behind. She gave up the possibility of getting any of her things back from Paris—she didn't want to get in touch with them and she was far too humiliated to do so in any case. She had no money, her credit cards were overdrawn, the bank would not give her a loan and the rental income was not enough collateral for them. Nobody would take her in, and her friend on whom she was counting had moved away. She had to rent a single room in a rooming house, and now she did not have enough money left for the next week's rent. She was hoping that Margaret would help her out and send her a train or at least a bus ticket to Budapest and let her stay with her until her finances could be worked out. Maybe she'd get a job there and live with Margaret for the time being. She had a second bedroom, after all, and she would not refuse to take Edith in when she was in such a desperate situation! She was a good friend and a good soul who never refused to help, no matter how badly Edith behaved. But for five days in a row now she had not answered or called back.

"What am I going to do?" she pondered as she walked aimlessly on the streets.

She thought about those distant relatives with whom she had stayed after arriving from Hungary in 1956, but ever since Gabor died, she hardly saw them. She dutifully visited them before she moved to Paris. It was a short and frustrating visit, and they didn't have anything to talk about. The old couple was hard of hearing and didn't understand half of what Edith told them, and she left as soon as she could without hurting their feelings, promising to get in touch from Paris. She knew they would not be any help—they were not well off, living on their old-age pension in a small, cluttered house in the outskirts of London. She would be forced to call them if there nothing else came up. Maybe they'd let her stay with them for a while. But even the thought of that possibility sent shivers down on her spine.

Margaret must call, she will, she will! Edith assured herself.

She stopped in front of a pub, but counting her money realized that she could not get more than two drinks. So she walked on until she found an all-night store in a narrow alley behind the main street. There she bought a bottle of the cheapest whisky. While leaving, she saw the proprietor bend down behind the cash register to pick up the change that had fallen off the countertop. The shop was empty, and before even realizing it, she had picked up a bottle from the basket beside the door, hidden it behind the bag of the bottle she had paid for and hurried out of the shop. She broke into run until she reached the busy main street. There she hid in an empty doorway, panting. Nobody took any notice of her in that rundown neighbourhood. After she caught her breath, she started towards the rooming house. She was disgusted with herself—she stole! She stole for the first time in her life, and it was alcohol, not bread! How could she sink so low? At every step, her self-loathing grew and she blamed the whole world for it. She blamed Gabor for dying, her lovers who used her, Antal who did not stay alive to be with her, Margaret who didn't call her back and her so-called friends in Paris who cheated her and wanted to use her. She went on and on, mumbling to herself.

She didn't run into anybody in the rooming house, and she could hear the owners having dinner in the kitchen. The doors on her floor were all shut, but from behind one of them she could hear music and laughter. That made her even more enraged, that someone could have a good time when she was deserted by everyone and full of misery. She took out the whisky and finally looked at the other bottle—it was cheap rum. She locked her door, undressed and put on a bathrobe. Sitting in the rickety easy chair by the window and looking at the dark sky, she started on the whiskey. Feeling sorry for herself, she drank glass after glass. When she felt sleepy enough, she took out a bag of pills Barb had given her once when she had difficulty sleeping, saying that they were mild sleeping pills. She took a handful and swallowed it with the rest of the whisky. She had a hard time getting to her bed, but she collapsed on it and fell into a deep sleep almost immediately.

She didn't know how long she slept, but she woke with a splitting migraine. It was dark, and only the streetlights through the window lit the room. Edith didn't turn on the light, but she got up from the bed, found the bottle of rum on the table, took a long, deep sip and washed down the leftover pills with a long swallow.

She suddenly needed to go to the washroom, which was at the end of the hallway. The hallway was dark because the landlord, wanting to save on electricity, never left the light on during the night. There was a small, solitary night light beside the door of the washroom. Edith started out towards it. Her legs wobbled like jelly, her head was spinning and she had to support herself with shaking arms on both walls of the narrow corridor. When she reached the stairway, one side of the wall ended. She lost her support—her balance was gone. She tripped and fell down the hard, wood steps, hitting her head on every one until she reached the bottom. After that she didn't feel anything.

She probably screamed when tumbling down, because the landlord woke with the rest of the tenants. They found her lying motionless at the bottom of the steps. The landlady started to scream, "Call an ambulance, call an ambulance."

One of the tenants bent down and reached for Edith's pulse. There was no sign of life.

"It's too late for the ambulance. I think she is dead. Probably broke her neck during the fall. You should call the police too. She reeks of alcohol."

Chapter 33

"Hello, I was worried that you missed your flight!" Jànos Horvath greeted Margaret as he stood up to let her take the window seat.

"Hello, Jànos, thank you," said Margaret. Jànos took her carry-on and put it up in the compartment. "No, Elsa and I were just too long saying our goodbyes and the line was long at security, but I made it!" She made herself comfortable in her seat with sigh of relief.

"How was your visit, Jànos?"

"It was really good, but I was ready to leave. I think I'm getting too old and grumpy for the constant activities and noises of two little kids. I love them all dearly, it was great to be with them and I will miss them for sure, but I think I'm going to enjoy the peace and quiet of my old apartment. How about you? How was your visit?"

"It was great. My friend took me all over the place—we went up north to the cottage country and visited Niagara Falls. She wanted to take me over to the states, but I didn't have a U.S. visa so we only looked at the two national flags on the Peace Bridge. Did you go anywhere?"

"Yes, but nowhere far because of the kids. We had a few outings to the country. Besides, this was not my first visit as you know. When my son was single, we would just take off to visit faraway places like

Montreal and the east coast. Those times I saw a fraction of that huge, wonderful country."

They exchanged their experiences during drinks and dinner, and they looked over each other's photographs. When the lights were turned down after dinner neither of them felt like watching the in-flight movie. They settled down as comfortably as was possible. Jànos helped Margaret open her blanket, asked for one more pillow for her and helped to adjust her seat. Both of them drifted to sleep lolled by the constant, monotone hum of the engines.

Margaret felt relaxed and almost happy if she didn't think about Elsa and the difficult times ahead of her. Jànos's kindness and attention also made her mellow. She admitted to herself that no matter how often she declared herself as a self-sufficient female who doesn't need anybody, his presence could be the thing she sometimes felt was missing in her life.

During breakfast, they continued their conversation, and before they landed Jànos asked, "Margaret, I would like to see you again. We are able to talk with each other about everything with such ease. You are an intelligent and kind person. Can I call you in a few days?"

"I would like that, yes," Margaret answered. "But it will take me at least a week to get back into my normal life here, I'd guess. Call me at the end of next week—we can meet for a coffee or some such. Here is my card." They looked at each other with warm smiles.

As they waited together at the luggage carousel, Jànos asked, "Is somebody waiting for you? Can I give you a lift? A friend of mine is waiting for me with my car."

"No, thank you, Jànos. I'll take the minibus as always. Here is my suitcase. Oh, thank you," said Margaret when Jànos lifted her bag up and put it on her cart. "I'll be looking forward to your call. Goodbye, happy homecoming."

Finally home, Margaret unpacked and suddenly felt so tired that she decided to have a nice, long soak in her tub and leave everything else, like mail and messages, for the next day. She called her daughter and son just to say that she was home safe and would call them in a few days to tell them about her trip. She soaked in the tub for a long time. She nodded off a few times too. She sent an e-mail to Elsa to let her know she got home all right, and then she went to bed and fell asleep almost immediately.

She awoke in the late afternoon and couldn't go back to sleep, so she got up, made herself a strong coffee and started to look through her mail. There was nothing interesting, just a few bills and a note from the university about a meeting before the semester started. Then she looked over her phone messages. There were several calls from an unknown number but no messages. When she got to the fifth call, there was a message from Edith.

Her voice said, "Margaret, where are you? Please call me back."

She looked at the numbers again and realized by the area code that all the unknown calls were from London but not from Edith's apartment. Margaret could not understand why Edith would call from London but not from her own place. Thinking that perhaps she went back to settle some official business and stayed with a friend, Margaret got to the next message. It was again Edith, but her voice was shaking and was hardly distinguishable. It was the angry, hysterical voice Margaret knew so well. Her friend was in distress.

"Margaret, why don't you call? I need you, don't abandon me, please call! You must call!"

It was late evening and Margaret didn't want to call the London number, so she decided to call the next morning. In the meantime, she finished unpacking, and she cleaned and aired the apartment. She couldn't sleep too much during the night and was up again at dawn. At six in the morning, she went to the market to fill up her kitchen shelves and refrigerator. She called the London number after ten, but there was no answer. She called several times during the day but the phone kept ringing and nobody picked it up. Finally, after six o'clock in the afternoon, she got an answer. It was a male voice with a harsh British accent.

"Hallo, hallo?"

"I don't know if this is the right number, but I am looking for my girlfriend, Edith. Is she there?"

"I don't know. Let me get the landlady, just a sec."

Margaret waited for a long time and was ready to hang up when a woman answered, "Yes, who is this?"

"I am a friend of Edith Kalmar, calling from Budapest, Hungary. She left me this number a few days ago. Is she there?"

There was long silence. Then the woman said, "She was but not any more."

"Would you know her new address or where can I find her?"

"You can't find her, she is dead."

"What do you mean, 'she is dead'?"

"She died four days ago. Fell down the steps and broke her neck because she was stinking drunk! I've had enough trouble with the police, so I don't want to talk about it anymore. If you want more information, call the police!" The line went dead.

Margaret was dumbstruck. Edith was dead! Why was she in London? Why was she drunk? Something awful must have happened to her in Paris! But her last letter was full of happiness and good news! True, it was more than a month ago, and she didn't write at all after that. What could have happened? Why didn't she seek Margaret's help as she always did when she couldn't cope with things? How can she get more information? Call the police? Where, what police station? Her mind was racing, and the reality of Edith's death didn't register for a long time.

When it did, Margaret got sick and had to rush to the bathroom to throw up. She felt awful. She had to call Elsa.

"Elsa?"

"Margaret! I am so glad you called. I was just thinking about you, I miss you! Margaret? Margaret? Is anything wrong?"

"Edith died!"

"Died? When? How? Are you sure?"

"Yes, I just talked with a woman where she stayed. There were several calls from Edith on my answering machine, and when I called back the number, an unfriendly, hostile woman told me."

"Did she call from Paris?"

"No, from London. I don't know why she was there! And that woman told me that she was drunk, fell down the steps and broke her neck!"

"Oh, Margaret, that is terrible! I am so sorry!"

"I feel dreadful. If I had been here to answer her call, she would be alive today!"

"Don't torment yourself! It happened and it couldn't be helped! Would we ever know what really did happen?"

"That woman said that she had enough problems because of Edith and hung up me after she said that if I wanted to know more, I should call the police! But I don't even know the address where she stayed!"

"Maybe if you call the London operators and tell them the phone number you called, they can get you in touch with the police in that district."

"Yes, that's it! Why didn't I think of that? Thank you, Elsa! I am going to call right now."

"Margaret, are you all right?"

"Yes, I am now. It's still a shock, but my mind is clearing."

"Okay, but please call me as soon as you know the details. And see if I can do something for you!"

"I will, thanks, Elsa."

It was late in the evening when Margaret finally collapsed on her sofa and put down the phone. It left a red ring around her ears, and her right hand was numb from gripping the handle. The police had been very helpful after she identified herself. She learned they had found her name and a few letters from her among Edith's belongings, and they found some distant relatives who identified the body. There was an autopsy which established that it was an accidental death caused by a combination of the fall, alcohol and drugs. There was no will, so the next of kin would inherit and look after the funeral arrangements. The friendly police officer had asked if she knew the relatives or wanted their number, but Margaret had said no and then thanked him very warmly for the information. It was late in the evening at the small, district police station, and the officer on duty must have been bored and happy to talk.

Margaret sat on the sofa for a long time. She grieved for her friend for dying in such a horrible way, and alone. Now she would never know what happened to her in Paris.

What went wrong with that short-lived happiness she wrote so much about? Margaret wondered, holding her head in her hands.

It was well after midnight when Margaret went to bed, but she could not fall asleep for a long time. And after she did, she had dark dreams about Edith. Edith was screaming for help, and Margaret wanted to go to her with all her strength but could not reach her in time. Edith faded away, but her scream hung on.

Margaret woke up suddenly to find her body shaking. She got out of bed and walked around the apartment until she became so fatigued that could not move. She was drained physically and mentally. Collapsing on her bed, she succeeded in sleeping fretfully for a few hours.

In the morning, she felt as if she had been run over by a steamroller. Her whole body ached, and she could hardly get out of bed. She forced herself to do a few stretching exercises, and after that she drank her coffee. She felt better physically, but she was still lonely and miserable. She couldn't get Edith out of her mind. It would be so good to talk about the tragedy to another living human being—and not just on the phone.

She looked at the clock on the kitchen wall—it was after nine o'clock. She rummaged through her handbag and found the card she was looking for. Then she took a deep breath and dialled the number on the card.

"Hello, Jànos. This is Margaret."

"Margaret, what a pleasant surprise! I was just thinking about you! I've been trying to decide between waiting until next week or being a nuisance and daring to call you now. What can I do for you?"

"Jànos, some very bad news was waiting for me at home, and I can't cope with it alone. Would you come over for a talk?"

"Well, of course. I'll be there as soon as I get dressed. I know your address ... it will only take me thirty minutes to get there. See you soon."

As he had promised, Jànos arrived in a half hour. He looked at Margaret's pale face and the dark circles under her eyes, and his first reaction was to put his arms around her and hold her. But he restrained his feelings—he didn't want to frighten her away, so he just greeted her warmly and kissed her hand. Margaret broke down and fell into

Jànos's arms, sobbing out of control. Jànos held her without a word and stroked her hair gently.

"I am sorry to be such a crybaby. I don't know what came over me to bother you with my call!" she said after a while, once her sobs quieted down. Disengaging herself from his arms, she pled, "Please forgive me!"

"Not at all. What are friends for? And I hope we are friends? What happened to make you so upset? I am a good listener," he said, smiling at her.

"Oh, Jànos, it's so horrible I don't know where to begin! I did tell you a little bit about my other friend who lived in London?" Jànos nodded, and Margaret continued, "Well, when I came home I got the news that she died …"

Margaret told the story of Edith—her unfortunate life, her moodiness, her depressions and what she knew about the last parts of her life. Jànos listened without interruption, and whenever Margaret's voice broke, he just held her hand tighter. After she finished her story, there was a long silence. Jànos let Margaret calm down before he moved and got hold of both of her hands.

"Margaret, this is a terrible tragedy, and I fully understand how you feel. But you have to realize that something like that was bound to happen to her sooner or later. As much as I learned about her now, it seems she was a weak, depressed personality who couldn't or didn't want to help herself and saw herself in the role of a martyr. You did what you could during your friendship to help her stand on her own feet and look into herself before blaming the whole word for her misfortune. It was an unfortunate situation that you were away when she last needed you, but you can't blame yourself for her death. The only thing you can do is to try to overcome this tragic accident."

"It is not easy! I'm afraid it will be a long time before I can think about her without any regrets or sorrow. I can't help feeling responsible for her death. I should have tried harder in the last few years to help her. Do you think I should get in touch with her relatives?"

"I don't think so. It would just stir you up again. You don't know them and they have probably never heard of you, so let it be. You don't need to hear the horrible details of her death. They probably didn't know anything about her life, and you'll never know what happened in Paris. You don't know the people there. You can't do anything to change the fact that she is dead. Think about your good times together, and try to forget about how it ended."

Margaret's tears were flowing, but slowly she calmed down. "Yes," she said, "I think you are right. Thank you for listening! I feel much better."

"And now get your coat. It is a beautiful day—let's have some fresh air and a long walk. What do you say?"

"Great idea, but I have to call Elsa first and let her know what I found out."

They went up to Castle Hills, walking in rhythm side by side like two old friends, like they had walked together for many years.

Jànos listened to Margaret's stories about Edith and sometimes asked questions. After a while, Margaret talked herself out. They walked in comforting silence for some time, and then Jànos said, "I am hungry, and I hope you are too. At the next block there is a small bistro that serves lovely sandwiches and great coffee. You would like it—they have a small patio too."

"Sounds good, let's go there."

Waiting for their coffee, Jànos looked at Margaret for a long time, merely smiling.

"What are you thinking about?" asked Margaret.

"You have beautiful blue eyes, and they turn darker when you smile. Did you know that?"

"Oh, come on, Jànos. You are not going to court me, are you? I am a senior!"

"Senior or not, you are still a remarkable-looking woman! And besides, who cares about age? We are as young as we feel!"

"True, that's my sentiment too, but sometimes I feel hundred years old. Like I did this morning."

"Margaret, I like being with you. I like you a lot! I've been a lonely, old widower for so many years. My wife died more than five years ago—she had cancer. It was a good marriage. We were soul mates and loved each other to the very end. I was devastated by her death and fell into a deep depression. My son almost forcefully took me to Toronto. There, he got me a Hungarian therapist, and slowly my son's love and the therapy got me out of the deep. I am fine now and have been for a few years. I lived quietly, reading a lot, listening to music and liking my solitude. I never thought I could find someone again whom I could talk to about my life and be interested in hers. And now I feel that I can talk to you about everything. I am so comfortable with you! Do you have any feelings for me?"

Margaret was touched by his confession but also frightened. She was silent for a while, playing with her napkin and not looking at him. Then she looked up and said, "Jànos, if I didn't feel for you as a friend, I wouldn't have called you in my distress. I like you very much, and I am very comfortable with you too. I think I want to be your friend. But I am an independent, strong-willed woman who has lived on her own for many years. I never let anybody in to share my life. I don't think I would be the kind of friend you might hope I would be. I could never give up my independence."

"I don't want you to do that! But it would be good for both of us to share a few concerts or movies or even talk about books whenever you feel like it. I will not interfere with your life. I am not a demanding person, and I wouldn't ask for anything more. Both of us could live our own lives because we wouldn't be depending on each other. We could say no if we felt like being alone without hurting any feelings. But both of us will know that we are there for each other without any further obligation. Would you like to have a friendship like that?"

Margaret wanted to say yes immediately, but she held back and sat in silence. She was not sure she could be a friend of a man, no matter how undemanding he was. Maybe it would be good to have a male friend with no sexual attachment, but judging from her feelings she knew that attachment would be there soon. The fact that she was over sixty didn't diminish her sexuality. Sometimes she was almost painfully aware that she missed having sex, but she never did anything about it. During her life, love had only hurt her. She suffered because she loved, she suffered because she hated and she suffered because she was alone. There were a few colleagues and some distant friends who had tried to get her interested, but she always stepped back, not wanting any distraction in her life.

She never stopped dreaming of happiness because she knew if she did, her soul would die just like her body would without nourishment.

It would be so nice to curl up in Jànos's arms and wake up beside him instead of hugging her blanket for comfort on lonely nights. But how long would it last? And what would happen then? She didn't want any complications and new pain in the winter of her years. But this could be her last chance to change her life for the better, and she couldn't be too afraid to do something about it. Why not try to get out the best of it and not worry about what might happen?

She looked into Jànos's warm, brown eyes and said, "Yes, I'd like to give us a chance."

Chapter 34

Elsa sat in the waiting room in the doctor's office at the Toronto General Hospital's tropical diseases unit. After long days of talks, Tom had agreed to stay in Toronto and let her take care of him on one condition: Elsa had to talk to the chief doctor of the unit about Tom's situation. She had to understand all of the problems, hardships and difficulties that could develop because of his sickness. He refused Elsa's offer to move in with her, but he agreed to find a place close to her apartment. Elsa was hoping that if she could make him agree to let her take care of him, she'd find a way to change his mind about that too.

The secretary called Elsa's name and showed her to the doctor's office. The doctor sat behind his desk, studying several folders in front of him and talking on the phone. He looked up when Elsa walked in, pointed to the chair in front of his desk and motioned for Elsa to sit down. He kept talking for a few minutes, then hung up the phone and smiled at Elsa. He had a nice, friendly smile.

"I'm sorry to keep you waiting, but that was an important call—I had to finish it. What can I do for you?" He looked down his desk. "Mrs. Martos?"

"I am here to get information about your patient, Tom Berontel. He asked me to talk with you about his present condition and the future problems of his illness. I think he told you that I was coming."

"Yes, and he asked me to be brutally honest with you. I understood that you want to take care of him. Is that right?"

"Yes, but he wouldn't let me decide before you made it absolutely clear what could be involved."

"As much as I've heard from him, he is a very lucky guy to have somebody like you."

"Well, ours is a long story, and I don't want to lose him again," said Elsa. She looked at the doctor questioningly and whispered, "Please?"

The doctor looked straight into Elsa's eyes and replied, "Tom is very sick. When he got infected, his immune system was at a dangerously low level because of the poor food intake—no vitamins and so on. Also, he didn't get treatment soon enough to get rid of the disease. Later, they used every possible treatment, but he had frequent relapses. The dormant parasites reactivated, mostly in his liver. We treated this problem almost successfully, but we could not get him entirely clean. At present, he is fine and can cope with the occasional relapses, but we can't guarantee if things will stay like that."

Elsa listened to him with a determined expression on her face, and when he stopped talking, she asked, "Please tell me the worst that could happen—in non-medical phrases so I can fully understand the situation."

"Well, you must know that we can't predict his reaction to the drug treatment 100 per cent. He could recover fully in time, if he can build up his immune system. That will take a sensible diet, lots of vitamins, a long therapy program and rest. But the disease could be stronger than him. In that case, he could have fluid buildup in his lungs, which causes respiratory distress, he could suffer from acute kidney failure, he could have a decrease in blood platelets or worse—cardiovascular collapse and shock."

"Does he know all about that?"

"Not so fully. We didn't want him to know the worse possibilities, which might or might not happen, because he would not be able to fully concentrate on the amelioration. We have seen people give up after the first few relapses and lose faith that they can get better. Tom needs all his strength and hard determination to keep fighting against this disease."

"I see your point, Doctor. I'll try my best for him, and I'm sure that he'll do his best to get better. When can he leave the hospital?"

"We have one more test running, and we need him to be here for that. Let's say in about a week. But he has to check in with us every month at first but less frequently later on." The doctor looked at Elsa closely. Then he asked, "Are you sure you want to do this? It could be very tiring, and you'll need a lot of patience. He could be cranky, difficult and fall into long depressions if he gets a longer-lasting relapse. He could be a full-time and sometimes hopeless job."

"I am positive I can look after him, and if it gets too difficult for me alone, I can always hire part-time help. Thank you for your concern and time. I truly appreciate it. Can I go and see him now?"

"Yes, but it is needless to say to keep the possible worse part to yourself. Let's hope that it will never happen."

They stood up, shook hands and Elsa left the office.

Before she went to look for Tom, Elsa sat down in the lobby to collect her thoughts. She wanted to search her heart, mind and soul and really know if she was strong enough to take on such a responsibility. Does she really love him so much as to change her life for him? Years ago she wasn't—she left him because her family was the first priority in her life. But now, with her family scattered, there was ample room for him. She was also sure of her deep love for him, and she felt a certain kind of guilt that Tom went to Africa because of her abandonment. She was convinced she had the strength to stand beside him in his fight for a longer life. She wanted to be needed, and she was sure that this time she would not turn out to be the needy one. True, her life would change and her freedom and independence would suffer, but she'd cope with it!

She pulled herself up from the chair and went to Tom's room. It was empty, and the nurse told her that Tom went out for a walk in the garden. She gave her the directions, and Elsa found him on a bench in a sunny spot. His face lit up when he noticed Elsa approaching. She sat down beside him, kissed his forehead and snuggled close to him.

"So," he said, "what did you talk about with Dr. Friar? You think he told you everything you should know? I asked him to be honest about me."

"Yes, Tom, he was. He is a very good man and wants to see you cured. And he also agreed that I could be a great help to you."

"Yes, but did he explain all the things that could result from this?"

"I don't see any reason why I wouldn't be able to deal with any kind of situation involving your sickness! I love you and want to be with you. I don't want to lose you again. You must get well! Two is better than one—we will beat this, I am sure of it!"

"But, my love, I could be an impossible burden. I am useless, irritated and impossible if I get one of those relapses. I cannot be a lover anymore, or at least not for a while, and who knows if my sexual powers will ever come back? You are still an active, beautiful woman who deserves a good lover, not just a useless companion, no matter how loving he is! Why would you take such a liability into your life? You are a free woman, why would you take on such an obligation?"

"As I've told you many times, because I love you! At our age, the loving companion is more important and meaningful than a sex partner! So stop making excuses! No more arguments! You have to stay here for a week, and during that time I am going to search for a suitable apartment for you on my street or around it. It would be much easier if you would give up your stubbornness and move in with me, but okay, I understand it will be a very sudden change for both of us. Let's do it slowly. If you give me your permission to choose the place without you seeing it, I can rent you one in two days. I have my eye on a specific one currently, and it's just about three buildings away from me. It is a bright, one-bedroom place with a balcony overlooking the park."

"Of course. Do what ever you think is best for both of us. I am well provided for because of the company's insurance, and I have sufficient money saved. I don't have to worry about living expenses."

They sat there until late afternoon, reminiscing about their first meeting in Venice and their years in Vancouver. Neither of them wanted to talk about what the future could bring, but both of them trusted that their love would overcome every obstacle and they were going to be happy together. It was after five when the nurse came and called Tom inside.

They parted with a long, warm embrace, and Elsa stayed in the garden until Tom disappeared through the entrance.

Elsa called the real estate agent on her cell phone and made an appointment for the next morning to see the apartment she had in mind. On the way home she stopped at the supermarket and bought some groceries and a grilled chicken for her dinner—she didn't feel like cooking. She pushed the thought that she would have to starting very soon deep into her mind.

After she ate, she called Lili and told her about her decision to take care of Tom.

"You are crazy, out of your mind! How could you take on such a burden? Are you going to be Florence Nightingale? You are going to be tied down for the rest of your life or his! I know what I'm talking about—I'm tied down with Michael, but he is my husband. You couldn't want that from your free will!"

"Lili, you know I love him. It doesn't mean anything that he is not my husband. I want to do it simply for the reason that I want to be with him."

"I'm familiar with your stubbornness, so I will not argue. It's your funeral. This means, of course, that you are not coming here this winter as we planned? You are neglecting me for him as usual!"

"Oh, Lili, don't be a bitch! You are my best friend always. I am here for you if you need me, you must know that! This will not mean that I can't travel alone!"

"I know you. You won't let him out of your sight for just a short time. How many times did you cut our trips short and run home, feeling guilty about being away from your darling family for too long. And I don't have point it out that they left you alone without blinking an eye!"

"You are pitiless and cruel, but I must admit you have a point. But you know me—I have to feel to be needed to be happy."

"Bullshit, my dear! But as I said, it's your life. I am still counting on your visit this winter, okay, mate?"

"Okay, I promise I'll come. How is Michael?"

"He has his good days and his bad, but he is getting along. He occupies himself with the stock market reports on the Internet. If his stocks are going up, he is well, and if they are down, he is miserable and worries about his future finances. The weather has started to cool off and he forces me to take walks with him. It is good for his health, but it tires me out."

"It's good for you too. At least you are getting some exercise and not just sitting around drinking coffee and smoking all day. Are you over your last fiasco? Did you explain to Michael the sudden change in your plans about the business?"

"I just told him that I didn't see any future in it and called it off. He didn't ask any questions."

"Do you think he sensed the real reason?"

"I didn't think about it. I deleted it from my mind and so should you!"

"I'm sorry, I didn't mean to pry."

"Okay, I confess I am still hurt a bit, but it will go."

"That's my friend! Take care and count your blessings."

"Yes, Mother. Keep me posted about the happenings, call me!"

Elsa looked at the clock to figure out what time it was in Budapest. She wanted to call Margaret, but it was late at night there. She decided to call the next morning before her appointment with the real estate agent.

"Hi, Margaret!" Elsa said when her friend answered the phone.

"Elsa, how good to hear your voice! I just got in from the university. On the way home I decided to write you a long e-mail, but this is much better! How are you? How is Tom doing?"

"I am good, and Tom is getting better. I talked to his doctor, and I decided to take care of him." She told Margaret everything about her talk with the doctor and the decision about the apartment.

"Well, I can understand your feelings," Margaret said, "but did you really think it over thoroughly? I know you love him, but it is going to be a complete change in your life. Are you sure you could do it without regrets after?"

"Yes. I have been thinking about it long and hard. I need him in my life! I was very lonely without him, and I think that if fate brought him back in my life again, it must be for a reason. How are things working out with Jànos and you?"

"It seems it will work. He is a great friend. We talk a lot, go to concerts and sometimes to a theatre. I am very comfortable with him, and he is not demanding at all. He is a really nice partner to have around."

"I am glad to hear that. Lili would ask you if you've gone to bed with him, but I am not that nosy, am I?" laughed Elsa.

"You are, but it didn't happen yet, which doesn't mean it will not. I think I am close to it to committing myself. But, Elsa, I haven't had a lover for over twenty years! I don't remember sex—only how to spell it!"

"It will come back to you, just like bike riding! Don't worry!"

"Elsa, I am over sixty!"

"So? Age doesn't matter, you'll see. Don't be afraid. You are much younger than your years!"

"Okay, I believe you! How are you and Tom doing?"

"He is still too sick and weak to even think about sex, but we have our memories, and we can live on them for the time being."

"Elsa, I hope that this big decision will not put too much strain on you and will work out as well as you hope. Did you tell Lili?"

"Yes, and she told me I am out of my mind as usual. But you know her. I promised that I'd still go to visit her this winter, so she mellowed out a bit. Margaret, I have to go, I have an appointment with a real estate agent about the apartment I want to rent for Tom. I'll call you after everything has settled down, okay? Say hi to Jànos for me, and be happy!"

Elsa liked the apartment. It was a big, one-bedroom in an old, two-story house just like the house her apartment was in. The steps up to the second floor were a bit steep, but there were not too many of them. The big bedroom had a small balcony overlooking the park, and it would get the morning sun. The living room had big windows facing west, giving it plenty of evening sun. The kitchen was small, but it had new cabinets and appliances. It was free, unoccupied and just needed to be painted so she could rent it starting the next week. Most importantly, it was the third building down on the other side of the street from her place. She signed a one-year lease and could hardly wait for the afternoon when she would tell Tom about it.

Tom was excited about his new place and was sure that it would be just great for him. Elsa asked him to give her all the information and papers about his storage in Vancouver. She wanted get the moving process started as soon as possible so the apartment would be ready for him when he was released from the hospital. If his furniture couldn't be there by then, she said he would move into her guest room until everything was be ready. When Tom started to argue that he'd rather move into a hotel, Elsa put her hand on his arm.

"Tom, we've been through that argument many times," she said, "please understand that I want to have you in my life. Because of that there is no inconvenience! And if you love me, you must know that!"

"Yes, my dear, I do love you more than I can say. The more I think about living close to you, the happier I am! I want us to be happy and make up for those lost years."

That night Elsa could not fall asleep. She turned and tossed and finally gave up. Getting out of bed, she put on a warm robe and sat down on her terrace without turning on any lights. The sky was dark. There was no moon, and the stars were burning very bright. On the big maple tree, a bird gave out a short peep and was quiet again. From the distant main street, she could hear the noise of the late-night traffic, but it soon faded away too. Her potted plants were waiting motionless with closed petals for the dawn dew. She felt that the world stood still. Looking up to the blinking stars, she realized that the tightness in her body was fear. She had finalized the situation quickly, which was against her usual nature of thinking things over many times and considering every possibility.

Tom's sudden reappearance in her life, the memories of those loving years and the sorrow she felt for his sickness hadn't let her seriously think the facts over. Was her love really as strong as she thought it was? Would it last through the future years of being a nurse and a companion? Or, after the sensation of the rejoining had passed, would it be a burden on her life? They were apart for many years; both of them must have changed as their lives went on without the other. They were seniors now, with habits and peculiarities brought on by the solitude of their separate lives. Would it be too late now for a happy, comfortable relationship? Would they be able to complement each other's habitual routines of life? Sex was not a crucial issue anymore, but understanding, sharing, love and togetherness were. She knew herself very well—she knew that no matter what happened she would not leave him. She would stay with him as long they lived, happy or not. She could lose her independence entirely, her freedom to travel and her freedom to live her life as she liked it. And how would David would feel about it? Maybe it would ease his conscience if his mother was not alone and less lonely. Or would he be against their relationship just as he was then? Would he say that Tom with his sickness was taking advantage of her soft heart? Would it mean their mother-son bond would cool off?

The sky had started to lighten on the horizon when she finally stood up and went back to bed without finding any solution for her dilemmas.

The next week passed quickly. The furniture arrived, and Tom could leave the hospital for a few hours at a time. He loved the apartment and selected what he needed to furnish it to his liking and sent the rest to the Salvation Army. Elsa unpacked his clothing, bought the necessary kitchen utilities and made the apartment into a warm home with drapes, pillows and plants. She did all the chores with pleasure and cleared all her earlier worries from her mind. She was sure she could deal with whatever problem occurred in the future.

Tom was finally discharged from the hospital, and Elsa drove him home. He stood in the middle of his living room with tears in his eyes. Elsa went into his arms and the two embraced, holding each other tightly for a long time while their tears mixed on their faces.

When they finally let each other go, Tom looked at Elsa shamefacedly and said, "See how old and sentimental I got? I don't remember the last time I cried. But I couldn't help feeling that after so many lonely years I am home for good. You gave me back the will to live … how can I thank you?"

"By getting well, doing everything the doctors say and always remembering that I am here for you and love you forever!"

Holding hands, they walked through the small apartment. Tom was overjoyed.

"Elsa, you are a marvel! I'll be happy here for sure. And to know that you are just a few steps from me makes me even happier."

They sat on the balcony, looking out over the park and the big maple trees, holding hands with peace in their hearts. The leaves had started to change colour—some were still green, but others mixed yellow, dark red and orange in an orgy of colours. Birds were zigzagging between the branches, chasing insects. Black squirrels played running games up and down the trunks and jumping acrobatically from one branch to the other. Tom and Elsa sat there in silence, occasionally looking at each other. They didn't need to talk, as both of them knew what the other was thinking, just like so many years ago in the Vancouver apartment. Later, Elsa served a light snack and opened a bottle of champagne that she had cooled in the fridge before she went to pick Tom up. They toasted their new life and togetherness. By that time Tom looked tired.

"Tom, it is getting late. You must have your rest. I am going home. Here is a cell phone with my number in it. Please call if you need me. Promise?" Looking down at the phone in his hand with wonder, Tom nodded. "And call me in the morning when you are up so we can go out for a walk in the park. I'll show you around the neighbourhood."

"Elsa, I don't want to dominate your life. Please don't feel that you have to spend all your time with me! You have to keep your freedom to do what you used to do before I invaded your life."

Chapter 35

Lili sat on her new patio at dusk, sipping one of her numberless daily Nescafes, looking into her newly redone kitchen through the new, large, custom-made glass sliding door. The kitchen gleamed with new mahogany cabinets and brand-new appliances, all of them the best money could buy. The recessed ceiling lights made the sand-coloured marble countertops look like warm velvet. She took a sip from her designer mug and turned her attention to the garden. It was newly planted, and the orange trees, grapefruit trees, bushes and flowerbeds were designed in a way that gave the sensation of being in an enchanted garden. She let out a long sigh of despair. She had achieved everything she ever wanted. She had redone the whole house to her liking. She couldn't do anymore. She had hoped that all the changes would make her feel satisfied, relaxed and maybe even happy.

Michael had died some time ago. Soon after her unfortunate affair with Tivadar, of which he didn't know about (or did he?), he had a second mild stroke that seriously disabled him. He could not walk, and getting out of bed or a chair was a problem. Lili wouldn't let him go to a nursing home, so she hired nurses around the clock, and the doctor visited him weekly. Soon after the second stroke, he had another seizure, and this one made him a vegetable dependent upon a life-support system. He had a living will—he didn't want to be kept alive by machines, so the life support was turned off, and he died without regaining consciousness. He didn't suffer, and his passing was mercifully fast.

During the time of his bedridden state, Lili did everything she could to make him comfortable. She sat with him for hours, talked to him and played cards and scrabble. She wanted to make up for her often indifferent behaviour during their marriage. She was patient and loving, put her own importance on hold and Michael was happy. She couldn't do more, and that belief cleared her soul of any doubts about being a good wife. She did cry a lot in the weeks after the funeral—she found she missed him terribly.

She was lonely, and her days were empty. She had certainly lived her own life before and had done whatever she wanted regardless of being married, but now it was different. There was no Michael anymore who adored her, who was proud of her and who was always there when she needed him. He had been the rock in her life, someone to come home to after her escapades and travels. His quiet understanding towards her eccentric, selfish and self-centered personality gave her such security that it made her relaxed and more or less satisfied with her life. To get out from under her cycle of self-pity, she started to redo the house the way she has always wanted but Michael was always against because of the mess, the inconvenience, and the money.

As it turned out, he had much more money than he thought. During his last month when he was unable to follow his stocks (he never trusted anyone to do it for him), two of them skyrocketed, making him a very rich man. He had no relatives, and Lili was the only beneficially of his will. She talked it over with her own financial adviser and decided to sell most of the stocks. She invested in blue stocks to be safer from the ups and downs of the market, which she felt she did not know enough and never trusted anyway. She also had her own money and her own income—overnight she became an independently rich woman. She started to spend recklessly. Besides redoing the house, she bought her dream car—a white, convertible Jaguar—and a home entertainment unit for the wall of her living room.

But all this did not make her happy. She was miserable and restless. She tried to wake up her interest by bringing home dozens of travel folders and spending days on Web sites searching for exotic destinations. But nothing aroused her interest.

The dog scratched her leg, wanting attention. Lili picked him up, and the dog licked her face and curled up on her lap with a deep sigh. Lili patted his head, stroked his ears, reached for a cigarette, lit up and turned her attention to the travel magazine on the table.

A distracting, unwelcome noise rose from the neighbour's garden— a baby's cry. New people had moved in a few months ago with a toddler and a baby. The children were outside often. Lili met the nice, young couple a few days after they moved in. They got acquainted but never went beyond a, "good morning" or "how are you" when they ran into each other on the street. The family was well off, a nanny took care of the kids and they had a housekeeper too. Hearing the baby's cry made Lili upset.

There was a part of her life that she had never talked about to anyone but Elsa. She had wiped it out of her mind and soul utterly, but she was helpless when at times it surfaced from somewhere very deep in her consciousness. The baby she lost.

He was born a healthy seven pounds and had an angry cry and dark, silky hair. She had mixed feelings about him, as she never had the motherly instinct and did not want to have children. It was maybe because of her unhappy childhood or because of her self-worship. But when she accidentally became pregnant, Peter was so happy and proud, and besides that she couldn't do anything about it. She hoped that in time her motherly feelings would wake up and she'd be a good mother. She never had a chance to find out, however.

Her boy was close to two months old. She put him down in his crib one night after the midnight feeding, covered him up and stood there looking at him. A warm feeling washed over her body, and she welcomed it, hoping that after all she was on her way to becoming a loving mother. She went to bed, glowing. There was no sound from the crib all night long. Peter got up very early as usual and went into the nursery to look at his son. Lili woke up to an almost animal cry and ran into the nursery. Peter was holding the baby's limp body, shaking and screaming. The child had died during the night of SIDS, sudden infant death syndrome.

The following days and weeks were blurry. She was under professional care because of a nervous breakdown. When she was discharged from the sanatorium about a month later, her marriage was in shambles. Peter blamed her for the tragedy. He pointed to the bottle-feeding, the choice of crib, the choice of blanket, not checking on him during the night and so on. He claimed he could not stand the sight of her and moved out. The divorce was fast, and she got enough of a settlement to start her fitness business.

As time went by she became her old self again, living recklessly and seeking after outrageous lovers and affairs, but she couldn't fully get rid of her pain. Most of the time she could overlook a mother pushing a pram or hearing a baby cry without any feeling, but sometimes it struck her unexpectedly like a sharp knife in her heart. She got up, dropped the dog to the ground, went into the living room and turned on her giant TV to watch the evening news. She couldn't concentrate, and her mind wondered to thinking about Elsa.

Her friend had come for a visit after Michael died and stayed with her for three weeks. She helped Lili through the hardest times to accepting the fact that Michael was no longer. They talked, or rather Lili talked, from morning late into the night. They sat on the patio, enjoying during the day the view of the blue, sparkling bay spotted with white sailboats, and at night they watched the many dwindling lights of the harbour and the city. Elsa listened to her patiently, but she did not hesitate to interfere when Lili got too deep into her self-adoration and steered her to the more realistic track. They hardly left the house and ordered in meals. A few times, when they got tired of talking they went down to a secluded part of the beach and just sat on the sand, listening as the waves beat the shore and immersed in their own thoughts. When the time came to say goodbye, Lili became upset, wanting Elsa to stay longer. But Elsa had to get back to Tom, who was slowly recovering of his malaria sickness.

"I don't understand why you can't stay longer!" Lili had demanded, even though she knew quite well. "Tom will be okay for a few more weeks. You did look after his well-being during your absence! I need you here much more than he does!"

"Lili, you know that I'll do anything for you. I am your friend. But my being here can't fill Michael's absence in your life. You must accept the fact that he is no longer alive and adjust your life accordingly. And this you must do alone. Fortunately, you don't have any financial worries, which would make your life difficult. You can spend as much as you like, do whatever you like and go wherever you like. And later you could even run into someone to share a bit of your life with."

"Your cheerful disposition can be annoying sometimes! What can I look forward to? I am alone and over sixty. There are no more affairs or lovers to seek out or to look forward to. I learned my lesson the last time. Never again!"

"It does not have to be an affair or a lover. It can be a male friend to talk to or go out with. Look at Margaret! She is very happy and content with Jànos. Their relationship started out like that and now they live happily together in a nice, homely apartment close to the Danube in a small community on the outskirts of Budapest. She retired from teaching, and they both listen to music, read and take long walks on the shores of the river!"

"I am not Margaret, your compassionate friend! And I am not you, who gave up her independence to care for an old-time lover! Do you want me to believe that you are satisfied with your life? Elsa, don't lie to me!"

"No, I am not always satisfied with my life. I have my difficult days too! Who doesn't? Sometimes when Tom has a relapse and he becomes difficult and edgy, I ask myself why I am doing this. But I am grateful to have Tom back in my life! I would not have it any other way. He is the only one who needs me after my family moved to the other side of the world, and to be honest, they never needed me as much as I would have liked. I am the opposite of you—to be needed makes me content, and to be needed makes you exasperated."

"I can't argue with that! You know me too well! So, I need you now. Please stay a bit longer!"

Elsa stayed for one more week after a long chat with Tom, who was well with no relapses. He said he missed her, but she should stay as long as she liked and shouldn't worry about him. During the week, Elsa forced Lili to go for long walks, go out for dinners, a movie and a concert. They reminisced about their passed youth, their travels and made plans for future visits with each other. By the time Elsa left, Lili had recovered from her depression and started the plans for the house remodelling.

Lili turned off the TV, put the leash on the dog and went for a walk. The street was deserted, the palm trees were whispering in the balmy breeze from the bay and the dark sky was full of stars. Lili looked up to the star-studded sky, searching for the brightest one as she and Michael had often done. She felt calmer than she had for a long time. She lifted her head, straightened her back and with energetic steps walked home.

The next morning, she called her travel agent and booked a cabin with a balcony on a luxury liner for a trip around the world.

Chapter 36

After Elsa came home from Sydney, she thought about Lili a lot and worried about her emotional well-being. As time went by, however, Lili became more cheerful and egocentric in her phone calls, and she was soon talking endlessly about redoing her house, her new car and her future plans.

Tom had lost some weight and looked pale, and he confessed that he had a bad relapse while she was away. He didn't want to go to the hospital to alarm Elsa, so he arranged with his doctor for a few visits at home. The doctor helped him to balance his health. He could not hide his joy about having Elsa back.

In time, their life fell into practice. Elsa realized that Tom was right about not moving in with her. They spent most days together and some nights in either his or her bed, but knowing each other so well they sensed when to part and be alone. Tom looked after his own breakfast and most of the time his lunch too, if Elsa was busy elsewhere. They ate dinner together at one of their places or just walked out to the main intersection where dozens of restaurants offered as many different kind of cuisine. They took long walks or drove out to the lakeshore, took the ferry over to Toronto Island and had lunch by the lake. They went to movies, and when Tom was strong enough to sit through one, they went to a concert or a play.

Their relationship was loving but platonic. Tom never regained his sexual powers and often became morose. During those times, Elsa tried to convince him that she was not missing anything—she was happy to lie in his arms and feel the love in his embrace. Sex was not nearly as important as the feeling of sharing and belonging to each other. Tom had some bad relapses, some longer than others, and it was hard on both of them. He would become depressed, want to be left alone and wouldn't respond to any of Elsa's attentive concern. He withdrew from her sometimes, very agitated. Elsa was hurt but tried to put on a good, cheerful face, and it burned up all her mental and physical energy.

Sometimes she was ready to give up and let Tom go back to the hospital. Her life had changed—she was not free anymore—but she had taken on the responsibility by her free will. She knew that she would never give up hope because she believed that his love and his need for her made her life rewarding.

David was not happy when she told him her decision to have Tom back in her life. Elsa was worried when they came for their first visit from Buenos Aires, but she relaxed when she saw that after their first awkward meeting, David and Tom became friendlier. David was older and understood life much better. He saw that his mother was loved and that the relationship made her happy. If he sensed that her life was not as easy and happy as she wanted him to believe, he didn't let it show.

The partings remained tearful and painful, especially with Andrew, who was very affectionate toward his grandmother and spent days with her in the park and in the Zoo. He became close to Tom as well.

They all talked regularly on the phone, chatted on the Internet and remained a part of each other's lives regardless of the many thousands of miles between them. Elsa and Tom were planning a visit to Buenos Aires as soon as Tom could undertake such a long trip.

Lili called her to let her know that she was going on a cruise around the world, and who knows, if she found a place that interested her, she might stay there for longer and take the next boat when she felt like it. But she was going to stay away from men. The boat called in to Halifax for a few days, and maybe they could arrange a meeting. She sounded herself again, full of problems about her wardrobe for the three-month-long cruise.

Margaret kept in touch too. She and Elsa talked on the phone and corresponded by e-mail. She gladly gave up her old life, settled down with Jànos and retired from teaching. Both of them sold their places and bought a comfortable, two-bedroom apartment outside of Budapest. Both of them were nature enthusiasts and enjoyed watching the wildlife on the nearby Danube and its inlets. Jànos was writing a textbook for a course for the university, and Margaret sometimes substituted for colleagues who were sick or on sabbatical. She saw her granddaughter more often, as the new home was only a half-hour drive from the town where her daughter's family lived. This made her happy, and Jånos saw a third grandchild in Annie. He had a good pension—they lived comfortably and travelled often. Margaret wrote Elsa about their first trip together to London, where she searched for and found Edith's grave. They put flowers on her tombstone and lit a candle for her soul. She told Elsa about standing there for a long time with tears in her eyes, remembering their friendship and her terrible death and feeling guilty that she couldn't do more for her. And about how she took comfort and reassurance from Jånos's arms around her. She was grateful to have a partner to share her life with after so many long, lonely years. They were thinking about a visit with Jånos's family next summer, and both of them were hoping to spend some time together as a foursome.

Elsa tidied up the kitchen after dinner, went into the living room, lay down on the sofa and put her head on Tom's lap. He closed his book and kissed Elsa's forehead, gently smoothing her hair just as he had so many years ago. Both of them were tranquil, looking out the window. The snow-covered park was breathtakingly beautiful in the last rays of the cold, winter sun. They didn't need to talk—their love engulfed them, leaving out words. As the sun sank down behind the tall buildings beyond the park, the snow became sparkling white again. The park froze into the stillness of the winter evening.

They held each other tenderly as the clock ticked away the time, and after a while Elsa put the book back into Tom's hand, they kissed with warm familiarity and said goodnight. She walked over to her apartment. The warmth of the embrace stayed with her, and she didn't feel the biting cold wind sweeping over the street.

She lit the logs in her fireplace, sat down at her desk and opened her laptop. Sitting motionless, she let her mind wander for a while with the dancing flames. Then with a deep sigh, she started to work on the last chapter of her novel—it was about the happiness, sorrow and anxiety of the twilight of life.

About the Author

Vali Gyenge won a gold medal in swimming at the 1952 Olympic Games. Her previous novels The Way They Were and The Promise were published in English and Hungarian. She is also a photographer and author of My Hungary, a photo album. She lives in Toronto and Budapest.

Printed in the United States
136874LV00008B/5/P